GUYNUR SCHWYN

A Short Story Collection

RAYMOND S FLEX

CONTENTS

THE WATCH

JAK'S HEART tickled his throat. He could taste nothing but ash and sweat and flesh. That was all he ever smelled in Guynur City. The only thing that he could get from it. And it made his mouth taste sour. Off in the distance, he could hear the juddering choke of a car starting up, somewhere out of sight.

Up here in the Bell Tower, a crooked, cobbled-together brick tower right smack in the centre of Guynur City, Jak kept his eye out on the night-time streets down below. On the shadows which clung to the alleyways, unmoved by the streetlights, to the darkened doorways, just as unmoved, and to the shadows of the buildings which splashed right out to cover the whole road in places.

This was as good of a lookout spot as any, for him and his companions: the ones who held magic at bay from the human citizens. They were the ones appointed to protect the humans from the more unpleasant aspects of living with magic. No, that wasn't it . . . they were here to keep magic out of the city *altogether*.

And Jak was in charge of the whole operation. The whole of the Watch.

Over his shoulder, he heard the swish of a robe. Someone approaching him.

He held his position at the window, glassless, only the ragtag brickwork to give the impression of a window at all. He waited for the whispered words to enter his brain. Those in the Watch never spoke or, at least, never had use for their mouths.

They had far more . . . *efficient* means of communication.

The words merely appeared in his mind, as if out of those shadows that prowled the midnight streets below, the ones barely lit by the light purple glow of moonlight.

"Master?"

Mathwell. His most trusty aide. Come to think of it, he could sense his very presence. But only now that he had heard him speak within his mind. It was a little odd. These days, these last few weeks in fact, he had been having trouble reaching out beyond himself, speaking with outside magical forces . . . the forces the humans might've called *mystical*.

He supposed that just about anything was *mystical* to the blind.

Jak held his position. Still staring down into the streets. He had been coming to this spot, staring out through this makeshift window, really little more than a hole in the side of the brick tower, of the Bell Tower, every day since he'd felt that oppressive presence about Guynur City. To tell the truth, it frightened him somewhat.

And the worst part of it was that he could share his fear with no one.

He had no family, no wife, nothing.

No member of the Watch did.

That was the trade they had made. For their power. To neither live in this world or the next. To dedicate their lives to servitude and to protection.

Could what Jak had even be called 'life' at all?

He sensed Mathwell standing about five or six paces behind him. At his heels. And Jak also sensed that Mathwell had some news to share. Most likely a callout. Some citizen who had had a run-in with some kind of magic tonight. And they needed the Watch's aid.

That was their job, after all.

The only thing that Jak was in existence to do.

Because, and he could never allow himself to forget, if he had no purpose to serve the humans of Guynur City, they would cast him out, just as they had all other magical beings.

That was the agreed function of Guynur. It was to be a sanctuary for the humans of Schwyn. And, he knew this just as well, the humans themselves knew so little of the magic that surrounded themselves that they feared it instantly. They were driven trembling with it.

But Jak supposed that was better for them, in the long run, that way they wouldn't come to the realisation of just how quickly the steady hand of magic could sweep them away if it wished.

That would turn it from living with fear to living with *death*.

Just like Jak and the other members of the Watch had to.

Jak glanced back at Mathwell, took him in, standing in the standard-issue shimmering, beige, gold and black robes of the footmen of the Watch. Just like his own, Mathwell's hood was drawn up over his head to leave his face in shadow, just like the streets below them.

The streets wracked by darkness.

Jak, though, himself, wore all-black robes. That was an honour bestowed upon him as the leader of the Watch, and one that would pass onto another when his time finally came.

When magic overwhelmed what remained of his body.

He shifted a final glance into the streets below, and then, together, they floated off down the spiral brick staircase, staying a few centimetres off the ground as they went right down to the basement of the Bell Tower where their vehicle waited.

T HE UNDERGROUND car park, beneath the Bell Tower, was dank and wall-to-wall cement. When Jak floated his way across the cement floor, he could hear the *scuttle* of rats off in the distance. Could smell the rancid odour of rat urine all around him. Like someone had fitted a gag over his mouth and nose. He could taste the tang of it on his tongue.

He felt a tingle pass through his bones as he took in the van, the Watch's van, in the sallow fluorescent light that beat out from the bulb over their heads.

He supposed that in another life the van had belonged to a contractor of some sort: perhaps a painter and decorator, a carpenter, or a simple builder. Before it had maybe been painted white whereas now it was black. And its paintwork was chipped all over, seemingly in all the places the bodywork hadn't rusted right the way through.

Those spots where he could see right into the interior of the van.

While Mathwell rounded the van, opened up the driver's side and then slunk up in behind the steering wheel, Jak hung back.

He had a deeply uncertain feeling about this. About tonight. About that oppressive cloud that had seemed to hang down over him for these past few weeks. As he hadn't been able to put a fully-fledged description upon it, let alone a name, it scared him all the more.

And now, more than ever, he felt it pressing down on him.

A warning?

Really, there was no way of telling. And he had his duty to perform. As the leader of the Watch *he* needed to set an example for the rest of his men. Though, he supposed, if he was going to take on a confidant then tonight seemed to be a better time than most.

He would be alone with Mathwell.

Just the two of them answering the call.

Jak took up his place in the passenger's seat, and strapped himself in as Mathwell drove them through the underground car park. Mathwell's hands were steady on the steering wheel. A firm but relaxed grasp. Just the lieutenant any leader could be proud of.

And Jak was certain that he was proud of him.

They passed through the darkened city, only that dim orange glow coming off the streetlights. Jak watched the odd mangy cat skitter along the cracked asphalt pavements, and more than a dozen rats digging through dumped, black plastic bags of rubbish left at the roadside for the scroungers to carry off to the Tip.

Sometimes he wondered just how well the humans might cope without magic amongst them. Why, they would most likely descend into utter and complete chaos.

And then they would die.

The magical forces of the world would prey on them without their protectors.

Without the Watch.

Mathwell drove the van on for a long while, through the deserted streets. Jak lost himself to the gentle *hum* of the engine, and those soothing vibrations passing up through the barely upholstered passenger's seat. He could feel the jagged springs poke him in the spine.

When he breathed in now, all he could smell was flesh—human flesh, all around him. He imagined them as all great big chunks of meat, constantly sweating. Giving off that unpleasant salty taste. The one that he'd once exuded, he supposed.

But that was a long, long time ago now.

A long time since he could've called himself mortal.

They carried on down a deserted street, or one that appeared deserted. All the steel rubbish bins burst with the plastic rubbish sacks just barely squeezed inside of them. And Jak could make out yet more of the furry forms of rats, pawing their way through the human waste.

Mathwell brought the van to a stop on the curb, and, all of a sudden, Jak felt a quiver pass up from the pit of his stomach, felt it quiver up through his crooked bones, and enter his skull, shake it from the inside.

He blinked a couple of times, trying to rid himself of the feeling.

"Are you okay, master?" Mathwell spoke into Jak's mind.

Jak held himself still a moment, not because he was considering his reply to Mathwell, but because he was still attempting to grab a modicum of control. To reel his mind back in. To prevent it from escaping him.

He didn't answer Mathwell, and merely let himself out of the passenger-side door, and down onto the road.

He took in the house before them. A simple, three- or four-bedroom house. Just like all the others on this street. And, just like all the others, it had cracked window panes, an overgrown garden, grown so wild that the tips of the plants' tendrils now loomed so high as to touch the window ledges of the next floor up.

Guynur City was filled with many such neighbourhoods. As a city it had been shrinking for years. Humans taking against some essence of the city and deciding to leave. Whether they found something better for themselves or they only succeeded in throwing themselves into greater chaos, the only thing that could be said for certain was that no one ever heard from them again.

The house was darkened, of course. No light glimmered from the inside. Neither did any of the streetlights on the street function. They were all totally extinguished. After all, if no one lived on the street then what was the need to have them switched on at all?

Or so he imagined the arguments of the city authorities going along those lines.

Jak waited for Mathwell to get himself down from the driver's side, and then the two of them, without so much as a nod, or a word spoken between their two minds, made their way up through the overgrown front garden and to the front door.

3

THE HALLWAY, just inside of the front door of the house, was infested with spider webs hanging from corner to corner. They draped down like netted curtains, and Jak supposed this place had been deserted for decades. Unlived in. Unloved. Those were terms he understood about a home, though he didn't have one himself . . . perhaps he had had one in his past, though he never would've been able to remember even if he tried hard to. That was another aspect of his job, of the position he occupied within the world.

His past was simply another thing he'd had to give up.

Through the hallway was a kitchen. It festered with unwashed and discarded crockery, piled up in the sink which had apparently long ago run dry. At least, there wasn't so much as a drip falling from the tap.

The moonlight streamed in through the cracked windowpanes, splashed across the surfaces manky with grease and rat droppings. But when Jak breathed in deeply here, when he really allowed the air to reach the very bottom of his clapped-out lungs, it tasted clean, *smelled* clean. There was none of that meaty, salty flavour that followed humans about. That sent his gut crunching in on itself or commenced that ringing in his ears.

Aside from a few overturned wooden barstools, some with legs snapped off, apparently by intruders intent on using them for firewood, there was nothing else in the kitchen.

All the food had long been snaffled from the cupboards, and, again, only grease and rat droppings marked these places.

But it was here.

Here was where the distress call had come from.

This house.

Jak held himself still. Tried to feel about him. To extend himself into the darkness. To sense the magic. That stirring that he had felt all these weeks past.

It had grown weaker. In fact, he could barely sense it.

Whatever that magical force had been that'd weighed him down for so long, it seemed like it had left now . . . left Guynur.

Or had it simply grown closer?

Was he now standing in the eye of the storm?

Could this . . . this place be the centre of that disturbance, of that which had sent fear spiralling through him on the long and lonely nights, those longer and lonelier days while he'd stood up there, back at the Bell Tower, staring out across the city, sniffing out any disturbances, any magical sparks that might be flying. Threatening this human experiment.

He turned to look at Mathwell, and, just like Jak himself, he was no more than mere robes. His hood kept his face in permanent shadow, just like Jak's own hood did his. Because their faces were not important. Not for who they were now.

For *what* they were now.

Jak took care as he crossed the kitchen, those black and white cracked tiles, streaked with grime and footprints in the dust, and he headed for the staircase.

The light green carpet had worn thin down the centre of the steps, so thin in places that Jak could make out the dented wood beneath. When he breathed in here the air seemed cleaner still, if at all possible, and he could feel his heart, for the first time in weeks, give a couple of vaguely youthful leaps. As if the blood that flowed through his veins really still mattered. As if it really mattered whether or not his heart continued to tick along at all.

The only thing that kept him going was the magic that flowed through his veins, and one day even that would cease to work. And he would drop down into the ground like the bag of bones and dirt he really was.

Jak made his way up the steps, floating a couple of millimetres above the surface of the carpet. Listening to the light sweep of the hem of his sable robe as he went. Listening to it brush the carpet beneath him.

He emerged up onto the landing, and to the moonlight which streaked in through the roof windows. The roof windows were not cracked but sprinkled with a fine layer of dirt and dead leaves so as to allow the light dribble in still.

Up here it was calm. So calm. Jak could hear himself think. He could feel the peace envelop him and draw him downwards. And, for the first time in a long time, he wished he might be able to share the feeling with somebody. With some mortal.

But it was far too late for *that* now.

He looked to the empty doorways, bathed in shadows. That same calmness remained with him, though the uneasiness was difficult to shake. He moved from one doorway to the next, looking in on all the bedrooms and finding nothing at all.

When he had finished his preliminary inspection, and found nothing, he turned his attention upwards. To the raggedy, torn-up cord which hung down. A plastic fob beating back and forth at the end of it.

He felt Mathwell close to him, sensed Mathwell's slight stirring of fear. Nothing more than a stirring but, all the same, Jak had learned to trust his instincts, especially when it came to his team. Though he liked to tell himself that he knew each and every member intimately, he had to admit also to himself that really that couldn't be the case.

Each of them had passed through similar experiences, true, but that didn't mean they carried the same wounds too.

Jak tugged the cord which dangled from the ceiling. Listened to a gentle *groan* as the apparently rusted-up hinges above let the door loose. And the door yawned open to reveal a large, black hole in the ceiling.

The entrance to an attic.

Or so it seemed.

Again, that uneasiness from Mathwell made an impact on Jak, but this time he disregarded it, told himself that they were here to do a job now, and he should put his own issues to the back of his mind for the time being.

Whatever this *thing*, this *disturbance* was that he'd been experiencing over the past few weeks, he looked to be on the brink of finding his answer now.

He drifted upwards. Neither his hands or feet quite touching the rungs of the steel ladder.

When he reached the top, he breathed in the dust and the leather scent of the place. He could say with certainty that it was a long time since any mortal, any *human*, had been up here. He peeled back the darkness with his penetrating glare.

And, off in the corner of the attic, over by a tiny window which looked out, down onto the street, he saw a huddled up figure.

Hardly much more than a bundle of rags.

4

JAK FELT himself go cold all over. And, it seemed, that all at once that intense feeling of relaxation dissipated completely. He was sure this figure couldn't be a human, he hadn't experienced that sweaty, fleshy scent since they had pulled up here in this neighbourhood.

He could hear light breathing. A slight rasp at the back of the throat as if the huddled-up figure had a cold, or was about to have one.

The dust seemed to catch in Jak's mouth, and to steal away any sense of taste that might've been there before. For some reason he did recall, back when he had been human, that he had had allergies. One of those odd facts that somehow managed to come back at him out of the obscurity of his past. And he remembered how he'd always carried a packet of tissues around with him wherever he went, for the inevitable sneezes and coughs.

Often these reminiscences infuriated him . . . made him wonder whether, if he could only put some effort into it, he could recall more of his past.

But what was the use of that?

He was a different being now, and anything that he had once known in his mortal life was long dead to him now.

. . . Or should have been.

Jak felt Mathwell close to his shoulder, and he caught the urge to tell him to wait back at the attic door. As if Jak was concerned for his lieutenant's safety. Being killed in the Watch was some kind of mercy really. At least they would finally leave this world behind. Leave Schwyn behind, once and for all.

Or so went the theory.

Jak stole closer to the hunched-up figure, reached out to their mind with his own. Waited for some kind of response, but received nothing but silence.

When he tried again, he was direct, to the point. "Were you the one who called for assistance?" he said, into the figure's mind.

But, just like the last time, there was no response.

Jak felt Mathwell close by. No doubt he wished to communicate with him. To speak into his mind. But he also knew, as well as Jak did, that it was better for them to stay back for the time being. Not for them to reveal the full extent of their telepathy till they had fully scouted out the capabilities of this figure themselves.

They had to know just what they were dealing with.

Jak stole closer still. Now only four or five paces away . . . if Jak had ever taken paces at all. The figure's breathing was louder now, and that slight *snick* of phlegm much more easily heard. Jak held back another second and then, knowing that it would have to be done sooner or later, he allowed his withered hand, hardly more than leathered skin melted onto bone now, and lightly touched the figure on the shoulder.

The figure, it turned out, was wearing a rough material—nothing more than rags, just like the scroungers who scoured the city for scrap to hock down the Tip.

But this wasn't any scrounger.

Scroungers were human.

For a long while, it seemed, the figure made no move to suggest they had so much as noticed Jak's touch. But Jak kept his fingertips jabbing into the figure's shoulder, determined that he would be able to get some sort of a response from him.

After they had passed what seemed like hours, but wasn't likely to have been more than a minute in reality, Jak decided to take a chance.

He gripped tighter on the figure's shoulder and then rounded the figure, lowering himself into a crouch before him.

He tried to make out the figure's face, but, just like with the members of the Watch, the figure's face was obscured by a constant shadow lingering down over it.

"Speak," Jak said, into the figure's mind. "Speak to me."

The figure remained still.

Jak tightened his grip a little more, and spoke more firmly into the figure's mind, determined that he would get a response, or at least that the figure would hear him.

"Speak to me," Jak said.

The figure stayed still for another moment and Jak wondered if he should speak again, try another time to get into the figure's mind.

But, before he got the chance, the figure finally spoke to him.

Spoke into his mind.

Clear. Even. And distinct.

"You are a *rat*—a rat in a *maze*."

Those words tumbled about Jak's mind. He turned them over and over, again and again, trying to get them straight, attempting to get some sort of significance from them.

Meanwhile, the figure remained in the same position, apparently unmoved by having spoken into Jak's mind. Jak could feel Mathwell close by, ready to step in if there was any danger forthcoming. But Jak didn't feel threatened, not in the slightest.

On the contrary, he got the feeling that whatever this figure was, *whoever* this figure was, he was here on account of Jak. That he had something to tell Jak. Some little nugget to reveal to him.

"What do you mean," Jak said, "when you say I am a rat in a maze?"

The figure stayed still. No motion whatsoever. Or any implication that he had spoken at all. Perhaps that was all the Jak was going to get. The only thing that he was going to manage to extract from the figure.

One thing, though, was for certain. Jak hadn't felt at ease like this, not had that cloud hanging over him, for a long time now. And with this figure, he felt intensely calm, almost *too* calm. As leader of the Watch, he had grown accustomed to constantly feeling slightly on edge—ready for whatever might be lurking out there in the shadows.

That was his role after all.

To protect Guynur City from the ill will of the magic that enveloped it.

The important thing was that Jak knew this figure here was magical, having a telepathic ability assured him of that.

And, as was his duty, he knew just what he must do.

So, without so much as word between himself and Mathwell— what use were words when they had instinct?—between the two of them, they lifted the figure up, and lugged him out of the attic, down through the house, and out to the van.

They would drive him back to the Bell Tower, and then they would see what they might do for him. Just like always, it would be a simple case. Whenever a magical being managed to penetrate the city walls of Guynur City, they handed him off to the Gaoler, who came by with his cart every market day. And he would take the magical being . . . well, back wherever he had come from.

Maybe they disposed of them.

That was all beyond Jak's remit.

5

BACK AT THE BELL TOWER, Jak, with Mathwell's help, steered the figure into one of the cells in the basement, down below the underground car park where they kept the van.

As they descended down the spiralling steps, the air thickening with that musky stench of rat piss, but at least not curdling with the much more repulsive stink of meaty mass and sweat . . . of *human* . . . Jak attempted to penetrate the figure's mind once again.

But it was blank.

It was as if he was merely drawing on a blackboard in a long-forgotten classroom, in a school far away from anywhere . . . and that hadn't been touched by a soul for centuries.

As they proceeded down the stone spiralling steps, Jak listened to the slight rustle of their cloaks scrunch back at them from the walls. As they descended further and further, the air got damper, and, it seemed, Jak's mouth grew staler.

Morth was on duty, another member of the Watch, currently serving as gaoler. He sat on the simple wooden chair reserved for the on-duty lock-up gaoler and stared into space. His face just as concealed in shadow by the hood of his cloak, as those of Jak and Mathwell.

Morth rose silently, and his hand, just as withered and leather-skinned as Jak's, swept his cloak aside and withdrew a loop of keys to the gaol cells.

He then floated to the nearest cell, unlocked it, and then brought the door open wide with a narrow, teeth-gnarling *squeal*.

Mathwell and Jak deposited the figure inside the cell, and then, with a word of thanks for Morth, Jak and Mathwell made their way back up the spiral steps, back on their way up the tower.

Only when Jak had returned to his lookout point, that point that he spent most of his days and nights at, did Jak begin to feel that same uneasiness dawn back over him.

He stared out into the darkness, as if it would reveal some secret to him, something that he had neglected to notice before. But, unsurprisingly, there was nothing at all.

He could sense Mathwell standing behind him, in the doorway to the tower, and he could sense further that he had something on his mind.

Literally.

Could it be that Mathwell had felt the same ominous sensation in the air these past few weeks . . . like a storm cloud gathering on the horizon, and that eardrum-crushing pressure that accompanied it. The scent of rain thick on the warm breeze. And that vague salty taste at the back of the throat.

Until that divining peal of thunder broke through it all, and brought on those cold waves of relief. Was that what awaited Guynur City now?

How was Jak supposed to know? He just kept magic in check. He had no idea of what the grander plan might be, or even if one existed at all.

He was a mere foot soldier, doing his job the best he could.

"Is there . . ." Mathwell began, his words forming themselves in Jak's mind. "Is there something on your mind, master?"

Jak held himself very still. Tried to focus in on the city that swept out from him down below. But it was impossible to focus. Not with Mathwell standing there. Boring holes into his back with that stare of his.

Jak thought for a moment, feeling Mathwell's mind melding with his, but keeping him out of his more personal thoughts. And, finally, Jak said, "No, nothing at all."

Mathwell remained in the doorway to the lookout room for what seemed an age, before he said, "Very well, master. Then I shall go and rest."

Jak almost found himself smirking at that comment. At the very ridiculousness of it.

Because, for them, for the members of the Watch, there would be no rest. Not till the day they were all swept off the face of the world.

But all he said was, "Yes," and then waited for Mathwell to leave him in peace.

When Jak was sure Mathwell had gone, once he'd sensed that he had floated off to his own room of the Bell Tower, Jak turned his attention back to the city.

Off on the horizon, Nephmur was rising, gleaming its pinkish glow over the distant rooftops of Guynur City. For some reason, Jak caught some recollection of having once been a boy, and having watched their star rising up in the mornings. Being there for first light. He supposed, in a way, Nephmur was the only constant that remained in his shadow life, the only aspect of it that gave any such strand of logic to his existence.

Nephmur and the moon, of course.

But whereas the moon chilled, Nephmur warmed.

If Jak had still had blood, he supposed that he might've been glad for Nephmur. He supposed that was the reason that humans were glad for Nephmur.

But if he had once been human, he wasn't any longer.

And this gloomy sensation was back with him. And, try as he might, he couldn't get the figure's comment off his mind.

'A rat in a maze.'

In a way, Jak supposed the figure was right. This was his duty.

His duty to the Watch. And it was the duty he would see to right through till the day he was wiped off the surface of the world.

And carried off into hereafter.

. . . Or, at the very least, that was all he could allow himself to expect.

PHAYSHAWE'S BOY

T HE PIPES OVERHEAD clunked and creaked about. A couple of them leaked little globs of the scolding liquid, whipplesnife. It skittered down through the air giving a light, snakelike *hiss* before splattering down onto the ground.

The stuff smelled like sulphur. And it got inside you. Got into your airways: through you nostrils, through your mouth. Even if you breathed through the sleeve of your shirt or the neck of your jumper, it'd find a way in.

Magical, that was what it was.

And deadly in large doses.

But it also powered near enough everything in Guynur City.

The whipplesnife splashed about on the ground, puddling around Blof's ankle-high, leather boots. The ones with the steel toecaps and the rigid treads. The ones that he had used in more beatings than he could remember. The ones that protected his feet from this unpleasant stuff now.

Being in the Crul meant stuff like this. Being one of Phayshawe's boys meant having to take the responsibility of doing this. Because, no doubt about it, Blof knew his place well on the totem pole, he knew that he was *way* down. Kind of like a maggot.

But even maggots have their uses.

Blof dug into the pocket of his tattered suit coat, the one which was jet black, kind of like coal. All the rest of the Crul wore suits like this. Some, like him, had them battered up just a little. This wasn't one of those gangs where you had to dress up like a pansy. Nah, this was the type of gang where you dressed up for *business*.

And though it was unpleasant, what he was doing here, down —*way* down—in the basement of Phayshawe's HQ: Hornheim

Manor, Blof knew that it was work that had to be done. Had to be done by someone like him.

But that didn't make it any more pleasant.

Nope, not one bit.

From inside of his pocket, he recovered a miniature lamplight, or a 'lamper' as most people of Guynur City put it. One of the gas devices that served for situations like this. Or, at least, he was pretty sure it ran on gas . . . did it really matter as long as it worked?

When Phayshawe had told him to come down here, to head down to the basement and check on some dial or readout or something, he had stressed that he shouldn't use a lamper, but what the fudge. If Phayshawe couldn't be bothered to get his hands dirty once in a while then just what did he really know about the intricacies of things?

Of course Blof knew there wasn't anything down here that was flammable. That would've been Stupidity 101. And so he knew that it was fine for him to spark up his lamper.

He depressed the spring-loaded switch and squinted as the veil of pinkish light glowed out from the lamper which he clasped in his fist.

Suddenly there was a little light on the world.

A little more perspective down here.

As he'd been walking, he'd caught the impression that this place was endless, that it was this great big expanse nestled beneath Hornheim Manor, but now he saw that the ceiling was only a few feet over his head, and only a couple more feet wide.

He was a big guy, always had been, just as tall as he was broad, or so they'd say. And so he was always subconsciously—and sometimes consciously—on the look out for bumping his head on ceilings or whatever dangled down on him.

Funny what tricks darkness could play on the mind.

Blof, more than anyone else, should've known that, since he'd used that knowledge to his advantage on people who Phayshawe had wanted to press for info. Covered their eyes with a blindfold for a few hours or so to try and leak details out of them.

And, more often than not, it worked just fine.

He guessed there was a reason why gaol officers did that to people in the Can.

Stripped away an all-important sense by way of punishment.

He took in the sprawling network of pipes too, made of copper and spiralling about here and there, sometimes snaking round in loops. Funny that in a place as grand as Hornheim Manor there was such messy workmanship just beneath the surface.

He never would've thought Phayshawe would've stood for it.

The pinkish light from his lamper gleamed back at him off the pipes, and he could see the puddles, could avoid them. He pressed forwards, much faster now.

It was a wonder what just a little light could do.

After he'd wandered on for another ten minutes or so, taking several jack-knife bends and plunging deeper into the darkness, he found himself emerging into a larger chamber.

It opened out above him and around him, which was to say that the walls and ceiling retreated, went beyond the pinkish glow from his lamper completely.

Overhead . . . well, all around him, in fact, he heard the sound of that whipplesnife gushing through pipes, washing through fast enough to make them clank.

Blof paused a moment, and then headed on.

He took a step here and there, into the darkness, trying to find some sort of direction, before he finally saw it. Found just what it was that he was looking for. What Phayshawe had told him to come looking for.

An oak cabinet nailed to the wall.

Though Blof wasn't usually all that observant about details like this one, he found himself drawn in. The thing was just so sturdy, and carved out in ornate designs. With dainty little loops and jutting cornices. It looked a little fancy to be down here. But what did he know about it? He was just a henchman, one of those that Phayshawe could pluck up and send to do whatever his whim happened to be that particular day.

He prised open the cabinet. It wasn't locked. And he held the lamper up to observe the insides. There, nestled within, was just what Phayshawe had told him to come down here looking for. Here was the dial he was supposed to read.

He looked to its face, a skinny pair of hands, one longer than the other, kind of like a clock face now he thought of it. The backing of the dial was a yellow paper that was peeling off its base. This dial looked old. He guessed that it'd been here ever since the piping had been put in down here.

From within his suit coat, he withdrew a heavy, leather-skinned pen. And he scribbled out the readings on the back of his hand, supposing that Phayshawe would know what they actually meant, and then he slammed the cabinet door shut once again, and made his way off back into the darkness, holding his lamper down by his side as he went.

Fancy Phayshawe expecting him to go all the way down here, down into the basement, without so much as a match. What did he expect of him? How had he expected him to read the dial at all without his trusty lamper?

Blof allowed himself a smug little grin down there all alone, thinking about how his boss might well throw a fit if he knew the truth—knew that he'd defied a direct order so readily.

Used his lamper.

Sure, Blof might be a henchman, but he was no lemming.

One of these days he would stand up for himself, do some change. Something that'd make him standout, once and for all.

He would show them all how he wasn't just *any* old hood.

As he took the route back along the tunnel, back along the slope and up towards the mansion, he heard the piping all around him creaking louder. Growing louder as he went.

The *drip-drip* of the whipplesnife from the pipes grew louder. The stench of sulphur sharper, almost as if it was singing his nostril hair. His mouth tasted dry and stale, and he was desperate for a drink of water. He squinted up at the pinkish glow that the lamper opened up for him, to the way back up into the mansion.

And then, all at once, with a loud and final *creak*, he heard the pipes give way around him, and the *gush* of the whipplesnife all getting free, spilling all about him.

Lapping at his ankles like a rising tide.

2

OR A MOMENT, Blof didn't think at all about the connection between the lamper he clutched in his fist and the whipplesnife that now splashed all about him.

In the pinkish glow from his lamper, the whipplesnife was a greenie-black colour with a metallic glean to it, kind of like molten lead, something like that. But he knew that it wasn't lead. That this *stuff* was much more dangerous than lead.

And it was pooling about around him now, like honey drooling out of a jar, it ebbed from the pipes and slithered about at his feet, sucking at the soles of his leather boots.

He could hear the *hiss* as it bit as the toe, could feel the warmth of its unchecked power as it heated up the steel toecap. But, more than anything else, he could feel that sting of the sulphur-like acidity in the air. Burning his skin, causing a nausea to creep up from the base of his stomach. He tried not to think of the chicken drumsticks he'd chewed right down to the bone not an hour ago.

He had to get out.

As he sped up, he remembered the lamper in his hand, finally put two and two together and realised just what he'd done. How he'd defied his boss's orders . . . perhaps they had been given for good reason after all.

He extinguished the thing with another flick of the switch and let it fall back into the pocket of his suit coat.

He could feel his heart tickle his throat. And the sweat seeming to ooze out of every pore. This time he had really done it. He had done something *really* stupid.

And he knew, even if he managed to escape from the basement, that Phayshawe would be furious.

He breathed in deep, sucked in that sulphuric stench, felt it sting the pits of his lungs and send a tingle racing up his throat. He ignored those sensations. He had to if he wanted to survive.

As he ran onwards hard, he could still hear the whipplesnife squeezing itself out from the pipes, and sucking at his boots. Threatening to drag him right down, below the surface. But each time, somehow, he managed to extricate himself. To tug himself free.

But he could feel the burn on his calves as fatigue began to over-whelm him.

In that moment, he wondered if he might've been better off having given up a few brews with the boys in favour of getting down to the gym once in a while, just to get himself a little better in shape. Ever since he'd found himself promoted to Hornheim Manor, to actually being within the inner group of Phayshawe, he had let himself get a little complacent. Hadn't really seen the need to work hard any longer.

Though he guessed he should've been working harder than ever.

As he continued on up the slope in the pitch blackness, the whipplesnife getting thicker, and oozier, and tugging harder at his boots, he could feel that sulphur-like stench getting the better of him, smothering him like a pillow to the face. Dragging him down, into unconsciousness.

His steps got heavier. His breathing too. And he felt his heart throb hard in his chest as if trying to eject a poison from his system.

As he felt his mind swim and his blood pump harder still, the toe of his boot caught the path before him and before he knew it he was tumbling forwards.

And, before he could stop himself, he landed face down in the whipplesnife.

For a moment he was surprised at how warm it was.

How *pleasantly* warm it was.

And then, as if someone had spun the dial on a furnace, the pure heat of it struck him.

Scorched him.

3

DREAMS CAME FLEETING AND FRANTIC.
    Blurred faces.

Jagged shapes.

Blotted and smudged colours.

And then, right at the end of it all, as Blof felt his mind slowing down, coming back to some semblance of reality . . . of *sanity* . . . a pink shade took over everything.

That same pink glow that he'd observed coming off the lamper.

That *pissing* lamper.

"Told . . . told . . . told . . ."

The words floated about him. About Blof. He couldn't hang onto them. It was as though he was standing at the opening of one side of a rocky valley, and the person on the other side was shouting to him. But the words got all mangled by the echo.

"You . . . you . . . you . . ."

Gradually, Blof felt a prickling sensation over his skin. The pink shade faded off. To be replaced by darkness. He breathed in, and then out. There was none of that sting remaining. Though he still had that bitter taste of sulphur in his mouth. Could still feel it harsh as paint stripper against his cheeks.

But he wasn't still down *there*.

Down in the basement.

No, he was . . . he was . . . someplace else.

Now the prickling sensation subsided. He felt a fresh warmth sweep through his blood. He focussed on his body. Realised that he was lying on something soft. A pleasant fabric. Silk? Was that what it felt like?

And then he opened his eyes.

A bed. That was what he lay on. Just a simple, single, iron-framed bed. Tucked in bed sheets. All white. And if he squinted hard, he could make out the bulge *way* off in the distance where his feet, his toes, poked up against the bed sheets.

He looked on a little further. Expanded his horizons.

Though his vision was a little blurred, he was certain of what he saw.

Phayshawe standing at the foot of his bed.

He wore his signature clothes. That pale pink suit, the cream shirt underneath opened right down to the downy grey hair that sprouted at his chest. And he wore his smart straw hat, with a pink silk ribbon also, of course. The brim of his hat was drawn down just so as to leave his features in shadow.

Blof breathed in. Caught the peppery fragrance of his boss. And, considering that his mouth still tasted stale, *dry*, the pepper was a nice contrast. Almost full of flavour in comparison with that sulphur taste.

And then Blof remembered what had happened.

The mess he'd left down there in the basement.

But before he could attempt an apology, Phayshawe was speaking to him again.

He wasn't smiling, that much he could see, that much his hat didn't hide, and as he spoke he held his hands stuffed into the pockets of his suit. That made Blof a little uneasy.

Did he have a gun or something on him?

Undoubtedly.

"So, I see you didn't follow orders," he said.

Blof parted his lips to speak, but he found he had simply no energy to spend. It was like someone had sapped all the strength out of him.

In any case, Phayshawe hadn't phrased it like a question.

34

"Yes," Phayshawe said, with a slight sigh, "that's the problem with hired help—let them out of your sight, even for a *second*, and they're going off gallivanting, doing their own thing, you know, messing with carefully calculated plans, picking apart the seams that hold everything together."

Slowly, as Phayshawe spoke, Blof took in the room around him. It was a small room. Not much bigger than the bed he lay in. The window was wide open, and it was a sunny day outside. He could see the green of the elm trees that marked the whole of Hornheim Manor.

When he turned his attention back to his room, he saw the pine wardrobe opposite his bed, and the red-ribbon patterned wallpaper on the walls. And the bedside table, also pine, that stood alongside him with various syringes and different coloured liquids in glass bottles.

Had they stuffed him full of that stuff? To keep him alive?

He turned his attention back to Phayshawe, standing at the foot of his bed.

Phayshawe tilted his head back, giving Blof a brief glance at his face beneath the shadow of the brim of his hat. "Wouldn't you say?"

Blof managed a glum nod. He reached for his silky bed sheets, grasped them in his right fist. Felt the blood pumping hard to his skull. He was powerless now. He was weak and ill, and if Phayshawe wanted to rub him out then now was the time to do it.

All he had to do was put a bullet in his brain and walk away.

Blof wouldn't be able to do anything about it.

There was a long silence, and Blof wondered if Phayshawe was waiting for him to say something, though he knew that he wasn't strong enough to do so. But, just as he was sure they'd reached a tense standoff, Phayshawe broke out into a smile, and strode over to the window of the room, gazed out.

As he did so, he held his hands clasped in the small of his back. Phayshawe's smile gave no sign whatsoever of leaving his lips. "I'm sorry about what I had to do, Blof, but it wouldn't have been possible to have done it with your own knowledge."

What was he talking about? Blof had no idea what Phayshawe was talking about.

"You see," Phayshawe continued, "I've been looking through my ranks for the longest time, trying to pick out just the *perfect* person. The one who might be up to the task."

What 'task' was he talking about?

"Someone who was well built, you know, *heavy*, like yourself."

Blof guessed he had a point there, what with him never having been the lightest kid at school, and he had certainly piled on the pounds ever since his promotion, there was no turning away from that. It was just a cold, hard fact.

"I don't know if you've heard about the experiments with whipplesnife, the ones to do with mixing it with humans."

This time, Blof found his voice, though it was croaky and feeble. "They . . . uh, *die*," he finally got out.

Phayshawe slipped Blof a sidelong glance and smirked. "Yes, for the most part. But the men I've got working for me seem to think they've made a breakthrough." He took a step towards the bed, the smirk gradually slipping off his lips. "I mean, I heard the stories— just like everyone else—about the people . . . *freaks* who had taken on brute force strength following exposure to whipplesnife. But, until now, there was no proper means of testing out that claim."

Blof felt a shudder pass over him. His muscles tensed up all over. ". . . If you wanted to choose me then why didn't you just *ask?*"

"Because, my dear boy, you might've said no, and then where would I have been? I had you appointed to the position close to me because of your size, because of your *weight*, someone with a chance to withstand exposure. I simply couldn't allow you to have a chance to say *no* to me, why, you might've taken it as a slight, and come back to haunt me later on, wouldn't you say?"

Blof considered this. He had to admit to himself that, if Phayshawe had asked him if he would be prepared to expose himself to whipplesnife then he would've certainly had second thoughts about it. Whether or not he would've agreed in the end, he didn't know.

But one thing still sat uncomfortably with him.

He tightened his muscles and propped himself up on the pillows, leaned back against the iron-framed bed, making it squeak just a little, and then said, "Why did it happen . . . I mean, why did it all explode about me? All the whipplesnife come loose from the pipes."

Phayshawe smiled again. "Because you used the lamper of course."

"Yes," Blof said, "I know that, but *why?*"

Phayshawe narrowed his eyes to slits, but kept up his smile. "I have to say that you have quite an enquiring mind for an aspirant mobster."

Strangely, Blof felt his cheeks growing hot, himself blushing.

"I suppose you've never heard of bunter?"

"Bunter?"

His smile widened. "Yes, *bunter*."

4

AS PHAYSHAWE EXPLAINED, and Blof listened in on, *bunter* was another energy source. It was much more stable than whipplesnife, though considerably weaker.

When whipplesnife and bunter were combined things became unstable.

Bunter was what everyone loaded into their lampers, and other portable items. There was no need for a central furnace, no need to keep it flowing through pipes as was the case with whipplesnife. And, come to think of it, Blof had most likely heard of it . . . but it was something so commonplace that he guessed he'd just never really thought about what powered all those portable things. Maybe he had really believed it to be gas.

Maybe he'd just had his eyes shut this whole time.

Come to think of it, he'd only really begun to realise the scope of whipplesnife a year or so ago, when he and his gang had been given orders to starve a neighbourhood of energy, as some kind of recompense for defaulting on payments. That was when he'd watched a more schooled member of his gang sabotage the whipplesnife pipes leading into the sector, and he'd asked just what it was.

And the guy had told him.

Really, thinking about it, Blof guessed that it wasn't all that strange. He had never been to school. His parents had just left him to do his own thing. He had just worked his whole time, preying on richer little kids, taking a beating from their dads now and then, until he had managed to get his foot on the rung with the Crul.

And this was what Phayshawe wanted from him now.

Phayshawe had expected him to go against his orders, to flare up his lamper, and Blof hadn't disappointed.

The idea had been to give him a gigantic dose, a dose only really possible to administer through an 'accident' such as the one that'd happened to him down in the basement.

He had just done exactly what was expected of him.

Later on, he met with the scientists, with those working for Phayshawe, the ones who claimed they'd done all the research into whipplesnife, and its combination with people.

Blof let them stick needles in him, take his blood out, put it back in . . . rinse and repeat. He did everything they asked because he knew that he couldn't possibly piss off his boss.

He had to trust him.

Trust that he knew what was the best for him.

After a long, drawn-out session, Blof sat up in bed, feeling his arm tingling, feeling numb and all worn out from the various needles they'd stuck in him today. He felt better today. More clear headed, or, at least, a little more clearheaded than before.

And stronger. He felt much stronger.

Stronger, in fact, than he had ever felt in his entire life.

The scientists, while he'd been in their care, had had him try out various things, take various tests. At first they brought him a standard wooden log—like the ones used in the open fireplaces, and in the wood-burning stoves—it had been about twice the thickness of his arm and he had managed to break it easily in two.

Then they had brought him gradually bigger things until they had ended up bringing him a brick, and taken a step back to watch and see just what he would be able to achieve with it.

Blof had broken it in half.

He could still remember that triumphant—slightly surprising—

puff of brick dust up in the air, and then he had crumbled the remaining pieces with his bare hands.

His strength had surprised him.

He had shaken for a long while afterwards, and he still remembered those self-satisfied smirks on the faces of those scientists, that bumping of fists that he was sure they hadn't thought he would see.

And now he was ready, ready to go and see Phayshawe, to ask him what he had to do for him now.

Blof trod his way through the mansion, taking in the cold, brick floors, and the staunch wooden rafters that divided up the plastered walls. He felt a kind of magic inside of him now. Tingling away. Though he knew that it was just the whipplesnife. That it had, well, somehow supercharged him. The scientists had seen to that.

As ordered, he headed up to the sun room, to go and meet with Phayshawe, and found him there, in the room made mostly of glass, standing with his back to him, staring down onto the cityscape, down onto Guynur City and all its sprawling alleyways, and bustling action. The cars heaving their way along. And the shouts of vendors coming from an unseen marketplace.

Phayshawe, like before—and always—wore his pink suit, the straw hat with the silky pink ribbon, and he turned around, glanced Blof over once, and then smiled.

He stepped towards Blof, his smile seeming to get wider with each of his steps until he drew right up before him.

Blof was surprised at how he towered right over his boss, though he guessed he always had done. Was it the whipplesnife? Was that what had given him confidence to stand straight backed in the presence of his boss? Did he . . . no, that was too crazy to think about . . . but he *had* thought it, had considered if he might be able to physically *crush* him . . . if he ever felt the need.

And he knew he could.

Apparently unaware of the thoughts on Blof's mind, Phayshawe smirked and then clapped Blof hard on his ripped bicep. And Blof felt the tingle of the whipplesnife now melded in his system rise to the surface of his skin.

"I think we're going to have a good old time now," Phayshawe said, and then glanced back over his shoulder, back to Guynur City. "I think we're just going to teach this town some lessons."

Blof gazed past his boss, out the window, to Guynur City.

And he knew that he was built to serve Phayshawe.

This was all he had ever fought for.

To be Phayshawe's boy.

UNIVERSITY OF LIFE

AMUNDDA drew her deep purple robes tighter about herself, and stared long and hard at the sign.

It was embellished with a gold and silver weave, with the same flowery lettering that she recognised from the whole of Guynur City over:

Edgebrudge University

And then, just below, in even more flowery script:

Heart and Soul and Knowledge

She could feel her blood pounding up to her temples, and that toast she'd scoffed down before donning her robes, and bombing it out the door, tasted sour now at the back of her throat. She could smell the plants beyond the well-armoured, black iron gate standing before her. They were strong, and potent smells. And, just off in the distance, almost at the edge of her consciousness, she heard a voice.

". . . Help you, ma'am?"

She took a sturdy breath. Tried to get a grip on her eyes. To bring them back into focus. Away from that sign. And back to the real world.

Yes, this was all real.

She blinked a couple of times, trying to get the image straight. Trying to take away that fuzzy gloss that seemed to hang about the periphery of her vision.

Edgebrudge U. Right before her. There it was.

With its castle-like appearance. Its mounted turrets that seemed like they'd been transported direct right out of the Dark Ages . . . to the lead-lined windows that all caught the light from Nephmur and turned it into that impenetrable, impossibly white glint.

Ivy sprawled its way up the stone walls. Inched in and out of the nooks and crannies, spiralled about the edges of the windows, apparently on a mission to reach the very top of the university. To reach those turrets that formed the roof.

And then the gardens. They flowed out from the building kind of like a lush, verdant carpet spread out before a king. And, in just a matter of seconds, she'd get to walk that very same carpet.

Did that mean she was a queen now?

She turned her attention to the guard. To the man who wore the deep purple uniform, the same colour as the robes she herself wore. He was dark skinned and had on a matching cap, drawn down over his neatly trimmed hair. His shoes were black and well polished, and she couldn't help but notice the handgun which he had holstered at his belt.

A .22 Pictlewhip.

Just like all governmental officials in Guynur City carried. Just like her mother had carried back when she'd been fuzz . . . before she'd been killed in a gangland shootout, and left Amundda and her two younger sisters orphaned.

The insurance pay-out had helped, of course, but it hadn't made up for the fact that Amundda had had to bring up her sisters as if they were her daughters. Had had to care for them till they were old enough to fend for themselves.

Till the middle of last year when the youngest had finally fled the nest, had found herself a decent job in the city centre, working as an apprentice at one of the financial firms.

And that had meant that, finally, Amundda could follow her dreams, that she could finally take the entrance exam to Edge-brudge U.

She could still remember the day, about three weeks ago now, when she'd got the letter, detailing out her first day at the university, along with the letter allowing her to purchase the robes from an approved outlet.

She could still recall the warm glow in her cheeks that'd stayed with her all through that sleepless night, and she could still recall the gentle burn of that cup of coffee she had overturned in her joy, and the smell of the coffee all puddling at her feet. And how she'd squelched through it in her slippers before picking up her mobile and calling her two sisters to tell them the news.

They had been overjoyed, of course.

Just as they'd have been overjoyed when something wonderful had happened to their mother. A de facto mother at only fourteen years old.

Now she was twenty-three, and full of hope for the future.

Amundda turned her attention back to the guard, who was giving her a thin-mouthed smile. "Papers, please," he said.

She handed them off to him, and he took them with a firm nod, before retreating into his booth and, as she could see through the tiny window, he smoothed them all out on his table and began rubbing at the university seal there with his thumb. Squinted at the paper as if he was certain that it was a forgery.

In the end, though, he re-emerged from his booth, and handed her back the papers with a smile. "Go right on in, ma'am," he said, touching the visor of his cap, and disengaging the lock on the black, iron side-gate with the dry *buzz* of the locking mechanism.

Amundda trod through the gap, thanking him more than a dozen times it seemed.

But what did she really care about seeming like a bimbo, coming across as a giddy girl on her first day at school?

This was *all* she had *ever* dreamed about.

THE ENTRANCE HALL of the university was all oak panelling. And she breathed in that deep smell of polish, felt it tickle her nose hairs, and dry up her mouth. Leave a stale taste there.

She could still feel her heart pounding hard in her eardrums and she knew that it was only first-day nerves. That things would get better as this became routine. After Edgebrudge U had revealed its secrets to her.

She was sure of it.

As she walked, she heard her flat-soled shoes making a hollow *thwack* against the oak floors, and she wondered if there was anyone about.

There didn't appear to be a reception of any sort, and she guessed that all the scholars were off studying in their rooms, or else giving tutorials.

As she proceeded down the hallway, she noted the several oil paintings which hung down off the walls, with their gilded frames and mean-looking scholars all staring down at her, she did noticed one other thing.

They were *all*, every last one of them, male.

That didn't intimidate her, though. It was just enough that she was here at all. She could leave all that political stuff behind her for the time being . . . though she did have to admit to herself that, from the outside, she'd always found the male-dominance of Guynur City's premier university somewhat unsettling.

She prowled about the hallways, peeping into the odd room, doing her best to see if she could see anything at all. Anything that might suggest a little life about the place.

Finally, she reached a dead-end, a hallway with another bunch of leathery-skinned, elderly past scholars of the university. All of them peering down out of their frames at her.

This time she felt a slight skittering sensation over the surface of her skin, all the hairs becoming erect. It was kind of like the reaction she had to spiders. Or to mice . . . with rats she was usually grabbing for the nearest broom, rats usually kicked her into action.

She eyed up the firmly shut oak door before her, looked to its gleaming brass handle. Saw the name etched into the tag on the door, in silver lettering. It read:

Prof Newbirth

Though she didn't recognise the name, she couldn't see anyone else around the university to ask questions on just whereabouts she should head next.

Other than the guard at the gates, of course. But that would've meant backtracking all the way back through the gardens, having to admit to him that she had no idea what she was really doing here at the university.

And she had no intention of doing that.

She gave the door a good couple of raps with her knuckles, and then waited, listened tight for any sound within.

There was a throaty cough followed by a shuffling sound.

Through all this, Amundda got the distinct impression that she was waking Professor Newbirth up. And, indeed, when he finally opened up the door, and peered out through the crack, she saw, just like the stereotype, he was wearing blue-and-white, striped pyjamas with a nightcap pulled down snug, right over his ears, its bobble snaking down to his collarbone.

He looked about sixty, maybe even older, he had mounted wrinkles about his eyes, and his eyes themselves were webbed with throbbing red veins.

"Yes," he said, looking at her blearily.

Amundda held back a moment, now feeling totally out of place. But she reminded herself that she had a right to be here, that she had her letter of acceptance all in order. And that this should be the best day of her life so far . . . a day she'd never imagined would come ever since her mother had been killed all that while ago.

"I . . . uh, I . . ." she just about got out.

He squinted at her, causing his furry, grey eyebrows to hustle over his eyes. And the cracks in his skin to widen, the wrinkles about his eyes to mount even further.

She caught a faint whiff of cologne mingled with the sour taste of sweat, and Amundda began to regret having knocked on his door at all. She could feel all her muscles drawing tight, and her heart hammering hard. When she flexed her fingers, she realised that they were clammy with sweat.

Then, all of a sudden, the lights, or whatever was behind Prof Newbirth's eyes, just seemed to blink on, and he said, "Ah, you must be one of the new ones, eh? Day for enrolment and all that, I suppose?"

Glad for his filling in the gaps, Amundda nodded vigorously.

"Hmm," Prof Newbirth said, and then stifled a yawn with the back of his clenched, leathered and pockmarked fist. "Then you'd best be off along the main hall—take a left, then another left, and you'll see the way to the Great Theatre. Then it'll all make sense I'm sure." He blinked another couple of times. "Say, what time is it?"

Amundda told him.

Prof Newbirth widened his eyes, apparently out of disbelief. "Oh, is that right? Then you *are* early. And," he said, through another yawn, "I'm not exactly late getting up for the day ahead either, so, if you'll excuse me, I'll head back to bed."

And he did, turning off back into his room, and shutting his door before Amundda had the good sense to say "Thank you."

3

AMUNDDA FOUND the Great Theatre easily, and she saw that, just like the professor had said, there was no one around at all. She *had* got out of bed early this morning, but she'd thought that getting here first thing was the best she could do. The best way she could make a good impression right off the bat.

Because she was determined to make her academic career at Edgebrudge U a runaway success.

The doors to the theatre were open, and so she simply went inside, and took in the enormous auditorium, surely large enough to fit many hundreds of students at the same time.

The layout was circular, so that the seats swept about the stage.

The walls were a flourish with cornices, and golden and silver paint, of all sorts of figures from mythology, or whatever, that she was sure to learn about at her time at the university.

There was a gentle scent of furniture polish in the air, and it made the back of her throat tingle just a touch. Reminded her of being back home. Of being back with her sisters.

It seemed like she'd lived another life back home looking after them.

But now she was living for herself.

Finally.

She took a seat in one of the folding-down, velvet-upholstered chairs a couple of dozen rows back from the stage. And she just sat there, allowing herself to sink back into the impossibly comfortable material of the chair. Feeling as if it was melting into her.

At first, when she sat, she was convinced that she might fall asleep, that she might simply drift off. But she needn't have been worried. It seemed like her heart was pounding out several hundred beats per minute. She couldn't have slept even if she'd wanted to.

Over the course of the next hour, as she sat there in that seat, she watched her fellow undergraduates all file into the theatre—most of them five years younger than her, of course—and soon enough, within another twenty minutes or so, she observed them all around her. All packed into their appropriate seats, and waiting, just like her, for the address to begin.

Once the theatre was more or less packed, and the feverish, excitable chatter had seemed to reach a fever pitch, Amundda noticed the appearance of several scholars up on the oak stage. That they were all there, dressed in their deep purple robes, and waiting for the ceremony to begin.

There were six or seven of them in all, but the only one among them that she recognised was President Mawkley. But of course she recognised him. Just about everyone in Guynur City recognised him, with his owl-sharp yellow eyes and his rigid posture. The way that he dug his thumbs into the fold of the lapel of his robes. What distinguished him from the rest of the scholars was that he wore also a pink ribbon which hung about his neck.

The sign of the president of the university.

Amundda was aware of her neighbours, her fellow undergraduates at either side of her, and how they stared up at the stage, just as intently as she did.

They must've been just as excited as her.

She watched as President Mawkley surveyed the theatre, tilting his head back slightly, looking down his nose at them all, in a way, before picking his way across the stage to the lectern which had appeared in the middle of the stage . . . that some stagehand had brought out of the shadows all ready for the president's use.

He stepped up onto it. Looked down at the notes he apparently kept there. Turned a page, and then cleared his throat.

He had no microphone.

No microphone was necessary for that dulcet voice of his . . . or, at least, that was what Amundda had observed from a distance, whenever he appeared on TV or the radio or whatever.

"It is my duty first to welcome you to our proud academic institution, to Edgebrudge University. You are all *quite* exceptional, in that of the millions and millions of inhabitants of our noble city, you are the ones who have been determined to have the best proficiency of any who have taken the entrance exams here."

Amundda felt a tingle pass up her spine. A slight fizz shoot through her blood.

It was funny, even though she'd had the validation of her acceptance letter, it wasn't till she was sitting right here, in this theatre, that she could really go some way to grasping the real gravity of what she'd already accomplished.

Not that she'd rest on her laurels, of course.

She was determined to be the greatest student she could be during her stay at Edgebrudge U.

For a long while President Mawkley went through the rest of the business—all those day-to-day details that were necessary for each and every student to know.

And though they were mundane, Amundda soaked them up like a sponge.

Felt them saturate her brain.

After what she saw, glancing at her mobile, had been forty-five minutes, President Mawkley brought his opening speech to a close.

"And now," President Mawkley continued, "I ask you all to bear in mind the motto of the university. The one that you shall see etched into doors, onto walls, and"—he slipped a slight smirk —"even scratched onto the sign at the entrance to the university."

He held back for the longest time, so long that Amundda thought something had gone wrong . . . that he had, somehow, forgotten the motto to the university, and the wait was made all the more strenuous by the fact that she could say that motto over and over in her mind.

But then, *finally*, President Mawkley put her out of her misery, as he said, "Heart and Soul and Knowledge. Those are the virtues of Edgebrudge University. And those are the three words I urge you all to bear in mind whenever you find yourself—as I'm sure you will— doubting your presence at this university. Because those are the foundation stones that the whole institution is built upon, as it always shall be."

And, with that, the whole theatre burst out into applause.

For a few seconds, Amundda was so awestruck by the situation, that she didn't think to join them till several moments later. But when she did, she was sure to clap extra-specially hard.

4

LATER ON in the morning, after Amundda had managed to get herself to where she was meant to be . . . which turned out to be Prof Newbirth's chambers, where she had gone that morning to knock on his door, she found things coming more naturally to her.

When she came to Prof Newbirth's door, she noted the slight look of shock that gripped his craggy features, just for a moment, before he broke out into a smile and allowed her to slip past him and enter his chambers.

Along with her, in her tutorial group, she had three other students. All of them aged younger than Amundda.

And all of them male.

They went about introducing themselves, saying a little about their lives.

And Amundda took the decision to hold back. Thought it better not to drown everyone with her sob story, as she'd learned not to do over the years . . . learned to see how people's eyes often glazed over whenever she got to talking about her mother, and how she'd raised her two younger sisters herself . . . etcetera . . . etcetera.

It was only when they were nearing the end of the tutorial that something caught her attention.

One of the students, blond and piggy-nosed, and with twinkling emerald eyes, muttered a comment to his neighbour. And though he made *some* effort to keep it from her, Amundda picked up on it right away. Heard the words just fine.

Crystal clear.

". . . Didn't realise Edgebrudge U had lowered itself to accepting girls . . ."

Amundda kept her eyes fixed on Prof Newbirth who was wittering along merrily about something, completely oblivious. It was a little funny that, even from her first day here, at the university, she had learned just when she could tune herself out of whatever it was a scholar was saying . . . but, then again, she also guessed that today—her *first* day of all days—she was hypersensitive to the burning issue.

The one that had gnawed at her heels in the long run-up to today—inauguration day.

She thought long and hard about leaving it, about forgetting that she'd overheard the comment at all, but it was only when they all got up to leave—after Prof Newbirth had declared the session over—that she decided that she was going to do something about it.

And so, sucking in her gut like some sort of superhero, she picked her way through the oak-panelled hallways, keeping an even pace as she followed after the two boys.

She followed them out to the gardens outside the university, and kept on going after them even when the blond boy glanced back over his shoulder to her, arched his eyebrow in her direction.

Amundda guessed that he had quite a bit of spirit for a snot-nosed little kid, but that just made her all the more determined to bring him down a peg or three.

"Hey!" she said, just as he turned back to his friend.

The blond boy jerked his head back in her direction, eyes wide, and lips pursed, apparently waiting for some sort of a reaction to his comment back there in Prof Newbirth's chambers.

She marched up to him, feeling the gravel of the path through the soles of her shoes. She stopped when she was just close enough to him to make him feel terribly uncomfortable, and then said, "I heard just what you said back there—back in Professor Newbirth's room."

The blond boy gave his companion—a mousy-haired, and quite round boy—another of his wide-eyed specials, before looking back to Amundda with what she supposed was meant to be a look of innocence. "No idea what you're talking about," he said.

She screwed up her eyes. Peered deep into his. "You said that Edgebrudge U's 'lowered itself' to accepting girls."

The blond boy just pouted a little more. "Don't think I did."

"You *know* just what you said."

The blond boy just shrugged at his companion, and then he made to continue walking, to apparently head out of the gates of the university—maybe off to go fetch some lunch from somewhere close by . . . no doubt with his daddy's pocket change.

She lurched forwards and grabbed hold of his sleeve. Clamped on tight to his dark purple robe, just like hers. "Listen to me," she said, with a lip-curling snarl, and then she told him all about her past. Just what she supposed—in retrospect—she should've told her *whole* tutorial group back there in Prof Newbirth's room. Right from the start. Maybe then they would've respected her right off the bat.

The blond boy and his mousy-haired companion just listened tight to her, didn't make so much as a *squeak* as she went through it all again.

And this time, Amundda was pleased to note, there was no sign of so much as a single glazed-over eye between the two of them.

They *were* listening tight to her now.

When she'd finished, the blond boy and his companion exchanged glances.

She waited for something . . . an *apology* perhaps . . . but it didn't seem to be forthcoming, so she decided that she might as well head off to go and get her own lunch, and presume that here today a lesson had been learned.

Only as she took a step away from them, did she hear someone call out.

But it was neither of the boys who did so.

When Amundda looked up, she saw a redhead girl trotting towards her. She had fair skin, and was wearing the same deep purple robes of the university.

She fixed the two boys with a snarky glare, and then turned to Amundda with much softer features. "I heard it all," she said. "Heard the whole story."

Amundda glanced up over the girl's head, to the pair of boys, who looked like they'd very much like to skitter off somewhere, but looked far too sheepish to actually do anything about it. She turned her attention back to the redhead girl, who was shaking her head.

"Unbelievable," she said, "I mean, after all we have to go through to get our foot in the door, and this is just what we end up being faced with."

Amundda shrugged. "I don't mind, I guess, I mean it was pretty much what I was expecting."

The girl held out her hand for Amundda to shake. And Amundda took it off her.

"Tera," the redhead girl said.

"Amundda," Amundda said back to her.

And then, when Amundda looked up again, she saw that the boys had already skulked away, that they'd made a bid for the university gates, apparently hoping to escape any further confrontation.

Tera took hold of Amundda's arm, and Amundda felt her giving her a slight squeeze, looping her arm through hers, and leading her through the university gardens. "You know," Tera said, "I was thinking that there weren't any other girls about here at the university, that *I* was the only one that they'd decided to let in. You know, kind of like a token . . . so they could bring me out whenever there're media hovering about—that sort of thing."

Amundda shrugged. "What makes you so sure you're not?"

Tera studied her for a few seconds before answering. "Well, because you're here too."

"Maybe they wanted a pair of tokens."

Tera went all straight-faced for a pair of moments, and then she returned to her glimmering smile. "Nah," she said, "I don't reckon that's it at all . . . I think I just caught the wrong idea right from the start. But things should be different now—I mean, now that we've got the two of us. That we can be friends and fight back against them together."

"Against who?" Amundda said.

Tera smiled wider. "The boys of course."

Amundda allowed those words to tumble about her brain. It all sounded so juvenile and yet, at the same time, it kind of made a sort of sense to her.

Well . . . what exactly had she been expecting from Edgebrudge U? Not just the greatest and most prestigious academic institution in the city, but also the biggest boys' club.

She felt Tera give her arm another squeeze, and tug her onwards, towards the university building. "Come on," she said, "I'll show you the trophy room, where they keep all the old-style photos and stuff . . . then you can *really* see how ridiculous this place is."

Just as they headed on up the stone steps, Amundda couldn't help but sneak a swift glance back over her shoulder, back to the pair of boys now stealing their way out of the university gates and back out into the street.

And she caught the blond boy's eye. And, even from a good

seventy or eight paces away, she was sure that she could see that little glint of fear there . . . or, as she liked to call it, as she'd started to recognise it from constantly scolding her sisters, *education*.

She guessed that he'd think twice before repeating those stuffy remarks . . . at least when Amundda was in earshot.

But, if he didn't, then she'd just have to up the ante.

Now she'd met Tera, she knew that it wasn't just for her, but it was for *all* womankind at Edgebrudge U.

But that was fine since she was perfectly used to fighting battles.

And now, at least, this battle wouldn't just be her own.

CORRECT THINK

I

JASMINE BALDERBAXTER fished about in the pocket of her sleek, black dress trousers. The fabric was all frayed, and it felt damp with sweat. She scraped her chewed-up fingernails right to the bottom and caught hold of a few scraps of lint right there. Nothing else. But, then again, just what had she been expecting?

Had she thought that she'd refind the lamper: the device that man down the market had given her?

Even though she'd seen it fall right between the metal grating of that storm drain.

Watched it tumble down into that obsidian pit.

Just because it was magic, did that mean she really expected to find it just *magically* back inside of her pocket, as if it could regenerate in some way?

No, and much better that she didn't find it, too, what with her standing here, in line, alongside all the others filing about the corner of the *Correct Think Institute*, all of them waiting in line in the hope that a job offer would be at the end of it.

Just another normal day.

Just like *every* day of hers.

She would wake up in the morning, look through her post for any sign of correspondence—a job that she'd applied for *somewhere* in Guynur City. Then, if she did have a letter from someplace, someplace offering her an interview, she would skulk through her wardrobe: nothing more than some wood off-cuts all slanted into one another and then held together by some wonky-hammered nails, and pick out her Work Clothes.

The clothes she wore now.

The white blouse that'd been ironed into oblivion.

The jet-black dress trousers: the pocket of which she'd slipped the lamper into.

And the over-polished, flat-soled shoes that she could feel bringing out sweats from her thickly-socked feet.

She still had that lingering taste of toothpaste in her mouth, that kind of empty, promise-less taste. The one that made her think of days like these—*every*day—these job interviews with the snub-nosed men in ill-fitting suits, and the business-like women with their gelled-down hairstyles and wily eyes.

Just challenging her to slip up.

To make a mistake.

She was standing at the front of the queue now. Only a meathead standing between her and the entrance to *Correct Think*.

As she stood there, she craned her neck upwards.

Took in the building.

It was sleek, and white, and . . . well *glossy*.

The windows, too, had that same kind of off-white hue to them, and it made her think about a photograph that's been taken just a little out of focus.

Yes, like a photograph of a snow drift.

Something like that.

The meathead, just like all meatheads, it seemed, wore a trim, black suit which seemed to be struggling to contain his bulging muscles. His eyes were like pinpricks, almost afterthoughts, smudged on in there just above his angular cheekbones.

Just like all meatheads, he never seemed to meet your eye.

Constantly swivelling about, never seeming to settle.

Never seeming to give up the prospect that here—that *anywhere* —there was a fight to be had.

She remembered back when she'd been a girl, maybe sixteen or seventeen, and how she'd lay in bed at night thinking over those rippling muscles, thinking over those buffed-up, bald heads . . . and she'd find her mind wandering, and her fingers somehow—almost of their own accord—drifting south . . .

"Watcha waitin' for?"

Jasmine snapped to attention. Somehow summoned a, "Hmm," from the back of her throat.

Then she realised it was the meathead who had spoken to her.

That he was glaring at her with those piggy eyes of his.

His hands bunched up into fists down at his sides.

"I said," the meathead replied, "Watcha waitin' for?"

Looking ahead, Jasmine saw that the doorway was clear, that there was no one else ahead of her. No one else waiting to head on into the building of *Correct Think*.

With a slight flush, she bundled on forwards, the lamper now pretty much shaken from her mind.

And her thoughts already sweeping ahead of her, turning to think about the job interview that awaited her.

That awaited her only a few paces from here.

2

THE SILENCE in the large boardroom, up on the seventeenth floor of the *Correct Think Institute*, made Jasmine think about the cutting edge of broken glass. Looking over the three figures: all of them wearing grey suits, and even greyer expressions, she couldn't help but wonder what she was supposed to be doing with her hands.

She decided on keeping them down at her sides, to bunch up the fingers into fists, and then to flex them out. For some reason, she found herself wondering about whether she might be an octopus secretly, and whether she was merely inhabiting this . . . this *human* body for a little while.

There were two women and one man on the board here.

One of the women wore glasses.

The other didn't.

The man had his light-blue tie, with a diamond design, all knotted up to his throat in a way that Jasmine was certain must be choking him.

Though Jasmine really had no expectations, she felt for her pocket yet again, felt for the lamper there.

And was unsurprised, all things considered, not to find it.

Did she *really* believe in all that guff . . . all that *stuff* about magic?

Why, she'd lived here, in Guynur, her entire life.

And she'd never *seen* anything to do with it.

"Ms Balderbaxter?" the man said, making the 's' of the 'Ms' buzz in such a way that made Jasmine think about beehives.

Only then did Jasmine realise that he was indicating that it was time for her to sit down. That she should take up the seat at the end of the long, shiny boardroom table. The table that seemed, ordinarily, to seat about twenty or so executives. But which today seemed a little empty, there only being four of them all together.

She examined the chair a second: a smooth, black leather chair with a curved back to it. It was one of those chairs that always looked pretty unfeasible to her, what with its curves, and the way that it made her think that if she was just to sit down there that she would slip right off . . . slip off the chair and land with a *thump!* on the thin, grey-blue carpeted floor.

But she rode this slight outpouring of neuroses, and took her seat there.

Against all odds, her rather slanted bottom managed to maintain full contact with the seat below.

She wished she still had the lamper, though what good it'd do her now sort of escaped her.

Maybe it just acted as a sort of comfort blanket, kind of a . . .

The man shuffled some papers, slapped them into flush on the desktop and then peered over at her.

Jasmine noticed that neither of the women had so much as looked at her.

That they were apparently engrossed in writing out something.

"Thank you for coming to see us today," the man said, a professional smile in his voice, but not on his lips. "We, ah, have spent quite a while considering *your* application, Ms Balderbaxter, and it might please you to know that we really are quite taken with it— with someone of your . . . uh, *experience*."

Jasmine felt her heart skip in her chest. Once again she patted her pocket, thinking that she might be able to find her lamper there. But, of course, there was nothing to be found.

All this talk about magic, it was just a mirage.

And in a way she'd *always* known that, though never really had the full heart to accept it.

Jasmine turned her attention over to the three people at the other end of the table, squinted just a little to bring them better into focus. She swallowed hard in a way that she was sure would communicate to these people that she was some-what nervous about this whole thing . . . because, well, she was . . .

"My experience?" she said.

"Hmm," the man said, turning his attention downwards, back to the papers before him.

It was only then that she twigged he had a copy of her CV before him.

Well, of course he did.

Of course he had her CV.

She'd sent it here, to *Correct Think*, after all.

How else would they have judged her a suitable candidate to call for interview?

Jasmine sat there, in the chair, feeling distinctly uncomfortable. She looked over her interviewers once again, and then she said, "But I don't *have* any experience, that's the problem, see, that I've never got a job, though I've been looking every day, no one *ever* seems to want to accept me."

As Jasmine shut herself up, she looked over the people on the other side of the desk yet again, watched them giving each other kind of knowing glances. And she wondered just what that meant. Just what they were trying to communicate between themselves.

Were they ready to toss her out on her arse?

Were they realising that they'd made a *dreadful* mistake?

. . . That they'd got the wrong person after all, that . . .

"Ms Balderbaxter," the man said, this time with a little more steel in his tone. "May I ask just what you know about *Correct Think?* About our company here?"

Damn, just the question she'd been worrying herself about.

She hadn't had *time*, there just *hadn't* been time.

No time for her to look into the company.

She'd only got the letter that morning.

And now, here she was, in this interview, with these *people*, and they wanted to know just what *she* thought about *their* company . . . she'd already taken too long with these deliberations, in her head, already taken too much time to think things over.

They would know that, the next time she spoke, she was simply *winging* it, making things up as she went along.

She only got as far as parting her lips before the man spoke up once more.

This time he had a light smile pinned on, and a tiny little gleam to his eyes.

"*Correct Think Institute*, Ms Balderbaxter, has existed for just as long as Guynur City has left the Dark Ages."

The Dark Ages? . . . Yes, she'd studied them, back in school, those times before there had been any sort of a magical influence on Guynur, before the whole city had been revolutionised by the magic which now flowed right through its veins: the magic that powered its cars, that warmed its homes . . . that made its lampers *gleam* . . . that same lamper that she had lost.

"*Correct Think*," the man continued, "exists to help maintain the separation between *magic* and everyday human existence."

Jasmine wondered whether she should speak up now, whether she should make some sort of a comment on this. The way that the man had spoken, he had left that thick, *pregnant* pause out in the air . . . a pause for her to fill in for herself.

Then something *did* strike her, something that she had heard throughout her life in Guynur City . . . but, then again, which kid hadn't heard the stories, those mentions of the group known as the Watch . . . the group of shrouded figures who kept blunt, brute-force magic out of people's lives . . . made sure that magic was *only* used to *aid* human existence, not to damage or belittle it.

Just thinking these things over, it made her wonder, made her think that this man here, that he might be onto something, that he might even know her better than she even knew herself.

Could *that* be the truth?

The man, as if he was reading her thoughts . . . had he been reading her thoughts? . . . smiled just a little wider, his mouth opening up like a gash breaking out of virgin skin.

"Yes," he said, "I think that you can appreciate just what this means. What this whole thing *means* for you, and for others like you . . . the ones that *really* think things through, that don't leave things alone like Good Little Citizens."

"I . . . I . . ." Jasmine began, a little uncertainly, but, before she could finish, she caught the two women looking up from their writing, the two of them staring at her, and before she knew it she was dismissed by the man . . . told that she would be starting on Monday.

3

THINGS HAD GOT to the point, in Jasmine's life, where the days had simply worked their way *in* and then *out* of her brain, as if this would always be The Way That Things Were.

So, with the acceptance at the *Correct Think Institute* right on the surface of her mind, she could hardly restrain her enthusiasm, the enthusiasm she had for her first day.

She arrived on Monday in the same clothes as she'd gone to the interview in, of course. She had no other clothes that would've been appropriate. None that didn't have *holes* in any case.

As she swept on in past the meathead on the door, and into the already, and strangely, familiar building of the *Correct Think Institute*, she tried to get a hold on her stomach. Tried to stop it cramping up on her, tried to stop those surges of blood billowing up to her brain —stealing away her attempts at logical thoughts.

She emerged out on the thirteenth floor, the floor that the man . . . who'd turned out to be called Mr Herald Frantson . . . *Mr Frantson* . . . had told her to go to on her first day at *Correct Think*.

She stepped along the well-polished, chalk-white floors, and smiled pleasantly at a rapid-fire typing secretary—about Jasmine's age—and wearing a navy blue jacket over a white blouse. The secretary nodded Jasmine into the office—into Mr Frantson's office—and Jasmine could hardly restrain her excitement—or was it just unchecked nerves?—as she rapped her knuckles against the thick oak door, and then entered when she was summoned with a slightly weathered, "Come in."

Mr Frantson's office was quite large, and had enormous windows which looked on out across the whole of Guynur City. For just a few moments, Jasmine lost herself in the sweeping, diving alleyways that steered on out away from the building of *Correct Think*, and out into the shadows.

She looked to Mr Frantson, who was seated at his CRT computer monitor, two-fingered typing out something or other.

She supposed *that* was the reason why he *needed* a secretary.

He finished up what he was doing then turned in his desk chair.

Took Jasmine in with his intense gaze.

"So," he said, "how're you feeling on your first day?"

To tell the truth, Jasmine felt a little at home . . . in a funny way like things were back to normal, as if she'd spent her entire life seeking out a routine that would be right for her, and now it appeared like she'd found it . . . or maybe it was just her mind moving on at a thousand miles per hour, hardly able to make sense of any of this.

"I'm glad to be here," she finally settled on.

Mr Frantson gave her a sturdy nod, glanced to his computer monitor, and then looked back at her. "So," he said, "do you fancy going back to school?"

"What?" she said, confused a moment.

He smiled, understandingly, and then he glanced back over his shoulder. Out to Guynur. The way that he looked, the way he *considered* the city, it was almost like someone who's found a speck of dust on a windowpane and is determined to clean it right off . . . *profoundly* . . . when they get the chance.

He turned back to her, his desk chair creaking just a little as he did so. "One of *Correct Think's* responsibilities, some might say one of its *highest* priorities, is *education*." He paused a moment as if to let the abstract concept of 'education' have a little room to breathe in the not-unsubstantial office. "So, your job," he said, reaching down to a desk drawer, shifting it out and then removing a beige-coloured folder—"is to go and speak with kids." He met her eye. "All you've got to do is read through this package, tell them just what's written here."

Jasmine gazed down at the beige folder that rested on the desk before her. She wondered if she should snatch it up, buck her way on out of the room. But first she decided that she had some questions—questions that needed to be answered.

She swallowed hard and then said, "Why me?"

Mr Frantson had his eyes fixed on his computer screen, out of sight for Jasmine. "Hmm?"

"Why did you choose me?" Jasmine glanced down at the folder once again as if it might be a bomb that was about to go off. "I mean, out of all those other people—the other ones that came here, wanting a job with *Correct Think?*"

Mr Frantson squinted at whatever it was that he was looking at on the screen, and then he turned his attention back to her. Gave her a fairly infuriating smile. One of those smiles that Jasmine instantly recognised as saying, 'First day on the job—guess it *is* time for some stupid questions.'

"Working here," Mr Frantson said, "it has everything to do with a person's innate talent—their innate *ability*. Really, it's something which can't be taught. You're either born to work here, or you aren't."

Jasmine blinked a few times. Tried her best not to look totally stumped by what it was that he was saying. It all just sounded so . . . *mystical* . . . was that the word she was looking for?

Mr Frantson squinted hard at his computer monitor and then, a couple of clicks of his mouse later, he turned his attention full onto her. He steepled his fingers and gazed over them in that way that villains in films always do.

"What do you *really* know about Guynur?" he said.

JASMINE HARDLY had a heartbeat to think of her reply, but, as it turned out, she had no need to say anything at all since Mr Frantson went on.

"Guynur City," he said, "is a *refuge*—think of it as a gated community that keeps us from the outside world, that keeps the rest of Schwyn out."

Jasmine drew a deep breath, and it felt kind of frosty, sort of prickled about the inside of her ribcage in a ticklish way. She focussed in on just what Mr Frantson was saying, flushing all other thoughts from her mind.

"We . . . *us* . . . *humans*, we are kept here, we are *born* here, and, fate permitting, we shall die here, in Guynur, too . . ."

This time, Jasmine couldn't resist interrupting. "But *why?*"

Mr Frantson smiled thickly and, just for a micro second, his eyes switched to the door, became interested in the closed door all of a sudden . . . before Jasmine had a second to think about just what this might mean, he turned back to her.

"There are *things*," Mr Frantson said, "*things* out there, in the wider world—in Schwyn—that would crunch humans to mincemeat without so much as looking at them." He drew a long breath and then sighed it out. "You see, to many of the magical creatures who inhabit Schwyn, we are really nothing more than ants." He cocked his head to one side. "Tell me, Jasmine, can you tell me with any certainty the last time you trod on an ant? The last time you *killed* an ant?"

Jasmine felt her heart thrum. ". . . Um," she just about got out, only right then realising that the question had been rhetorical, because Mr Frantson went on.

"That's *why* Guynur City exists—a refuge from the outside world, an incubator for this *ever-so* fragile *human* life. That is why the *Correct Think Institute* exists. We answer the questions of the populace while doing our best to keep the truth . . . the *wider* matters somewhat concealed."

Jasmine had just about a hundred questions tumbling through her mind in that moment. But the only one which she got out was, again, "Why?"

Mr Frantson smiled warmly at her once more. "Why what?" he said.

Considering her surprise at all of this, Jasmine marvelled that she somehow managed to keep herself together. To answer in a somewhat lucid stream. "Why keep the truth from the people of Guynur City? Why *can't* they know?"

Mr Frantson shrugged. "Because the truth might turn them crazy—might send everyone into a *panic*. Not even the Watch know the *full* truth. Only the Council, and us: *Correct Think*." His smile dissolved just a little on his lips. "Tell me, how do *you* feel right now?"

Maybe she should've kept her thoughts to herself, remained an enigma, but the truth of all this was that she simply didn't have the presence of mind *not* to blab her mouth—blab everything that was on her mind.

"I . . . I . . ." she said, "I guess that I'm feeling just a little confused."

"Hmm."

"Well, I have to say that I find it somewhat unbelievable . . . I mean, if all you say is true then how do we manage to keep these magical creatures *out* of the city?"

Mr Frantson smiled again. "That," he said, "is beyond even *my* remit."

Jasmine felt her stomach tighten. It was odd that Mr Frantson was admitting a limit to his knowledge when, just now, he had enlightened her so much, had made himself seem like he was all-knowing.

Mr Frantson tapped the folder on his desk then said, "Everything you need to know is here, inside."

Jasmine found herself going all numb, but, at the same time, reaching for the folder there. She slipped it off the desk, tucked it under her arm, and, before she really knew what she was doing, she was padding her way to the door of Mr Frantson's office. Only when she heard the two-fingered typing recommence over her shoulder did she think to turn around and say, "But, Mr Frantson . . ."

"Please," he said, "Just call me Herald."

"Mr . . . uh, *Herald*, you haven't answered my question, told me just why you chose me."

Herald gave her another of his thick smiles, blinked a couple of times, and then he said, "People like you—people like *you* and *me*, everyone who works at *Correct Think*, who has any sort of an access level along the lines of the one we share, they have magical blood gushing through their veins. We *do* make a point of sweeping up all those we can get our hands on. Getting our hands on the ones such as yourself. Why? Well, those with magical blood . . . they—how should I put this?—they are most likely to twig, at least at some point in their lives, that this is all just a rat's maze, that Guynur City is an illusion . . . and that they live here *merely* for their own protection."

Jasmine sidestepped the bombshell about her having magical blood, she could shudder to herself about the revelation of *that* fact when she got outside, got out into the city. For now, she just picked another question with Herald. "What would've happened to me if you hadn't found me?"

Herald shrugged, glanced for a second at his computer monitor, then turned back to her. "One of two things," he said, "you would have been banished from Guynur—thrown out into the Big, Bad World of Schwyn, left to fight for yourself, with that *magical* blood of yours." He turned his attention back to his computer screen, apparently having forgotten the second thing.

"And the other?" Jasmine prompted.

Herald drew a slight gasp between his lips, as if he might've forgotten himself . . . though Jasmine was almost certain that he hadn't. "Well," he said, "the most likely *other* option was that you might've been *killed*."

"Killed?" she said.

"Hmm," Herald said, then turned his attention back to the computer monitor. "In one way or another."

Jasmine took this as her cue to leave and she reached for the doorknob. Only then, as she felt the mechanism twitch beneath her grasp, Herald spoke one more time.

"Jasmine?"

"Yes, Mr . . . uh, *Herald?*"

"Now that you work with *Correct Think* you *must* remember your role at all times—you are to speak of nothing that I have told you today." He nodded at the folder in her hands. "That information should serve as the guide for the cover story you should feed the kids."

Jasmine lingered for another second, another moment in which she thought of asking yet another question, but, in the end, she speculated that, really, there was no need for it to be asked.

Because she already knew the answer.

The question over what might happen to her if she chose to share her knowledge—to tell someone else the full truth she had just discovered about Guynur, about her home.

And she knew that the answer would be simple.

Clean, empty, decisive.

Death.

5

J ASMINE COULDN'T HELP but think of the lamper she'd lost, back on the day of the interview.

The recollection struck her now, as she padded along, counting out the building numbers on her way to her mission.

On her way to the school.

Why, it had simply disappeared, hadn't it?

But what did she really mean by that?

Like it had just slipped out of her pocket, slipped through the metal grating of a storm drain?

. . . No, she was wondering whether her *magic* might've had something to do with it, if *she* had had something to do with its disappearance.

Was that *really* what Herald had meant when he'd spoken about magic, or was it just her imagination?

He hadn't really defined that at all.

She shifted the load of the beige folder in her arms. She had flipped through the information nestled inside while she'd been travelling on the metro. It was familiar. Blood-churningly familiar actually. And she knew the reason for its familiarity was because she'd heard just about the same thing—near enough verbatim— back when she'd been at school, back when she'd been an eager . . . or should that have been *not so* eager . . . schoolgirl.

And now it turned to her.

Now it was her turn to *lie* to a bunch of schoolchildren.

Could she really do that, when she put the whole matter so bluntly?

. . . She supposed that she'd have to . . .

She closed in on her assignment, on the school name.

Gunderbrudge Primary School.

She was to give her talk to around thirty six-year-old kids.

Just thinking of those sixty-something eyes all gazing up at her in some kind of wonder made her heart kick on a little harder. Made the blood flow just a little hotter. A little thicker. What if she made a mistake . . . what if they asked her questions?

Questions she wouldn't be able to answer.

Questions she wasn't *allowed* to answer.

She swept through the school, a kind-faced secretary pointing her off on the right track, and Jasmine took the opportunity to flip through the first few pages of her information pack one more time. Just so that she could get the knack of it. She guessed that it would take only a dozen or so of these sessions before all this information —all these *lies* she was about to dish out—would become second nature to her.

The classroom was larger than she'd imagined. With full, shining windows which let in the late-morning sun. And brought the warmth rising up from the carpeted floors. She looked over all the expectant faces, those latched-open mouths as they took in this *stranger* in their classroom.

For the longest time, Jasmine just stood before them, the silence only disturbed by the gentle scratching of the teacher behind her, sitting at her desk marking books, or something or other. The teacher that was rounded, bundled-up, and who reminded Jasmine of her grandmother, and who had her hair sticking up in manic tufts as if she was maybe just one crisis away from being committed to the Nuthouse.

Jasmine held her folder down at her waist. Already having the information, or the beginnings of it, memorised so that she could dispense it to the children.

Knowing that there was only one way out of this thing, out of this encounter, she started.

"Does anyone know why we're here?" she said.

The kids remained silent. Their eyeballs remained fixed in their sockets. Their stares totally blank. Mouths *still* latched open.

Jasmine took a deep breath, thought over the second question in her instructions. "Does anyone know *why* we live here, in Guynur City?"

Blank stares all around, yet again.

Jasmine tried to get things straight in her mind. Tried to work out whether she might've said those questions wrong. And then she recalled something else in the information pack: about the expected responses from the children she was dishing this information out to . . . and how they often wouldn't participate early on in the talk.

And then, on the periphery of her vision, Jasmine saw a raised hand. She zoned in on it swiftly. For a second Jasmine just stared at the little girl with her arm raised. She had her blond hair done up in pigtails. Her blue eyes gleamed in the sunlight which dribbled in through the expansive classroom windows. Jasmine remembered her role here, pointed to the girl then said, "Yes?"

The girl grinned back at her, and Jasmine saw how the rest of the kids all stared at the girl now as if they were some sort of savages all held in awe by some idol. "Um," the girl said, "it's because we have everything we *need* here, in the city. Um, because we have the magical fuels here. Um, so that we can all have a much easier life."

It was odd. The answer was so rote, pretty much verbatim to what she had written within her folder, that Jasmine was struck dumb for a few seconds—and in those seconds she was sure that she could hear the kids all breathing as one, those biting, semi-*asthmatic* breaths.

Then she remembered herself. Gave a grin, and then said, "That's right."

The girl with the pigtails grinned and then brought her hands down into her lap, to rest on her crossed legs.

Jasmine couldn't shake the thought that they were in a prison—that Guynur City was a prison. That humans were kept here . . . well, there really was no other way to say it, *against* their will . . . but going out on a limb would mean Jasmine risking her own life, and it wasn't like these kids would even grasp the impact of such a statement in any case . . . no, it would be Jasmine who would suffer if she told the truth to these kids, and for no reason at all.

Jasmine forced on a smile, and then she said, thinking back to the contents of her folder, "That's right—yes, that's one of the many reasons why Guynur City is such a wonderful place for us."

She paused, thinking things over, trying her best not to spill what was on her mind . . . those thoughts that could get her into a whole *world* of trouble.

Remembering her audience, Jasmine thrust her finger up in the air in a semi-comical way that at least brought out a slight *titter* from the kids all sitting cross-legged on the carpet before her. Then she said, "But, there's another reason—another reason why we should stay here, in Guynur City, can anyone tell me just what that is?"

Another raised hand. This time a boy with green eyes and black hair. A jumper that looked like it had been washed too many times and pretty much had a layer of fuzz sprouting off it.

"Yes?" Jasmine said.

"Because, because"—the boy paused for several moments, apparently to catch his breath, having put his hand up before he'd truly had a chance to get his thoughts together—"there's *bad* things out there, outside of the city," he said.

Again, Jasmine was surprised at how well these answers corresponded to just what she had written down in her folder. In fact, the only thing that she could think to do was nod along with the boy's answer.

"And, and, and," the boy continued, "it's much better for us to stay here, to stay in the city, where we can be nice and safe and not get into trouble or nothing."

Jasmine felt her professional smile slip just a little, but, as soon as she realised, she pinned it right back on.

Again, the kid had answered right in accordance with her information.

Some of the key phrases within the materials she had were about her being as vague as she could possibly be—to neither confirm or dispel certain beliefs the children had.

The most important thing was for them *not* to associate magic with the *badness* outside of the city, that would have been a travesty . . . the main things they were *supposed* to associate with Guynur City was safety, a future, a place where they could *be* human . . . and it was to their benefit to obey that considering what their fate might be if they chose to leave the city.

If they chose to *die*.

Jasmine swept through the rest of her materials, the rest of the activities all written out within her folder. Those included group games, and rote chanting, along with a song which Jasmine did her very best to get out in a somewhat melodic way.

When the school bell clanked tunelessly above her head, Jasmine couldn't help but feel a skitter up her spine, that sensation she got when something caught her off guard.

The teacher thanked her with a neutral smile and, just like that, Jasmine was off on her way, leaving the school—and her first assignment behind.

6

I T WAS WHILE she was walking through a nearby park, meandering her way back towards the metro, and her next assignment, that she felt that same uncertainty stirring in her belly

That shrill buzz passing through her blood, that innate sensation that she'd learned to recognise as her body's reaction to her doing something *wrong* . . . for want of a better word, *immoral*.

Was that right?

Was she doing something *immoral?*

Was her job *immoral?*

Was wanting to save her own skin *immoral?*

. . . Because that was what she was doing, what she was tasked with doing.

There would be no backing out of the job she had accepted now, not with the knowledge she had gained, of the way that things *really* were.

She thought back to that class, to her first assignment, to those kids back there, and she wondered if any of them had magic in their blood, if they were like her.

If they would have to face a similar decision in their own lives.

If they would live their lives damned.

And here, in Guynur, forever more.

DOWN IN THE DUMPS

T HAT FAMILIAR, sickly sweet stench of rubbish wafted all the way across the Tip in the early-evening fading sunlight. Naufrenzy breathed it deep into his lungs. Felt that tang at the back of his throat. It tasted like sugar on his tongue. He could feel the warmth coming off the mulchy brown piles of discarded things that towered up high around him.

This place was his kingdom, and he was its king.

In the distance, Naufrenzy could hear the gentle hum of the afternoon traffic. The car engines thrumming back and forth, filing in turn as they headed to wherever it was they were headed.

The sound spilled into the compound of the Tip, over the rolled-up, barbed wire that was strung all over the tops of the three-storey-high brick walls that guarded the Tip against *intruders* —those that Naufrenzy hadn't given permission to come inside and scavenge.

People might accuse him of lots of things, but one thing he wasn't was a mug.

No one got one over on Naufrenzy and lived to tell the tale . . . at least that was what he would often tell his kids when they all came round him, all wide-eyed and scrubbed up from their bath, looking for a bedtime story.

That was always the moral of the story, whatever story he thought of telling: that *no one* got one over on Naufrenzy . . . he could even admit that to himself.

He wasn't too proud of a man not to see it for himself.

Humility was one of the truest tests of a leader.

And no one could doubt that he *was* a leader, even if it was just of the Tip . . . it did have a habit of making him chuckle, just a little, when people tried to downplay the importance of the Tip to Guynur City.

Quite simply put, the Tip was where *every* last scrap of rubbish from the whole of the city came. It all ended up here, in these five, or so, square blocks: a far bigger spread than most of those so-called *uptown* buildings. To be rummaged through by Naufrenzy's noble scroungers, for it to be thoroughly scavenged to see if there was any value to be had . . . and then, that which had no value would be taken out in carts, out to the edge of the city, to be buried in those great big holes and forgotten.

Left for forthcoming generations, his grandkids' grandkids to worry about.

For all he knew about that stage of the process, it might've been magicked away by some magician or other . . . that was another of his rules: steer the hell away from magic in all forms.

For Naufrenzy, it might as well have not existed at all, though he wasn't so near sighted as not to realise that magic was everywhere, that it powered Guynur City, and it wasn't going away any time soon.

However much he would like it to.

Nope, no matter how much people would try and downplay the Tip's importance to Naufrenzy, he always, though often just in the back of his mind, declared just how wrong they were.

Naufrenzy popped the collar of his cream-coloured shirt, bringing it up to cover the flabby mass of his neck. He always took care to cover it up. The one problem with his job, with him being in charge of the Tip, was that he didn't often get a chance to get all the exercise he needed.

He found himself spending a disproportionate amount of time having dinners with business people, people looking for contracts on his scrap, people looking to leave their waste to him and his workforce. And so, quite inevitably, he'd got a little porky these last few years—the amount of time he had been in charge of the Tip.

And he'd just got back from one of those meetings, and so was still wearing his suit. It was a charcoal-shaded one. His wife had bought it for him for one of his birthdays. And he'd noticed, over the past year or so, how he'd been having increasing difficulty prising his rolling stomach into the waistband.

He'd managed today.

But only just.

Naufrenzy crunched his fingers into fists and set them at his waist, driving his knuckles into the fine black leather belt a scrounger had scavenged last week from a heap of discarded clothes. Had his wife clean it up, of course. But it was as good as new. Had a few jewels encrusted into it, even.

It was amazing sometimes the sorts of things you could find down at the Tip. Perfectly good stuff that would otherwise get thrown away.

Why, only last week he'd uncovered a perfectly good pair of smart shoes too. They were sturdy, only a hole in the sole of the left shoe, but he'd soon taken care of that with some putty. He'd got the wife to polish them up and they were good as new. All ready for the meeting he'd had today. No one at the meeting had noticed. He had blended in with the rest of them. And it did send a chuckle tickling through his throat to think about it sometimes, about how these people that called themselves businessmen often splashed out a good amount of quid just to get themselves looking all dapper, when, really, there were impossible and unending riches to be had at the Tip.

But that was a secret that would die with Naufrenzy . . . unless, of course, one day one of these businessmen came to him, *really* hard on his luck, pleading for work. To be a scrounger. Just like those that worked for Naufrenzy.

The scroungers made light scrabbling sounds at they dug through the piles. Each of them looking to turn up some treasure of some sort, and if not treasure then at least something of value, something they could hock to Naufrenzy. Something *he* could see some value in selling on.

Though the workers weren't *technically* his *employees*, he *was* the one who let them all work here at the Tip. So that was how he termed them. It sounded better than *scroungers*, anyway, and having once been one himself, he guessed that they'd go for the euphemism.

He took them in. Their shabby rags. All of them reduced to that same raggedy, brown-grey colour. Some of them not even having so much as shoes on their feet, just chewed-up, bloodied rags.

Oh, he felt pity for them, of course he did. But this was all about business. This was the world of business. And those that couldn't survive in it, well, the simple truth of the matter was that they simply *went away*. Like rats, they'd turn up drowned in a sewer, or gutted, or sometimes both. Robbed for the few quid they had in their pockets, or maybe just for the packet of food scraps they'd dug up out of some alleyway bin or other.

In Naufrenzy's time as a scrounger, in his time in and around the Tip, he had the whole hierarchy of the place totally internalised. And he could see that the scroungers, the ones that were reduced to actually coming here, down to the Tip, to sift through the endless piles of rubbish, they were the lowest of the low.

Next up on the totem pole were the scroungers with the carts, the ones who went around the city. They pulled the carts themselves: cobbled-together wooden contraptions with vaguely round wheels.

Naufrenzy had been one of those too.

The next ones were the scroungers who had managed to avoid those common pitfalls: the drugs, the stabbings, the hunger, and scrabbled together a few quid to buy themselves horses for the carts they'd once drawn themselves.

They could bring in far more scrap. And get paid by one of Naufrenzy's men off at the entrance to the Tip. Then they'd turn back around and head off through the city to bring in yet more scrap. Getting paid each time.

The way Naufrenzy remembered it, the way he saw it now, being in charge of the Tip, was that those who drew their own carts only managed one, at most two, loads of scrap to the Tip a day. Only got paid once or twice a day at most.

But those with the horse-drawn carts, they could make as many as half a dozen, sometimes more, trips down to the Tip with their load of scrap.

They were the ones who would start to make it.

And then, if they were smart—if they were like Naufrenzy—they'd buy up more horses, more carts, and put people to work *for* them.

It was easy to make a few quid that way.

Naufrenzy should've known, he had done that himself.

Built up his empire till he'd managed to run for Proprietor of the Tip.

To arrive to just where he was now.

Just as Naufrenzy completed his swivel-eyed surveillance of the Tip, taking in the heaps of rubbish from one end to the next, his attention fell onto the entrance, to the great big, iron-tipped spikes which stuck up on the gates—currently open—and then to the cart standing there right now.

It appeared that the scrounger was having a confrontation with one of his guards—one of the men he employed to take money off those who arrived with their carts laden with scrap.

Though Naufrenzy would normally leave such disputes to his noble employees, to be fair to himself he was usually too *busy* to deal with such mundanities, he decided that he might as well step in here.

It was good to keep a visible presence down on the ground at times.

Kept the employees—the *workers*—on their toes.

2

A S NAUFRENZY drew closer, he caught a strong whiff of rotten eggs. Now, considering that Naufrenzy was well accustomed to *bad* smells, odours of all kinds, it took something especially rancid to catch his attention.

But this certainly did.

It threatened to bring the wonderful prawn noodle soup, and accompanying crunchy garlic bread back up his throat. But he kept it down.

He felt a cold chill pass over him.

An omen?

And as he got closer still, crunching along the broken pieces of stone that formed the gravel floor of the Tip, he could hear the scrounger babbling on at the guards at the entrance. There were two of them, both dressed in the neat, emerald-green uniform of the Tip. Their handguns holstered at their sides.

The standard issue: .22 Pictlewhip.

Steel-grey with a rigid, pocked black grip.

A gun beloved and handed to all city employees.

Why, Naufrenzy had one of his own, at all times strapped to him by a shoulder holster beneath his suit jacket.

Both of the guards had their fingers hovering down at the grip of their guns, apparently ready to whip them out at a moment's notice.

From looking at them in profile, Naufrenzy saw that they were both fresh faced, *young*. And, on closer examination, he saw that their fingers were shaking as they reached for their guns. Now, taking in their uniforms properly, Naufrenzy did realise that the emerald shade was still bright, not washed out at all . . . a pretty much giveaway sign of a callow employee.

Yes, a good job that he had stepped in after all.

Naufrenzy reached into the jacket of his suit, felt for his own gun nestled inside there. And flipped off the safety catch, unbuttoned the flap keeping it in place. Ready to tug it out if required.

The two employees—the *guards*—flashed a pair of glances back at him, and he watched the shock register in their eyes, in the wrinkling of their foreheads.

He never tired of that expression, loved it really. How they never in all their lives would've expected the administrator of the Tip—their *boss*—to come down here to the entrance and get his hands dirty.

But he had.

And he was certainly here now.

Naufrenzy allowed himself a smile as he took in the scrounger. Saw that he was still gripping tight onto the rectangular-chopped wooden handles which protruded from his cart. That his knuckles had turned white from gripping so hard.

The scrounger had a fuzzy, ginger beard, and Naufrenzy could see that he had a twitch in his right eye, and that his complexion—beneath the beard—was mottled and rosy. That he was most likely coming down off some drug or other.

Naufrenzy really had *no* time for addicts, of any type or creed. He supposed that his prejudice came from his own time spent as a scrounger, and from the basis that since *he* had managed to get through it without drugs then everyone else bloody well could.

He kept his voice steady, even and made an effort to meet the scrounger's eye. Just like all the others, this scrounger wore only rags as clothes and as shoes. "What's the matter here?" Naufrenzy said.

The scrounger's eyes widened, and Naufrenzy looked beyond him, to his cart's load. Saw all of the castoff scrap metal piled up there. The stuff that he had scavenged out of the various back alleys of Guynur City.

He caught another wave of that rotten-eggs stench, and couldn't help but turn his face away, gagging. When he turned back to the scrounger, he could feel the sting of bile in his throat, his dinner really coming back this time. He swallowed it down. Tried to forget about the churning in the base of his gut, and tried again.

"Scrounger," he said. "What's your business with my guards here? Haven't they offered you a price?"

The scrounger averted his eyes. His eyeballs swivelled about their sockets. His hands gripped the handles of the cart tighter still.

Naufrenzy shot the pair of guards a look. "Where's your supervisor? Where's Hedder?"

The two young guards just looked back at him with their wide eyes. Apparently no idea between the two of them.

This time Naufrenzy slipped his gun out from his shoulder holster, clicked the first shot into the chamber and held it down by his side. Right where the scrounger could see it.

He tilted his head upwards, up to the top of the brick wall, to the watchmen he had patrolling along it. And he saw that a pair had assembled there. He could make out their forms in the fading sunlight, in the twilight sky. Could see the silhouettes of their rifles.

In a minute or so the automatic lights would flicker on, illuminating the whole of the Tip for the night. This situation might've been eased with a little better lighting. But there was really nothing to do.

Naufrenzy had come down here to take care of business, and so that was exactly what he would do.

"Scrounger?" Naufrenzy said. "State your business, or leave, that's your choice. Else"—this time Naufrenzy brought his gun upwards, pointed it at the scrounger's chest—"I'll have no choice but to take care of you right here and now. You *do* understand that this is city property, and that if I decide that you're trespassing the law covers me to take you out?"

The scrounger was mumbling something under his breath.

Naufrenzy caught the worried look off one of the young guards a moment before he heard the almighty *crack!* spread through the air, echo about the compound of the *Tip*.

A blinding white light filled the air. Forced Naufrenzy to close his eyes. And even then, even with his eyes clenched shut, and his arm brought up to shield his eyelids too, he could still feel the burn against his retinas. Could feel the strain burrowing in through his eye sockets.

All of a sudden it got hot. Too hot for him to stand. And then he was whisked from his feet.

He felt himself tumbling back through the air. His balance long lost. And he felt his gun slip from his fingers and heard it clatter down onto the ground beneath him.

He wasn't just tumbling.

No . . . he was *flying*.

And he only stopped when, with a hard *thunk*, he struck a heap of rubbish. Listened to the gut-churning *squelch* as he slipped in deeper. Being shoved in deeper by some mysterious force . . . though *was* it so mysterious? . . . Because he knew just what it was.

Magic.

3

FOR A LONG FEW SECONDS, Naufrenzy lay there, in the heap of rubbish. He knew that he should've been absolutely covered with that sickly sweet scent, but, instead, he could only catch a whiff of those rotten eggs. The rotten eggs from the scrounger . . . that *magician*, who had just cast that spell. Sent him to where he now lay.

His heart tickled his eardrums and he expected the killing curse to come at any second. His mind's eye filled with his family: his wife, his kids. Him having told them all one of his stories, watching them wide eyed with shock before seeing the smiles burst out on their faces as they realised that the protagonist—*himself*—had overcome all the odds and won the day.

Would he ever see their faces again?

His brain felt thick with blood pumping to his temples, and he was sweating all over. As covered in sweat now as he was with the rubbish that he lay upon. At least he had been lucky enough to land on one of the soft piles—on top of a pile of scrap fabrics, something like that, and that it had gone all soggy in the rain.

His mouth tasted of a mixture of salt and blood. He wanted to scrabble up. To reach for his Pictlewhip, but at the same time he knew that it lay a long way off from him.

He was in a position he'd hoped—*prayed*—he would never, ever find himself in.

He was at the mercy of a magician.

The magician could finish him off.

Right now.

If only he wanted to.

Naufrenzy waited out a few more seconds before he dared to

raise his head a fraction. To open his eyes even a slit. He took care not to make any sudden movements, and he gazed about himself, trying to gauge what he could see.

Looking through the blur of his eyelashes, he could just about make out the mulchy brown surroundings. The heaps which surrounded him. He squinted off towards the entrance of the Tip, managed to spot the entrance.

At least twenty paces away.

That *magician* had somehow managed to toss him, with his magic, twenty paces.

Magic was outlawed in Guynur for good reason. Only registered practitioners were permitted to use magic, and then only with long and drawn-out regulation from the city authorities. And if anyone should've known about city bureaucracy, it was Naufrenzy. He had been through a tidy sum of it himself in his climb up to the top of the Tip.

He would have to call in the Watch: the city authorities who looked into magical matters, if one of the guards hadn't already done so.

He looked about himself. Couldn't make out the magician's location. *That* put him on edge. But, really, there wasn't much he could do about it. He wasn't about to go *mano-a-mano* with a magician. Especially with one that he couldn't see.

He jumbled through the inside pocket of his suit, jiggling through to try and find his mobile. Finally he managed to fish it out. Checked the coast was clear. Then he dialled up the Watch, listed, as always, as 678.

He got through to the operator, fed him the location as quickly, and as quietly, as he could, and then he pocketed his mobile once more.

When he looked up, blinking hard to try and break out of the daze . . . maybe it had been brought on from his landing in the rubbish heap . . . he saw that a couple of guards, those same young ones, had emerged from wherever it was that they'd been hiding. And, with their handguns down at their sides, they were trudging along the broken-up rock floor of the Tip, apparently hot in pursuit of the magician.

Naufrenzy was caught in two minds. He could just stay here, lying here in the middle of this sodden, foul-smelling cloth . . . though it was no match for that stench of rotten eggs the magician gave off . . . or he could take charge, go find his handgun, and stand up to show his employees the leader he truly was.

But what was he thinking? This was a *magician*.

A matter for the Watch.

And they were on their way.

Perhaps . . . perhaps he should just . . .

"Sir?"

Naufrenzy glanced up. First saw the smooth, emerald-green uniform, before he got a glance at the face. Saw the stringy moustache on the upper lip, a mousy brown like the rest of the remaining hair that collected about the crown of his head.

Hedder.

The supervisor.

The man beneath him, and in charge of the guards down here on the ground.

Naufrenzy had to admit that he'd never been happier to see him.

He saw that Hedder offered his gloved hand—the finger pouches all cut off at the joint, like the gloves all the guards wore, to help with grip on their trigger fingers—and he accepted it, allowed Hedder to tug him back up to his feet.

When Naufrenzy got himself back upright, he toppled from

one side to the other, his legs having apparently turned to jelly following his flight through the air. But, a couple of moments later, he got a hold of himself. Managed to rediscover his sturdy, trusty stance.

"Where is he?" Naufrenzy said.

Hedder's eyes darted away. Back over Naufrenzy's shoulder. To the entrance of the Tip, and then they scoured the area, picking through the piles of rubbish. And then, in a hoarse, uneven voice, he pointed and said, "There, sir. Over there."

Naufrenzy followed Hedder's knobbly, tangle-haired finger. And he looked off to the rubbish heap in the direction he pointed. It was one of the smaller heaps, off just inside the wall. And he could make out the magician there, his cart behind him, having apparently tugged it all the way into the Tip without any resistance.

When Naufrenzy glanced up to the brick wall, to where his watchmen were placed, he saw that they were only just then staggering up to their feet.

Something about what had just occurred suggested to Naufrenzy that a direct, all-guns-blazing approach might not be the best plan of action right now.

Especially with the Watch on their way.

He glanced up to the brick wall, and gave them a limp-wristed wave, ordering them to stand down. And then he turned his attention back to the magician.

If there was one thing he had learned about magicians, even with his limited experience of them, it was that they had to be kept an eye on at all times.

"Sir?" Hedder said, and then Naufrenzy saw that he was holding his Pictlewhip in his hand— Naufrenzy's Pictlewhip—the one that had slipped from his hand when the magician had sent him soaring.

"Thanks," Naufrenzy said, taking it from him, feeling just a little warmth rising to his cheeks as he did so.

Naufrenzy took the lead, treading over the crunched-up rock underfoot, that smell of rotten eggs getting more rancid still, and those noodles not leaving him alone. He swore to himself that it would be the last time he would indulge himself in a business lunch before coming back to the Tip in the afternoon—having to do battle on a full stomach certainly couldn't be recommended.

He kept his handgun down at his thigh as he picked his way across the broken-up rock, made his way closer to the magician, who had his back to him.

It stunned him, really, to think that he had been so convinced that this was just an everyday scrounger. A second-class scrounger, too, him having a cart and all. Just a horse away from rising to the aristocracy of scroungerdom.

But he had the same rags, the ones he wore, the ones on his feet. His face was bearded. And he looked like just another drug addict.

He had missed something, though. Some detail. There was *one* thing that he would take forward from this experience.

He wouldn't make the same mistake again.

He would become more sharp-eyed from now on.

Never let *another* magician slip past him.

But, first things first, he had to take care of this one.

Naufrenzy stalked on closer, hearing Hedder's heavy breathing just over his shoulder. He wanted to tell him to shut up, to stop breathing, just like back when he'd been a kid and he would some-times tell his brothers while they were playing hide-and-seek, or some game that required them to stay quiet.

He looked to the magician's shoulders, hunched over as he dug through the heap of rubbish. He looked infinitely busy, digging through the scrap with his bare hands.

Naufrenzy wasn't sure what it was. Maybe the blood buzzing in his brain. Maybe his heart just took that opportunity to give a double tap. Or perhaps his innate hatred for magicians just won out over his logical brain.

Because it was then that he raised his handgun, held it straight and looked along the barrel, lining up a shot, aiming for the space between the magician's shoulders. His trigger finger trembled and then squeezed hard.

The bullet cracked through the twilight air.

And caught the magician right where he'd aimed.

4

NAUFRENZY FELT every muscle in his body go tense. A cold sweat broke out all over him. Beneath the surface of his suit, which acted now like a sponge, soaking it up. All at once that stench of rotten eggs grew impossible to bear. Just sour, and unwieldy in his nostrils. When he breathed in, it seemed to burn his lungs right from the bottom and up to the top.

He caught that bloody taste on his tongue again, though he was certain he hadn't bitten the inside of his cheek, that there was no raw blood for him to taste at all.

But, over everything else, the thing that struck him was the silence.

The *deafening* silence.

He looked to the magician. To where he had crumpled down. No more than a heap of rags now. His heart seemed to break out of its pause. To tick right on again. And the world soon followed.

He heard a chuckle at his shoulder. Hedder. Then Hedder walked round him, into Naufrenzy's vision, and he saw that he was shaking his head, apparently in disbelief.

Then again, Naufrenzy wasn't sure he believed it himself.

Couldn't quite bring himself to believe what he had done.

He heard laughter all around him too. Bouncing off the brick walls of the Tip. Coming back at him like they were a bunch of diseased hyenas, or something.

Naufrenzy, though, remained serious, continued to stare at the magician's carcass, didn't bring his handgun down, kept it pointed right at the point where he had shot.

At the spot between the magician's shoulders.

Perhaps if he hadn't taken so much care, hadn't been the only one among them to keep his wits about him, then they could've all been dead.

Right there and then.

But Naufrenzy saw it. He saw the cobweb-like sparks dance over the fallen magician's body. Over his rags. And, before he could truly tell what he was saying, he found himself bellowing out. Warning his people away.

Another blinding light filled the Tip, but this time Naufrenzy had the presence of mind to turn his back to it, to avert his gaze, and when he recovered, saw that the light had dimmed, he saw that his people had done the same.

"Come on," he said, beckoning his people away from the downed . . . though apparently *alive* magician . . . and he got them all clear of the site.

All of them waited off by the entrance till the Watch showed up.

Like always, they were dressed in those shimmering, beige, gold and black robes. Their hoods drawn up to hide their faces. To leave them steeped in shadow.

The Watch always sent a shudder passing across Naufrenzy's skin, and they did so now. He always found himself in awe of their tall, skinny, almost sticklike forms, and how they seemed to hover rather than take steps.

The Watch, as Naufrenzy saw it, were a necessary evil. Magicians that were just about this side of tame, just about worthy of trust.

But only just.

He watched them go to the magician's side. Saw them all crowd about the magician, hide him from view, and then, that unearthly *hum* filled the air. That chant of theirs that still gave him nightmares.

He could remember having heard it back when he'd been a child. Back when he'd once got up in the middle of the night, and gone to his bedroom window, looked out into the street to see the Watch there, all of them crowded about a man lying in the street . . . very similar to what played out before his eyes right now.

Naufrenzy stood his ground now. His handgun dangling down at his thigh, but there was no chance he would holster it. Not till magic had well and truly left his premises.

He watched the Watch leave, watched them carrying the magician between them. He had no idea what they had done to him. If they had given him a sedative, knocked him out, or if perhaps they had stolen whatever life remained within him.

Whatever they had done, the leader of the Watch, as Naufrenzy recognised him from the plain, black robe he wore, made towards him.

Just like the others, his face couldn't be made out from beneath that hood, there was only shadow there. He often wondered if they had faces at all. If they had bodies.

Or if their robes were all that was to them.

If, really, they were nothing more than wisps of air.

Jak. The leader's name was *Jak*.

When he spoke, it sounded like a knife being dragged over a sharpener. A tone that made Naufrenzy want to close his eyes shut and wish the experience away. "Dead," Jak said.

Naufrenzy had his answer at least. He waited to see if the head of the Watch would say something more. But he just lingered there, staring out from under his hood, his features totally obscured, though Naufrenzy guessed he had very little curiosity to actually make them out.

Naufrenzy just gave a nod, and an almost imperceptible, "Okay."

Jak tilted his head to one side from beneath the hood, as if regarding Naufrenzy in some way, and then, without another word, he shimmied off away from him, headed off out through the entrance, in pursuit of the rest of the Watch, and the scrounger / magician they carried between them. Held *floating* between them.

Naufrenzy watched them all the way, out into the street. And then watched them all the way off around the corner and out of sight.

Only then would he allow himself a well-won sigh, to turn his attention back to his guards, all of them seemingly, standing around him, blank, slightly shocked expressions on their faces, all of them still bearing their arms.

Naufrenzy returned to his senses. Felt his blood come off the boil, and he addressed them all. "All right, you lot," he said. "Back to work for you now."

And then, with Hedder striding alongside him, Naufrenzy made his way back towards his office. He would drive back home now. He had had enough of the Tip for one day.

As he strode hard, already thinking of the hot coffee that awaited him back home, and his children, no doubt in the process of being bathed by his wife, he couldn't help but feel his sanity returning to him.

Sure, he had always known that magic was close, like what people said about rats, about never being more than a couple of metres away from one . . . yeah, like that.

But the fact remained that, in this world, they lived with magic everyday, that it powered their cars, heated their homes . . . for goodness' sake, it even powered his mobile phone, the one he'd used to call up the Watch for assistance . . . but, even so, he often fantasised about waking up one day, and it being simply gone.

Then they would be on their own, of course, they would have to return to the Dark Ages, to those days before the magicians had seen right to reveal themselves to ordinary mortals, and to give them a 'helping hand' in their lives.

But Naufrenzy had always believed that they could live alone.

That *humans* could live alone.

They had managed for thousands, or tens of thousands—millions?—of years without magic, so why did the magicians simply take it upon themselves to step in and *decide* that they, the humans, needed their help?

It was a mystery for greater men than Naufrenzy . . . or was it?

Could he, perhaps, make a change if he was truly determined?

Come to think of it, back when he had been a scrounger, a scrounger of the first class, he had never so much as entertained the idea of one day being the head of the whole Tip, but he had managed that.

Was there anything to say that he couldn't run for office, that he couldn't take over the city and run it the way that he saw fit?

Banish *magic* from the place, once and for all.

Naufrenzy only realised that he had reached his car, that he had even got down to the car park, when he heard Hedder, who he had forgotten about, chirp up and say, "All back to normal, eh, chief?"

Naufrenzy paused a moment, still caught with his daydreaming, and then he turned back to the supervisor, a slight smirk nestling in the corner of his mouth, and he said, "Yes, everything back to normal."

Hedder gave him a solid nod, then turned on his heel and beat it back to the Tip, to go and supervise his men, to dish out the orders for the nightshift before heading home himself.

Naufrenzy unlatched the door handle of his rusted-up car. It had holes all over and barely clung on to the glass from its windows.

But it ran thanks to the magical juice that pumped through it. Through the specially adapted engine.

The whipplesnife. That magical fuel that powered all of Guynur, it seemed.

That had made human technology and innovation redundant.

There was no need. Whipplesnife would heat or power anything a human could think of. And all through the currently existing technology.

There was no need for manufacturing any longer.

But it meant that humankind had had to strike a deal with the devil.

A deal with *magic*.

And now they had to live with it forever.

Or did they?

As Naufrenzy turned the ignition, listened to the *thrum* of the whipplesnife passing through the pipes in his beaten-up old car, he thought about how things would be different.

If *he* was in charge.

SWOTS

GUYNUR CITY COMPREHENSIVE was nothing short of a madhouse.

Why, Timon Grunt guessed that anybody—any *kid*—could get away with just about anything at all. He remembered, back when he'd been in primary, that he'd heard all sorts of stories about GCC, about how kids there would drop cherry bombs down the toilets, or you'd get yourself beaten up in the toilets by a gang of older kids, or if you were especially unlucky, you'd get your head flushed down the toilet itself.

Timon had just thought they were a sort of urban legend, something to think about, be scared of for precisely six seconds, and then to forget about.

But, as he stepped over the threshold, hearing the swearing and laughter from the big kids standing inside the toilet on the ground floor of the school, all those stories seemed to return to Timon.

He tried to back out.

To retrace his steps.

He could head on up to the second floor.

That toilet would be empty.

He was *sure* of it.

But it was too late.

"Hey!"

Though Timon knew that he should run, he found himself, almost stuck in a trance, looking in the direction of the call. He had always thought that, if he was any animal, he would've been one of those bunny rabbits that froze and always got eaten first.

"You!"

Timon stood rooted to the spot, and that was all it took for one of the big kids—one of those kids that seemed *inconceivably* tall—to grab hold of his arm and jerk it back behind his back. Timon winced at the pain, but he made no noise. He didn't want to give them any sort of pleasure in this, not for any real reason of pride, at least not beyond the fact that he didn't want them to do this again.

He wanted this to be a one-time deal.

Get bullied.

Then get out.

There were five of them in all.

Timon recognised them as all being in the oldest year of the school—five years older than him. He had no chance. None whatso-ever. Even if he'd brought a knife with him, like he'd often considered, he wouldn't be able to take them out.

Not *five* of them.

Their talk sort of dwindled into a heavy cloud which lingered above Timon's head. He could almost feel the pressure pushing down on him. Making his eardrums feel under high pressure. The only slight weapon he had in his armoury was his ability to—*blindly* —take off running in some direction. But even that was gone now that the kid held him tight.

As Timon stood there, in the middle of the five-strong group, he breathed in the heady stench of disinfectant in the toilets. He could taste it right at the back of his throat. He could *feel* the burn of it on his tongue. His hand throbbed from where the kid held him so tight that it cut off the blood flow. Timon wanted to ask the kid to let off just a little, but he knew that there would be zero response to that.

"So," another kid, not the kid who held him, said. "Whatcha got to say for yourself, huh?"

Timon kept his lips shut tight. What *did* he have to say for himself? That he'd come in here, to the toilet, because he'd been busting for a piss? That he'd only wanted to duck in here before he started up the stairs to mathematics?

. . . Yeah, telling the truth, like his parents always nailed into him as just about the most important virtue on the face of all of Schwyn . . . that just wasn't going to get him any place at all with these guys. At least not to any place that *wasn't* Painsville.

Timon swallowed hard, still doing battle with the unholy stench of the disinfectant. "Uh, nothing," he said.

The kid staring at him, looking for some sort of an answer, cracked a smile. "You queer or something, huh?"

"What?" Timon replied. "Uh, no," he added, but too late before the kids had already leaped on it and started to chant.

"Queer! Queer! QUEER!"

The last repetition was much punchier than the previous few. It sent a tremor through Timon's eardrums, and he impulsively shut his eyes as if that'd make the loudness easier to bear.

"Whatcha say, huh?" the same kid said.

Timon could now feel that his need to piss had turned to a burning sensation at the base of his gut. It was how he got whenever he felt like he had to go to the toilet. There was a moment when something told his body that splashdown was imminent. And it was almost impossibly difficult to back track once that feeling—that *signal*—got through to his bladder. But he had to hold it in. The alternative was unthinkable.

Perhaps the kid was a mind reader, or maybe—more likely—he was more perceptive than most, better at noticing the subtleties of body language, and he said, "What, you gotta *piss* or somethin', huh?"

Timon wasn't sure what to say. The way that his parents had built him made it *so* difficult to lie. He had almost a physical aversion to it, and he felt like all the boys' eyes were fixed on him as he gave it his best shot. ". . . No," Timon replied.

The kid gave a smirk and then took a step forwards. "Guess we'll see about that, huh?" He took one more step and then he reached out, with a bunched fist, and he pressed hard against Timon's stomach, pushing hard against his bladder.

Timon could feel all the piss inside of him pressing to escape.

But he held it in still.

Didn't want to surrender himself.

He wasn't going to lose this battle.

If he did it would be the beginning of a war—a war against humiliation for him, and one which he didn't suspect he would be able to win.

But it was difficult now—the boy kept on pushing so hard against Timon's bladder.

He felt the warmth within him.

That sensation of pins and needles.

Then came the moment when he . . . *had* . . . to . . . let . . . *go!*

It came as a single stream, unstoppable. He felt the warmth dampen his trouser leg, felt the steady trickle down his leg. Instantly, it seemed, the sharp scent of urine cut through the air of the toilets.

The kid who'd been pressing Timon's bladder took a step backwards, and released his fist from Timon's now-relieved bladder. He was smirking all the wider still, and he had his eyes fixed onto Timon's stained trousers. "Guess that'll teach you to say lies, huh?" the kid said, and then, with a brief nod to the others, he led them away. "Fucking swots," the kid added, over his shoulder.

He left Timon to clean up his own mess.

2

TIMON GOT THROUGH the rest of the day somehow.

He managed to clean himself up as best as he could.

He washed his trousers in the sink with a good squeezing of hand soap.

Walking about all day in trousers that were soaking wet with water was at least preferable to walking about in trousers soaking wet from *piss*.

When Timon got back home, he shot right up to his bedroom, ditched his trousers, and then plucked out a bucket from some-place. He filled the bucket with warm water and then dunked his trousers inside to leave them to soak in the corner of his bedroom, out of sight.

That evening, he said nothing about what had happened that day at school.

Of course he didn't.

That night, he hardly slept at all, just staring up at the ceiling above him, thinking things over, wondering what his life would be like. Because now he had a reason to dread school, a reason for him to *not* go there. And he had been so certain that none of this would *ever* happen to him. And yet it had . . .

And, as sure as fate, the next day at school, though Timon had never before yesterday seen those kids in his life, he found himself running into them again.

This time it was out on the school field.

Timon had thought that he would go on a long walk about the school grounds during break time. That he would do his best to avoid the kids who had brought a new misery to his life the day before. But, as it turned out, they weren't *always* hanging around toilets.

No, they liked to hang around the school field just as much.

They grabbed Timon right away, of course, and they goaded him about what had happened the day before. They asked what had happened to his stained pair of trousers. Timon didn't bring out their delight by informing them that they resided inside a bucket of soapy warm water.

Today, using the chain-link fence which ran about the periphery of the school field, they snapped off some pieces of wire and tied him up. They tied his ankles. His wrists. And his waist. There was nothing that Timon could do to resist them.

Then they left him there, Timon simply hanging off the fence.

Being tied up there meant that Timon missed the bell for the next class, and it wasn't until a PE class came out, and one of the kids noticed him there that there was a prospect of salvation. Thankfully, as the kid worked to untie him, the teacher running the class didn't notice Timon.

The last thing he wanted was for teachers to get involved.

Because that would inevitably mean *parents* getting involved.

And that would be the beginning of the end.

As the kid untied Timon from the fence, he introduced himself a Koarl—asked Timon just what had happened. For some reason, Timon found himself opening up about it. Telling him from the start, from the toilets the day before, to what had occurred today.

Koarl listened intently to Timon and then asked, when he'd finished, whether he wanted to join with his group of friends, and where they hung about at break times.

Timon said that he would.

They only stopped their conversation when the PE teacher

emerged from somewhere and called Koarl over to go back to class —and for Timon to hop along to his own.

Timon obliged the teacher.

As he stepped into his alchemy class, he couldn't help but feel a smirk twitch its way onto his lips. Somehow he got the feeling that things would be better from now on. That now he had somebody he could relate to—somebody who could help support him in the face of the other kids.

3

A FTER SCHOOL THAT DAY, Timon found himself invited round Koarl's house.

On the way over, as they padded along the roads which led away from GCC, Koarl told him about how he had something to show him. Something that could well change *everything* for Timon.

They dug through the various school books, and through the discarded pieces of school uniform in Koarl's room, and Koarl eventually found just what he was looking for.

It was a transparent vial with a thick, black, oily liquid within.

Koarl held the vial up to the light which came in through his bedroom window and said to Timon, "You ever seen this stuff before?"

Timon shook his head. "No, what is it?"

With a slight smile, Koarl said, "Magic."

Timon frowned. "'Magic?'"

"Uh huh, you heard of that, right?"

"Well, yeah, of course I have, it's just . . ." and his words seemed to drift away because he was about to say that magic was illegal— that there was no way that he could take it off him because to do so would be to break the law.

Few laws were more readily defended than the banishment of magic from Guynur City.

"Look," Koarl said, "I know that you're feeling just a little apprehensive about using this but you've got to trust me that dealing with those bullies—"

"They're not bullies."

Koarl shrugged. "Well, if you want to deal with those kids, then this little vial right here"—he gave the vial clutched in his hand a little flick with his finger—"is your best bet."

Timon held still. He stared into that black, oily substance and he wondered what might happen to him if he got caught with it. Of course he'd heard of the Watch. He'd heard that the Watch arrived pretty soon after any sort of magical substance—not to mention *creatures*—cropped up in Guynur. But was that an overblown thing? Was that just something people said that wasn't *really* true?

Timon looked deep into Koarl's eyes, tried to work out whether this might be another cruel game. The problem was, ever since those kids . . . those bullies . . . had started into him at school he seemed to have lost something of his ability to trust.

He was constantly watching to see what people's angle might be —what it was that they wanted from him, what kind of a *reaction* they were hoping to extract.

But that couldn't help Timon's attraction to the little vial.

"What should I do with it?" Timon said. "I mean, if I do want to use it?"

Koarl shrugged again. "A drop here, a drop there, that'll do it."

Timon stared long and hard at the vial, and then, decided, he reached for the vial and took it out of Koarl's hand.

When he looked up again, he saw that Koarl was grinning from ear to ear, but not because he was anticipating some great embarrassment . . . at least not *Timon's* embarrassment.

4

THE NEXT DAY AT SCHOOL, Timon paced his way along the pavement. He took in the towering mass of Guynur City Comprehensive. The grey cinderblock towers that stretched upwards for twenty storeys or more. Each was assigned to a particular department of the school. Timon recalled his first day, when he had felt extremely intimidated about so much as walking through the cast-iron gate. About entering the school.

And he felt the same today, but for a different reason.

A reason which had nothing at all to do with the grim architecture.

And which had everything to do with the little glass vial which he had stashed away in the pocket of his jacket. He was ready for them. Ready for those bullies.

Just let them *try* to get the upper hand on him this time.

He would show them.

He would show them all.

Overhead, the sky was overcast. One of those days which Timon secretly enjoyed. It was one of those days which seemed almost set to crush the whole city. To float down and smother everything beneath it. Sometimes he really *did* wish that the clouds would crush everything beneath them.

Timon strode on in through the school gates, ready for those bullies, ready to confront them. He reached into his pocket and he clutched the glass vial. It felt smooth, cool against his skin, and yet there was a warmth there too. A warmth which seemed to send a slight pulsing sensation through his blood.

Just let them try.

As Timon strode over the grounds, he heard them right away.

Those sniggers, the gentle pad of trainers over tarmac.

And he knew they were lying in wait for him.

He squeezed the glass vial even tighter still.

Waiting.

Biding his time.

"Hey there queeroid!" one of the kids said.

This word . . . *queeroid* . . . was what they'd settled on calling Timon—it apparently had to do with the location of their first meeting, and that nobody who *wasn't* gay would ever dare use a toilet. Timon had turned that logic over in his mind while he'd laid in bed at night. He had tried to get to the foundations of it, but had come up empty-handed. But, then again, he supposed that logic was pretty far down on a bully's totem pole.

"Hey *queeroid!*"

This time Timon did look around. He spotted the kids there, all five of them waiting for him. He wondered if they did this everyday, if this was maybe some sort of a highlight for them. Did they all fire text messages between themselves before he arrived to school? All of them plotting just how they were going to 'get him' that particular day?

The kids all trudged towards Timon, and Timon held his ground.

Though they'd already got him twice before: once in the toilets, that first day, and then again at the school field, yesterday, Timon was determined that today they would fail.

Today they wouldn't have the success they'd pressed for.

They surrounded Timon quickly, and there was nothing to be done. He gripped tight to the glass vial, feeling its cool glass against his palm. He could feel the cork stopper on the vial with his thumb.

He felt one of the kids shove him in the back. Though it wasn't much more than a prod, Timon was so tightly wound that he stum-

bled forwards a couple of steps, almost losing his balance and falling. Before he did fall, one of the kids reached out and stopped
him.

Timon couldn't help but reach out and use the kid as something
to prop himself up.

The kid pushed him away with a smirk.

"So," the kid who'd pressed Timon's bladder said—the ring-
leader apparently, "Whatcha gonna do about us today, huh?"

Timon didn't reply. He just kept his fist tight around the vial.
What he knew to be his only hope. What if . . . what if Koarl had
been lying to him? What if there was nothing more than just a ton
of muck nestled within this vial here?

Timon felt his heart give a little skip at the prospect.

He really wouldn't be able to bear that.

No way could he allow himself to think about it.

Because it would be the worst betrayal yet.

To have somebody *pretend* to be his friend only for them to stab
him in the back at the last.

He felt one of the kids grip hold of Timon's wrist, sink his
fingernails in until Timon was sure that he could feel the blood
creeping out, lolling in beads across the surface of his skin.

"Whatcha gonna do, huh?"

Timon felt all the anger within him tighten into a little ball,
right down deep in his stomach. He could feel it pounding so hard
that—just for a second—he was sure that he'd grown a second
heart.

But he *could* do something today.

Something which none of them would suspect.

Not for one second.

And so he dipped his hand into the pocket of his jacket and
brought the little glass vial out for them *all* to see.

He heard some grunts of disbelief . . . *animal* noises of bullies.

But Timon acted quickly, knowing that time was of the essence.

Any one of them could easily knock him to the ground.

Leave him flat on his back.

He popped the cork with his thumb, listened to it bounce up off the ground.

A coil of steam rolled out from the vial.

Timon knew, on instinct, not to breathe it in.

He tightened his grip on the glass, now deeply aware that all five of the kids were watching him, that they were interested in what that liquid *was*.

And it was then that it came to Timon—when he knew exactly what he must do.

Keeping his feet planted on the tarmac floor of the playground, he tossed the vial down hard. Right *smack* at the ground right between his feet.

And then he ran.

5

AS TIMON TURNED THE CORNER of the playground, he could hear a high-pitched *hissing* filling the air. But he wouldn't allow himself to look back. He could hear the bullies all groaning too, no doubt out of pain.

Timon tore onwards, not wanting to stop for a second, because to stop would mean that he would be in the biggest trouble of his life, and not just with the bullies themselves.

But with teachers too.

When he reached the first of the tower blocks—the alchemy department—he tore up the staircase, taking the stairs two, and sometimes three, at a time. All that was on his mind was to put distance between himself and the bullies. That was the only way that he could possibly get away with this thing.

It was only when he'd got up to about the seventh floor, and he stared out along the dulled, sticky beige floor tiles that he saw them.

Kids. More kids.

Not the bullies, though.

Kids who were all collected together, over in the corner of the hallway, obviously doing something extremely confidential. He scoped them out. Noticed that Koarl was among them.

It was then that Timon felt a rush of relief. He couldn't quite believe his luck. That he had managed to escape up here, to be with *allies*.

But when Koarl looked back at Timon over his shoulder, when he met his eye, Timon saw that there was no glee at all in Koarl's expression. With a deadpan expression, Koarl gestured for Timon to go over to the window and stare out with him.

Timon did.

He looked out through the glass, down into the playground.

It wasn't difficult to spot the bullies.

They were surrounded by a puff of jet-black smoke.

All of them lay on the surface of the tarmac, clutching their faces, crying out at the tops of their voices.

When Timon looked down at them a little harder still, he could see that they each had throbbing red welts that popped up out of their skin. Welts that seemed, to Timon, to be extremely serious.

"You've gotta run," Koarl said, without looking at Timon.

Koarl just continued to stare out of the window.

"What?" Timon said.

This time Koarl did turn back to him. He met him with a steady gaze, and then threw his hand up to indicate the others around him. "These are the SWOTS—*we're* the SWOTS. We fight back against the bullies at GCC . . . but we don't *maim* them."

"But . . . what, I . . ." Timon began, and then finally got out, "I did what you said, what you *told* me to do."

At this, Koarl just shook his head. "Nah, I told you to use a couple of drops, nothing more. And I certainly didn't tell you to toss that thing like a dumb cherry bomb."

Timon's mind flexed back. He tried to work out just *what* Koarl had told him.

Yes, that did ring a bell.

Just a few drops.

That had been Koarl's instruction.

But in the intensity of the moment, with all that anger that'd been rippling through him, Timon had simply been unable to control himself. And he had *had* to toss the vial.

He could still hear the snake-like *hiss* in his ears from when the liquid had struck the tarmac.

"Timon?" Koarl said. "You've gotta go now."

Timon remained hypnotised by what was happening below them, in the playground. And how his former bullies continued to roll about on their backs like ants frying in fierce sunlight. When Timon spoke again, he felt just that . . . *hypnotised*. "Run where?"

Another of the kids—another of the SWOTS—murmured something under their breath.

Koarl hushed them by saying, "It's not his fault that he hasn't heard yet. Not all of us can have such an encyclopaedic knowledge of Guynur that you have." When Koarl turned back to face Timon, his expression wasn't exactly unkind, but it certainly carried no warmth either. "Look, Timon, you've got to get going right now. You need to seek out Beggy, he'll be able to sort out all your troubles."

"My troubles?" Timon said.

Koarl gave a thick nod, and then a dry-throated, "Yeah." He pointed back out the window, down at the bullies writhing about below. "You see what's happening to them?" he asked.

Though Timon was fairly certain of what he saw, he didn't reply.

He didn't want to say anything wrong.

Didn't want to say anything stupid that would make the SWOTS think he was some kind of an idiot.

He shook his head.

"They'll be dead in the hour," Koarl said. "The amount you tossed on them."

Timon felt a new heaviness in his heart.

"Won't just be the fuzz that'll come," Koarl continued, "it'll be the *Watch*."

For a second—and no more than a single second—Timon could feel that he was on the verge of sobbing. But he managed to push the feeling away, to tell himself that he didn't want to embarrass himself in front of the closest thing he had to friends.

The closest thing he had *had* to friends.

Because, as he got back to his feet and made for the door, he knew that the end had come. When he reached the door to the staircase, Koarl called out to Timon, told him how to get to Beggy's.

Timon thanked him and then he left.

6

I T WAS FUNNY, Timon had always wondered what it was
exactly that kept kids at school. Why, if they hated it so much,
they didn't simply sneak out through the gates, slip off into the city
and never come back.

Guynur City was a big place, after all.

Had the teachers here really done such a good job at brain-
washing them all that students felt *compelled* to come to school
simply to appease them?

He really had no idea.

And, as Timon skirted the side alleys of the city streets, slowly
making his way away from GCC, he thought about his new life, and
what it might mean.

Because now he was a tainted kid . . . he had used magic.

And his only hope would be to follow the address which Koarl
had fed to him.

To find Beggy.

FUZZ

D ETECTIVE SUUMAN passed beneath the stone archway which marked the entrance to the main station of Guynur City Fuzz Headquarters. Already he caught that draught that skittered about the upturned collar of his charcoal overcoat, and sent a chill shuddering all down the front of the white shirt and black tie he wore beneath.

He chewed up the last of the tobacco that he kept smudged on the inside of his cheek, and then he spat it out into the steel-rimmed bin which stood to his left.

He didn't break pace as he spat, but his aim was true.

And he heard that satisfying whisper of the plastic bag nestled inside of the bin as his wad of tobacco dropped inside.

He breathed in deep, breathed in the stony smells of the place, of Guynur City Fuzz Headquarters. He pushed his homburg hat, the same charcoal as his overcoat, down smarter onto his head. His mouth felt bone dry, chewing on tobacco always did that to him. But he also liked the recently-departed tobacco taste he got just those fair few moments after spitting it out. Sometimes he wondered if the whole reason he chewed tobacco in the first place was just so he could spit it out and get the feeling he had now.

As Suuman pounded on, hearing his well-heeled, and well-polished, ankle-high boots echoing back up at him off the concrete slabs that made up the floor of the station, he caught a slight whiff of his perspiration mixed up with his cologne. He'd gone for the woody-smelling one today . . . he couldn't recall the name of it for the life of him.

Didn't really see much point in recalling it, to be honest.

It was one of the ones his ex-wife had given him for some long-forgotten birthday.

Fuzz officers, all dressed in their dark grey uniforms, trudged about, some of them with their hands hovering over their sidearms, in that nervous way that fuzz in uniform had a habit of doing.

Secretaries and assistants, all dressed up in their mini skirts, almost like tropical birds compared with the dour-uniformed fuzz, clutched papers to their chests and tottered along on their heels, apparently always on the very brink of toppling over, but somehow managing to overpower the laws of physics right at the last with an elegant swerve to the left or right.

People seemed to be weaving in and out of just about every doorway along the hall.

The place was all flustered.

Suuman had seen that much from the outside. Seen the fuzz cars all drawn up to the curb. Just now, as he'd pulled along the road leading up to headquarters, he'd been stopped by three separate traffic fuzz, all of them asking for his identification.

When he'd flashed his detective's badge at them, they'd waved him right on through.

But this kind of panic was unprecedented.

Even for Guynur, it struck Suuman as odd.

He guided his way through the clustered reception hall, trying to keep his elbows tucked in so he wouldn't jab anyone on his way through. He didn't have so much as a chance of getting a glimpse of the mahogany reception desks, or of that new brunette receptionist who'd caught his eye and he hadn't yet had a chance to approach.

Hopefully the other receptionists hadn't been chatting to her, hadn't got to the point of telling her about his reputation.

But, even if they had, he could almost bank on her being curious of him.

That was how he had bagged just about every receptionist Guynur City Fuzz had had . . . they all got curious.

He padded gently along the thinning, pale-green carpet that led up to his boss, Hulason's office. He had memorised the gilt-framed, sepia-ridden pictures that gazed down on him from where they were nailed up on the peeling wallpaper of the walls. All different generations of fuzz, all done up nice in their ceremonial uniforms, and all wearing that same straight-faced, *serious* expression of theirs. God, they all looked like they were army boys, squaddies . . . tin soldiers, some shit like that . . . ever since Suuman had joined the force he'd abhorred all that uniformity, that thing whereby everyone had to look just like everyone else.

And he'd only really begun to feel comfortable again, *individual* again, once he'd shed his uniform on his promotion to detective.

And now, from what he'd heard, they wanted to take it away from him.

He gave a couple of smart raps of the mahogany door to his boss's office . . . that same mahogany they used out in the reception on the desks there.

The trick here was to stay calm. He had to keep a lid on things.

Though since he'd never had a problem with his temper getting out of hand, unlike probably a dozen fuzz he could name . . . and all still uniformed, probably for that reason . . . he thought that he would handle himself just fine.

He just had to stop his boss getting on top of him.

From deep within the room, he heard Hulason answer him with that throaty, almost toad-like, "Yarp," and Suuman shoved his way inside, like he always had to give the door a little shove with his shoulder to get it moving.

2

ULASON had his back to him. He sat on his chair, staring out the window that looked down on the main entrance to the station. Here they were about two, three floors up from ground level so Hulason had a pretty good vantage point on watching people come and go. No doubt he had seen Suuman trotting up those steps not too long ago.

The air smelled of dust, and soap, and mushroom soup.

That last detail reminded Suuman that he'd skipped lunch. That when he'd heard he had to drop everything and come right here.

Outside the window, birds chattered about in the bright summer's day. And the sun warmed up the glass of the office, making it either pleasant or sweltering depending on your prefer-ence. Put it this way, it sent Suuman feeling for the collar of his shirt and loosening his tie a couple of degrees.

"Sir?" Suuman said, tasting that hollow tobacco flavour as he did.

"Detective," Hulason said, in a dry voice. Not turning around.

Suuman hung about at the closed door, not quite sure whether or not he should take another step into the office. He hadn't quite had time to work out a strategy about how he was going to exactly play this, if he was going to go balls out, or if he was going to be all sweet and passive. Both ways could work with chumps, but, unfor-tunately, Hulason was a long way from being a chump.

"I heard the news," Suuman said, seeing that Hulason wasn't going to initiate the conversation round here.

"That so?"

"Uh huh."

"And what'd you hear?"

Suuman stared at the back of Hulason's head. Today he wore a grey-blue suit, recently pressed, and he could see the arms of his glasses jutting out from the backs of his ears. His ears, today, looked particularly rosy. For a second Suuman wondered if Hulason had been drinking before he twigged that Hulason didn't drink.

That he was teetotal.

Poor fucker.

"I heard," Suuman said, his mouth drying out all of a sudden, "I heard that I'm getting the big ol' boot off the case."

"You heard that, huh?" Hulason said, tilting his head slightly to one side, but stopping short of turning around to face him.

Suuman glanced about the room. All mahogany. The desk, the bookshelves, the pair of chairs which sat in front of the desk. Hell, when Suuman blinked sometimes he was certain that Hulason had turned mahogany *too*, with the rest of this place.

Just another reason that Suuman was glad not to have to spend any longer than he absolutely had to about the station. He guessed that he'd find all that coordination nauseating after a while, and if he didn't find it nauseating then it might mean something worse . . . that he'd got used to it.

"It true?" Suuman said, still lingering at the door, not bothering to remove his hat even. Removing your hat was something you did when you were being invited in by someone, and there was no inclination whatsoever that Suuman was invited at all here.

"Who's to say?" Hulason said.

Suuman felt his heart struck numb. "'Scuse me, sir?"

Hulason tipped his head further to one side, and Suuman wondered if it was because he wanted to make his point clearer, or because he'd seen something that had interested him out of his window.

"Been some changes about here, Suuman."

"What changes, sir?"

Suuman had to admit that one of the problems with being a detective, with being out there in the midst of the city, out there in the thick of it, was that he got somewhat out of step with office gossip and rumour.

Or was it an advantage?

"Got word, from the Watch."

Suuman felt a chill scutter up his spine. His blood cooled. His heart jumped a few good leaps, apparently making a good go at beating out through his ribs.

The Watch? The Watch kept track of magic, they kept tabs on just about everything inside of Guynur City. Some said that they were the real fuzz, but whenever Suuman heard that, he always corrected people.

He told them that they were more like the *government*.

Hulason finally turned around in his chair. He had deep black circles beneath his bespectacled eyes, and his cheeks looked sunken, his complexion pale. Suuman got the impression that it wasn't just him who was wrapped up in . . . well, whatever the hell it was that was going on around here.

Hulason's shirt seemed to hang off him today, like a puffed-up, juiceless blister. He looked like he'd been dragged through a mangle or two the night before.

"Anything you can tell me 'bout it?" Suuman said.

Hulason shook his head, then stuck out his bottom lip as if he'd momentarily changed his mind.

But in the end he kept schtum.

"So that's it?" Suuman said. "It's over?"

Hulason swallowed, and Suuman saw his Adam's apple bob long and hard.

"What . . . what happens to the case, then?"

Hulason shrugged. "They'll take it over, most likely, they've the expertise."

Suuman felt his chest tighten. That chilly feeling that'd been following him about all day, this was what it had been trying to tell him. And, strangely, for the first time that day, he felt himself warming up. Felt himself filling with confidence even. With injustice.

Better not to show his hand, though.

No point in really showing his hand.

Time for a little distraction . . . and a little curiosity.

"Boss?" Suuman said.

"Yarp."

"What's with all them cars out front—all the people just rushing all about the station. This's bigger than the case I was working, right? I mean, the way people were moving I'm pretty certain that there's some sort of panic setting in about the place."

Hulason eyed him lazily, and then gave a lop-shouldered shrug. "You could say that the Watch decided to come on in here and take a look at stuff."

"What?" Suuman said, feeling his eyebrows rise up his forehead, make some inroads on what remained of his thinning-out fringe of brown hair.

"An audit," Hulason said, his voice dry, eyes unfocussed.

"An audit? What . . . I . . . really?"

"Uh huh."

Suuman thought it over. Though the Watch had long had precedence over just about everything in Guynur City, this was the first time in more than fifteen years on the force that he'd ever run into something like this . . . something so *direct*.

"Take a day," Hulason said. "Come back fresh bright and early tomorrow—might look different then." Hulason turned to look back out his window, out to the swarming uniforms ploughing their way up the steps to the station, all of them with their arms full of cardboard boxes containing whoever knew what, then he added, "Get some sleep."

Suuman lingered for another moment, thought about pressing home just what he thought about all this bullshit, but, in the end, decided just to leave it.

He was better off saving his energy if he really wanted to cut to the quick of what was going on here.

3

OUTSIDE THE STATION, Suuman wormed his way through the never-ending stream of anxious-faced officers, those same cardboard boxes in their hands, and surfaced at the far end of the street where he'd parked up his car—a beaten and bruised pale-brown estate that would have looked more at home serving for a five-member family than a bachelor detective.

But that was just another part of the disguise.

He could park up just about anywhere in the city and no one would *dream* that he was fuzz . . . at least, not the lesser criminals, the higher-ups would take a little more fooling than that, but he couldn't catch them all.

He slipped his key into the lock of the driver's door and looked over that deep, rusted-up dent there from where a scrounger had taken a kick at him. He'd taken a wrong turn, ended up down a dead-end alley, and before he'd known it the scrounger had jumped out of nowhere—high as all hell—and given his car a solid kick with his bandaged-up foot.

To be honest, Suuman had been more impressed than angry at it, considering the scrounger had taken that shot without so much as wearing shoes.

Then again, that was probably just a demonstration of the numbing effect of the drugs the scrounger had been on.

He should get it fixed one of these days, that was what his colleagues were always going on about. But he just couldn't find the will to care all that much at all. What did his car matter anyway? He needed his car to park up in all sorts of undesirable spots of Guynur City, so chances were, even if he did get it patched up, it'd only get kicked in all over again within a week.

The sun slipped behind a cloud overhead, and he felt a chill set into the air. Kind of like that frosty sensation carrying on a summer's breeze. Just a reminder that winter was waiting around the corner.

He clambered in behind the brown, leather-upholstered wheel, brought the door shut, and just sat there for a minute, still absorbing all the fuss taking place on the street right at the moment.

The Watch? What did the Watch want with Guynur City Fuzz? What did they want to go through the records for?

Why hadn't they thought to contact him?

But he had to hold that thought because his mobile was buzzing away in the inside pocket of his overcoat. He dipped his fingers in, caught a hold of it, and brought it out.

An unknown number.

He didn't *usually* answer unknown numbers, but something about today, about this whole fucked-up situation, told him that he should answer.

That he would be making a mistake to let the phone ring itself out.

That he'd *regret* it.

He accepted the call and brought his phone up to his ear. "Suuman."

The voice on the other end made his phone speaker buzz with a high-pitched static, annoying, but just about bearable. What Suuman couldn't deny, however, was just what that meant, and that was what turned his gut.

Magic.

The voice on the other end was like a dying whisper. "Detective? We would like to speak with you."

Though Suuman hadn't ever spoken with him before, he knew just who he was speaking with.

Jak.

Leader of the Watch.

Suuman got that prickling feeling, all over his skin, that feeling that he'd learned to recognise, ever since he was a child, that someone was watching him.

He gazed out from beneath the windscreen, looked along the street, to the low-lying buildings on the street . . . though most buildings were at least three or four storeys, the Guynur City Fuzz Station towered above them all both in height and girth.

He couldn't see anyone watching him, but he hardly had time to scour every single window which looked out over the street.

"When?" Suuman finally got out, recalling that Jak was on the other end of the phone.

"We'd like to see you in the Bell Tower right away."

The phone went dead.

Suuman held the phone to his ear another few seconds before snapping back to consciousness. He blinked the daze out of his eyes, and then, heart ticking in his throat, he turned the ignition and made for the Bell Tower.

4

QUITE SIMPLY PUT, the Bell Tower had the best vantage point in all of Guynur City. Suuman remembered, back when he'd worn a uniform, back when he'd been naïve, fresh from the academy, how he'd wondered why the fuzz didn't use the Bell Tower as a lookout point, as a centre of operations. Even as the central station itself.

Those were the days before he'd fully comprehended the Watch, before he had fully fathomed just what they meant to the city on a street-level, everyday scale.

Of course he'd always known of them, always known that they were concerned with magic, more specifically with rooting it out of Guynur, but what he hadn't realised was just how far their influence truly stretched.

Like it or not, they really were the ones running the show.

Running Guynur City.

That was the truth.

As he trundled the car forwards, into the shadow of the Bell Tower, he looked about the buildings which surrounded it. For blocks and blocks, almost every single building was dilapidated, no more than piles of brick, puffs of cement dust, rickety, rusted-up metal frames, like a pigeon all pecked down to the bones.

The Bell Tower itself wasn't in much of a better state. It rose into the air unconvincingly, its grey-blue bricks all crooked and seemingly ready to topple over in a stiff breeze.

But he knew the Bell Tower would stick together.

For as long as the Watch wished to use it as their headquarters.

There was no glass in the windows, no lights that shone out from within, though night had fallen a good hour or so ago.

Everything about what Suuman saw suggested 'creepy' to him.

But this was where his case had brought him.

He had no choice.

No one *ever* ran from the Watch . . . not if they wanted to remain alive.

Though he'd driven past the Bell Tower several times before, he'd never once so much as pulled up at the place, let alone driven into the underground car park, which was what he was doing now.

He looked to the yawning blackness of the hole awaiting him. And the downward concrete slope beyond it. No one manned the barrier, because there was no barrier. All that remained of it was nothing more than snapped-off wood, any paint it had once had all stripped away.

He breathed in deep, dug into his pocket, into the same inside pocket where he kept his mobile, and he plucked out another paper parcel of tobacco. Slipped it in between his lips. Chewed on it. Instantly felt the saliva wetting his mouth. And the waves of warmth from his chewing action bringing him back around. Sharpening his senses.

When he breathed now, he could smell that overwhelming scent of decay that clung to this place, that pounded at him out from the ventilation ducts of his car. He wondered how anyone at all could live in a place like this—what kind of a person would *choose* to live in a place like this.

But then he reminded himself that, whatever they were, the Watch weren't human.

Not any more.

He listened to the muscles of his jaw click and click as he chewed harder and harder on the tobacco and then, feeling his chest tighten and that sour taste of the tobacco put him at ease, he pressed down on the accelerator, urged the car forwards, down the slope, and into the underground car park.

Into the darkness.

5

A PALE YELLOW LIGHT illuminated the underground car park. Other than Suuman's car, there was nothing else there, save for an aged van—washed in black paint, chipped all over, and rusted up too. Suuman guessed that, at least, his car wouldn't feel out of place.

After he'd parked, he sat at the wheel for a good couple of minutes, apparently stuck to the cushion of the driver's seat. He gave his tobacco another good few vigorous chews, caught another few waves of the tobacco in his mouth, and then spat it back out into the same paper he'd taken it from just a moment or so ago.

When he stepped out of the car, he saw the figure, standing off by a set of steps, off in the shadows. Wearing those gold and black robes. Face hidden, steeped in shadow, from the hood of the robe.

Suuman had had dealings with the Watch before, of course, and so he knew what a footman looked like when he saw one. This wasn't Jak—Jak wore plain, black robes, as the leader of the Watch. Though he knew these little titbits about the Watch, it was just about the whole scope of his knowledge. Whenever, on a case, anything clearly magical took place, the first action was always to get in touch with the Watch, to dial 678. He had always followed that protocol. Learned that there were things in Guynur City that he would never comprehend, let alone be able to fight back against.

He had made peace with that, or so he'd thought.

But why had they brought him down here to the Bell Tower?

What did they possibly believe that *he* could give them?

Without a word the footman of the Watch, turned around and appeared to float on up the staircase, to head up the spiral stone steps.

Suuman took a final glance over his shoulder, back to his car all parked up in its place, before following the footman.

They climbed for at least five minutes, perhaps much longer, Suuman lost the ability to keep track of time soon enough. His muscles soon got worn out and he felt his skin seep with sweat. He was on the brink of asking the footman, half joking, if there wasn't a lift in the Bell Tower, when the footman ceased heading up the spiral staircase, and floated on, out away from him.

Onto the current floor.

Suuman held back, he felt the thick darkness wash over him. Ahead of him, out onto the floor that the footman had gone along, he could see the cold bluish-white moonlight washing on in through the windowless windows.

But the light didn't suggest safety.

Nothing of the sort.

Suuman felt better in the shadows.

Though he knew, deep down, that the Watch could see him all the better in the darkness.

Finally, he got a hold of himself, tried to forget his pumping blood, the sound of it swilling up around his ears, and his heart pounding against his ribcage. And he took one step forwards. Then another. And before he knew it, he was standing in the doorway to the room which he'd seen the footman disappear into.

He looked about the place. Immediately located the footman. His gold and black robes, before he turned his attention to the taller figure, to the figure who seemed to be a clear seven feet tall, if not taller, and skinny as a newly planted sapling.

Both robed figures had their back to him, and were looking on out of the window, out across the night-time cityscape. Suuman could see the orangey lights of the city all spread out like fireflies, almost so miniscule that he could've easily crushed them with a well-aimed index finger.

He focussed in on the gloomy room, which *was* still gloomy despite the moonlight which beamed on in through the windowless opening in the side of the Bell Tower. And there, right in the centre of the room, he saw the straight-backed, rectangular-angled wooden chair. It seemed to be waiting for him.

He thought to raise his voice, to announce himself to the figures there, in their robes, looking on out through the opening, but got the feeling that, somehow, they already knew he was there. And that he had no need to say a thing.

So he stepped onto the floor, noticing the concrete beneath his feet was sopping wet with stagnant rainwater—he could smell it was rainwater, that unruly, musky mixture of stale water and sewage. Even the rain in Guynur stank. As he walked, the soles of his boots made a stomaching-sickening *squelch*. He tried to ignore it. Tried to think back to that smoky flavour of the chewing tobacco he'd been chewing on. That reassured him somewhat.

Not completely.

But somewhat.

He shot off another look to the pair of robed figures before taking his place on the wooden chair. Hearing its ancient nails keeping it together give a *groan* of protestation as he sat.

And then he just sat and waited.

Slowly felt his buttocks go numb against the hard, flat, wooden seat of the chair.

Finally, the pair of Watch members turned away from the opening.

Both of them faced him, looking out from the impenetrable darkness of their hoods.

When one of them spoke, Suuman knew that it was Jak.
He would've known that deathly, bone-dry tone anywhere.
"Thank you for joining us, detective."

6

SUUMAN didn't quite know where to look. If he looked to their faces, *tried* to look each of the figures bearing down on him in the eye, he simply lost himself.

Did they even *have* eyes?

When Suuman breathed in now there was no trace of that tobacco in his mouth, and he wished that he hadn't spat it out into the paper. Surely these two wouldn't much care whether or not he was a well-mannered human. Since he was only a human, after all.

Now when he breathed in there was a heady stench of fish guts, and of the damp which clung to the whole of the Bell Tower. Over his shoulder, somewhere out there in the midst of the darkness, he heard a rat give a *squeak* . . . and he somehow managed to keep from flinching.

"Your most recent case," Jak said, his voice like the grinding parts of a machine. "That is what we wished to know about. That is the reason *why* we are taking a look at the files down at the station."

Suuman had no real idea what to say to that. So he just stayed quiet. Gently, moving slowly so as not to bring their attention to what he was doing, he slipped his hands beneath his buttocks, to give them some relief from the unforgiving hardness of the chair.

"Detective, if you wouldn't mind."

Another few seconds passed before Suuman clicked just what they wanted from him. They wanted him to recount the case. For him to take it from the top.

He felt his eyes widen as they did battle with the gloom, and he did his best to keep his voice straight, tried his best *not* to think of that *drip-dripping* sound coming from some corner of the room.

"Didn't you, uh," Suuman said, "read the file?"

A brief pause, then Jak said, "We wish to hear the matter from *your* lips."

Suuman blinked a few times, still battling with the darkness, and that pair of figures bearing down on him. The footman who'd led him up here, in those gold and black robes, and then Jak in full black dress. He wondered if there might be more members of the Watch up here, lurking in the shadows, or close enough to come . . . well, they didn't *run* per se . . . *floating.*

Better just to do what they asked. And to think about this other stuff later on.

When he was a long, *long* way from the Bell Tower.

"Well," Suuman said, "it all started about three, four weeks ago. I got this call . . . uh, got called out to this location on the edge of the Bluff . . . the Gllunarks neighbourhood, you know the one?"

Suuman waited for an affirmation, but seeing that he wasn't going to get one, continued.

"Straight-forward case, on the face of it. Murder. This guy lying facedown in a pool of blood. Middle of his kitchen. Knife lying beside him. Blood covering it. Fingerprints all over the place, too. Hardly got the samples down the lab before we'd had a confession —the guy's wife, turned herself into the station, all bloodied up, his blood . . . anyway, we got her in—"

"Detective?" Jak said, butting into the story.

"Hmm?"

"If you wouldn't mind moving onto the next stage of the case?"

Suuman's mind went blank for a moment or two. "I'm sorry, what?"

Though Suuman got the impression that, surely, he was testing Jak's patience just a little, Jak's tone remained flat as ever, as shrill and uneven. Apparently unaffected. "You had the suspect put in the

Can in the meantime, awaiting her trial." Jak paused a second. "Then what happened?"

Suuman felt his chest tighten. His throat too. It got hard to breathe all of a sudden. He felt a shudder pass over his skin. He could *really* have done with some tobacco to chew right about now, and half thought about dipping his hand into the pocket of his overcoat, popping one into his mouth. And he might well have done that if his hands hadn't been shaking quite so badly.

He tried to compose himself, told himself that these guys would know the whole story. They just wanted him to confirm what he'd already turned up, and filed in his report.

"I . . . uh, there was another case—I was called out to another case, and, well, I could hardly believe it, but it was the same one, the . . . the *exact* same circumstances. Same body, same knife lying there. And, uh, the same . . . the same . . ."

"Detective?"

Suuman swallowed hard. "It was the same woman—the same one who we locked up before, the one who was in the Can awaiting her trial."

Suuman waited for Jak, or his companion's response, hoping that he might get this matter cleared up for him. That it might get put to rest.

He decided, from their silence, that this was his cue to continue.

"The woman, we thought she was in the Can, thought that, ah, she was right in there . . . only, when we went to go take a look she, uh, she wasn't."

"And what did you do then, detective?"

"Well, we put the woman away again, locked her up fresh. Wasn't anything else we could really do."

"What about the report? Did you find the paperwork

connected to her case—from the first time that you brought her in?"

Suuman nodded, and then, thinking about the gloom that enveloped him, and that perhaps Jak and his companion couldn't see the gesture, he answered, "Yes."

And only then, after he'd spoken the word, did he think that, most likely, they could both see him quite clearly.

He thought long and hard, that *drip-dripping* sound got louder, but remained just as invisible in the gloom. He thought on the case, then said, "It was, uh, strange, you know. I mean, the funny thing was that the paperwork—the paperwork that we'd all done, I had it on my desk, all ready for it to be looked over, for it to be, ah, matched up with the recent arrest record."

He felt his chest tighten as that same old frustration came back at him. "It was right *there* flat on my desk. But, when I went to look it over the next day, all that was left there was blank pages. Nothing on them. Plain-white sheets of paper."

He could feel his pulse pounding at his temples now, that sensation he got about his eyes that told him that, soon, he would have an absolutely cracking migraine. "But the weird thing about it was that, when I asked around, when I brought up the matter, the case of this woman, they didn't seem to see anything odd about it at all . . . it was as if it was the first time that I'd brought the case into them—the first time I'd locked up the woman. None of them, uh, remembered."

It was like the darkness sucked up his voice, like water soaking up a sponge. He wondered if he'd been speaking barely above a whisper, if the two figures had actually heard any sound leaving his lips . . . or had they simply read his mind, and he hadn't known it?

Jak's voice breaking through the silence took him off guard.

"Detective, your home life, your *personal* life in Guynur City, might I be so imprudent as to suggest that, well, for want of a better way of putting it, is *non-existent*."

Suuman felt himself numbed by this change in direction. His heart hung in his throat. He knew that he ought to be outraged, but, really, he couldn't find it within himself. What was the point in being angry about the truth, however bluntly it was put?

"That's as good a way of putting it as I can think of," Suuman said, and then rolled his shoulders, trying to shake loose the numbing effect the hardness of the chair had on him—the way that it put all the muscles in his back to sleep.

When he breathed in profoundly this time, he caught that reassuring scent of tobacco, got that same glorious, tarry, *familiar* smoky-wet taste of it. And this time it seemed to compliment the dank air, not make it so unwieldy to his lungs, or, at least, not quite as unwieldy as it had been before.

He waited for Jak and the other member of the Watch's response to this.

But, before it came, he felt them draw nearer.

Felt the air about him get colder.

Had that animal-urge to flee, for him to take off running right there and then.

Or for him to put up a fight.

Subconsciously, he padded his overcoat then realised that his gun was still nestled in the glove compartment of his car. In the underground car park below. Strange, he had never forgotten to take his gun out with him before, but he had forgotten today.

He thought that he would feel those jagged, bony fingers of theirs up against his skin, thought that they might squeeze his windpipe till he was dead.

Though the why of it all would have escaped him.

"Detective," Jak said, his voice a chilling whisper in Suuman's ear, "would you like to join us?"

7

A PRICKLING SENSATION broke out, all across the surface of Suuman's skin. All at once his blood ran hot, then cold, and a sweaty film broke out on his forehead. He realised that he held his hands down on his thighs, and that he was gripping so tight that he'd cut off the blood flow at his wrists.

"What?" Suuman said. "I . . . I don't understand."

Suuman heard what must've been an approximation of the drawing of breath, coming from Jak, and the other member beside him, the one who had led him up the spiral steps from the underground car park. And now, all at once, Suuman was aware of more robed figures appearing out of the shadows, shrugging off the folds of gloom, and bearing in on him.

He knew he was surrounded.

Somehow, at the back of his mind, he had known that he was surrounded here.

"Detective," Jak continued, "you are well connected to the magical fields which confluence about Guynur City—you are much better connected to them than you imagine. In this case, this case that has drawn forth our attention, the one you have just described for us, for any average mortal about the city, any *normal* detective, this would have triggered an infinite loop—a constant coming and going of this woman being taken into custody, and then being rearrested the very next day.

"However, because of your ability, your connectivity with the world about you, you have been able to see this for what it was, a magical being playing tricks on the minds of the mortals."

"But . . . but," Suuman said, "why?"

Though Suuman could see nothing in the gloom that enveloped

Jak's face, the gloom that was generated by the hood of his robe, he could've sworn that Jak was smiling.

Or perhaps he only heard the smile in his voice.

"This woman, this *magical* being, she has been playing this trick for no one knows how long, but the important thing is that now she has been captured—her trick has been put to rest once and for all.

"Once we conclude our audit of the Guynur City Fuzz Station, we shall have all the answers we require, there shall remain no evidence of this case, or, indeed, your involvement with it. No one shall so much as remember your name, or that you were ever a detective there. Or that the Watch even ever audited the premises. All this shall scurry once more into the shadows of their minds." Jak paused a long moment. "Just as things should be."

Suuman's mind got caught in a whirl, and he tried to piece the bits of the puzzle together for himself. And came up empty handed. There was nothing to be put together—nothing that he could find to put together, in any case.

"And me?" Suuman said. "What happens to me?"

"Detective, or should I say, Mister Suuman, you now have a choice ahead of you—a very much binary decision to make."

Suuman felt the beginnings of the migraine now. When he opened his mouth to breathe he found the air so thick that it felt like an invisible damp blanket covered his mouth and nose. That dankness tasted mangy on his tongue. "What?" he said. "What is it? What do I have to decide."

"We, as the Watch, cannot allow you to remain in Guynur City, not with the abilities that you possess, not simply running loose, getting into whatever trouble you might get into."

When Suuman spoke again, he felt himself shaking, right down to his bones. "Then . . . then you'll send me away?"

"Hmm, yes, detective, you should be sent away—away from Guynur City, far away from here. But, maybe you would enjoy it, maybe it would be better for you."

"What is there?" Suuman said. "Outside Guynur City."

"We do not know—it is outside of our capacity to know, just as it is outside of yours. It might be a wide, open new world, or it might simply be the end of existence." Again Jak paused, apparently thinking the matter over strongly. "But after our discussions it is not our belief that you would choose such a path in any case, it is our belief that a duty to serve Guynur City, to protect it from disorder, runs strong within you. Is that belief correct?"

Suuman thought this over. He thought about how when he'd been at school, and how he'd only ever dreamed of serving the fuzz, of doing all he could to take on the criminal elements of the city. It *had* seemed natural to him. Second nature. And now, with Jak saying it out loud to him, it seemed like, consciously, the right thing for him to do.

What he had been put on the face of the world, on the face of Schwyn, to do.

"You want me to join you—to become a member of the Watch, or you want me to be outcast, is that correct?"

Jak made no reply, but Suuman knew that he had understood the nature of the offer, and that it was up to him to decide.

Suuman hadn't much need to think this one over. As little as he had binding him to Guynur City, he knew that there was only a single facet inside of him. That facet for wanting to protect the place—for keeping its citizens safe.

"I . . . I . . ." Suuman began, "I'd like to join you." Then, when he spoke again, he found that his voice had a reinforced steel to it . . . almost verging on desperation. "*Please*, let me join you."

There was a long silence about the room, and the *drip-drip* sound grew louder still, seemed to echo all the more about the darkness. For a second Suuman was certain that he was alone. That the members of the Watch who'd only just now surrounded him had melted into the shadows, that they had left him here alone.

But then, from the very blackest of the darkness, he heard Jak's voice once more. Speaking to him. And only to him.

"Very well," Jak said. "You shall become one of us."

And as Suuman breathed in again, he felt the darkness swell about him, felt his brain swimming off, whatever had once bound it to his body being let free. And he left it behind him willingly.

Because he knew what awaited him.

Knew that ahead of him he had a new existence.

One which, he had somehow known, had dwelled in him all along.

INFIRMARY

DOCTOR MATRIS WHOLSUUN dug between the gaps in her teeth for any of the remaining grains of peanut butter, from the toast she'd just about rammed down her throat before coming down here, to the Infirmary emergency ward. And then to here, to this examination room, after she'd been off into the store cupboard to get a few sutures, and a hypodermic needle. She caught one of the peanut butter grains, chewed it up, lost herself in the thick, earthy nutty taste for a moment. She wished she'd had the time to get a proper breakfast down her . . . if 'breakfast' was what you could call eating at eleven o'clock at night.

The nurse, wearing her pale-pink, short-sleeved scrubs, her matching plastic pink sandals just about poking out from beneath her untapered trouser legs, stood proud with a stout, snub-nosed expression pressed all over her face. She stood on the other side of the empty crash trolley, opposite, Matris.

The green paper sheet of the crash trolley was all scrunched up and mottled with still-fresh blood, turning the paper itself a dirty purple colour.

Matris stared daggers at the nurse. She could feel her heart welling up in her throat, and was quite unable to believe what she'd just heard—what the nurse had just told her.

"Would you care to repeat that?" Matris said.

Matris knew this nurse, had seen her about the place before. She always wore that same expression, the one she was wearing now. That look of total and complete superiority, that holier-than-thou look that told anyone who cared that *she* was in control of everything about here. And that they'd better not try to cross her path, or they'd be taking their lives into their own hands. It was the kind of expression that cut through the air thick with disinfectant, and sent even the most satisfied, lunch-filled stomach gurgling with apprehension.

And it pissed off Matris all the more to know that if there was anyone here who should've felt superior then it was *her*. She was the fucking doctor about the place, after all. The senior doctor on the nightshift, no less.

Even the way the nurse's lavender-scented perfume wafted through the air seemed obnoxious to Matris, as if she'd engineered for it to be that way. That the nurse had perused the counter of whatever shopping centre she'd bought that *damn* perfume at, only settling to select the one that'd cause the maximum amount of passive-aggressive conflict down the Infirmary.

Or maybe Matris was just in a bad mood.

Maybe it was because she'd spent the first half of tonight, the time when she was *supposed* to be catching a few hours of rest, up with her six-month-old daughter Julie, trying to get her calm while she was burning up from a temperature. It was *always* almost too much for her to bear leaving her behind—turning her over to the babysitter who she paid a fortune to show up at midnight on these night shifts and look after Julie.

But Matris knew that they needed the money. And that, if she decided to quit her job as a doctor at the Infirmary now, then it would also mean herself, and Julie, drowning in the mountain of debt which had piled up from all the years of medical training . . . and she could hardly face going back to those part-time jobs, waiting tables, or serving drunks in some scumbag bar. That just wouldn't bring in the money she needed any longer.

The money she needed to bring up Julie the right way.

Slowly, Matris allowed her eyes to dip down, allowed herself to read off the nurse's nametag.

'Beajrix.'

Beatrix, with a 'J.'

Even her name was obnoxious. Matris would've had a hard time trying to pick out a better-suited name for the nurse.

"He just got up and left," the nurse said, with the same smug grin.

Matris blinked a couple of times, maybe trying to shake off her complete sense of disbelief. "The guy was bleeding out of *everything* —don't you tell me that he simply got himself up and shoved on out."

The nurse, Beajrix, held up her palms, in surrender. "Both you and I know that he was mixed up in, goodness knows what." She quietened down her voice, and added, "From the looks of his tattoos I'd have said he was Crul."

Matris snorted, a kind of chuckle of disbelief. She knew all about the 'Crul,' those mobsters that ran just about half the city it seemed these days. The Crul were responsible for a good proportion of the traffic into the emergency ward—especially at this time of night.

But that made no difference, not to Matris.

Everyone who passed on through those sliding doors of the ward, they were all equal in her eyes.

They were all patients that needed to be treated.

And they'd stay that way till they'd been all patched up and sent on their way, healthy once more.

But Matris brushed past the nurse's briskness, and said, "Did you see which way he went?"

The nurse shrugged, then screwed up the soiled green paper sheet which covered the crash trolley, made a ball of it and tossed it into the bin over in the corner of the examination room.

It landed neatly inside with a *swish* as it came into contact with the plastic bag lining the inside.

"Out the doors?" the nurse added, unhelpfully.

Matris cursed the woman under her breath as she tottered on out of the examination room, grabbing her moleskin coat off the back of the door as she went.

2

MATRIS SHRUGGED her coat on around the shoulders of her flimsy, light-blue scrubs, as she barrelled on out through the sliding doors of the emergency ward. She emerged into the crisp, half-frozen night air, and felt it instantly send a sharp tang right to the pit of her gut. Made her feel ten times more awake than she had done before.

The air was thick with fumes on account of the low-hanging cloud. There had been no way for the air to clear, not even at night when most of the city was sleeping.

She could feel her pulse on her tongue, had a stale, bloodlike taste in her mouth, that kind of taste she got after inadvertently popping an ulcer in her cheek.

She stood stock still on the pavement and listened hard, trying to hear anything at all that might help her.

Off in the distance, she could hear that faint sigh of the traffic going by on the ring road that ran close by the Infirmary, and which the ambulances would pummel along with fresh emergency cases.

Protocol was clear, Matris wasn't supposed to leave the Infirmary behind in the event of a patient leaving the premises, she was supposed to call up a meathead from security, get one of them to go off and prowl about, to see if they could recover the escapee . . . or however else the patient had managed to get away from the Infirmary.

But she felt such a strong duty, almost as strong as the feeling she had for Julie in leaving her behind every time she had to take on a nightshift. This sensation deep within her that she couldn't leave a job half done.

She had to see it through to the end.

She stuffed her hands into the soft moleskin pockets of her jacket and she walked on quickly, feeling just about every nook and cranny of the cracked-up pavement beneath the rubber soles of her sandals.

Like a scrounger checking out scrap, looking for something to drag on down to the Tip for a few quid, she twisted her head from side to side, taking in each of the alleyways she passed by, in expectation of finding her patient there.

She had gone about three blocks before she found the trail of blood.

And she thanked the weather this night, the crisp air, and the looming, soggy-bottomed clouds, for not bringing any rain with it.

If it had been raining she never would've had a chance in hell of finding the bloody mark.

She followed the trail, catching just a whiff of that familiar metallic odour in her nostrils. That odour that still sent a twitch up her spine despite having been a fully-qualified doctor for five years now, going on six. She guessed that some things were just deeply instilled in human nature, and no matter how much training was put into a thing, no matter how much experience was injected into someone's skull. There were some things that could never be shaken off entirely.

The trail led her around the corner, and then to a recently white-washed wall. Even in the dim gleam of the orange street-lights, she could still see the graffiti, all loopy and scrawling, showing through the coat of paint.

She found her patient slumped on the ground, lying in a vague recovery position.

Her heart dipped in her chest, feeling like it was on the verge of touching her stomach. She rushed up to him, looked him over.

A man of about forty. He was unshaven, and had pudgy cheeks.

He wore the same grey suit, the one which seemed at least a couple of sizes too large, despite his bulky shape. He had the same over-polished shoes too. The laces of his shoes were undone, she noticed, and she also saw that they now had more than a few spots of blood on them.

She could see where the blood was still oozing on out through the fabric of his suit, where it had turned the grey fabric to black, and given it a gleam.

From what she recalled of studying his injuries, about an hour before, she'd found puncture wounds on his chest and back. One just above his right knee, though that was just a flesh wound, it appeared to only have sliced off skin, leaving any nerves or veins unharmed.

She looked to his face, took in his pallid complexion, and she saw that he was breathing hard . . . *gasping* really. It seemed to her that each breath he took was a fresh struggle.

As she crouched down over him, she heard a rustling sound over her shoulder.

She pivoted round, looked off in the direction of the sound.

But she saw nothing but shadows.

Being out here, in this neighbourhood, on her own, made her feel deeply uneasy. There was a reason for the protocols being in place. A reason that the Infirmary sent meatheads after escapees rather than doctors.

New meatheads could be rounded up on any given night in the Bluff, whereas fully certified doctors were something of a rarity in Guynur City.

She reached out and lightly touched her patient on the shoulder pad of his suit. She had to squeeze hard before she could feel his flesh beneath. "Hey," she said. "Hey?"

Another *rustle*, off in the shadows.

She turned back again.

Again saw nothing.

Her heart sped up. She felt her skin go clammy down the back of her scrubs. Could smell the salt of her sweat and body odour wafting up at her.

"Come on," she said, "let's get you back to the Infirmary, yeah? Back there . . . I can get a good look at you, get you feeling better, okay?"

She shovelled her hands beneath his armpits, the only logical way she could think to lift him. And she gently brought his weight onto her, felt him leaning into her. She couldn't quite tell if he was conscious at all. If he could hear her. It wasn't like he was a dead weight.

He *was* helping her out a little.

Grounding herself, she brought his weight onto her, and gently got him onto his feet.

He seemed able to stand, though she wasn't going to push her luck by experimenting to see if he could stay there completely unsupported.

She held on tight with her arm about his shoulders, and his arm draped over her.

She looked him in the face, feeling his weight getting the better of her now. "We're just going to go on a little walk, okay? Just a few blocks to get back to the Infirmary, then we can sort you out, okay?"

No response.

But he appeared to hold onto her.

They shuffled on, making steady progress along the pavement, and headed back in the direction of the hospital. Already Matris was thinking up how she would file the complaint for that nurse that had acted so nonchalantly towards her patient.

She would have to be disciplined.

No two ways about it.

She never had liked the way that nurse acted.

They were just on the point of turning the corner and heading back towards the sliding doors of the emergency room when Matris heard a car engine behind her. And then the *screech* of tyres as it pulled up.

With her patient's weight dragging her down, she couldn't look around to check, so she just kept on loping on.

The capacity that people had to create car accidents out of nothing always amazed her. There were some people in Guynur City—people she'd treated for whiplash, burst spleens, or whatever else—who could somehow get into trouble on a deserted street like the one which led up to the emergency ward of the Infirmary.

Behind her, she heard car doors creak open on their hinges.

She heard smart footsteps, seemingly half a dozen of them.

Then came the low, throbbing tone of voice. "Hand him over, love."

3

MATRIS'S PULSE QUICKENED. Her sweat seemed to chill her flesh all over. Bring it out in pimples. That bloody taste in her mouth got worse, and it mingled with the bloody stench coming off her patient. A slight ringing sound started up in her ears.

But she pressed on.

She kept on lugging her patient forwards, pretending not to have heard the voices. She knew, from experience, that it was better not to speak to strange men on the street after dark. She had fallen for that one many times over. Her kind nature getting the better of her when they asked for the time, or to be directed to the nearest metro station . . . only for them, when she looked back, to be brandishing a knife or a gun and demanding she give them her handbag.

"Miss? You just hand him over here, now, y'hear?"

She focussed on the sallow light which spilled on out from the illuminated windows of the emergency ward up ahead and ignored the man. Twenty, maybe thirty, paces away. Just a little further on. Why, if she was to call out now, she could well bring a meathead running . . . yeah, or just as likely get herself into big trouble with these guys.

Something told her not to make any sudden moves.

Nothing that might piss them off.

Don't turn back. Don't pay them any attention. Don't . . .

She felt a sturdy hand on her shoulder. Felt the brush of calloused skin against her exposed neck. And she felt the weight of her patient leaving her. Felt someone taking on his load. She grappled for a moment or two, trying to cling onto her patient's jacket, but she could get no purchase and the fabric slipped through her fingers.

She turned to see four men, all of them dressed in sable suits, with matching ties, lugging her patient between them, still lolloping along on his feet, towards a shiny black four-by-four, pulled up at the curb. The four-by-four had tinted-out windows. And all she could see was her own reflection staring back at her, open mouthed and wide eyed.

She watched on, powerless, as they maneuvered her patient towards the open door of the backseat of the car. Somehow she summoned the strength to speak. ". . . Wait," she said.

Once they'd got her patient slumped down on the backseat of the car, one of the men dressed in a suit glanced up at her.

He had pinched cheeks and full, thick purple lips, tanned skin that looked almost a shade of green in the orange streetlights.

"He . . . he needs *medical* attention," she said, already feeling an idiot for having spoken out. She should've just kept on walking. Should've got back to the emergency ward, gone back to her duties.

But, deep down, she knew that, right now, this patient here was her duty.

If he died, it would be on her.

The other men piled on into the car, leaving the solitary suited man there.

From inside the car she could hear the *slap* of flesh on flesh, and she instinctively knew that they were slapping her patient's cheeks, trying to bring him round.

This was her chance. "He'll be dead in a few minutes without my help," she said.

The suited man, the only one outside the car, tilted his head to one side, and narrowed his eyes. He pouted long and hard, then ducked down, looked into the car, spoke to someone inside. When he straightened back up, he looked Matris over in that lecherous way she'd grown accustomed to whenever she passed by a building site or a pub.

"You come with us, then?"

Matris felt like her eyeballs were lolling out of their sockets. Her heart was beating hard against her tonsils, and her tongue tasted like an ashen coal. She could smell the blood of her patient, still thick in the air, and she wanted more than anything to be with him.

To do all she could to save him.

She nodded to the suited man, who nodded to her in return, signalled for her to get in.

4

BEFORE GETTING INTO THE CAR, Matris made a bargain with the carful of suited-up men, that she could return to the emergency ward to fetch the supplies she needed. The supplies she had dumped at her feet in that examination room when she'd found that crash trolley empty, and the smug-looking nurse standing there.

As she went to fetch the supplies, she toyed with the idea of alerting security, of getting a few meatheads to bear on this thing. But, somehow, what the nurse had said to her came back at her now. About how her patient looked like he was involved with the Crul.

Now that Matris had got herself this far ensnared with whatever it was her patient was wrapped up with, she knew that she'd have to see it out.

If she gave them so much as a whiff of being out to crash their plans she reasoned that they'd know *exactly* where she worked, and from that they'd find out where she lived . . . and from that they could get to Julie, and that was something Matris couldn't allow.

She managed to extricate herself from the Infirmary, and got herself back into their car with everything she needed.

With two sets of eyes on her, from the two suited men who also sat on the backseat of the four-by-four, she set about her work, doing just what she had intended to do before her patient's escape. With the men's help, she got the suit off her patient, and set about getting him cleaned up and stitched up.

She was almost finished as she felt the car slowing and taking a hard left turn before coming to a complete stop.

As she dabbed away at her patient's bloody flesh, she glanced out the window and caught the light-pink signpost with the swirling, silver lettering that read: Hornheim Manor.

Something about that name was familiar, though she couldn't place it.

She continued to look out the window as they passed through a pair of tall, steel gates, all painted in immaculate white, with ornate swirls in the design.

As the car slipped on through them, the gates closed automatically behind them.

She worked on at her patient as the car engine ground onwards, leading them all up a gravelled drive. She could hear the rocks from the driveway leaping up and pinging off the bottom of the four-by-four.

The car came to a stop with a *crunch* of gravel as the wheels all locked in unison.

She looked over her work, over how good of a job she'd done in patching up her patient, and decided that she was finished.

There was nothing now that bed rest wouldn't take care of.

It was only then, when the car engine clicked off and all the doors opened up around her, that she felt fear sneaking on into her mind. She had been so occupied, been so dedicated to keeping an eye on her patient that she hadn't thought about their final destination, or having to handle anything about it.

But she would have to think about it now.

That same suited man who'd asked her along, the one with the pinched cheeks, the tanned skin, the purple lips, said, "Out the car."

Matris did as he said, and slid her way along the backseat, which she only now noticed was leather—*black* leather. Again, she'd been so wrapped up in what she'd been doing that she'd really not taken stock of her surroundings.

She found the man with the pinched cheeks holding out his hand for her, a gesture that, in any other circumstance, might've seen gentlemanly to her.

In this situation, though, something about it struck her as being infinitely seedy.

But she took his hand all the same, allowed him to help her get out and up onto her feet.

She had to take care.

Wherever this was that she had ended up.

As she listened to the rubber soles of her sandals crunch onto the gravel driveway, she glanced upwards, about the car, and looked to the . . . well, she supposed from the name on the signpost outside that it *was* a manor.

And that seemed no overstatement.

From her experience of manors, of course.

The whole place was washed in that same light pink of the signpost outside, offset with the occasional white-washed feature: the doorframes, the window ledges, the drainpipes.

Neatly trimmed bushed surrounded the stone steps which led up to the towering oak double doors. Ivy crept its way up the façade of the house, ebbing in and out of an unseen trellis beneath.

She hardly had time to take stock of the driveway, of the gravel they'd passed along to get here, hardly any time to take in the pine and elm trees which lined either side of the driveway, before she felt a sure touch at the centre of her back.

That same guy with the pinched cheeks. "Come on," he said, and led her in the direction of the front doors to the manor.

As he led her along to the doors, she tilted her head back and took in the windows above her. Slick, almost fluorescent, white light flowed out from within. It reminded her of the light back at the Infirmary, and she wondered how anyone would be able to live with lights like that all the time. Why, at night, when she was relaxing, she liked to have soft light, low-wattage bulbs.

And then it struck her.

The type of person who'd want lights like that was someone who primarily worked at night. Someone who had to be awake to do their business. Just like they did back at the Infirmary. Whoever this manor belonged to, there was no doubting that they worked at night.

The guy led her on through several hallways, all with that same light-pink shaded wallpaper. Oil paintings hung off the walls, almost all of them portraits of uninterested-looking people, striking uninteresting poses. Staring out from within gilded frames.

Several vases stood up on pine stools, all of them containing fresh flowers: roses, posies, lilacs, all, she guessed, had been plucked from the garden.

As they carried on through the house, she caught sight of the hallway ahead, and the wide, stone staircase leading upwards. She saw her patient there, now lying prostrate on a stretcher, being carried up by two of the suited men.

Instinctively, she broke away from the man escorting her, but she felt him snatch a hold of her wrist before she'd taken so much as three steps.

"Where you goin', huh?" he said.

She didn't resist his tight hold on her.

"Yeah, tha's righ'," he said. "You gonna go see the boss. You gonna see Phayshawe."

5

THE GUY led her away from the staircase she'd seen her patient disappear up. Her heart skipped a beat as he led her along a narrow hallway, deeper into the manor. When she breathed in, she caught a strong smell of polish. And it stuck in her throat. Tasted dry in her mouth. She let the guy steer her along, him still clutching on tight to her wrist, apparently not trusting her enough to let her loose. His footsteps were smart and echoless, totally absorbed by the thick wallpaper which surrounded them.

A couple of minutes later, after them taking several flights of stairs upwards, higher into the building, he brought her to an archway, and to a pair of wide-open oak doors that seemed to reference the front doors to the manor. The guy glanced back at her, gave her the sliver of a smile, and then led her on through the doorway.

As she took in the room, she felt her breath ebbing on out through her lungs. She took in the ceiling made of glass, and most of the walls too. Only the wall which she stood with her back against was wallpapered.

If it had been a clear night, she might've been able to look up and see stars blinking in the night sky, but since it was cloudy, a *moody* night, she could see nothing much at all.

But, off in the distance, she could see the cityscape stretched out.

Guynur City in the darkness.

Just a flickering glow of light.

And a dozy snore.

She was so struck by the view out through the windows, that she almost didn't notice the figure, dressed in a pale-pink suit, with his back to her. He wore a straw hat with a silky pink ribbon tied about its crown to match his suit. She guessed that that vague peppery smell in the room was down to him—some sort of exotic cologne that Matris had never experienced.

Phayshawe, she supposed.

She waited a couple of beats, felt the guy who'd led her through the manor thus far, let go of her wrist, and she took a couple of tentative steps into the room.

As if he was responding to her footfalls, the figure in the light-pink suit turned around and looked over to her. When he took her in, he gave her a full-faced smile, the kind that meant a whole host of wrinkles breaking on out from the pit of his chin right on up to his forehead.

"I hear you've been seeing to our guest," he said, his voice sounding bright . . . much brighter than Matris would've imagined it.

He took a few steps towards her, that smile of his not showing any signs of dialling down so much as a wrinkle.

"Really quite marvellous of you," he said.

Matris decided that this was the point where she was meant to say something. "I . . . I was just doing my job."

He held up his hand, as if he were a musician silencing an audience going wild for his encore. "Of course you were, of course." He held his smile and narrowed his eyes a little. "Though you must understand that it really would've been quite acceptable for you to turn over our guest to my rather noble helpers, I can assure you that he would've been quite all right with them."

"He needed urgent medical attention."

"Yes, I can imagine."

From the way he said it, Matris got the impression that he knew just what had happened to her patient, just how he'd got into the state he had.

She decided to speak up for herself some more. "He'll need medical care throughout the night, too, or at the very least some nursing, he'd uh . . ." she paused a moment, not sure whether she should add any more, but decided that this man seemed reasonable enough ". . . he would be much better off back at the Infirmary. He would have a much better setup about him."

"Oh, my dear, please understand that the setup we have right here, in this very manor, shall be more than sufficient for his requirements."

Matris thought twice about offering her medical opinion to the man's pure belief, and decided to just leave things where they lay for the time being.

She'd not get anywhere arguing with him.

Not here in his own home.

"Still," the man said, trailing it out as he dipped his hand into the pocket of his light-pink suit, and removing a pocket watch. He glanced at the face of it, and then looked back at her, that same smile pinning back his cheeks. "I think we *would* be extremely interested in your services, you know, in you looking him over for the night if that would be possible?"

"Oh, I . . . I don't know about that," Matris said. "I mean, I'm meant to be down the Infirmary—there're other patients I need to see to, that's why I say he'd be better off there, where I can keep an eye on him."

There was a long silence in the room, and Matris had herself convinced that she'd just gone and said precisely the wrong thing. She was on the brink of trying to talk her way out of whatever hole she'd got herself fixed in, when the man spoke up again.

"Listen, doctor, I, uh, think I have a proposal for you—one which you might find *extremely* interesting, if you'll just hear me out?"

Matris stood still, now afraid of what was coming next. She felt torn. She knew that she had to be back at the Infirmary, but, at the same time, that she needed to see to her patient. Had to be on hand if anything went wrong with him.

And she could do that much better back at the Infirmary.

"Okay," she said, her voice sounding reedy and uneven.

The man smiled some more, then dipped his hand into the other pocket of his suit, the one which he *didn't* keep his pocket watch inside. When his hand re-emerged, he clenched a whole bundle of quid in his fist. Notes and notes and notes.

An untidy crunched-up mess.

But just from looking at them from here, from the doorway of the room, she could tell that right there, in his fist, there was at least a month's worth of wages.

She thought of all the things she could do with that money . . . repay a significant portion of her debts, maybe take Julie out somewhere on a daytrip, somewhere that wasn't her boxy studio flat in what seemed like the busiest junction of all Guynur City.

It would be just nice to have some breathing room . . . for once.

But she couldn't.

There were *other* patients waiting for her, back at the Infirmary.

Without her saying anything at all, the man—Phayshawe—seemed to read her mind, and he nodded to himself as if in subconsciously understanding.

She listened to the *creak* of the soles of the shoes of the suited man with the pinched cheeks behind her, and she watched him stalk off into the room, over to a pine cabinet that she hadn't noticed previously. He brought the cabinet door open and dug about inside, producing a large, bright-pink, steel safe box, which he, in turn, carried on over to the man in the pink suit.

She felt her heart throbbing in her throat, and she felt the blood pumping hard into her head, almost stealing away her capacity for lucid thought . . . but what need did she have for lucid thought if that steel box contained what she thought it contained?

Slowly, the man in the pink suit dipped his hand into his inside breast pocket and withdrew a key. He slipped the key into the lock of the steel box and turned.

Even from where she stood, a good twenty paces away, she heard the mechanism *snick* and *click* into place. Listened to the hinges of the box opening with a nasal *whine*.

The man in the pink suit turned the box around for her to see inside.

Right there, laid out, in neat little rows, she saw more money than she could ever have imagined . . . though, if she'd been forced to put a figure on it, she might've guessed it to be somewhere in the region of four or five *years'* worth of wages.

"Deal?" the man in the pink suit said.

Though Matris's head was swilling, and every bone in her body was telling her to run, she found herself nodding back in reply, and then saying a firm and committed, "Yes."

6

PHAYSHAWE DETAILED OUT what her role was to be. What he had bought with his money.

He told her plainly that he wanted the patient alive by sunrise, and in good enough health to answer questions. What questions those were, he wouldn't say . . . and Matris wouldn't ask after either. The way she saw it, the kind of money he was paying her, that was so that she wouldn't get all inquisitive on him.

The suited man with the pinched cheeks led her on through the manor, up and then down several flights of steps before they emerged into a hallway with a door guarded by two suited men, one at either side, sitting on wooden chairs.

Neither of them so much as looked up as they passed by, as the man with the pinched cheeks turned the doorknob and led her inside.

Right away, just stepping into the room, Matris could smell the familiar mixture of blood and disinfectant, along with that unplace-able, but unmistakable odour, that she always associated in her mind with the Infirmary.

The room was simple and windowless. There was a single bed shoved up against one of the light green walls, and her patient lay on his back, dressed only in his underwear—just the same as when he'd left her back in the car.

He lay on top of the fuzzy, marmalade-coloured blanket, and he slept with his arms down at his side.

Good, that was good.

Just what he needed.

Bed rest.

To sleep off his trauma, all the pain he must've been going through.

She'd slipped him several doses of painkillers on the car ride over, of course, but those were surely wearing off by now, and she hadn't brought any more along with her.

As if in answer to a unspoken question, the man with the pinched cheeks, unsmiling, trod through the room and up to the pine bedside table. He pulled out all three of the drawers to reveal the medical supplies nestled within.

She guessed that Phayshawe had been speaking with confidence when he'd informed her that here she would find everything that she would need to treat her patient.

She felt herself grow a little steelier inside, felt herself get a little more confident in herself, as if only now was this seeming like it might actually be a feasible thing.

She tried not to think of the Infirmary, and all the patients she wouldn't see to tonight.

Though she reassured herself that, when the Infirmary saw that she hadn't returned to duty, they'd call in another doctor, get someone else with the expertise they needed out on the emergency ward. They'd be fine.

She tried to think of Julie.

And everything they could do with that money.

There would be no more stress, that was for sure.

And only for a night's work.

The man with the pinched cheeks left her without another word, though she doubted that meant that he trusted her, that she was now totally trusted to toddle about the manor as she pleased. No, most likely they were watching her somehow . . . at the very least one of those men sitting on guard at the door would be keeping a sharp ear out for any sound within the room.

Matris put that out of her mind, though, and busied herself with taking care of her patient. She dosed him up with more painkillers, checked his vitals, and then the dressings she'd given him. Everything looked fine. It was just a case of nursing. Of keeping an eye on him.

And so she took up the chair beside the bed, and lost herself in the light green colour of the walls, in a way it reminded her of the Infirmary, and then she wondered if Phayshawe had set up this room specifically as a kind of treatment room.

If he'd engineered the feel of the place.

Perhaps hours passed by, or maybe it was only minutes, but Matris found herself lost in all her inner ramblings, thinking things through, mentally spending the money she was earning right at that moment.

It was just as she'd found herself and Julie the perfect house, on the outskirts of the city, in one of the pleasant, leafy suburbs that hadn't yet become lost in urban sprawl, that she heard her patient give a slight *groan* in his sleep.

A skitter passed up her spine, and she felt all her muscles draw tight.

She glanced over at him, wide eyed, seeing what the matter was.

He had one eye crooked open, staring out at her.

7

MATRIS FELT her heart thrum in her chest, and all the blood within her seemed to pump harder still. Instinctively, she looked to the door of the bedroom, as if she expected the man with the pinched cheeks, or one of the suited men standing guard, to burst on inside.

But, of course, nothing at all happened.

Her patient kept on staring at her with that solitary eye.

When she spoke, she kept her voice low, afraid that one of the two suited men standing guard might overhear. "How are you feeling?" she said.

Her patient kept up his staring. His other eye remained shut tight. And he didn't so much as blink as he looked her over.

She rose up off her chair, and reached out for him.

Then he did speak.

". . . No," he said, his voice similarly gruff and almost too quiet for her to discern . . . as if he also realised the peril he was in here, that there was a pair of guards ready to burst into the room.

She flinched, then backed off, not wanting to distress him in any way.

He drew a profound breath, and she watched his chest rise and fall as he did so. She examined his sweat-soaked brow and had the urge to wipe it with a damp cloth . . . but, at the same time, only wanted to do so with his permission.

Given the injuries he'd sustained, she knew it was important to keep him as calm as could be possible, so that he didn't overwork his heart, already working overtime to fix up his tired and wrecked body.

"Are you . . ." she began, but he cut her off.

"Where am I?" he said.

She thought about it for a moment. "I don't think I can say."

He opened his other eye, slowly, as if he might've been punched there and was just now waking up on the floor, staring up at his opponent. He pressed his lips together, as if thinking this over, then, "Why? Have they, uh . . . got me?"

Again, she thought it over before nodding.

He squeezed his eyes closed, pursed his lips, as if he was in pain, though she was sure that she'd given him enough sedation to do him till the following morning.

"Is there . . . is there anything I can do for you?"

He didn't respond to her.

She had no idea what to do next, if it would be better for her to leave him alone . . . but, at the same time, she knew that she couldn't, the whole thing that Phayshawe was paying for was for her to stay here, by his side.

She was convinced that he'd slipped away from her, that he'd dozed off on that tidal wave of drugs she'd given him to help him sleep.

But then he spoke.

"Kill me," he said.

"What?"

He opened his eyes, and his eyes lolled about, sleepy beneath their lids, and he took her in with a fever-drenched stare. "Kill me. Please."

Matris blinked a few times, trying to bring the scene clearer. Maybe it was because she hadn't got enough sleep the night before. What time could it possibly be now? Surely approaching dawn, and with her work almost done?

All told this was going to be one of the easiest shifts of her life . . . and certainly the most lucrative.

She could go back to the Infirmary with new energy—with energy she'd never before felt within her, now that she had that much-needed cushion Phayshawe's money would afford her.

"You know," her patient said. "You know what Phayshawe *wants* from me?"

She shook her head.

"You know *how* I got myself like this?"

Again, she shook her head.

He blinked long and slow, clearly dazed out of his mind, then said, "You have heard of the . . . the *sprites*?"

"No, I haven't."

"They . . . one . . . it attacked me."

"A"—she tried to think over just what he'd said—"'sprite?'"

"Hmm."

She thought this over. Of course, like every other citizen of Guynur City, she knew that magic beat at the heart of the place— that the energy produced from the magical sources of bunter and whipplesnife kept the lights glowing, and the car engines grinding along.

But this . . . 'sprite?' . . . It sounded like some magical creature, and that, at least for Matris, was something she had never once in her life run into. Most likely, of course, her patient was delusional. He was drugged, after all.

All the same, she allowed him to go on.

It was important not to distress him unduly.

"The . . . the thing, they set it on me . . . when I was . . . uh, I was . . ."

She reached forwards for his hand, took hold of it in hers, felt his fingers cling to her skin as if he was terrified, as if he was afraid that he was on the brink of death.

She wished she could reassure him, tell him that everything was going to be all right, but the state he was in at the moment, in this wild, outpouring state, she couldn't see any way for her to break away.

"Here," he said, "Here is where *he* has the sprites—he *has* them here."

"Who?"

He drew a long, long breath, then breathed it out again. "Phayshawe."

Outside, she heard a *scuffle*. She craned her neck around, looked to the doorknob, certain that it would turn at any second and that one or both of the men guarding the room would burst on in. But the doorknob stayed still, and once she was content that no one was coming, that no one had overheard that her patient was awake, she turned back to him.

"He . . . he wanted to *infect* me," her patient said.

"To infect you?"

"Yes, yes, to infect me, with the sprite, with the magic from the sprite—*that* was his plan. That is just part of his experiments, of the experiments that Phayshawe conducts here, in his manor. Life will be . . . will be, *unbearable* for me here, do you understand?"

So, he'd figured out just where they were, though, if what he said was correct, that he worked for Phayshawe, then it didn't take an enormous leap of logic to realise that, most likely, he recognised his surroundings.

That he was intimately familiar with the manor itself.

"Please," he said, "I will do anything"—his eyes sought hers out, he moved his head slightly on his pillow, looked her right in the eye —"*kill* me."

Matris felt a tingling sensation pass through her chest, and through her blood. The sensation trailed right through her body and all the way down to the base of her gut. She felt nauseous, like the walls of the room were pressing in on her. Like the air in the room had grown stilted, *stifling*. Her clothes seemed to be sticky with dried sweat, and she could smell the mixture of blood from her patient's wounds and the metallic smells from the disinfectant.

She wanted to get out.

Desperately.

She *needed* to get out.

Her heart rose up and tickled the back of her tongue, and she tried to stand, but her patient held on fast to her hand, and repeated, "Kill me."

His request, of course, was absurd.

First of all there was her medical ethics to consider. Her role was to keep patients alive for as long as she possibly could—that was the oath she had taken, the one that she still believed in even to this day, even with all the stresses and strains of those nightshifts.

Even with the stress and strain of being out here.

Asked by Phayshawe to look after this man till the morning.

To bring him around.

Her patient glared up at her now, apparently using every scrap of energy he had, all the energy that he *should* have been using to recuperate, to look at her, to say, "He will take me. Down . . . and down . . . to his labs, and he will . . . he will . . . put me in a *cage*."

Finally Matris summoned the courage to break away, to tear her fingers loose from his.

The other factor, the other reason why she couldn't kill him and, to be honest, with all that had happened tonight, the one foremost on her mind, was the money Phayshawe had offered her, to keep him alive.

"Please," he said again, and this time, with his voice dropping to a rasping whisper, "*Kill* me."

Perhaps it was the desperation in his eyes, or how his hand, the hand that had only just now been holding hers, draped down off the bed, flimsy and spent, its fingers numb and unfeeling.

Or maybe it was the intrinsic feeling that Matris had that, tonight, she had done so many things wrong—she had taken so many wrong steps—but she found herself pawing through the drawer, popping through the vials, digging out a hypodermic needle, filling its plunger with a lethal dose of the only thing that she could find . . . the only thing that would do the trick.

And even then, her standing over him, bearing down on him, and him with his eyeballs rolling beneath those droopy eyelids, she couldn't do it.

She was simply frozen in time.

Unable to move a muscle.

His lips brushed against one another, and his voice was hardly more than a sigh now. "Kill me, please."

Then his eyes shut.

And he drifted off into drug-addled sleep.

She thought about the cash, about Phayshawe's offer.

Surely it was only a matter of hours before the money would be hers.

This place all long forgotten.

Her patient, here, forgotten.

Unless he managed to find his way to the hospital again . . . escaped those labs that he had jabbered on about.

Her mind was made up.

She administered the dose, and then, exhausted, collapsed back on the chair beside him.

And felt her mind ebbing away from her.

8

THE CREAKING sound of the door hinges brought her round.

She blinked away her dazed sleep, looked over. Saw the man with the pinched cheeks standing there, in the doorway. She straightened in her chair and then, out of shock, looked to her patient.

He was still now, his face still damp with perspiration.

He wasn't breathing.

And his cheeks had gone a pale shade of blue.

What they often called 'deathly pale' back at the Infirmary . . . black humour often got them through shifts.

The man with the pinched cheeks seemed to realise right away what had happened, and he flashed a glance to her before retreating from the room.

While he was gone, Matris got up, made her patient look more comfortable. And she felt, a little against her expectations, a tiny tear spill down her cheek.

It was warm and wet, and it was like a breath of life direct into her lungs.

When Phayshawe arrived on the scene, dressed in a light-pink, silk dressing gown, he gave her an understanding smile before offering her a decent chunk of the cash in any case.

Though she didn't want to take it, she knew that it would only be more trouble for herself, further down the road, if she didn't.

After that, she left the room behind, and Phayshawe had the man with the pinched cheeks drive her back to the Infirmary . . . though he asked for her home address, she told him to take her to where they'd picked her up. Though she didn't doubt that they could find out where she lived if they really wanted to, she wasn't about to make things easy on them.

If they wanted to find her, they'd have to work for it.

She settled everything back at the Infirmary, giving them a story about how she had felt ill and gone back home to lie down . . . and next thing she'd known it was morning.

She promised them that it wouldn't happen again, and she made it up with the covering doctor—the doctor they'd had to raise up out of bed to take her place when they'd found her missing.

As she trudged through the neighbourhood of the Infirmary, off to catch her metro, and to go off home, she spotted a scrounger, pottering about with his wooden cart. He was prying through a rubbish bin, having shucked the black plastic lid.

She called out to him, and when he approached her, handed him the money.

He could hardly believe the quid he held in his hand, but he made no attempt to hand it back to her. He thanked her over and over, before he returned to his cart with a smile lighting up his face.

Matris was glad that at least *something* positive had come out of the day, and she promised herself that she would never get herself into a similar position again.

The Infirmary employed meatheads for a reason.

It was just as she stood at the metro stop that she saw her.

The nurse.

Beajrix, as she remembered.

She sat on the faded red plastic seat which protruded out of the brick station wall, and she stared at the spot between her feet, stared at the patch of concrete there.

Matris thought it over a moment, and then approached her. Sat on the seat beside her.

The nurse turned her head. Beajrix turned her head.

A look of confusion passed over her face, her forehead wrinkling.

"I'm Doctor Matris," she said, holding out her hand for her to shake.

Beajrix took her hand, shook it back, then said her name.

After they'd broken off the handshake, the two of them just stared out into the space before them, at the bricks on the opposite side of the platform. Matris didn't think there was anything more to say . . . but then she came up with one thing.

One more thing.

Still facing forwards, she said, out of the corner of her mouth, "You were right, about that patient. He was Crul."

Beajrix slipped her a sidelong glance, then gave her a slight smile.

Matris smiled back at her.

Then they went back to waiting for their metro trains.

The two of them knocking off their shift for the day.

Back to their respective lives, their respective families.

And Matris could hardly wait for it.

THE DOCKS

1

R UMPARD SNOHANDS couldn't quite put his finger on just what it was that was so special about the Docks. As he laid the steel container—a well-beaten-up, faded-pink colour—down on the cracked concrete surface, he raised his head to the breeze.

A fresh, warm lime flavour carried on it.

Could that be the specialness he was trying to get at?

Certainly he could say that was an aspect of it.

He peered out over the metal railing and to the towering ships sitting in the dock, bobbing lightly in the swell. There were all kinds. Sailing ships, with masts that seemed to be trying to scrape at the overcast sky which hung above the Docks. And then there were the container ships, jammed full with stuff from all through Schwyn.

Just like the ship *Rumpard* had arrived in, all those years ago, looking so hard for refuge, and then finding none at all.

Not here.

Not in Guynur City.

On the decks of the ships, Rumpard could make out several blurred forms: men going back and forth, *creatures* going back and forth.

Which was he?

"Oi, Sno-*dick!* Get a move on, yeah?"

Rumpard glanced back over his shoulder. He saw his boss—his *human* boss.

Bradness Ivenoor, in his white, string vest, as always, stood with his fists crunched at his waistline. Stare intense. Eyes all scoping. Moustache greasy and twisted.

Rumpard snorted at him, sucking back the amalgamation of oil and salt within his nostrils. He sucked it all down to his throat, and then, just like his boss said, he went back to his work.

He shifted his weight downwards, bent his knees, just like he'd always been instructed, and he listened to the gentle *creak* of the rigging of a nearby sailing boat. As his fingers found the ridges of the container, he squeezed hard, feeling a little dulled pain from where he had filed down his claws so that he might be able to pass as human.

Why had he bothered?

Why did he *still* bother?

He had found out soon enough—soon enough after his arrival to Guynur City—that he simply wasn't *wanted* here.

With a *grunt* Rumpard lifted the container up to his shoulder and risked another glance back over his shoulder. Back to Guynur City itself. And to the large wall which wrapped itself about the place. Which hid any sense of the buildings beyond, at least from here, this low down on the ground, at the Docks.

He still remembered coming steaming in on his boat, breathing in that sweet smell of cinnamon. They'd been telling the truth, all the travellers he'd spoken to en route to his destination. Telling him that the air smelled strongly of cinnamon.

As he'd gripped tight to the metal railing, encrusted with rust and sea spray, he'd looked out over the cityscape, taken in all those buildings nestled together.

It had struck him how the buildings stood so finely upright— how they were so unlike the jagged teeth in rotten gums, like the buildings he had grown up with in his place of birth.

In Eyeoor.

He had guessed, as he'd been approaching Guynur, that it had to do with how humans would flatten the ground before putting down the plans for their buildings. And how they'd make everything nice and straight using *mathematics*, among other things.

Rumpard had wanted to get straight to the matter of that. He had wanted to investigate it all personally for himself. But he'd never got the chance. He hadn't even managed to get past the City Gates. They had seen through his disguise. Seen right away that he was a half-blood, that the Grumer in him far overwhelmed the Mortal. And he had been turned away.

But, unable to give up so easily give up on his dream, on that dream which had dimmed his vision ever since his mother had told him the truth which Rumpard had suspect all along—that he had had a human father—Rumpard had found employ here, in the Docks.

And so here he was now.

A stranger with no place to go.

Simply bobbing about.

As Rumpard lugged the container along, he felt the curvature of his spine, the coiling of all those muscles there. He kept his eyes fixed on his destination, on the container ship up ahead. He wondered . . . he *did* wonder.

Perhaps *one day* he would get into Guynur.

Maybe *one day* they would realise that he was human *enough*.

As Rumpard stepped over the creaking gangplank, he caught the eye of one of the deckhands. Like Rumpard, he was a Grumer . . . or, at least, this deckhand was like *half* of what Rumpard was.

He had a triangular-shaped head, almost like somebody had taken a *human* head and then pinched it between finger and thumb. The pair of eyes, moving independently of one another, like what a human had once described to him as being like a chameleon.

Rumpard had those eyes too.

Though he had learned control.

He had learned to keep them together.

And, all that time ago, when he'd presented himself at the City Gates, he had felt that he had *almost* passed. That he had almost managed to fool them into thinking that he was fully human. In the end, it had been his bone structure, the way that they had inspected his skull, the way that it was *almost* drawn to a point at the top of his scalp. And then, of course, they'd noticed his curved spine. And that had been the beginning of the end.

Rumpard knew that he would never be *pure* human enough to ever pass through the City Gates . . . to ever *truly* integrate himself into Guynur.

As Rumpard passed by the deckhand, he thought about how the Gromer's slick, orange skin was also a dead giveaway. Yes, any inspector standing on the gates would've seen that in Rumpard too. And the way that the light-pink sweat oozed out of him.

Now that Rumpard had been here—at the Docks—and he'd seen so many creatures from all throughout Schwyn come and go, he could easily tell a human apart from the rest.

It was the way that they seemed to walk so nobly.

How they appeared to keep themselves upright as they went along.

As if nothing could throw them.

Rumpard recalled his lessons, back at school, about how he had learned—just like every other kid in Eyeoor, the Grumer capital— that they had all come from humans . . . that all the creatures of Schwyn had come from humans. But that creatures had become corrupted with magic. And so they would never again be able to reach the pure bloodlines of the humans.

As Rumpard stepped into the ship, he felt its gentle sway. He set his container down near the back of the ship's almost empty hold.

While he headed back out again—back out to the Docks—he could feel the eyes of the Grumer deckhand on him.

Sure enough, when Rumpard tried to make his way along the walkway, he felt the Grumer stick out his arm, blocking his path. "Hang about," the deckhand said. "You Grumer, right?"

Rumpard knew there was little he could do now. If there was anything he had learned during his time at the Docks, it was that he was an exceptionally poor liar. He simply gave the deckhand a grunt in reply.

He could feel the deckhand drinking him in with his constantly swivelling eyes. He knew what was coming next, so much so that he probably didn't even need to listen to what the deckhand said.

But he did.

"Half-blood?" the deckhand said, in the Grumer language.

"Yes," Rumpard said, taking care with his pronunciation, the pronunciation that he had spent *so many* years trying to get just right . . . so that he might pass for human.

He replied in the common tongue.

"Mm," the deckhand said, and then, also replying in the common tongue, "And whatie you doing here, huh?"

Down below him, below the flimsy gangplank, Rumpard could make out the grey, molten steel sea underneath. One false step here and he would tumble all the way down. Into the frozen depths. He had seen more than his fair share of dockworkers fall into the sea. Inevitably, their heads bobbed on down below the waves before anybody could think to rescue them. Many of the creatures who worked the Docks were allergic to water, or couldn't swim . . . though Rumpard had other theories. Theories that involved the dockworkers who fell in *giving up* on things. Just giving themselves up to their fates.

They *knew* that they would never be able to get into Guynur.

They had made their peace.

Perhaps Rumpard should make his own peace . . .

Rumpard gave a shrug to the deckhand's question. He tried to shove his way past him.

The deckhand held him in place. "You, uh, not looking to get into Guynur, naw?"

Rumpard felt his heart—his *human* heart—skip a beat. He looked to the deckhand, and then back along the docks, as if his boss might be watching on. Or if somebody might've placed this deckhand here so that he could catch anybody who was trying to get into Guynur through *any* means.

But what was the use of lying now?

What would be the worst if they caught him?

He would end up banished . . . sent on a ship and sailed far away from Guynur.

But, in some ways, wasn't he as far from Guynur as he could possibly get right now?

Rumpard turned to look at the deckhand and, in a dead, monotone voice, he said, "Yeah."

"Waitie here," the deckhand said, and disappeared into the shadows of the ship's hold.

2

R UMPARD DID CONSIDER springing out—heading off some other place. But, in the end, as he reasoned with himself, he might as well hang around to see just what this deck-hand had up his sleeve. If he brought along some fuzz to drag Rumpard onto a banishment ship then so much the better. Or, maybe, Rumpard should pre-empt fate and simply toss himself into the gentle, slopping waves below.

But first he would see.

See if there was anything at all to this deckhand's claims.

Rumpard waited up on the dock for what felt like an eternity, and when he finally caught sight of the deckhand again, it was from a direction he hadn't expected. And he saw that the deckhand was bringing along a human tagging at his heels.

A human just like his boss, Bradness Ivenoor.

Now Rumpard felt a little uneasy. Though he had never seen an undercover fuzz . . . who really had, beyond all the hearsay? . . . he suspected that they probably looked something like the man who walked beside the deckhand.

But there wasn't anything to do now.

Not except for tossing himself over the edge and into the waters below.

The deckhand and the human approached him. The human wore a tatty shirt and a pair of jeans with holes just about every-where. Even before the human had come close, Rumpard could feel the human sizing him up. Working out his angles. Trying to slot him into a box. So that Rumpard would be more easily understood.

The deckhand looked to Rumpard, said in Grumer, "This man should help you out."

As Rumpard watched the deckhand tread his way back over the gangplank which led into the ship's hold, he couldn't help speaking out, also in Grumer, and asking, "Why should I trust you say this man is who he says he is?"

The deckhand glanced back at Rumpard, his expression slightly bored, a little tired. "Because," he said, still speaking in Grumer, "none of us full-bloods would ever have so much of a chance. At least with you—with *you*—there should be an opportunity."

And, with that, the deckhand disappeared into the shadows of the ship's hold.

When Rumpard turned back the man who the deckhand had brought along, he caught a fresh whiff of that lime smell—that smell which, Rumpard knew, drifted across the sea from the continent.

The man was still looking Rumpard up and down, though now, if he had been subtle before, all subtlety had now completely vanished.

Rumpard got the strangest feeling that the man was almost undressing him . . . and then dressing him *again*.

"Whatcha wanna go into Guynur for?" the man said.

Rumpard was a little caught off guard by the question. By its directness. And by the implication that there was nothing worth going to Guynur for.

That was surely spoken just like a human, a human who didn't *truly* understand his worth in the lands of Schwyn, just what his historical role had been.

"I . . . I . . ." Rumpard began.

The man held up his hand, indicating for Rumpard to cease speaking. "Listen, bruv, that's personal, right? Couldn't really give a toss, to be honest." He snorted hard so that Rumpard, with his acute hearing could listen to the *dribble* of the phlegm down the back of the man's throat. "Name's Blichart."

It took Rumpard a couple of moments to realise that Blichart held out his hand, was almost jutting it right into Rumpard's chest.

Rumpard finally took it off him, gave it a firm shake.

As they shook hands, Rumpard watched on as Blichart turned their hands over, as he inspected Rumpard's hand. Blichart frowned and then gave a little nod as he caught Rumpard's eye once more. "You should pass," he said.

Rumpard felt his whole body caught in a warm glow.

3

THAT NIGHT, at the Docks, Rumpard crouched down between a pair of containers. He hadn't clocked off his shift, but, the way things went at the Docks, it wouldn't be treated as being abnormal. There were dozens of creatures who arrived here, to the Docks, looking to pass for human and enter Guynur, who were turned back from the City Gates and forced into working the Docks to scrape together enough to buy their passage home.

Those who didn't clock off their shift were assumed to have sailed off into the sunset, leaving Guynur behind them.

But Rumpard had no intention of doing that.

None whatsoever.

He would rather *die* than return to Eyeoor, somewhere, he had always felt, he did not belong.

By his watch, Rumpard saw that Blichart arrived right at the time that they had agreed. He watched the man, dressed just as he had been earlier in the day, but with a jacket draped about his shoulders, approaching him. The air was warm tonight, and the smell of limes almost strong enough so as to convince Rumpard that he only had to open his mouth and take a bite to end up with zest on his tongue.

Blichart said nothing, he only communicated to Rumpard with a slight gesture for him to follow. And Rumpard did.

They carried on along the waterfront, Blichart in front, and Rumpard trailing a few paces off his heels. As they went along, Rumpard examined the walls of Guynur as they passed them by. He stared up those enormous, great cemented monstrosities and he thought about what life must be like on the other side.

Were there others like him?

Other half-bloods?

Those who only wanted a *chance* . . . just *one* chance to try and pass for human?

When they came up to near the edge of the Docks, Blichart pressed his back up against the wall, and then looked Rumpard over. He spoke for the first time that night. "You got someplace to go?" Blichart said.

Rumpard felt his chest tighten a little. He sensed the tension in Blichart's voice and, for the first time in years, he felt like his dream of entering Guynur wouldn't be in vain.

Rumpard shook his head.

Blichart broke off eye contact. His eyes skirted along the wall.

Rumpard followed Blichart's eyes as he looked off towards the ships bobbing along the waterfront. Blichart's focus seemed to remain on a certain ship for a long while before returning to Rumpard.

From within his jacket, Blichart withdrew a small rectangular piece of cardboard which he thrust at Rumpard, thrust into his chest.

Rumpard, on instinct more than anything else, took it from him.

"That'll get you started," Blichart said.

Rumpard examined the scrawled writing on the cardboard. He read the common tongue fluently, of course, how else would he ever have hoped to pass as full Mortal?

"You know Pikenun Park?" Blichart said.

Rumpard was a little taken off guard by the question. "I've never been to Guynur City before," he said.

Blichart rolled his eyes. "Look," he said, "you gotta shake this whole tourist act you've got going on here, yeah?"

Rumpard nodded swiftly, realising that there was nothing else that he was supposed to do in this moment.

Blichart clapped him on the shoulder. "Good," he said, and then nodded back to the address which Rumpard held in his fist. "That's Beggy's Place, that is. He'll sort you out fine." Blichart glanced Rumpard over another time. "Surgery, refuge, food, the works."

Rumpard felt a little uneasy, though he couldn't quite identify why . . . another few beats of his heart later and he had his answer. He asked Blichart straight out, "Why're you doing all this for me?"

Blichart opened up his mouth in a wry smile, showing off a whole host of golden, and silver, teeth. "Why does anybody do anything, eh?" he said. "Because I get paid."

Rumpard blinked a few times, not sure how to break things to Blichart. Already Rumpard was scrabbling about in his pockets. Of course he had brought along all the quid he had managed to scrounge together during his time working the Docks.

Blichart, however, held up his hand. "Nah," he said, "don't bother." He dialled his smile down a couple of notches. "Nothing that you coulda saved working the Docks'll be enough." He seemed to register Rumpard's look of dismay, and he reached out, clapped Rumpard on the shoulder. "No worries, pal, you get in there, and Beggy gets you set up in the city and I'll get my money. Dontcha have any issue with that, okay?"

Blichart now turned his attention back to the wall once more. Then he looked to Rumpard and said, "You ready to bust into Guynur then?"

"Yes," Rumpard said.

4

B LICHART LED THEM through a crevice which appeared in the rock face. Rumpard thought about the many—*many*—times he had stared at the rock face which surrounded the Docks and thought about what sorts of secrets it might conceal.

Now, he guessed, he was getting some insight into the answer.

As they went along, the rocks smelled of salt and damp, and more than one rat skittered along the floor and across the toe of Rumpard's boot. But Rumpard tried not to show any reaction whatsoever. He couldn't blow this now. This was his big chance.

The crevice got extremely thin, so thin that they had to turn side on, and there was a point where Rumpard found himself cursing the curvature of his spine, and how, though he had performed straightening exercises near daily since his birth, he could never get his back to stand up perfectly tall.

It was only with an extra tug from Blichart that Rumpard was able to squeeze through the gap, and only then with several grazes across the surface of his stomach.

On the other side of the crevice, Rumpard was rendered stunned.

Down there—spread out below—he caught the orange glow of streetlight. And he marvelled in the way that the shadows all seemed chased into corners. How the buildings of Guynur City seemed to burst right up out of the ground. And how *straight* everything was.

He almost missed Blichart's continued movement as he lost himself in the sight below. Guynur City. His new home.

Blichart, of course, had no time at all to stand about and take in the view, and he was already descending the clay-surfaced slope which ran down, away from the crevice.

When Rumpard looked back, to where they'd come, he saw hardly more than a crack in the rock. And certainly no sign of the Docks beyond . . . though he couldn't say that he felt at all sentimental about having been robbed of a final opportunity to take in the view of the place that'd served as his home for the last few years.

Rumpard quickened his pace, caught himself up with Blichart.

They were down at the base of the concrete wall now, but the wall itself was shorter here, and Rumpard caught the idea that Blichart was looking for some way for them to climb up over it.

Rumpard's heart quickened as he thought about the prospect of them getting caught by fuzz now. What would happen? Would Rumpard be simply sentenced to banishment, or would there be something *worse* in store?

He knew the remit of Guynur, that it was intended as a refuge, as a place for Mortals to thrive, to be undisturbed from the influence of magic.

But it was all very well for them.

They were *inside*.

What about those who were kept out?

Blichart kept himself flush with the city wall, and Rumpard stayed close to him.

Perhaps it was the nerves, or maybe it was just a dose of high-spirits, but Rumpard found himself saying, under his breath, "I never realised that there were other ways into Guynur."

At first Blichart held his finger to his lips, but, another few steps later, he broke out into another grin and then said, "Thing about Guynur is that it's just about as secure as a torn-up sponge."

Rumpard wasn't quite sure what to make of this comparison, but he was kept from making any further comment when Blichart pointed at the wall and said, "We're here."

5

RUMPARD BLINKED several times at the point in the wall which Blichart indicated. Try as he might, he could see nothing special about this spot. In fact, it looked just like the rest of the wall they'd been striding along for the past hour.

Did Blichart intend for them to go over the top?

Or underneath?

Rumpard couldn't see a sign of a path to do either.

Then again, he guessed, as with the best back doors they were always kept well hidden.

Rumpard stood back, starting to think something might be wrong, that Blichart might've been fuzz all along, when, with a crystalline glow, a bright light hovered on the surface of Blichart's fingers, then, all of a sudden, burst right out and into the wall.

Rumpard watched on as the light hit the wall and then spread out, like a crashing wave striking the hull of a sailing boat. Slowly —*gradually*—it formed a rectangular shape. The shape of a door.

Blichart stood back from his creation, and Rumpard kept his eyes fixed to the shape till the glow off it completely dissipated and it formed, what seemed to Rumpard, a perfectly normal door.

Rumpard felt Blichart clap him on his shoulder. "All right, pal?" Blichart said.

"You're not coming?" Rumpard said.

Blichart shook his head, gave another grin. "Nah"—and then he jerked his thumb over his shoulder in a direction away from the Docks—"don't like my kind inside of their city walls, I'd get found out awfully fast, if you get my meaning."

Of course Rumpard understood.

What Blichart was saying was that he was a wizard.

And wizards—magic in general—could *not* be allowed within the walls of Guynur City.

"Send me a postcard, huh?" Blichart said, already walking away from the door he had opened up in the wall.

Rumpard felt his whole body seize up, as if he might have some physical reaction to walking through this door. But he knew that he must go through it. Wasn't this what he had worked his entire life for?

"Thank you," Rumpard said.

Blichart kept walking away from him, the only sign of him acknowledging his statement a back-handed wave. And then, just like that, melting into the darkness, Blichart was gone.

Rumpard reached out for the door handle.

And turned.

6

RUMPARD TOOK CARE to shut the door quietly behind him. It was like he was a boy again, and he was sneaking about the house after darkness, going to get something to feed his ever-growing body.

But now he was where he had always wanted to be.

Now he was standing here, inside the walls of Guynur City.

He glanced about himself, feeling the wash of the streetlights against his skin.

And he knew that he, truly, had come home.

MEATHEADS

JESSA COULD STILL TASTE that last coffee she chucked down her throat before coming on out here. She'd hoped it'd help with her stuffed up nose, and take her mind off the fact that the only thing she could smell at all was that rancid, biting phlegm stench. And that *sniffle* sound every time she breathed in.

She stuffed her hands into the velvety pockets of her overcoat—the overcoat that she'd only gone and pilfered from her older brother, Vinny. The overcoat that was pitch black and which made her feel stronger, less feminine, and which promised that she would have a chance.

A chance at becoming a meathead.

What she'd always wanted.

She'd spent a long while wondering about whether or not she should put on a tie too, and she'd decided, at the end of it all, that a tie was absolutely necessary. Because, without it, she'd stick right out like a sore thumb . . . or, another way of putting it, like a female meathead.

It'd taken her plenty of swearing and maybe an hour to get her tie all done up right. She hadn't wanted to ask anything of her brothers, for obvious reasons, and so she'd just suffered right along as much as she could with the help of a dust-covered book she'd dug out.

And then she'd had to slick back her greasy, black hair into a ponytail, and got it on down beneath her homburg hat—also black, and also her brother Vinny's.

That'd got her looking a little more manly, though she still wasn't convinced herself if she'd pass. And if she couldn't convince herself, then how was she going to manage to convince the meatheads?

. . . Impress Big Ricky, the one that she'd been told to go and get in touch with?

Though she'd only got out of school last year, she'd got herself all bulked up, bulked up enough, she thought, with all the weight training she'd been doing back at home while she'd been working miserable jobs in warehouses, or worse.

Not that she had all that much to show for it.

She always enjoyed it, when she met with people, and looked at the surprise on their faces when they saw she was lugging along something weighty, and then them seeing that she was 'just' a girly . . . and not a big one at that.

That was her trick—that was what she depended on.

She wanted to show these meatheads just what she could do.

That she could offer something they desperately needed:

The element of surprise.

The drizzle was coming down in a thick, foggy blanket. It made this night ever the more bitter and hard to stand. Made her stronger. She could feel the drizzle pooling into the rim of her hat. She was a bit apprehensive about that, about how she'd need to find some way of drying off the hat before she snuck it back into Vinny's wardrobe.

She could smell the fabric of it, a smell that reminded her of horseflesh for some reason, as the rain got into it some more. She snorted back he phlegm a little more, knowing that she'd have to speak firm and solid if she'd have any chance at all of impressing Big Ricky.

That coffee had seemed to bring the taste of blood to the surface of her tongue, and she relished it—she had always liked the taste of blood, it'd set off something inside of her, and was one of the reasons that she was so determined to have a career as a meathead.

She could give out a beating just fine if she had to . . . not that it'd seem at all like an obligation, it'd be a pleasure, in fact.

Though her hands sweated in the velvety pockets of the overcoat, she didn't dare take them out. She could feel the eyes staring out at her, from the shadows of this alleyway deep into the Bluff. They were all in there, just looking to sniff out some form of weakness, to blow her cover, to find out that she was a girl after all . . . and therefore never able to become a meathead.

But she trod onwards, in the two-sizes-too-big boots that she'd bought back years ago, and which she'd worn just about every day of her life since. The boots that seemed to act as a second layer of skin about her feet and ankles, and which made her feel like a giant.

They had toecaps to them, too, and she'd used them toecaps to knock a fair bit of sense into various boys over the years—boys from school that'd got fresh with her, or who'd tried to pick on her younger brother Knicky, easily the weediest member of her family.

But he was family all the same.

And so he deserved the protection.

She saw the place, up ahead, and she slowed herself, trying to make her heart follow suit. It was important that she go on in there calm, else they'd see right through her.

She'd been taking these pills, pills she'd got from some guy who'd said something about magic, though she hadn't pressed him too hard for a scientific explanation, and which had gradually worked at making her voice thicker, more masculine.

And now, tonight, she'd decided that she'd got her voice convincing enough for her to pass, enough for her to *try* and pass.

Mager May's Bar.

All lit up in green neons that fuzzed and fizzled in the drizzle.

This was the place.

The place where Big Ricky held his office.

Where she was likely to find herself some work.

If she was going to have any chance at all.

Because, as she and everyone else in the whole of Guynur City knew, if Big Ricky didn't give you the seal of approval, if you weren't one of his boys . . . one of his meatheads, then you were risking your neck by trying to practise a trade as a meathead in *his* city.

A couple of meatheads stood dressed in their overcoats, in the shadows of the entrance to May's. Both of them, like Jessa, had their hands stuffed into their pockets, and their faces covered by the rims of their hats.

Jessa pressed on harder, caught the occasional glimpse up at the doorway, to those curly, corniced loops that stuck out from it. She could already hear the light *throb* of bass notes from the music inside, could feel them vibrations passing right through the cement beneath her feet, and into the base of her gut. She caught a whiff of smoke and ale, wafting on out from inside. And that only sprung up a thirst at the back of her mouth.

An eighteen-year-old girl going face to face with Big Ricky, asking him for a job, wanting to pass for a meathead.

Jessa knew that no one would've ever believed it.

Not her brothers.

Not her father.

Her mother would've gone all frail and most likely have fainted.

As she bustled on, eyes fixed on the sallow light within May's, one of the meatheads on the door said, "Oi, you stop right there."

2

JESSA FELT her heart well up in her throat, and her blood run real cool through her veins. She thought that they'd seen right through her disguise straight away. The smoky smell that wafted on out from the inside of the bar cleared the phlegm from her sinuses and her throat, and she found that she could breathe easy now.

That was how she knew that she was entering her habitat, how she knew that she *belonged* here. And she was determined that no one would tell her that she didn't.

She stood still, and felt the meatheads move into her from both sides.

They padded down her body, starting from her ankles, and then moving their way slowly up her, up her legs, to her hips, stomach, and then, when they reached her chest, she breathed in strongly . . . willed the trick she was hoping to play on them to work, how she'd spent a solid hour of her time this evening binding up her breasts so as to make that whole area as flat as she possibly could.

It'd looked okay in the mirror once she'd shrugged on the overcoat, but she wasn't at all convinced that it would work when someone got as close as these two meatheads were getting right now.

She clamped her eyes shut as they ran their hands over her breasts, all bound down, but they made no reaction at all.

She only dared open her eyes when the two of them stood back and one of them said, "You got an appointment with Big Rick?"

She felt something stick in her throat. An appointment? She hadn't bargained for that. She'd only gone and taken the metro down here, down to the Bluff, walked on through all these shadowy and notorious streets to get here . . . and now it might be for nothing if these two meatheads here wouldn't let her on in through the doorway.

"Nah," she said, keeping her voice low and gravelly.

She felt the meatheads exchanging glances with one another before her, and then, the one that'd just spoke to her said, "In that case we can't let you in," before adding, "sorry, bruv."

Even though she was all too aware of just what this meant—that she'd just been denied what she'd set out to do, she couldn't help feeling a slight hop in her blood at how he'd acknowledged her as a man . . . and that was the first step to her becoming a meathead.

And it only pushed her on further, suggested to her that what she had in mind might really be possible.

But it looked like she'd have to prove herself first.

She sucked in her gut, and drew on that strength within her that them magic pills had given her—that confidence they'd instilled in her in their making her voice thicker, deeper.

"Ain't no way for me to see Big Rick?"

Again, the same meathead spoke, "Not unless you go through us first, bruv."

"And how'd I go about getting an appointment with him, then?"

The meathead scoffed a laugh. "If you gotta ask then you ain't never gonna *get* to see him, bruv."

Jessa scanned what he'd just said. Was that a threat . . . or had it been a challenge? Maybe what he wanted her to do was for her to prove herself. Was that what he was getting at? Or did she somehow have to get some kind of approval from some other meat-head somewhere who'd act as a go-between in getting her a meet-up with Big Rick?

She really had no clue.

But she knew one thing.

That she hadn't been building up these muscles of hers for nothing—not just to stand back and be brushed aside like a *good* little girl.

Nah, that really wasn't her way.

She felt the weight of the meatheads' gaze on her, and she knew that they were scoping her out, that they were checking her over to see if she might fit.

And it was then that she knew for certain that this was just one of Big Ricky's tests.

A way to separate the wheat from the chaff.

She wouldn't have wanted it any other way, thinking about it.

And so, she sunk back on her heels, made as if to spin around, and head on off, back into the Bluff, and to the metro station and the train that'd whisk her back off home, but, just as she was sure that she'd got the meatheads' defences down, she delivered a smart kick, right to the balls, of the meathead that'd spoken to her.

While the one she'd kicked doubled over, the other one made for the inside pocket of his overcoat—for his gun—but she brought her other leg up and swiped at his wrist, knocking it away, before she drew back her fist and plunged it right down on the button of his nose.

With a blood-curdling *crunch*, he went down in a heap, clutching his face.

The meathead she'd kicked in the balls was still doubled over, only just recovering enough to think of his own gun, and Jessa worked quick on him, delivering a hard blow to the back of his neck—that blow that she'd practised just about a hundred times back home, with the help of another book, and she watched him crumple down and lie there on the ground alongside the other meathead.

She stood back.

Pulse racing.

Heart on fire.

Breath like a sticky poison.

Neither of the meatheads was getting up fast.

She got a prickling feeling across her skin.

And she felt all them eyeballs watching her from out of the shadows.

Them eyeballs out in the alley.

She knew she couldn't waste time, and so she shoved her way on in through the door, and into the bar.

3

T HE WARMTH from the fireplace crackling off in the corner of the place seemed to send her breaking out into sweats almost instantly. But she had no intention of shucking her overcoat, not yet, even though she had Vinny's suit on underneath, the one that he'd used for his graduation, and which he used for special occasions when he was required to dress up.

She didn't want to give herself away yet.

No matter how well she might've proved herself with them meatheads on the door outside.

The ones that now lay in a heap on the threshold of the bar.

The place was done up in worn-down, kind of yellowed trimmings. Them kind of half curtains hung down from the windows of the place, and the bar had a dulled, unpolished brass railing that ran all about it. There was no one behind the bar. Just the rows and rows of corked bottles with the misty glass of all different tones of blue and green.

Smoke lingered up in the air, it wafted up into bluish clouds and just held there.

Up at the ceiling.

Her pa had always smoked and so she'd found it kind of a homely feeling.

And it felt welcoming now.

In fact, it was only as she heard a slow handclap, over her shoulder, off in one of the corners of the bar which sat level with the doorway . . . the only corner of the place she hadn't yet wandered her eyes . . . did she realise that, really, she was welcome here.

She turned to look. Saw the man slumped up there, sitting on the faded red cushions which lined the benches which ran all along the side of the room.

He wore a trim waistcoat and tight trousers which exposed his bulky muscles nestled beneath the fabric. He had a flagon of ale sitting on the battered, old wooden table before him. He was bald headed, and his overcoat, sunglasses and hat lay on the cushions alongside him. He stopped clapping, as if frozen in time, when Jessa looked over to him.

Big Ricky.

Yes, he was certainly big.

He was, at a conservative estimate, a good three times wider than she was, and at least one and a half times taller than her . . . not that height or weight had made much of a difference out there in the alleyway, at the entrance to the bar.

She had dropped those two meatheads all the same.

Without saying a word, Ricky gestured to a place on the cushion beside where he sat.

Jessa caught another shudder. She glanced about herself, half afraid that someone, another meathead, might leap out from the shadows, give her yet another test.

But no one came.

It appeared that she and Ricky were alone here.

As she trudged over there, Ricky upturned his flagon, pouring the contents right down his throat. She watched as a couple of drops snaked their way down the sides of his mouth, as they didn't quite make it through his lips.

Finished, he brought his flagon down with a wet *thwack* on the surface of the wooden table, wiped his mouth with the back of his hand, and turned his eyes onto her, a slight smile curling the corners of his lips. "So," he said, "wha' can I do for you?"

A quiver passed through Jessa's gut. She had thought about this meeting for so long. She had practised speaking into the mirror, trying out the new voice she'd got from those magical pills, and each time she'd felt more confident that she could do it.

That she could pass for a meathead.

But now it was like her stomach had turned to jelly, and her bones had all gone to mush.

Maybe her body was catching up with what she'd just done out there to the meatheads guarding the door.

Better just to get to the point. To speak direct, and be frank.

So that was what Jessa did.

"Wanna be a meathead," she said.

At this Big Ricky gave her a wide grin. She could smell his woody cologne wafting out from his sweaty armpits, and the ale on his breath thickening in the air too. "Certainly came dressed for it, didn' you?"

Jessa couldn't think of anything to say to that, so she simply nodded, and then looked away from his eyes, as if he might be probing her, looking for anything that didn't sit right with her appearance.

"You know," he said, slumping back into the corner of the bar, into the cushions, with both arms draped over the backs of the ledges at his shoulders, "ain't never had someone take care of my meatheads on the door before." He met her with a smoking, steel stare, and said, "So, you see, I reckon that you've got something special here, whadda you think?"

"I think I wanna be a meathead," she said.

He fixed her with a narrowed-eyed glance, and then he peered back to his flagon, as if he'd forgotten that he'd only just right now drained it. "And why's tha'?"

Jessa wanted to go through her reasons. She wanted to tell him all about how she was sick and tired of being treated like a second-class citizen in this city, and how everyone that had any power about the place seemed to have it because they had a dick and big muscles . . . and there was at least one of those she could obtain without surgery, or magic . . . that she already had got herself, and shown her true force.

But she couldn't say any of that.

Because if Big Ricky had known she was a girl all this, all she'd done right now, would have been in vain.

And so she gave a nonchalant shrug, then said, "I like pummelling people sometimes."

This brought out a thick smile from Big Ricky, and he glanced up at the ceiling of the bar, apparently lost in his thoughts. "Yeah, tha's as good a reason as most, and given whatcha did to my boys on the door, I think you've got some history to back up that swagger you got there." He flexed his fingers, seemed to focus his attention onto his fingernails which were all pretty much gnarled up and twisted—probably from beatings, Jessa thought. "So, where d'ya see yourself meatheadin'?"

Though Jessa had practised a shitload to get to this point, to getting herself an actual sit-down with Big Ricky, she had never envisioned what would happen if he asked her a question like he just had done.

But, the truth remained, that he had.

And now she had to answer.

She gave another shrug, trying hard not to make her feelings known outside of herself. "I'd be happy with whatever, to be honest, I'd take whatever you'd throw me."

"How about you tell me a little about yourself first, eh?"

Her muscles froze up, but she was determined, and she wasn't going to allow him to back her into a corner. He'd witnessed just what she'd done to his meatheads on the door so he knew all too well that it was better for him not to get to messing with her.

"I . . ." she began, "I always wanted to be a meathead, tha's all."

There was a long silence between them, and Jessa instinctively knew that it would've been much better for her to say something else. For her to not say something that sounded so *fucking* dreamy and bone-headed. For her to say that she was looking to make some seriously cold cash at this. That would've been a language that Big Ricky would've understood.

Now he'd be suspicious.

She was sure of it.

Heart in mouth, she looked back over to him, to where he was deliberating over his reply.

"Hmm," he said, and then he leaned forwards, clasped his hands in his lap and writhed them together. His sapphire eyes latched onto hers. "How about's you tell me what a *girl* is doin' wantin' to do some meatheadin'?"

4

IT WAS LIKE JESSA was made of glass and someone had just gone and chucked a massive, great brick at her, and sent her entire body tinkling about her into a thousand razor-sharp pieces. The smoke in the air, rather than reassure her, now gagged her nose and mouth, and she felt like she was sinking down and down, unable to stop herself.

She caught a bloody taste on her tongue, and realised that she'd been working at the inside of her cheek with her molars because of all the pressure she felt in Big Ricky's presence. A ringing sound began in the distance of her hearing. A sound that just kept getting louder, it seemed, with every heartbeat.

"Eh?" Big Ricky said, a gentle reminder as if she might've forgotten the question already.

Thick blood from the inside of her cheek oozed out over her tongue now, and she caught the metallic taste of it all smearing itself on her insides. She sucked it all up, and she swallowed it back, and she stared long and deep into Big Ricky's eyes, trying to get her body to behave for her once again.

"I, uh," she started, "I . . . I didn' see any other way."

Big Ricky held her gaze for a long while. And it was only then that she realised that he was gripping her wrist tight. So tight that she could see the blood beating out of her hand, and turning the skin there a greenish-white colour.

What would he do to her now?

"Pretty brave, dontcha think?" he said. "I mean, a girly like you coming on down here, into the depths of the Bluff, and what with you looking to be a meathead . . . *beating* up a couple of fully-grown meatheads." He paused. "How old're you anyhow?"

She could hardly keep her voice straight now, despite all them magical pills she'd swallowed, the ones that'd worked to make her more of a man. "Eighteen," she said, answering truthfully.

He puffed out his lips and nodded gently, and then he seemed to notice his too-tight grip on her wrist, he looked down at where he held her, and then loosened it.

Only now did she see that he was just as shook up about this whole thing as she was. And why shouldn't he be? . . . After all, if he'd been telling the truth, about never having had his meatheads beaten up, then he'd surely want to know just what she was up to.

He released her completely now, and sank back into the bench cushions. His eyes never left her, though, as if he was afraid that she might throttle him alive if he looked away. "You, uh," he said, "got something *magical* going on about you?"

There seemed no reason to lie now, and it was hardly like Big Ricky was going to call up the Watch any time soon . . . meatheads were known for *hating* the Watch almost as much as they hated fuzz, despite surely a lot of them being ex-fuzz . . . though, thinking about it, Jessa guessed that even more of them were *failed* fuzz, the ones that hadn't been bright enough to pass the exams that'd get them onto the force.

She gave him a nod.

Big Ricky parted his lips and she heard a faint, "Ah," at the back of his throat as if now it all made sense. He looked her over again, with that new glance of his. "And, where'd you get hold of this getup, huh?" he said, indicating the overcoat and the homburg hat which was squeezed down onto her head . . . crushing her girlish hair.

"My brother," she said.

Big Ricky kept up that kind of gormless expression of his, half disbelief and half awe, and then he seemed to blink out of it. And his easy smile returned to him.

Then he did something which Jessa didn't expect at all.

He chuckled.

And his chuckle soon graduated into a full-out belly laugh.

He doubled over in laughter, just like them meatheads on the door had doubled up when she'd smashed them down.

When Big Ricky got a hold of himself, propped himself back up against the benches, tears glistening in his eyes, he shook his head over and over, and then said, "Sorry 'bout that, it's just I never heard such a thing, y'know? Hard for me to believe, tha's all, wouldn't have believed it neither if I hadn't seen you drop my boys like you did out there."

Jessa felt her gut clench.

"Jus' one question, though," he said. "Why'd you think you had to come on down here, to the Bluff, all dressed up like a man? Didn' you think that I'd have thought you over if you weren' a man, or wha'?"

Though that was exactly it, Jessa didn't want to confirm it for him. She didn't want him to laugh at her again, though she knew that him laughing was just about the best thing that could've come out of this meeting. For all she knew, he might've had a whole bunch of meatheads hiding off somewhere in this bar, all of them ready to come rushing out to take care of her.

It was one thing for her to take on a couple of meatheads, but quite another for her to contend with what would've been a whole group of them.

In a couple of years, maybe, but her skills just weren't there.

Not yet.

Again, she shook her head.

There was nothing for her to say.

He fixed her again with that same narrowed-eyed glance, and then he said, easy and evenly, "But dontcha worry about any of tha' shi', you proved yourself jus' fine with them boys of mine, after all. Think I'll have a job for you, and pretty soon too. Tell me one thing, though, you know your way about a gun?"

Jessa could hardly believe her ears, but she knew just what she had heard, and there was no shaking it from her mind. There would *never* be any shaking it from her mind.

She felt a rich glow flooding up from the base of her gut, swarming its way through her blood, so hot now that it near enough boiled her from within. Her heart *thunk-thunked*, and that bloody taste was thinner in her mouth now. Almost back to normal. The self-inflicted injury in her cheek now well on its way to being healed.

But Big Ricky had asked her a question.

A question she had to answer, and honestly.

One more time, she shook her head.

He shrugged, and then said, "No matter, you got the skills, you have, and tha's all that matters to me. To tell the gods' own truth, thing is that any old lunk can cart about a gun, wave it in people's faces, maybe even shoot up some folk, but wha' you showed me, out there, with my boys on the door . . . well, tha' jus' sure as hell can' be taugh'."

Jessa felt her heart beat another few times. She couldn't believe this. Couldn't believe *any* of this. But it was all coming true. Her richest, most cherished dreams were all coming true now.

She watched him rising up out off the bench cushions, manoeuvring his enormous weight as if he had a time of it just lifting them muscles of his.

Then he held out his hand to her.

And she took it off him.

Gave it a good old shake.

"Wha's your name anyway?" he said.

"Jessa."

He gave her a smirk. "Welcome on-board, Jessa, you'sa meat-head now, and we take care of our own kind, and don' let anyone ever tell you differen'."

All Jessa could do was smile at that and just keep on nodding.

Because she knew that, now, nothing at all would stand in her way.

Now she would show them all just how tough she could be.

In a *man's* world.

DICEMASTER

O FF IN THE CORNER of the room, Peergolde could hear the gentle grind of an iron rod, turning a pig on a spit. Every couple of seconds there was a *sizzle* as its fat dropped down into the naked flames of the open fireplace. The stench of the pig just about filled out the place.

The Melder's Wail Ale House was not much more than some cobbled-together bricks with some roof tiles stuck on top. A battered old wooden plank for a bar, upturned barrels with roughly circular cuts of wood nailed on top served as tables. Wooden crates for chairs. That was the kind of place it was. Not really a pub as much as a place for getting some work done—for getting together some serious cash.

For making a *killing*.

Though Peergolde wasn't nervous—he *never* got nervous—he could feel himself sweating all over the place. It was the heat. The heat from that stuck pig twirling about over the fireplace.

He dipped his hand into the breast pocket of his peach-toned shirt—it definitely wasn't pink, like some unfortunate types had tried to tell him—and he slipped a cigarette out of the packet he kept there. He just held the cigarette between his lips, not yet wanting to light it. Just touching his tongue to the butt, just for that papery taste. Suckling on it, getting that promise of the good thing to come when he finally lit up.

He didn't like to smoke in the middle of a game of dice. Them little moments, them little *distractions* could cost you. Maybe you could put the case that, really, them little lost moments didn't matter all that much to the amateur player, to a player who'd come on down to the Bluff: most likely vying to be the seediest area of all

Guynur City . . . and that was an achievement of sorts . . . but it *did* matter to a professional.

A professional like Peergolde.

Everyone about the Bluff called him the Dicemaster, and he had no intention of letting that name slip, of becoming like all them other ones, the ones that had got themselves all broke and ended up as scroungers, sleeping in gutters, or worse.

The ones that no one could so much as remember the names of.

Peergolde looked across the table, to his playing partner, to the guy who'd come on in here, into *The Melder's*, wearing that snappy sable jacket with the silky lapels, with a crisp, white dress shirt underneath and with the collar popped.

He had a flop of golden hair that tufted up on the crown of his head, daring considering that pretty much anything that so much as whiffed of gold in the Bluff got itself pinched.

His skin was leathered up, though, and he had a crusty scar emblazoned into his left cheek, what looked to Peergolde, from his considerable experience, to be from some sort of a knife fight. Something like that. A decent-sized blade no doubt.

He had to be about Peergolde's age, or maybe a couple of years younger, though Peergolde never did like to think too much about years.

Mid-forties? Nudging fifty, perhaps?

The guy just oozed money, had his shoes all polished up, and wore a golden chain that kept on dangling out from the sleeve of his jacket, and even Peergolde, not even a snatcher himself, couldn't help being drawn to it every time it made an appearance . . . the way Peergolde saw it, he'd be better off taking this fool for all the money he had before some kid with a knife jumped him in an alleyway on his way back home.

Then again, if there was one thing that Peergolde knew about scars, it was that the people that had them had either had a ton of bad luck, or they could handle themselves just fine.

Still alive, weren't they?

And Peergolde was betting on the latter.

This guy *did* look like he could handle himself.

He watched the guy shaking up the three sets of dice in the wooden eggcup—Peergolde's *lucky* eggcup, the one that he'd only gone and whittled out himself when he was just a mangy little kid, and the one that he'd always insisted on playing with.

He never ran into much trouble with the demand that they use it, though other players did like to rib him about it from time to time.

But that was fine, let them rib, and he'd take all their money.

The guy shook up this one good, and let the dice tumble down onto the wooden surface between the two of them, making that *clickety-clack* sound that got Peergolde's nerves all jangling, and sent a severe pulse right up the nib of his dick.

He watched the dice, standard black-varnished with white dots, a little frayed about the edges, and worn down to show the wooden base beneath, as they tumbled on over the table, and kept on tumbling till they came to a standstill.

Three.

Four.

Six.

Peergolde allowed himself a smile as he reached on over the table, swept the dice up with his forearm, before gathering them in his palm and giving them a squeeze.

He looked over at the guy opposite, narrowing his eyes slightly in that way he hoped made people think he was in some sort of trouble, like he was skating out here on thin ice.

Though nothing could've been further from the truth.

Off to Peergolde's left, Marth, a scribbler, was taking notes of the game, taking down the score so that if there was any drunken dispute it could be sorted out quickly and, in theory, without blood and broken bones.

Like always, Marth wore a scrappy, faded beige waistcoat, with that iron chain clinking out between pockets, in a way that Peergolde guessed was meant to give him some kind of an air of a gentleman . . . something like that. And his eyes were quick and sharp, never missing a beat, all topped up from the mountains of caffeine the guy must've consumed daily.

His jet black hair, with just a few scraps of grey here and there, fit right into the Bluff . . . just about as much as this guy, this guy with the golden tuft of hair, didn't.

Just as Peergolde squeezed the dice tight, made to drop them into his eggcup, he felt a tap on his shoulder. He let out a long sigh, because there was little he hated more than getting his game interrupted.

But, all the same, with a slight roll of the eyes to his playing partner, the golden-haired guy, he sank back on the wooden crate he sat on and felt the lips brushing his ear, them same lips fleshing themselves out into a full-bodied whisper.

"Boss?"

Without even needing to look the man over, without having to double check, Peergolde knew just who it was that was chewing up his ear. If the voice hadn't told him, the halitosis would have. Timmoughny. His main boy. His lookout. His safety.

An assistant of sorts.

Sharper eyes even than good old Marth here.

"Hmm?" Peergolde said, not wanting to speak more than necessarily while in the middle of this here game, and, anyway, he still had his mouth full of cigarette butt.

"Careful with this one, yeah?"

Peergolde felt his chest tighten, and his blood heat up . . . maybe to somewhere about boiling temperature. He *hated* it when people told him to 'take it easy,' or to 'look before you leap,' or, like now, to 'take care.'

Fuck 'em.

All of 'em.

Loser talk, that was what it was, no real other explanation for it. It wasn't like there was fuzz around here neither. Not about here in the Bluff. Not in uniforms, in any case. No uniformed fuzz. Not if they wanted to get themselves out of the place alive.

Then something just clicked.

Something went *pop* in Peergolde's mind, and he could think about nothing else.

Thinking about it, the man opposite him could be fuzz. For all Peergolde knew he was a plainclothes fuzz. Fuzz liked to gamble just like the rest of mankind. Nothing wrong with that. Just as long as they left their badge behind them when they ventured down here, into the Bluff.

Still, better to be certain.

So Peergolde gave Timm a well-done pat on the hand, turned himself back towards his playing partner. Leaned himself over the table, propping himself up on the wooden surface with his elbows, hearing that slight *creak* of his joints as he did so, and he looked the guy square in the eye, right down into the very pits of them choco-late-brown irises, and said, moving his cigarette to the corner of his mouth, "You ain't fuzz, are ya, bruv?"

2

THOUGH PEERGOLDE had hardly spoken in a voice above a whisper, the effect of what he'd said was instantaneous, the way that just about all the whole of *The Melder's* went all hushed up. People stopped tossing down dice. The scribblers stopped their scribbling, and looked over. Even the crackling pig fat off in the fireplace in the corner seemed to quiet down.

Peergolde gnawed a little at his cigarette butt. Sucked a little air through the unlit tobacco, breathed it down into his lungs, half thought about padding the pockets of his dress trousers down to get his lamper out, but then remembered that he was in the middle of a game, clasping his eggcup, in fact, the dice all loaded up and ready to go.

The golden-haired guy opposite kept his face all stony, his lips all straight, and apparently without any emotion. His eyes stayed set on Peergolde, too, like he was some kind of a long-lost lover that he wasn't likely to let out of his sight any time soon.

Slowly, taking his time, Peergolde watched him reach for his drink, for the brandy ale he had there, in its wooden flagon, sitting before him at his place. He clasped his fingers about the flagon and then lifted it up to his lips. Drank long and hard, tipped the bottom of the flagon back as he took down the liquid.

Peergolde knew that everyone in the whole of *The Melder's* was watching him take his drink, and he had little patience for it.

No games were to be played while he was tossing dice.

So Peergolde, without taking his eyes off of the guy opposite, raised his hand, made a come-hither signal to Timm, who he knew was standing off somewhere in the shadows of the pub, all watchful and the like.

In the near-silent pub, Peergolde heard the *snap* of Timm unbuckling the case which carried his sidearm. His .44 Jackcannon. One of them guns that could take down just about anyone, or anything. Peergolde would've trusted his back with nothing less.

Sometimes a show of firepower was the best way to steer clear of a fight, and Peergolde preferred to steer clear of fights . . . for one thing they were bad for business, they meant pubs getting all popped through with holes, proprietors killed, that sort of thing, places shut down for a while . . . and with no places to toss dice, Peergolde had no means of income.

As the golden-haired guy set his flagon back down on the table before him, eyes back onto Peergolde as if his pupils were attracted to his by magnets, Peergolde removed his unlit cigarette from his mouth, held it tight between his crooked, dicemaster's fingers, and said, "Whatcha packin', then, bruv? You at least level with me on that, or do I gotta get my guy to give you the full-hearted welcome to the Bluff, or what?"

The golden-haired guy just stayed how he was. He rested his arms on the surface of the table. Apparently to show that he wasn't going to reach into that real nice jacket of his any time soon. But Peergolde had seen these sorts of tricks before, they didn't fool him none, in fact they just got him all pissed off and worse.

No mistake this thing, right here, could get an awful lot worse for this golden-haired guy, and fast.

Peergolde continued to crush his eggcup in his grip. He laid the cigarette he was holding down on the table, let it rest there. It'd stay there for him whenever he felt like lighting it.

The golden-haired guy held Peergolde's gaze then said the first thing that'd come out of his lips during his entire time at *The Melder's*. When he spoke, his voice was husky, just above a whisper, but still loud enough for every soul in the pub to hear him. "Jus' wanna roll some dice."

Peergolde continued to stare him down, looked deep into them chocolate-brown irises of his. He broke off the stare to glance over to Timm, wanting to check on him. Because he knew one thing, and he knew it well, his man, Timm, wouldn't come between Peergolde and his dice unless he had a mighty good reason . . . or a powerful gut feeling.

He turned back to the golden-haired guy. "Look here, pal," Peergolde said. "I ain't got no issue with you even if you are fuzz, but, the way I see it, if you are you might as well say it." He paused, gave a slight smirk, a type that, he knew, would show this guy just how comfortable he felt here, in *The Melder's*, how *untouchable* he felt. "But you gotta agree there's a big difference between off-duty fuzz and undercover fuzz, if you get me?"

The golden-haired guy made no reaction. His arms remained flat against the table, that completely passive pose that he struck. That told him that there was nothing to fear here. A couple of seconds later, the golden-haired guy nodded in the direction of Timm, still standing off by the wall, his gun still pointed at his chest . . . Peergolde had no reason to look over to know that, he knew that Timm fulfilled his role perfectly, that he was a real professional.

Was this golden-haired guy a real professional too?

"You think you could point that elsewhere?" the golden-haired guy said.

"Hang about," Peergolde replied, "you ain't in any sort of a position to be making demands, you hear? Jus' ain't how this thing's looking to play out."

The golden-haired guy flashed his eyebrows. "So how's it gonna play out?"

Peergolde felt his chest tighten a little, that familiar warmth in his gut warning him that he was on the brink of losing his temper. "It's a simple question, bruv, you answer it and we'll move on from there."

The golden-haired guy glanced from Peergolde to Timm—to Timm's gun—and then back to Peergolde. "Why's it matter who I am, hmm?" the golden-haired guy said. "There some sort of code here that I don't know about, some kind of a password, a secret handshake, that sort of shit?"

"Nah, bruv," Peergolde said, "there ain't no rules here, but you gotta respect the ground, you hear me? You gotta be on a level-pegging with the rest of us. How'd we know you're not posted out here by some snub-nosed fuzz to bust someone about here, eh?"

The golden-haired guy smirked, shook his head, but still kept his hands flat on the table.

Peergolde wondered whether he'd been in this kind of situation before, he seemed to know just how to handle it. Just how to put everyone in the room at ease . . . or as much at ease as was possible given the circumstances.

"You think," the golden-haired guy said, still smirking and his voice communicating a little disbelief, "you think that I'd come on down here, to the Bluff, wearing what I'm wearing and be doing some fuzz business?"

Peergolde had expected him to maybe use his hands to gesture to his suit, to underline his point. But he showed great discipline in keeping his arms flush on the table.

It was like the man was cold blooded.

Yeah . . . or maybe like he had a squad waiting for him out in the back alley, all ready to come busting in through the back doors of *The Melder's*, that kind of thing would give any self-respecting fuzz a whole shitload of confidence.

"I dunno," Peergolde said, staying straight faced, feeling like this guy was starting to take liberties . . . and if he was, then he wouldn't do it for much longer, "you tell me."

The golden-haired guy shook his head. His tuft of hair billowing about from side to side as he did so, just slightly out of step with the rest of his motion. "What'd ya want me to say?"

"I wanna know if you're fuzz, that's all."

Another shake of the head. Finally he lifted arms up off the table, brought his hands together, interlocked his fingers.

Peergolde made a point to see just where the guy was putting them hands of his.

Hands could make a whole lot of trouble, whether or not a guy had a .44 Jackcannon pointed directly at his chest.

"Can I?" the golden-haired guy said, indicating his jacket now.

Peergolde nodded.

The golden-haired guy reached inside his jacket, fished about in the pocket.

Peergolde could feel just about every soul in the pub holding their breath, taking them profound breaths, right down to the gut, waiting to see just what was going to happen.

Why, Peergolde himself felt his stomach dip, and he hoped that, if it came to it, Timm's aim would be true, and he'd teach this would-be fuzz just what the rules were here in the Bluff.

The golden-haired guy whipped a piece of paper out.

Not a badge.

Not what Peergolde had been expecting.

He slapped the paper down on the table between them.

A picture, a photograph.

Peergolde held off looking at it, kept his eye firmly on the guy for a few moments, before, reminding himself that Timm had him all sewn up with his gun, he dared look down at it, dared to take it in.

It was a picture of a young girl, maybe seven or eight, Peergolde had never been good with kids around them ages, they all kind of looked the same to him.

She had that same golden hair that the guy had, and them same chocolate-brown eyes too. It didn't take a mighty leap of logic to put the pieces together.

"Your daughter?" Peergolde said.

The golden-haired guy nodded.

Peergolde gave a shrug, slid the photo back towards the guy. "And?"

It was funny, like for the first time, the guy seemed to get a little flustered. He got all into a bunch of heavy blinking, as if he'd been caught in a daze. But he soon caught up with himself. Maybe he'd hoped that picture would do all his explaining for him, but, for Peergolde, it just raised more questions.

"I . . . I . . ." the guy said, "I'm doing this—I'm *here* for her."

Peergolde kept on staring into the guy's eyes, even though his attention was now drawn downwards, to the photo of his daughter. "You fuzz, bruv?"

"Detective," the guy said, his voice sounding hollow, as if his ribcage had become some sort of an echo chamber.

Peergolde felt a trill pass through his blood. His heart pump harder.

So there it was.

3

NO ONE SAID nothing then, there was nothing else to say.

But there was certainly some things to get cleaned up.

And Peergolde had every intention of doing so.

He could feel the weight of everyone's eyes in the pub all weighing him down, pressing down on his shoulders. The stuck pig roasting on the fire across the room had gone all quiet, and Peergolde guessed someone had tugged it right off the bare flames. He could smell that ashen flavour of pork on the thick air, and his mouth tasted stale, in need of a cigarette.

"Why didn't you say?" Peergolde said.

The golden-haired guy, the detective, reached for his photo—for the photo of his daughter.

Peergolde snatched out and pounded his fist down on it, stopping him from sliding it away, from replacing it in his jacket. He finally managed to wrestle the detective's eyes back onto his own. "You gotcha badge with ya, bruv?"

The detective wouldn't reply. He just kept up that blank stare of his.

Peergolde could see that the detective's face was damp with sweat now, sweat that glistened in the yellowy glow of the luminescent lights that surrounded them.

The detective gave a slight nod.

Peergolde glanced off to his side, off in Timm's direction, gave a little nod.

Timm moved quickly, keeping his gun still pointing to the detective's chest, apparently ready to fire off a shot at a moment's notice. Timm worked fast, padding the detective down as he sat there, his palms flat on the table as if he knew just what the drill was . . . well of course he knew what the drill was, that had to be the case considering he was fuzz.

He'd probably padded down a thousand suspects or more.

Maybe this was the first time he was getting padded down himself.

Perhaps he hadn't come on into the Bluff alone before.

Without his backup.

Timm uncovered the badge, brought it over to Peergolde, handed it to him.

Peergolde flipped the leather folder open, looked at the gleaming gilded coin within, the one which had an engraving of Council Hall, and then the lettering: Guynur City Fuzz, about the outside of it.

On the other side of the inside of the leather flap there was a laminated piece of paper with the detective's picture there, his number, and, most important, his name.

"Detective Urla Maakes, eh?" Peergolde said.

The detective, Urla Maakes, nodded.

Peergolde continued to look the badge over, not because he hadn't seen everything, but in a conscious effort to make the detective feel just a touch more uncomfortable for a little longer. "They not pay you on the force, eh?"

Urla remained still, looking down at the photograph of his daughter still lying, face up, on the table between them.

"Needed to come here, to the Bluff, to suppliment your paycheque, that it?"

No reply.

"Hey, bruv?" Peergolde said. "You gone deaf or something? You better get on with answering these questions, it's bad enough that you come on down here to the Bluff with that fucking badge of yours, but then not to let us all know who you *really* are . . . well, I have to say that there's a few knocking about the place who don't much care for that." He paused. "Myself included."

"My . . . my daughter . . ."

"Yeah, that's it, bruv, that's a start."

"She, uh, she's gone . . . she's gone missing."

"Sorry to hear that," Peergolde said, pocketing the badge in the breast pocket of his shirt—the same pocket he kept his packet of cigarettes. "And you, uh, what're you up to out here, eh?"

"I've . . . I've gotta, gotta . . ."

"Yeah?" Peergolde said, feeling like he was winding up the guy even more, that he'd finally managed to crack to the heart of this nervous guy's gut.

". . . Gotta quit the fuzz, and . . . and I need money, money to get things going, you see?"

Peergolde shook his head. "Can't say that I do."

"To search, I have to leave my job, have to scour the place looking for her—the fuzz they, uh, they won't touch the case, say that it's in the Watch's hands."

Peergolde felt a tingle burrow right down to the pit of his gut. Wow, did he not like hearing about that. The Watch, them skeletal, black-robed *things*, them *things* that wandered the city, kind of like a form of shadow fuzz, all of them skimping about looking for magical . . . *stuff* . . . stuff that had no place in Guynur City, no place at all.

"The Watch?" Peergolde said. "You in trouble with the Watch, bruv?"

This time the detective cracked a smile. It wasn't a healthy smile—not a smile that was betraying deep feelings of jubilation. No, it was a scared smile. The smile that showed the detective was at the end of his wits.

"Can we . . . can we just *play*?" he said, the final word he spoke catching in his throat.

Peergolde surveyed the situation, tried to see through this all. Of course *he* would never get himself mixed up in any of that shit, never get himself so much as onto the Watch's radar . . . that was a recipe for disaster.

But this guy, this guy right here, he was playing with scared money, and he was just plump for the taking. Just like a great big fat midwinter's goose.

If he didn't take him to the cleaner's then someone else would.

Peergolde felt the pub still pressing down on him, could hear all them about him glued to this scene, trying to see what he would do next, to see if Peergolde would sick his boy Timm on this rat detective, this fuzz that'd snuck on in here with that badge of his.

"You shoulda come here after quitting the fuzz," Peergolde said. "Or, at the very least, you shoulda left your badge at home."

The detective nodded quickly, as if he'd been struck by a bout of arthritis, kind of like a scolded schoolboy getting chewed into by a headmaster.

Peergolde tried to gauge the atmosphere. No one about the pub would bat an eyelid if he did give Timm the order to pull the trigger. Hell, they might even help him lug the body down to some drain and let him lose on the currents, send the fucker out to sea.

The fuzz wouldn't dare come on into the Bluff, not unless they wanted to start a war.

Peergolde, though only a minor player, had seen some underground rooms in the Bluff that made the fuzz's armoury look like child's play.

Peergolde held on for another moment, noticed how the detective was eyeballing him with them round eyes, the eyes that told him that he would jump if he said jump now . . . but, more than anything else, that whatever money he put on down on this here table, it would be gone within seconds of him laying it out.

And, after all, Peergolde was a gambler first.

A mob man second.

So he gave a curt nod, then brought the eggcup out before him, gave the dice inside of it a little shake. Listened to the hollow echo of the dice bouncing about.

Slowly, he heard the rest of the pub grind back into action about him, as the others went back to their drinks, and to their own games.

Out of the corner of his eye, he noticed Timm lower his gun, and saw him stalking out the periphery, no doubt taking a quick gander for any backup this detective might be packing.

But Peergolde was inclined to believe the detective's story. Really, there seemed little reason for him to lie about it all. Surely, when things had got all sticky back then, he could've just as easily rung in his hypothetical boys out in the alleyway.

From there on out, the story was a pretty familiar one, namely that Peergolde took him for precisely all that he brought to the table. It was interesting, if a little soul numbing, the way that he watched the detective break apart in the course of the game.

Each time that Peergolde was certain the detective was out, he dug his hand into his pocket and brought up a fistful of notes. More for him to lay down.

More for him to lose.

And he lost it all.

At the end of it all, Peergolde gave a satisfied smile but, to be honest, he felt a little shelled out inside, since he never liked to see someone headed off home in desperate circumstances like this detective had cooked up . . . but also knowing that that was the game, that that was how Peergolde earned his living, from the suckers and their problems.

But he watched him go, all the same, watched the detective cut a dejected figure as he slumped on off into the gloom of the Bluff to go find some other solution to his troubles.

He didn't even ask for his badge back, so it seemed like he'd been telling the truth about quitting the fuzz . . . or maybe he'd just file a missing report on Monday.

Peergolde really had no knowledge on how them institutions really worked.

Never had any inclination to get himself buried in one either.

As Peergolde headed on back to his table, the barman bringing him over a fresh flagon of brandy ale, he set himself down on the wooden crate, and sipped at his drink quietly.

Timm sat down on the crate beside him, and when he did Peergolde laid his hand down on his shoulder, gave him a squeeze of thanks.

He had good people around him, that much was clear.

People who looked out for him.

And as long as he continued to treat them well they'd look out for him for always.

Peergolde drew the badge out of his breast pocket, laid it down before him, and thought about how much he might be able to make from it. Someone would want to buy it, for sure, want to use it as a base for forgeries. There was people all through Guynur who had reasons for pretending to be fuzz.

When Timm tapped him on the forearm, Peergolde came round, glanced about him, saw the raggedy figure standing up in the doorway to *The Melder's*, dressed in a denim jacket, all puckered with holes. A grey, bearded face. And the look of All Beaten Up just dripping right off him.

Peergolde eyed him right away, invited him to sit down with him, bought him a drink, and then they set about playing. Because everyone knew that Peergolde *only ever* played for high stakes.

If they got lucky, they might be able to win it all off him.

But, more often than most, they lost it all to him.

That was why they called him the Dicemaster after all.

THE COUNCIL

G UNIA DOUDLY gave her breath mint a parting suck as it dissolved in her mouth. When she breathed out she could smell that fierce *minty* odour, so strong it might drop flies out of the air. That was the idea. On nights like this it was all about going on the offensive.

Her breath felt hot as it hit the backs of her well-soaped, and moisturised, hands. It was on nights like this that she was glad that she wore gloves whenever the sun showed its face, so that she could keep up the fetching, girlish, pale gleam to her skin.

The chatter rose up higher in the air.

Up to where Gunia stood up on the balcony of the banquet hall of Doudly Scoth Mansion, her father's mansion, the mansion that would *one day* belong to her.

She loved this room, often told Father that he didn't get *nearly* enough use out of it.

What with the crystal chandeliers which carried flickering candles—painstakingly lit an hour or so before the event by the waiting staff—and the ivory-smooth cornices which looped down from the roof, in little swirls and globes, and other designs that her father had reassured her had been extremely expensive to have designed and absolutely draining for the craftsmen to get just how he wanted.

The lush, regal-red carpet too, was simply *divine*.

She recalled, back when she'd been a child, stealing her way in here and throwing herself down onto the carpet. She would lie face-down and swim her arms up and down, savouring the feel of it against her skin.

When her nanny had caught her, and dutifully told Father, she had got into an awful lot of trouble. Thinking about it now, she could almost still feel the sting of the smacked bottom he'd given her.

The thick wallpaper complimented the carpet with its sweeping, lighter tone, one which gave that all-important, flirty suggestion. The one that suggested that naughtiness might be afoot here in the banquet hall this night.

And, goodness, there would be, if Gunia had anything at all to do with it.

And everything else in the banquet hall was set, the circular tables all covered in a simple, but *costly*, white cloth, with the velvet-upholstered chairs tucked in underneath for later.

For when the welcome drinks had been consumed, and the food had arrived.

Gunia eyed up the talent. The fetching men in their tuxedos, and their partners in their cocktail dresses with low cleavage. Rather like the dress which Gunia wore, though she was one-hundred-per-cent certain that she looked better than any given woman in the room. She had spent the best part of an hour shuffling through the dresses in her wardrobe, getting just the right one. In the end she had settled on a strapless, peach-toned number, with a pair of matching, very strappy, and very high, high heels. That should get the boys panting.

Or, at least that was what she'd said to herself in extreme confidence in her makeup mirror approximately fifteen minutes earlier.

Hmm, not a huge amount to talk about, and certainly nothing to get all a blush over.

But . . . *hang on a minute* . . . she turned her attention to the archway of the banquet hall, to the entrance. There she saw him. Bengerman Bengerbills.

Blond. Square jawed. Dapper.

And, *hello*? . . . No sign of that much-celebrated fiancé of his, certainly not on his arm tonight, in any case. This might well be the time to make a move.

Mid thirties. Loaded with money and influence.

Earmarked for the Council if the gossip she heard was to be believed . . .which, considering it came from Father's most-trusted aides, it was.

Goodness, now the party had really started.

She gripped her flute of elderberry wine tighter, taking care to keep her dainty fingers clutching the stem with the little finger pointed outwards at a jagged angle in the way that Ms Kjuggle, her etiquette teacher, insisted on.

The way that she claimed was 'ladylike.'

Normally Gunia wouldn't give two craps for what Ms Kjuggle had to say about anything, but, right now, right at this minute, she was standing before her, clasping the brass banister of the balcony, slipping Gunia disapproving sidelong glances.

And, as Gunia well knew from experience, if Ms Kjuggle saw anything that she disapproved of, she would report in to Gunia's father . . . and then Gunia would never hear the end of it.

If only she could slip away from that vulture gaze of hers, get away down into the reams of people streaming into the hall.

Then she would be able to do just about anything she wanted.

Gunia flashed a glance back down, down to ground level, to the bustling blacks and whites of the tuxedos, mixed in with all those cheerful, multi-coloured cocktail dresses.

She watched as Bengerman Bengerbills accepted a flute of elderberry wine off a passing waiter, she saw how he took it with a polite smile, which he soon shucked just as soon as he had the flute in his possession. He brought the flute up to his lips and drank, his eyes constantly on the move, going about the crowd, looking for someone.

Gunia felt her chest tighten, her heart skip a beat, and she knew that this was her chance. She glanced over to Ms Kjuggle once more, saw her severe, chopped-back, cosmic-blue hair, and her spindly body as she gripped onto the brass railing of the balcony, and she knew this was her chance. This was the perfect chance.

Gunia knocked back the rest of her elderberry wine for a touch of Dutch courage, and then she skittered her way out off the balcony, slipping past the velvet curtain which hung down and escaping her chaperone.

2

G UNIA FELT her cheeks flushing with the combination of the wine she'd just downed and the body heat that the crowd gave off. She was also willing to bet that it was just the excitement bubbling in her gut at having seen Bengerman Bengerbills—Bengerman *Fucking* Bengerbills!—here and all alone.

She still had the bitter taste of the elderberry wine on her tongue, but it gave her an edge, made her feel more awake, like a bitter black coffee in the morning.

The crowd got much louder. She could smell the mixture of colognes and perfumes, almost overpowering to her.

Down at ground level everything seemed much brighter, much more real. More alive. It was unfair how Father would instruct her to stick close to Ms Kjuggle during these events, have her looking over her shoulder for the entirety of the encounter.

So it was just *right* that Gunia had broken free.

She wasn't a child any longer, she was twenty-one, and she felt just as adult as anybody. Someday she would inherit everything Father owned so it made no sense for her to sit out these events, all quarantined off somewhere in the mansion as if she was poxed.

Gunia worked quickly, catching the white-waist-coated waiter coming up her left side, and, more importantly, his silver tray with the flutes of elderberry wine on top.

She snatched a flute off and held it at her chest, taking care to keep her elbow tucked in as she maneuvered about the crowd, zigzagged her way through the warm bodies to seek out Bengerman Bengerbills.

Several times people tried to speak to her, to *greet* her, and she brushed them off with a sweet smile, and girlish giggles. They seemed to get the picture. After all, no one came to these banquets because of her, no one came here to see *her*.

That was why she'd have to make the best effort she possibly could with Bengerman Bengerbills, to make him sit up and take notice of her.

Finally.

She swayed some more through the crowd, dished out another dozen or so polite greetings before she managed to get herself within the vicinity of Bengerman.

As she eyed him, through an elderly woman's lime feather boa, she saw, to her horror, that he had been intercepted by her Aunt Carul.

Gunia cursed under her breath.

She looked to her aunt now. She was recently widowed, what with her husband, Gunia's uncle, having died in a car accident.

Recently?

. . . Well, it had been five years since he had died, but there was something that Gunia found herself constantly spotting in widowed women, that permanent bagginess in their eyes, that look of fear deep within their irises, as if they surveyed every future possible beau with a kind of fatalism.

Even at her fifty-something, her aunt was attractive. Terribly attractive, in fact. She had soft blond hair which flowed down the back of her midnight-blue cocktail dress, and she had the skin . . . well, even Gunia had to admit that standing beside one another it was difficult to tell who was the younger by skin alone . . . somehow the woman just wouldn't wrinkle!

From here, Gunia could scent her aunt's distinctive honey and blueberry perfume, even through the cloud of other fragrances. Gunia wished that she'd manage to find some vendor, somewhere in

Guynur, who would do fragrances half as original as the one which her aunt managed to track down.

She recalled once, while they'd been having afternoon tea in the lounge, how she'd lightly asked her aunt just where she got her perfume from, more out of politeness than anything else, and her aunt had simply held her finger to her lips and given a slight giggle.

What a bitch.

And now here she was, making a *royal* fool of herself with Bengerman Bengerbills, no less.

Gunia planned her approach, checked on her surroundings. She flashed a glance upwards, to the balcony. Ms Kjuggle was gone. No doubt already hot on her heels. That was just another motivation. What would she be able to say to her if she saw her chatting with Bengerman Bengerbills . . . what would *Father* have to say about it?

He would be delighted, of course he would.

And perhaps it was just the prospect of how stormy and vengeful Ms Kjuggle would look as Father congratulated her that drove Gunia into her final advance.

She took care to watch where she was treading—another of Ms Kjuggle's pieces of advice—and she navigated her way up to her aunt's elbow.

Just standing there, grinning away, aiming her smile at Bengerman's face, she could feel the icy chill coming off her aunt.

"Well, hello there!" Bengerman said, cracking a smile at Gunia.

Only standing here and looking back at Bengerman's smile did Gunia truly realise what people meant when they said a *pearl*-white smile.

He leaned forwards, planted a pair of greeting kisses on each of Gunia's cheeks.

She breathed in deep, savoured his cinnamon scent, and could hardly keep the feathers from rising in her stomach, and blurting out her undying affection, when he withdrew, and took up his former pose. Reassuming, she was glad to see, his more dour expression for Aunt Carul.

Gunia knew she had to bide her time, that she had to stand her ground. Sooner or later her aunt would get the message and wiggle on off somewhere to go and try her luck at some other bachelor . . . hopefully one a little closer to her own age, though, at that time, Gunia couldn't have cared less.

That moment, thankfully, came sooner rather than later, with some rosy-cheeked, yellow-teethed, drunkard waggling in and draping his arm about her aunt.

Gunia watched on, delighted, almost seeing the thing play out in slow motion, as the drunkard's drink was tipped over the back of her aunt's dress.

With a smart *slap*, and a quick turn of heel, her aunt beat a retreat, heading off to the powder room, no doubt.

The drunkard, his job done, soon wandered off, away from them, and Gunia turned her attention back to the much more important matter of Bengerman Bengerbills, who stood before her making a wincing kind of expression as he followed the back of Aunt Carul's dress out through the crowd and, eventually, out of the banquet hall.

With a couple of blinks, Bengerman turned his attention onto Gunia, and he grinned that divine grin of his once more. It seemed like Aunt Carul had been quite swiftly forgotten. "I say," Bengerman began, "I didn't see you about here earlier."

Gunia gestured in the direction of the balcony. "I was up there," she said.

Bengerman cocked his head to one side and smiled pleasantly. "And what good might you do all the way up there?"

Gunia felt the warmth rising in her cheeks, but she couldn't help showing it, though she tried her best to hide it, taking another sip from her fresh glass of elderberry wine.

Bengerman turned his attention to the hall, and he regarded it in a fashion that reminded Gunia of a king looking out over the remnants of a victorious battle, and taking in his newly won lands. "Terrific little shindig here, really, isn't it? Your father really does put on all the best parties."

Gunia tried to think of something witty to say to that, but she came up with nothing. She couldn't help but stare into Bengerman's lightly tanned cheeks and try to come up with the precise colour tone of them.

He looked back at her, aiming those pale green eyes of his at her —drawing her in like a tractor beam. "I, ah, can't say that I've had the pleasure of taking in the Doudly Scoth homestead." He paused for a moment. "You, uh, wouldn't be interested in doing me the honour, would you?"

Gunia could hardly believe her ears. This was too good to be true. It *had* to be too good to be true. Quickly, sure that this was all going to be dragged out from under her feet at any second, she spun about and scoured the crowd, searching out Ms Kjuggle.

There! There she was. Skulking about on the other side of the banquet hall, her nose thrust up in the air, and those sharp eyes of hers on the prowl.

If Gunia didn't move on immediately she might find herself being thwarted.

It was now or never.

And so, with a flush of adrenaline, she grasped hold of Bengerman's suit sleeve and led him off through the crowd, away from the rest of them, and through the velvet curtain, guarded by a pair of meatheads, who, with their bald heads and tight-fitting tuxedos, nodded them right through.

3

THE BABBLE of the banquet hall diminished on Gunia's heels, she couldn't quite believe what was happening—or that it was happening to *her*. This really was turning into a dream now! If only she'd ever had the imagination to have a dream like this in the first place.

She felt her heart playing her ribs like a xylophone and in that moment recalled the flute of elderberry wine in her hand and swigged the rest of it back, laid the emptied flute down on the carpet, up against the pristine, beige wallpaper.

Most likely it wouldn't get knocked over there.

As she came back up, she felt Bengerman's hand slip down to hers, and his fingers interlock with hers. His palm was warm, but not clammy. And his breath smelled of hazelnuts, just wafting over her like that. She wished to explore that mouth of his . . . among other things.

She tried to catch up on herself, tried to slow the ticking of her heart and tell herself that she had to be a little more sensible here.

Yes, this might well be Bengerman Bengerbills but that didn't mean that she was going to throw herself on her back and be his *whore* for the evening.

Far from it.

She was playing the long game, and, as such, she needed solidly founded assurances.

And so, it would pay for her to be a little cold to begin with.

But those *eyes* of his . . . they near enough invited her in to test just how warm the waters were.

Have. To. Resist.

"Come on," she said, without giving his hand a squeeze, no matter how much she wanted to. "I'll give you the tour."

"Oh goody," Bengerman replied. "I *have* been looking forward to it."

As she guided him along the endless corridors, she felt a little ditsy, and not a little embarrassed, to admit that she'd got herself a little lost *in her own home*.

But Bengerman just seemed to find it terribly amusing, and so she just laughed along with him, and showed him to the rooms which cropped up in their path, and did her best to explain their histories, the ones she'd heard so many times as she'd trailed at her father's heels as he'd given his own little tours.

It was just after they'd concluded the fifth floor of the mansion and were standing on the marble balcony that looked out over the expansive mansion gardens that she thought it a good time to broach the tender subject of their relations.

. . . Why, listen to the way she was speaking, Ms Kjuggle would've been proud if she hadn't been so furious!

She had broken off her hand from his by now, deciding to play things a little cooler. And she held on firm to the marble wall of the balcony, and stared on down over the lush lawns which flowed out from beneath them and to the very end of the horizon, and then to the conifer trees which bristled about on all sides.

And then, far away over the sturdy rock walls which marked out the perimeter of the mansion, she saw the faint glimmer of Guynur City, and all those poor saps who had to live their lives among that smog—and within all those problems.

Whenever she went into the city, she tried to make it as painless as she possibly could . . . she always made a point of picking out her destination, and then having her driver wait with the engine running, ready to motor away at a moment's notice.

That was the only way to do Guynur.

She breathed in the night air, the freshly trimmed grass, could taste the dew carrying on the breeze too. The wind sent a shimmer along the surface of her skin—made her feel more awake, and more sober. From down below, she could hear the babble seeping out from the banquet hall. She supposed that one of the servants had opened the doors which looked out onto the lawn, so as to make the air temperature down there more habitable.

Well, it was now or never.

She turned into Bengerman, just as he turned into her, looked at her with those delicious pale green eyes of his, and she said, "Your fiancé, Mory, where is she?"

Bengerman kept up that easy smile of his, hiding his inner turmoil if there, indeed, was any, though Gunia guessed that a future politician, and all-round smooth operator such as Bengerman was well past the point of blowing his cover . . . least of all to a silly little girl.

He looked on out over the balcony, and to the horizon, out to Guynur. He reached up and ran his hand through his short blond hair, gathering it into tufts between his fingers. "Mory, Mory, Mory," he said. "Yes, that *is* a bit of a tale."

"Will you tell it to me?" Gunia said, and then, realising that maybe she should show a little more tact, added, "Or just give me the gist?"

He pressed his lips together, dialling down his smile by a few degrees. She could see the sheen of the moon in his eyes, and wondered what was going through his mind right at that moment. It was hard to believe that this was really happening, that she was *really* standing here with Bengerman Bengerbills and that he was on the cusp of spilling all of his most personal, most intimate, secrets . . . or, at least, considering *hinting* at them.

"Mory and I, I think it's fair to say, have some mutually exclusive interests."

Gunia tried to piece together what this might mean, but came up a long way short. She really had no way of interpreting just what he meant by that.

But she had to show patience.

That was the theme of her night, after all.

"You see, with Mory—with her *family*, they are so locked down in their business matters, and Mory's father is *determined* that she take on running that business one day." Bengerman heaved an authentic-sounding sigh. "And, well, with my political ambitions, with me wanting to one day sit on the Council, it's a bit of a sticky wicket." He turned to face her, gave her a light smile. "If you see what I mean?"

Gunia saw exactly what he meant now . . . or, at least, she was fairly sure that she did . . . saw what he was hinting at, that was.

Gunia's father, what with him being on the Council, Bengerman thought that marrying his daughter . . . marrying *Gunia!* . . . might be a sound career move.

In fact, from the way that he said it, it sounded like Gunia had been a keystone in Bengerman's decision to break off his engagement with Mory!

Just the idea that she had been on his mind was enough to send her heart to flame.

Gunia thought this over.

While it was true to say that this lacked quite a large amount of romanticism, she thought that it was fair to say that it *would* put Bengerman firmly into the commitment camp.

But there was just one thing, she would like some . . .

Just as she was on the brink of asking, she watched him dip his hand into the inside pocket of his tuxedo, fish about there for a moment or so, before he produced a ring from within. He held it up in the moonlight, and Gunia watched the light play out across the surface.

"She returned the ring," Bengerman said, sounding, for the first time that evening, a touch downhearted.

Gunia really had no idea what to say. She had never been engaged, let alone broken off an engagement . . . or at least not *directly*.

In a swift, single motion, Bengerman swept his arm back and tossed the ring long and hard, off into the deep patch of conifer trees, several feet down below the balcony.

Gunia heard the rustle of leaves as it fell down to the ground.

For a few seconds she just felt numb, inside and out, and she really had no idea what to say, whether or not she should comfort Bengerman . . . *commiserate* with him.

But, as it turned out, there was no need for her to do anything.

Because he was the one that grabbed hold of her hand, inter-locked her fingers with his, and whisked her back into the mansion.

It was funny, this place seemed so strange, so *unknown* to Gunia. And, as it turned out, all the doors on the floor were locked. They resorted to her and Bengerman cantering along the hallway, each of them trying the doorknobs as they went.

In the end, it was Gunia who finally found the doorknob which gave some. She turned it. And, delighted to find it unlocked, shouted back to Bengerman, for him to come over quickly.

It was only as she stepped on into the room, the room she thought was deserted, that she saw Father's face, sitting at the head of an oak table with another dozen stern-looking gentlemen also sitting around it, that she felt her heart drop like a stone.

4

BENGERMAN ARRIVED at her side with impeccable timing. He panted in and out, and she could feel the heat coming off his body from the running they'd done to try and find a door that wasn't locked.

His breath, which had once smelled so sweet, down in the banquet hall, now was a little sour, and sticky. She could feel her heart pummelling her from the inside, and could hardly believe all those men, with their flaky scalps, and their wispy hair just about clinging to their near-bald heads, all eyeballing them. Some with their mouths latched open, and others with unbelieving eyes.

Somehow Gunia managed to tear herself away from their reproachful looks, and onto Father, who sat at the head of the table, dressed in his tuxedo, and his face rapidly turning a shade of puce.

Father's expression wasn't one of reproach, it was well, well past that.

She felt like she should look down at the tips of her toes out of shame, but found that she couldn't, that she simply couldn't break off from that blazing gaze of his.

Slowly, he rose up out of his chair, his eyes swivelling between Gunia and Bengerman like he was just now totalling the sum of the evidence.

Why wouldn't he say something?

Why wouldn't he just scream . . . *do* something?!

But he just stayed quiet, his hands balled into fists down at his sides, with the other men, men who Gunia soon recognised as other members of the Council, providing a black-and-white backdrop with their tuxedos.

"Outside," Father finally said.

Gunia glanced about the room, feeling her heart flutter in her throat, her blood pumping right up to her brain, seeming to drench the inside of her skull and steal away any reason. Somehow she understood the command, did as Father instructed.

Only when her loose elbow caught Bengerman in his soft belly did she remember that he was there with her. But she couldn't bear to look up at him. To share this shameful moment with him. No, it was better for them both to suffer through this thing in silence, and then to pick through the pieces later on.

It was hard to believe what could've gone worse.

Gunia had just *known* that this was too good to be true!

Out in the hallway, Father brought the door to the room with the Council members inside closed, and he looked over the two of them.

Though both she and Bengerman were adults, her being twenty-one and him being in his mid-thirties, it felt like they were much younger what with her sixty-something father bearing down on them.

She looked to his sharp eyes, to his rigid nose, and she wondered how this could possibly get any worse. She had thought that Father would've been delighted for her, that she'd finally found someone who could truly play at her level in Bengerman Bengerbills.

Now, though, it had all gone horribly, seemingly irretrievably wrong.

Father swept over her with his flared nostrils and wide-open eyes, and then he turned his attention, square onto Bengerman. "Just what in the *hell* do you think you're doing rushing about *my* house?"

Gunia felt her throat seize up, but she knew that she had to step in here, that she had to explain. But when she parted her lips,

Father hushed her by simply holding his hand up for her to be quiet.

Bengerman blinked several times, and Gunia saw how his cheeks flushed, she knew that he felt under attack here, and maybe he blamed her too.

Oh, what must he think of her?!

What with her steering him about her own home, claiming not to know all the ins and outs of the place . . . had he *really* bought that, believed that she could truly be so pathetic?

But that had been the truth.

No matter how pathetic it sounded.

"Well, then, Bengerbills?" Father said, his voice hinting at being just a touch more reasonable, but certainly no more than a hair's breadth away from launching into outright fury once again.

Bengerman parted his lips, appeared to try to speak.

But he couldn't.

Gunia felt her heart beating hard in her chest—felt herself go cold, then impossibly warm. Bengerman's cinnamon-scented cologne seemed to turn sour in her nostrils, seemed to flip her gut inside out.

She watched as Bengerman's Adam's apple rose and fell in his throat, but no sound passed beyond his lips. Only a vague *hiss* of air.

Gunia could hardly believe what she was seeing, and the way that Father looked on at Bengerman, the way that he glowered at him, his eyes intent on Bengerman's which now bulged on out of their sockets as if he was being squeezed by some invisible force.

As if . . . or *was* he?

Feeling powerless, weak all over, Gunia studied Father's face saw the strain that appeared there, the way that his brow was all wrinkled up as if he was exerting a great effort.

She managed to find her voice at last.

". . . Father?" she said.

Another couple of moments passed. Silent moments. That *hiss* of air leaking out between Bengerman's lips the only real sound. And then, just like that, Bengerman staggered backwards, into the wall of the hallway, his arms scrabbling to find a new balance.

Then he turned, staggered from side to side, and beat a retreat along the hallway, back in the direction of the banquet hall.

5

FATHER GLARED on after him, not allowing Bengerman to leave his sight till he had turned the corner at the end of the hallway and gone for good.

At least Gunia was *certain* that he had gone for good.

Finally, Father turned to her.

She had expected his eyes to be wide, and his mouth thick with fury, but, instead, he only seemed a little tired, a little drawn. His thin, grey hair sticking up in wispy tufts and moving slightly in the draught which blew on through the hallway.

. . . It was like that old cliché, the one that went along the lines of not being angry, but being disappointed.

That was right.

She felt like he was disappointed in her now.

And it was *awful*.

"Where is Ms Kjuggle?" he said, his voice flat, and expressionless.

Gunia surprised herself when she spoke, about how she managed to keep her voice together, to keep it from sounding frayed or startled. "I, uh, I ran away from her."

Again, she expected Father to fly into a rage, to begin his cursing, to start into decrying how he had picked the wrong mother—*Gunia's* mother—the one who he always went on about being a feeble woman because she'd died while Gunia had still been a child, that she hadn't been about to raise Gunia in her own image.

As a perfect *lady*.

"You are to return to the banquet hall," Father said, turning away from her, apparently offering nothing more by way of punishment.

Maybe he would wait until later. Until the Council meeting had been adjourned, for whatever reason they were meeting tonight.

Gunia felt a flush of warmth through her. Her gut tightened. And now she couldn't help feeling bad, not for Bengerman, but for Ms Kjuggle.

True, Gunia had her daily battles with her chaperone, but at the same time she could hardly imagine herself coping with anyone else.

Ms Kjuggle might be the enemy, but at least she was known to Gunia.

"Please, Father," Gunia started, "don't punish Ms Kjuggle, she . . . she . . . it was all my fault, she never had a chance of tracking me down—of keeping tabs on me."

Father glanced back over his shoulder at her. Met her eye briefly. "Go back to the banquet hall, child, we shall talk about this later on."

Gunia felt her chest tighten.

She hated, *hated*, it when Father called her 'child,' like she was just some little girl that he could pluck up and set down on his knee. That he could just as easily cart off beneath his arm and lock away in her bedroom till she calmed down from whatever tantrum she was in the midst of throwing.

But, instead of launching another defence in the name of Ms Kjuggle, she found herself saying something quite different instead.

"Father?"

"Hmm?"

"What did you *do* to him?"

Father stopped dead, his hand on the doorknob to the room which housed the Council. He held on tight to the doorknob another few seconds and then let go. He turned around, looked back at her.

His eyes were . . . well, kind of *sad* now.

Almost dopey looking.

There was no trace of the fury he'd unleashed on Bengerman.

"I mean," Gunia said, feeling that if she wanted to get in her own point of view on the conversation that now was the time to do it . . . while Father had cooled down somewhat, "I thought you would approve of him—of Bengerman, I mean. He's of good standing, and he has political ambitions, he . . ."

But Father cut her off with a wide grin, a grin which didn't carry a note of joy to it. The kind of grin that just showed him acknowledging a grim truth . . . something that Gunia, in her little-girl world, couldn't possibly hope to comprehend.

She *hated* it when he did that.

"He is not adequate for you, my dear," Father said.

"Then at least answer me what you did, Father, please?"

Father loomed there, up against the door. He was the leader of the Council, and as she well knew, he was used to carrying himself with esteem and pride, to being a leader among men, the one that they could all look up to.

He let loose a slight sigh, and then took a few steps away from the door. He draped his arm about Gunia's shoulders, and led her on along the hallway, and back out onto the marble balcony where she had been only minutes before and under such different circumstances.

It was like stepping into an entirely different world.

For a minute or so, they stood there, the two of them, with the night-time breeze blowing up against them. At Gunia, there in her cocktail dress, feeling every chill of the wind brushing her skin, and Father, in his tuxedo, looking dashing as he always did dressed up, but, at the same time, just a little drawn, a little tired from the dark circles which dragged down the bases of his eyes.

"The problem," Father began, "with Bengerman, and his polit-ical ambitions, is in his blood."

"His blood?"

"Hmm," he replied. "He, well, you see . . . he doesn't have any *magic* in his blood."

Magic?

Gunia tried to reason this, tried to pull this all straight in her mind, to understand just what he was trying to say to her. What was he talking about *magic* in his blood? No one in Guynur City had *magic* in their blood, it was prohibited, in fact . . . aside for the members of the Watch, of course.

"Magic," Father continued, "like that which flows in my veins." He paused for a long while. "And like that which flows in *yours*."

Gunia felt the breath depart her lungs, it was like someone had just squeezed a bellows, let all the air out of her. She might have collapsed to the ground if it hadn't been for the sturdy support of the balcony wall which she clung onto.

"Father?" she said, her voice frail now. "What're you talking about?"

Father remained in profile and gave a light smile as he gazed on out into the garden which spread out below them. "Perhaps it *is* time you know more about what's going on—about what your legacy shall be once you are of age to claim it."

Gunia's heart pumped harder and harder now, seemingly unstoppable. She followed Father's gaze, out to where he looked. She realised now that he didn't look down on the garden, but he stared on off to the horizon.

To Guynur City.

Glittering with its orange lights.

It might have been considered beautiful by someone who hadn't ever seen it close up.

But Gunia had certainly seen it close up.

"The Council," Father continued, "is made up solely of men who have magical blood running in their veins—the ones who can see the wood for the trees, so to speak, the ones who have a better knowledge of just what Guynur City means."

Feeling weaker and weaker by the second, Gunia said, "Father, I don't understand at all."

He parted his lips, apparently considering just what to say next, but, in the end, he opted to press them shut, and to reach across, to lay his calloused hands on top of her own. His hands had always reminded her of sandpaper, the way they were so rough. And he said, in a voice so soft that she was certain he was afraid of being overheard. "In time, you shall come to understand it all, when you take your own rightful place on the Council."

Gunia's heart rapped harder and harder. She felt the heat rise in her cheeks. This time she couldn't find the strength to raise her voice to repeat, once again, that she didn't understand, so she just had to settle with a shake of her head.

"True," Father said, looking her over with a benevolent smile, "a woman has never before served on the Council, never before stepped into those all-important shoes . . . but I suppose that there are exceptions to be made, precedents to be set, as they should be with the trudging pass of time."

Gunia could hardly understand Father when he struck this sort of philosophical tone, but she thought that she could just about grasp the base of the idea.

That she was magical.

That she had *magic* running in her veins.

And that, one day, Father saw her rightful place as serving on the Council.

On her being a politician, overseeing Guynur City.

She could hardly believe her ears.

But she could just about comprehend it now.

In fact, she could feel lots of things all sliding into place in her mind, all those little misunderstandings as she'd been a child, as she'd grown up about Doudly Scoth Mansion and clumsily trotted about trying to find her place—trying to deal with her own good fortune.

Maybe, now, she had the answer she'd sought for so long.

Though it was an answer she'd not known she'd been looking for.

One more question, though.

Just one more for Father.

She turned her hand over, allowed his fingers to intertwine with her own, and she felt him squeeze her gently. Then she peered upwards, into his eyes, and she said, "Father?"

"Hmm?"

"What did you do to Bengerman?"

He stayed quiet for a long moment, a long while, and then he finally broke out of his daze, and said, "I laid a charm on him . . . something basic, something just to warn him of what he was dealing with." He paused, pouted for a moment, then continued. "I think he understands now, I think he understands just what he's dealing with. It was better for him to see it demonstrated than to have it told to him, I'm sure he will agree with that later on, later on when he eases himself into his true future, marries that *Mory* woman."

Gunia thought about protesting for a second, thought about saying how they'd stood right here, on this very balcony, no more than an hour ago, and how Bengerman had tossed the engagement ring off into the trees, down there, down into the garden.

But, right as she was about to speak, she heard a rustling down there.

Among the trees.

And, through the leaves, she caught a flash of white, of a figure dressed in a tuxedo.

Of Bengerman Bengerbills.

Apparently searching for his ring.

When she glanced back at Father, she saw that he was smiling, and, though the situation was a serious one, though she felt bad for Bengerman and the lesson Father had taught him . . . the lesson Father had taught *her* . . . she couldn't help but grin also.

And, after lingering there, on the balcony, for another few minutes, listening to all that rustling which accompanied Bengerman's search, Father led her on back into the mansion, and away from the garden.

As Gunia left Father behind, and headed on back to the banquet hall, to bury the hatchet with Ms Kjuggle, she couldn't help but keep up that same smile on her lips, and think about how, now, her future was all taken care of.

She simply didn't need to *think* about it any longer.

Because she had *magic* running in her blood, and now, thinking about it properly for the first time in her life, that confirmed to her what she had vaguely known throughout her life.

That she was special.

That she was superior.

And that *one day*, she would rule them all.

RATTERS

THREE GENERATIONS was nothing to sniff at.

Not at all.

No matter what your occupation was:

Doctor. Lawyer. Teacher.

Ratter.

It really wasn't important.

But Argoon Shween could've done with a reminder every time he came down here, to the Business Bureau, to renew his Working Licence.

The oak arches overhead looped above him two, three storeys high.

Intimidating?

Sure, that was how they'd been designed.

They were *meant* to make anyone who set foot inside the Business Bureau feel intimidated.

Beyond them the desks, oak too. And all worked at by men stuffed into the collars of shirts, and kept in there with their ties. Their suit jackets seemed to weigh down their shoulders so much that they could no longer move. That they were pinned down to their seat till the order came, at five o'clock, for them to mooch off home to their TV dinners, and their stay-at-home wives, and their babbling children.

The women were somehow worse.

Their frailer frames were left open-necked where their blouses showed off all different tones of skin. And their stares remained fixed on their radiating computer screens, that sick bluish light splashing out over their numbed faces.

Argoon's leather trench coat, which made him feel at least seven feet tall out on the street, seemed almost impotent here.

The heaters seemed all turned up in here, made his leather coat work on him like the jacket of a potato baking in an oven.

The wax off the floors smelled thick and sour to his nose, thoroughly *artificial*, and the floors were so shined up that it made the soles of his boots squeak out as he walked along.

He wanted to chew on some tobacco but he had none left after the meathead standing on the door: an ape squeezed into a suit, had forced him to spit it out into the bin before he'd allow him inside.

The meathead had almost not allowed him into the building on account of his trench coat—on account of him not dressing up in a *suit* and a *tie* like the rest of the rats about Guynur City.

Because that's what they were to Argoon.

Just like the rats he tugged out of people's drains.

Worse even . . . because at least for him rats meant money—money for the family business.

He hunched his shoulders and trudged on harder. Keeping eyes only on the scuffed-up toes of his boots. And making an effort to keep his mind as blank as he possibly could.

All this spit-and-polished wooden fixings: the banisters, the skirting boards, the edges of the stairs. They caught him right out of place. Made him feel out of place.

His domain was the piss-stinking alleys, the ones that were punctuated by the rubbish bins over spilling with refuse of all kinds: organic, and not, and of course there was the matter of the *rats*.

Rats, they were his business. Always had been. Ever since he was a little lad he'd thought of nothing else. His father had never *allowed* him to ever think of being anything else.

He could still remember school fresh, as if it'd just been the day before, the way he'd roll on in after a sleepless night out ratting with his dad, with them dark circles beneath his eyes, and how he'd try to keep the board in focus with his impossibly blurring eyes, and how the teacher's voice just lulled him to sleep till a sharp reprimand brought him back with a *thwack!* to the Land of the Awake.

Then how all the kids would talk behind his back, call him dopey and worse, and how he'd get pissed at them and maybe punch a brick wall, or another kid if he got it into his mind to do so.

. . . No, all things considered, he liked to be out and about, doing his own thing, running the family business now.

It was just these unpleasant little chores that got on his nerves every once in a while.

Clutching his paper ticket, he matched it up with the bright-red LED screen above him, headed for the booth that it indicated, staffed by a balding man of about forty. He had sweat patches beneath both his arms, and he was constantly pushing his horn-rimmed glasses back up the bridge of his nose as they slid down.

He didn't so much as look at Argoon when he sat down on the chair opposite him, the rattle of his fingers across his computer keyboard was the only thing that resembled a greeting.

Argoon sat there on the hard-backed chair, the cushions so worn down from the years and years of other people—other business owners—sitting themselves down here and waiting on the person behind the desk to give them a reply to their query.

Perhaps wanting to preserve the silence as greatly as the man at the desk, Argoon dipped his hand into the pocket of his overcoat, removed the folded-up piece of paper and slid it across the desk to the man.

Without a word, the man picked it up, unfolded it, glanced at it briefly, and then rattled out the details it contained on his keyboard.

He waited a second, maybe two, then his forehead wrinkled and he narrowed his eyes at his screen, as if unable to comprehend just what it was that his computer showed him.

A scratch of the scalp later, he tapped out the details once again, apparently giving the computer another go.

The same thing happened, the wrinkled brow, the confused expression, and then the apologetic glance that he aimed in Argoon's direction. "Sorry, sir, I'm afraid that your licence has been revoked."

2

ARGOON TOOK A SECOND to absorb the information. The heat in the place was almost overwhelming now, and he'd caught hold of yet another smell—a smell of polish which was tickling his nostril hair, and threatening to make him sneeze.

Beneath the desk, and beneath the man's line of sight, he balled his hands into fists, digging his well-gnawed fingernails into the soft heels of his hands. He felt the sting of the pinched flesh and he liked how it brought his mind around—made his thinking grow sharper.

He washed some saliva about his mouth, and tried to comfort himself with the vague taste of chewing tobacco that remained there.

When he breathed, he listened to the warm air come rampaging out of his nostrils, apparently unstoppable.

"You wha'?" Argoon said.

The man blinked several times, made contact with Argoon for a moment then turned his attention back to his computer screen. "It says here," he began, "that your licence has been revoked." He brought his finger up and used it to guide his way across the unseen lines of information on the screen. "Three weeks ago," he added, turning back to Argoon with a sheepish smile, and a cock of his head, as if that'd make things far more reasonable.

Argoon felt the heat getting the better of him. He should probably shuck his trench coat. That'd make him feel better. But, though, as often happened, his mind told him one thing, and his body did something quite different.

He leaned forwards, made sure that his tone was bitter, and no-nonsense.

His father had taught him that.

Had taught him that that was the way to get things in business.

"Why's it say it's cancelled?" Argoon said.

The man adjusted his glasses, gave a vague smile, looked back over his screen, and said, "No, not *cancelled, revoked.*"

"Wha's the difference?"

"Well, the definition we work with for 'cancelled' here is that it means the licence has permanently been taken away." His smile faded a little, maybe because he was aware of the fight he might be setting himself up for. "'Revoked,' well, that means that the licence still *exists*, but it has been suspended temporarily."

"And why's it been . . ." Argoon paused for a moment, wanting to do his best to affect the man's form of speaking . . . "'revoked?'"

With a few clicks of the mouse, but without meeting Argoon's gaze, the man replied, "The licence was revoked for the non-payment of quarterly fees."

"And how'd I get it back then?"

"Well," the man said, then, another click of the mouse later, "you will need to pay a fine to have your licence returned to you."

"How much?" Argoon said, hardly able to prevent the sigh leaking out into his tone of voice.

The man gave a figure Argoon wasn't best pleased with.

But he managed to keep his clenched fists below the table, where the man wouldn't see his rage at this.

"I didn't hear nothing about no quarterly fees."

The man spoke quickly, fluidly, obviously used to dealing with these sorts of protests, and no doubt having some sort of training to deal with them.

Some quick-fire strategies to nip them in the bud.

"Oh, you were sent *three* separate letters," he said, using his thumb and a couple of fingers to illustrate this number, apparently in case Argoon couldn't count.

Argoon shrugged. "Didn't get any of them."

"Then, sir," the man said, turning back to his computer screen, "I suggest that you lodge an official complaint."

He jerked his thumb over his shoulder, indicating—Argoon saw —a desk which stood up on a platform above the rest of the floor full of desks, and behind which sat a severe-looking woman of about sixty, skinny, dressed in a suit, and with wilted, leathered skin dangling off her neck. Wearing glasses too, just like everyone working the desks here seemed to.

He guessed his old dad had been onto something when he'd said that the only thing that offices did to folk was turn their spines all bendy and make their eyes all blurry.

Being a ratter, catching rats the whole time, that meant you didn't run into any of them problems at all. You had to be spry and sharp eyed else . . . well, you wouldn't make much of a ratter at all.

The sign over her desk read, 'Queries' in bold red lettering.

Argoon turned back to the man. "Ain't there nothing you can do . . . you know, with that computer of yours there?" he said, with a nod to the monitor.

The man smiled professionally, and said, "I'm afraid not, sir. You can either elect to pay the fine now, and we shall reactivate your licence, or you shall need to go and register a complaint with my superior at the Queries desk."

Argoon weighed his options.

The woman did look somewhat frightening.

He'd never been good at handling women, young or old, never really knew what to say to them. And as soon as he got into his occupation, told them that he was a ratter, that usually saw off any lingering interest in him.

Fuck 'em, that's what his dad always said, but Argoon also knew that Dad had an interest in him not going off with any woman, going off drawing and pilfering from the business, because, after all, that was the only thing that mattered in the family.

Argoon sometimes thought that he'd like a girlfriend, though, or some company at least.

Maybe he'd get a dog when he cleared all this stuff up about the business licence, yeah, a dog or a cat'd be great for ratting, probably help him out a great deal, all things considered.

"Sir?" the man said, peering over the tops of his glasses.

Argoon looked back at him, gave him a grunt of thanks, and then shoved off to the Queries desk.

3

THE WOMAN was way more severe up close. But, unlike the man that'd seen to him before, she at least looked at him straight in the eye, her lips pressed tight together so that she squeezed all the blood out of them, and gave her skin a greenish tinge.

"Yes?" she said. "How may I help?"

Argoon jerked his head to indicate the desk he'd just come from, and the man sitting over there who was just now seeing to another customer. "He told me that I can't get my business licence because it's been 'revoked,' says I shoulda got a bunch of letters in the post warning me about fees, and because I didn't pay them fees they've taken it away . . . the licence, I mean."

The woman arched an eyebrow, in that way that Argoon was sure meant that she heard this excuse several dozen times a day. He wished there was some way to make her see that he was telling the truth, that he wouldn't do anything wrong if he'd known it was wrong.

She took his details then clicked on her mouse and tapped away at her keyboard, putting all his details into her system. Finally, with a click of her tongue, she looked out from beneath her glasses at him. Her glasses made her pupils seem much larger, like a pair of drain holes, and if he stretched his imagination just a touch, he was almost certain that he could see a pair of furry forms—*rats*—scurrying about in their darkness.

"The letters were sent and received, Mister . . ."

"Argoon Shween," he said.

"Mister Shween," she continued, taking her glasses off, folding them up and then holding them in her hands. She held them tight in her bony, bloodless fingers and rocked them a little, almost like she was rocking a baby or something. "I would advise you to pay the fine and be done with it." She drew breath. "As I'm sure my colleague informed you, if you pay the fine you can be out of here with that licence in your hand in a few minutes."

Argoon thought this over. Thought about the quid he had nestled in the pocket of his trench coat. It wasn't nearly enough, but no way was he going to give this woman the satisfaction of telling her that he simply didn't have the money to pay.

Nah, she'd have to work really hard to get that information all squeezed out of him.

And, anyway, he hadn't received no letters in the first place.

She was the one who was lying.

"Mister Shween?" she said, this time a little testily.

Argoon snapped back to reality, back to the overwhelming polished-up smell that hung about the place, and that vague, distant taste of chewing tobacco in his mouth. His heart was beating quick now, that same quickness it got into when he caught sight of a rat out of the corner of his eye, or heard its squeaking, that moment right before he went after it, went off to pursue it with his wooden mallet dangling down at his side.

He wished he had his wooden mallet on him now, but he hadn't risked bringing it with him down here, to the Business Bureau, knowing from experience, them other damn times he'd had to come down here, that the meatheads on the door would take it off him right away, demand that he leave it behind if he was going to head on into the building.

He stared at her, into them oily pits that were her eyes, and he said, "Wha' is it, wha's it that you're up to, eh? I wanna know, come on!"

She glowered at him. "Mister Shween, please do not raise your voice. I have outlined your options—those letters, the warning letters, they are all marked as received on our system and so the fine stands as being legitimate."

"Are ya . . . are ya," Argoon started, wondering whether he should keep on going, if he should really head on along with finishing the sentence he'd started . . . then decided that he really didn't give a flying fuck, "are ya working with the authorities, eh? Them contractors they brought in to get all the ratting done? That it? Is that it?" he said, rising up out of his seat, and towering over the woman.

He half expected her to start to cowering, just like anyone that he faced up to in the street would do if he gave them enough of his height to worry about.

But she just crossed her arms over her chest, and looked up at him, kind of like a disapproving teacher he'd once had.

And Argoon knew that he'd just got himself into a whole *world* of trouble.

It was only a dim sensation, feeling the hands of the meatheads on him, and their gentle, but firm, grips guiding him on, off the floor of the building, and out towards the daylight which streamed on in through the front doors.

Argoon could hardly get a hold on himself before one of the meatheads gave him a good old shove in the back to send him on his way.

Argoon spun around, raging inside, but at the same time knowing just how useless a fight with these meatheads would turn out . . . why, they'd mince him, and his bones, up into a fine paste. These meatheads they just lived to pump muscle, to make themselves big and strong. While Argoon was quick and wily, and smart on his feet about the back alleys of the city, out here, in plain view, a level playing field, it wasn't really his domain.

And the meatheads seemed to realise it too, both of them, bald-headed, like great big potato sacks wrapped up in suits, turned around and headed back through the sliding doors of the building.

Neither of them so much as cast a glance back over their shoulders to him—to check that he had skittered off on his way.

No matter, though, Argoon knew that this wasn't a problem with this place, with the Business Bureau, he knew just who the real enemy was, the one that'd got in the way of them letters getting delivered.

Them contractors the city had brought in.

And he knew just where they were at.

4

ARGOON TOOK his bedraggled, half-dead van across the city. It was just about a shade of brown, though which one exactly he couldn't really say. And it had dings here, and dents there, the exhaust pipe just about kept its nose up from scraping on along the road beneath him. The windscreen had this sprawling spider web-like crack all over it, and meant that, whenever he wanted to make a left turn, he'd have to lean clear across the passenger seat so as to see the wing mirror there . . . or what remained of it considering that it was just about as clouded up as muddy water.

The engine rattled about, sending its vibrations up through the driver's seat and seemingly directly through his blood and muscle to jangle his bones. First thing he did, after switching on and pulling on out, was to fish for a fresh piece of tobacco. One that'd take away all them awful smells of the Business Bureau, all them memories of them rows and rows of suits and their *desks*.

As he chewed about on the tobacco, he released all them woody tastes that kept him so calm even when everything was all shot to shit around him.

Because, and this was for certain, he was all shot to shit if he couldn't sort this thing about the Working Licence.

No ifs, no buts, he'd be finished.

Plain and simple.

His family too, his ma and pa, the ones that he supported with his ratting.

He pulled on up to his intended location, off on the other side of the city, in one of them districts that seemed to be constantly getting renovated, and then all left behind just as quick.

Peelah District this one was called.

One of them places where there was always a crane about, always builders milling around, and the smell of churning cement thick in the air.

He shipped on past a beaten-down building that had them steel fences all surrounding it, and some yellow tape too, to seal the deal.

It was around here, Argoon knew that, it was his business to know about the competition, to keep himself updated on the latest comings and goings that concerned all manner of ratting in Guynur City, and this case had been no exception whatsoever.

He swept on around the corner a solid ten, fifteen miles per hour too fast, and he felt one of his wheels catch the edge of the curb as he went.

He eyed the billboard up there.

His adversaries.

Them ones that he was sure had done him wrong.

Rapid Rodents.

That was what the sign read.

It was all done in bright orange lettering on a white background, then a frame about it too, all looping and complicated. This kind of happy-smiling, cartoon rat on the sign too as if it was just dying to get itself all ratted.

And, having been a tried and tested ratter, Argoon knew that was way far from the truth.

He parked on up, and then beat on out of his van, trudged his way up the path that led to a temporary shelter that had a sign which marked it out as the Office of the place.

The shelter itself was only a single-storey high, and it looked like a good, stiff breeze would knock it right down flat, just like a bunch of the buildings about here in this district, in the Peelah District.

The reception desk was empty, no one was home apparently, and when he went to check the adjoining room he found that he was equally out of luck.

Nope. Nobody home at all.

He shifted on back out to the street, getting himself wound up even more, and chewing even harder on his tobacco, so hard in fact that after a particularly tough chew, he tasted blood welling up from his tongue and oozing its way about the inside of his mouth.

He couldn't give a shit.

Anything else could be patched up later.

What he needed right now was that fucking Working Licence.

And them punks what'd got in his way.

Just when he thought his anger couldn't really get all that much stronger, he reached on into his van and withdrew his wooden mallet. The one that he used to smush rats.

He really didn't know what he had in mind, though he did have just a few ideas blasting on through his brain.

He ended up having to wait for a solid twenty minutes, there on the curb, till he watched the brand-new, light-blue van, what with that same cartoon rat emblazoned on the side of it, just like the signpost for their whole damn place.

As he stood there, on the curb, Argoon clutched the handle of his mallet all the tighter.

The van pulled up, its back door slid on open and four people all stepped out of it, all of them dressed in that same light-blue tone, all of them wearing overalls zipped right up to their chins. Each of them carried this kind of steel rucksack that was rectangular and looked awfully bulky. And slipped onto the side of the rucksack was a kind of thing that resembled the nozzle of a hose. He wondered about that for a bit, and then reached the conclusion that they had poison there. They had poison there on their backs.

Each of them had baseball caps too, all of them with the same logo stamped on the front.

Argoon wondered just how they felt walking about all day dressed like that, to him they just looked a bunch of clowns that'd somehow got it into their heads that they'd all go out, get themselves some uniforms, and then play at being ratters for the day.

These people weren't ratters.

Argoon was sure of it.

Ratting was in his blood, and these people weren't it.

Two men, and two women, but they all resembled each other in those loose-fitting overalls, and the way they all looked just as bored as one another did.

Argoon picked out the leader of the bunch, the one that he'd picked out a long while ago, back when he'd done his initial research of Rapid Rodents.

Her name was Mishell Duggunal and she was the owner of the whole operation, she had recently got given the licence to run her vans all about town, to have her Rapid Rodents people all going about and sweeping up all the ratting business.

All the business there was.

No room for the little guy.

But that was going to change.

Right now, that was.

Argoon stomped on after her, heading after the group of them guys in their overalls, all headed on back to that temporary shelter that, he guessed, served as some sort of base for them. None of them looked back, or appeared to hear him stamping on, following their footsteps, and that was good.

Surprise was good.

The weight of his wooden mallet in his right hand felt good.

Argoon waited a moment till they'd all crossed on into the temporary shelter, and then he went in after them, taking in again the flimsy structure.

Ms Duggunal was already taking off that rucksack of hers, flipping her blond hair out from the straps of it, when Argoon caught her pretty little smudgy green-brown eyes, gave her that menacing smirk of his, the one that he'd practised a good amount of times in side alleys, on his own, right when he'd been clutching that wooden mallet of his.

Like he did now.

She looked to him, to his face, to his expression, and then her gaze dropped on down to his wooden mallet which he held at his thigh. He watched her lips pucker up and her eyes widen in surprise. She seemed to have to drag her eyes kicking and screaming back upwards so as she could look back at him again.

"Who . . . who . . ."

Argoon cut her right off there, ignored the three sets of other eyes all staring right at him. "Wha' you done with my Working Licence, eh? Whatcha said to them people? How've you gone tinkering about in my business?" He felt every vein in his body brimming full of hot, sticky blood, and he squeezed the handle of the mallet tighter still.

He got his answer right now.

He was determined about it.

"Don' play games," Argoon continued. "You and me, we hash this out now, ya hear me?"

Ms Duggunal flashed a glance about the others in overalls, her employees, and then she looked on back to Argoon. "You . . . you won't *hurt* anyone, will you?"

Argoon lifted his wooden mallet up, right up above his head, like he did when he went for a big smush on one of them king rats he often cornered down a gloomy old alleyway—them big, juicy rats that just seemed to pop on out after midnight.

And then he brought his mallet down.

5

ARGOON'S MALLET came on down with an almighty *thwack!*

The snapping of wood, and the mallet cracking on through it. Through the desk.

Woody dust rose up in the room, and he could hear the screams of the others all reverberating about his head. But he didn't really hear them. They were just like a kind of white noise, and they meant nothing to him at all. As far as he cared, they might've been from the direct cause of his mallet and it would've had no effect on him.

Because he was ratting now.

He was flushing out some *real* big rats right now.

Argoon drew back, every muscle in his body tight, and he felt a great big exhale just flush right out of him. He brought the mallet into his chest, protected it there as if it was a baby that he'd just gone and found and picked on up out of some long grasses. That some teenager mother had left there for the rats to take away.

The silence in the room just about swirled about him, and Argoon felt his skin all prickling up into pimples, felt several cold shudders pass right through his blood stream. He wanted, more than anything, to get on out of here, out of the stifling air of this room, and head into the cool night air.

Go to ratting.

But some business had to be taken care of first.

And so he eyed Ms Duggunal, took her in with his gaping eyes. Forced them green-brown eyes onto his. Though her bottom lip quivered, she got the words out fine, and without any hesitation, no sign that she was frightened at all, really.

"Wait outside," she said, to the other three of them, the others in the overalls.

For a moment, no one moved at all, and Argoon clenched his wooden mallet just a little tighter still. He brought it away from his chest, and held it before him, as if he might swing away again if anyone decided on causing a scene.

No one did.

Them other three, they all filed on out of the room without any more of a fuss, leaving Argoon alone with just Ms Duggunal.

She seemed almost frozen to the spot, behind that desk there—the desk that Argoon had only just gone and battered clean into two pieces.

"What do you want?" she said, arms down at her sides, and her face clean of any expression at all.

"Working Licence," Argoon repeated. "You people—I know what you done."

She made to shake her head, and then her eyes fell back onto his mallet, and it seemed like she got better ideas about the whole thing. "Uh, I . . . I don't know what you're talking about."

Argoon sneered and shook the mallet about some. "Dontcha play games with me, yeah? I know jus' wha' you did, jus' came from the Business Bureau, didn' I?"

"Please," she said, again dropping her glance to the mallet, apparently she was getting something of an obsession with it.

Maybe she'd never seen a proper ratter at work before, and didn't know just what kinds of tools real ratters carried about.

He could teach her a lesson if she liked.

If she wanted to learn how to *really* ply the trade she was robbing him, and his family, of.

"Them letters," Argoon said, repeating what that severe-looking lady back at the place had told him. "They said that we got some warnings—*three* warnings about not paying the rates on the Working Licence, and now they say I gotta pay a fine, how's that sound to you?"

Still all wide-eyed, but managing to break off that fixation of hers on the mallet, she looked up at him, and said, "Why don't you just pay the fine?"

Argoon opened his mouth, mentally ready to tell her just what the problem was, and then he remembered his pa's words of advice, about him not telling anyone outside of the business any more than he had to about it.

"Matter of principle," he said, again parroting something that his pa had always told him to go on about when people got all pissing and picky like she was getting.

"I . . . I . . . *really*," she said, "I have no idea at all about this Working Licence, about your Working Licence."

"Then what about your business"—he couldn't help but give a slight sneer—"what about *Rapid Rodents*, huh? Only makes sense for them to take care of the competition, dunnit? I mean, with us independent traders out the way it'll be a paradise for you lot, with your governmental contracts and all."

She clamped her eyes shut a couple of moments, as if she was trying to clear out some mad thought from inside her brain. Maybe she was thinking on making a grab for his mallet, on turning the tables on him. One thing was for certain, if she planned on doing that then she'd really have to be hellacious quick and, to be honest, Argoon couldn't see that she had it in her. She looked like a solid businesswoman, unafraid to get her hands dirty, but it was another matter entirely for her to go nose to nose with him and his strength, and his quickness he had on account of the years and years of ratting.

But let her try.

Just see what might happen.

She made no move forwards when she opened her eyes, neither did she say anything more about the business, and Argoon was starting to get awfully pissed off with this whole deal, and his fingers were getting all itchy as he held onto the handle of the mallet.

He decided that now was the time for him to push this thing forwards.

He took a step forwards, another one.

Raised his mallet in his hand.

That was enough for her to flare her nostrils, and for her eyebrows to just about fly right up and out of her forehead. She held up her hands as if they'd save her if he *really* got it into his mind to go all mental-like with his mallet.

"Look," she said, her voice sounded just a touch taut now . . . a little closer to becoming shrill, "I *was* the owner, this *used* to be my business, but I took on a different role, training up the first batch of ground-level recruits, y'know? I sold out the business when I got the contract with the government, a few weeks back, I only agreed to stay on here till I'd got the rest up to speed—got their new employees up to speed."

"And who's the owner now?" Argoon asked.

She blinked several times, fluttering her silvery eyelashes.

Argoon squeezed the handle of his mallet tighter. It shook a little in his fist as he did it.

Finally, she cracked.

She gave him the name and the address of the new owner.

His *home* address . . . nothing less.

Argoon allowed himself the faintest of smiles as he slid himself back into his van, got himself back into the driver's seat.

This might be over soon.

And then he could go on back to ratting.

6

ARGOON JUST ABOUT hit the rush hour as he pulled on out of Peelah District, away from all them constructions works, stuff like that. All them cars on the roads were tail-to-head-lights, and he could hardly see anything for the smog which wafted on up, and which pumped on out through the ventilation ducts on the dashboard of the van.

He had crammed on in another three pieces of tobacco and had got to chewing them just as furiously as he had the first. He knew it was important to calm down, and that nothing good ever got done when he was stuck into one of his hot-headed tempers.

But it was difficult, because he knew just what was on the line.

He knew that his family were on the line, and that his ma and pa were depending on him making things work, on getting this fine thrown out with the rubbish.

He thought about things, about how he'd been sailing just a little too close to the breeze for a longish while now. How he'd had trouble drumming up business but, at the same time, hadn't wanted to say anything at all to his pa.

He'd thought he'd be disappointed in him.

That he wouldn't want to hear excuses.

But maybe, just maybe, before all the finance issues had got on top of him, he should've said something. Maybe his pa could've suggested something for him to try.

But it was too late for that now.

Now it was down to Argoon to take care of the business.

Argoon first got worried as he hit the super slick tarmacked roads of the Fleed, that area where all the upper-class folk of Guynur seemed to stick down their homesteads. Plenty of towering blocks of flats, all of them near enough buffed to a shine.

And meatheads to spare.

Argoon felt like he might get himself pummelled just for driving on through the district, the way that he saw them suited-up, bald-headed meatheads all turning their fat necks in his direction. And their piggy eyes all hid behind their blacked-out sunglasses.

But he'd come too far to turn back now.

If he left, he would return home with nothing.

No business, no future, they'd starve.

Argoon was sure that he'd have to take up scrounging . . . and everyone knew just where that road led down, how it led on down to getting into being an addict, and worse.

For him it'd mean that his ma and pa would starve, because neither of them could do work any longer.

They looked to him to provide for them now.

And he was *determined* that he wouldn't disappoint them.

He rattled his van on up to the building that Ms Duggunal had said to him was where the new owner of Rapid Rodents lived.

There was something that struck Argoon right away about the owner, and that was that he wasn't short at all of a decent quid or too, not if the buffed-up glass building, towering up above him to what must've been fifteen or sixteen storeys into the sky, was anything at all to go by.

Or the meathead that was wearing his suit and sunglasses like the others that he'd seen about the district, and who was approaching the van, dipping his hand into the inside pocket of his jacket.

There was some things that Argoon could use his mallet against, but guns weren't one of them. Not even a Pictlewhip, one of them small ones that fuzz and meatheads all ran about town with.

But he just stayed his ground there, on the driveway which led on down to the underground car park of the building, knowing clear in his mind that this was his only chance at saving his business, at keeping his ma and pa safe from harm.

Of giving himself some kind of a future.

He'd get it all sorted out now, he was sure of it.

The meathead made a gesture for him to roll down his window, that twirly motion with his index finger, and Argoon did what he was told, not even having a thing in mind as the meathead said to him, "Better hop it now, pal."

Argoon clenched the steering wheel tight, with no intention of doing what this meathead said, he had no option now but to keep up what he was doing . . . if he was to keep his families' heads above water.

"Come to speak with Mister Neels," he said, speaking the name that Ms Duggunal had given him.

The meathead allowed the flap of his jacket to open right up, so that Argoon could clearly see his shoulder holster there, and the Pictlewhip snug inside, all ready to get pulled out and pointed at him.

Argoon was pretty sure that the meathead wouldn't blow his brains all over the place out here in front of this fancy-looking building, though, and he clung onto that belief.

"He's expecting me," Argoon said, keeping his voice straight, feeling those pleasant, warming waves as the tobacco took hold of his muscles and seemed to numb them, and give him fresh confidence. "Tell him I'm a ratter—one of them that his fucking business has done its best to do away with, yeah?"

The meathead cocked his head to one side, glanced up at the building above him, as if he might see Mister Neels staring right down at him, wanting to see what the hold up was with his guest here at the gate. Then he turned back to Argoon.

"Listen, bud, I'll put the call through, but if he won't see you—if Mister Neels won't see you, then you'd best be rocketing yourself right off down back where you came from, and if you so much as show yourself about these parts again I'll have no hesitation sticking a bullet through your forehead for your trouble." He paused, not to catch a breath, more likely to freshen up that poisonous bile he was spitting. "Dontcha think that I ain't got the privilege to do just whatever I want, I kill scroungers by the dozen, ya hear?"

Argoon flushed out his thoughts, turned his mind away from this meathead talk that he heard just about every time he had the misfortune of having to interact with them.

Oh, sure, they liked to dish out threats, liked to make themselves feel seven foot tall, but he knew, more than likely, he was just going on about this stuff to scare him.

And Argoon had a lifetime of experience behind him that stopped him getting scared.

He had never been afraid of the dark as a kid, or anything that went *scuttle* in the night, and he sure as hell wasn't afraid of no meathead like this one . . . no matter how nice the suit he wore was or how much heat he was packing.

Argoon kept on facing forwards, staring down into the underground car park, and his destination, ahead of him, then he said, "You jus' make tha' call, bro, okay?"

The meathead fixed him with a steely stare, one of those stares that just kept on lingering forever and a day, and then he retreated from the side of Argoon's van, disappeared off into the glass booth that sat beside the barrier that blocked off entry into the underground car park.

Argoon had no idea what to expect. He had just been improvising. Just buying time, really. He hadn't wanted to look like a fool, but he might look like an even bigger one now that he had got the meathead to go and phone up Mister Neels . . . because Mister Neels had no idea who he was.

He watched the meathead inside of that glass booth with the phone to his ear, calling up to Mister Neels's apartment, and he watched the man's stony face. Couldn't read anything in the reaction on the other end of the phone. The meathead showed no expression at all.

But, when the meathead came on back out from the booth, he was buttoning his jacket up, apparently wanting to keep his hands busy, and that was just fine with Argoon just as long as he didn't think to whip that gun of his out and fire him clean through the forehead.

The meathead said nothing. He just punched a button on the side of the barrier, and the barrier swooped on up, allowing Argoon to drive his van down the slope, and inside the building.

Argoon didn't feel anything at all about the thing.

He didn't feel bad or good, or even glad that Mister Neels had agreed to see him.

All he could think of was his wooden mallet lying on the passenger seat beside him.

7

ARGOON TOOK the lift on up to the penthouse, which was up on the top floor of the apartment building. On his way in, the meatheads, standing on the door, found his wooden mallet and took it right off him.

After they found that, they wouldn't let him take his leather trench coat in with him either, they demanded that he leave it outside.

Argoon felt somewhat naked just in his once-white, now-grey shirt tucked into the waistband of his black jeans. But he went on into the penthouse, a meathead standing at either side of him.

For a second Argoon couldn't deal with the bright daylight that flooded on in through the windows that occupied all the walls of the penthouse, or the beige, plush furniture that occupied just about every single nook and cranny of the place.

Neither could he handle the soft and thick carpets down beneath his boots, and he couldn't help feeling, what with them suited meatheads at his elbows, that he was pretty underdressed for this whole thing.

For this 'meeting' . . . whatever that might mean.

He had toyed with the idea of coming here to threaten Mister Neels, of staking his claim in some kind of way, showing him that there was no way that he would be able to flush out a family business that'd been running the city for three generations.

But now Argoon felt like it was Mister Neels who threatened him.

Mister Neels himself lounged about on one of the extremely soft-looking sofas, one of his arms draped over the side of it, with a cigar smoking away between his fingers. He wore a silver-grey suit, with a crisp shirt and a matching tie beneath. He was stick-thin, and had a skinny, grey-haired moustache which traced his upper lip.

For some reason, Argoon had expected him to be fat.

Maybe that was just what his pa had taught him about high-flying businessmen, about the ones who called the Big Shots in the city and who made life hard for Little Guys everywhere.

Mister Neels had his head clean shaved, and all buffed up to a shine.

For a second, Argoon dizzily wondered just what he put on his scalp to get it to gleam that way. He decided, whatever it was, that it was expensive.

Mister Neels dabbed out his cigar in an ashtray on the mahogany coffee table before him, and then he got up to his feet. He extended his hand towards Argoon, and a light smile played out on his lips. Only then did Argoon notice the blank, vanilla-coloured envelope sitting there on the coffee table too.

Argoon took his hand from him and gave it a firm shake.

Just as his pa had taught him.

"Well, hello there . . ." Mister Neels said, his voice trailing off as he waited for Argoon to state his name.

"Argoon Shween," Argoon said, meeting Mister Neels's coppery eyes—eyes that never seemed to stay still for a moment.

They reminded Argoon of a rat's eyes, and them eyes always put him on edge, made him think twice just what he was doing, and just what the rat might be planning.

Because rats, they was always planning something.

"Please," Mister Neels said, gesturing behind him, to the beige sofa, "sit."

Argoon waited a couple of beats of his heart and then he did what Mister Neels said.

The sofa was soft, and seemed to absorb all his weight. It was like sinking down into a featherbed, and he wondered just what material this thing was made of.

The smoke that lingered in the air from the recently extinguished cigar had the effect of putting Argoon a little at ease. The meatheads had insisted that he spit out his tobacco too before they'd allowed him to enter into the penthouse.

Argoon looked to Mister Neels, still smiling, as he draped his arm over the back of the sofa, as if this was just a normal day, as if Argoon hadn't just shown himself here, a totally unexpected guest brandishing a wooden mallet.

"A ratter?" Mister Neels said, that smile of his only getting wider.

"Uh huh," Argoon replied, looking over the meatheads who were still intensely watching them, each of them with their hands clutched behind their backs for now, but surely ready to reach into their jackets at a moment's notice for the Pictlewhips they kept there.

Argoon tried to put it out of his mind, and turned his attention back to Mister Neels who'd gone and picked up the envelope that'd been lying on the coffee table.

"I've been expecting you," Mister Neels said.

Argoon couldn't hardly believe that. "Yeah?"

Mister Neels gave a slight nod. "I've got quite a few calls from ratters, from ratters working all ends of Guynur, wanting to come down here to see me." He grinned wider still. "Wanting *assurances*." He stretched his fingers out as they rested on the back of the sofa. "That *is* what you want, isn't it?"

Argoon swallowed hard, breathing the fading cigar smoke into his lungs, and feeling it cool his blood, unwind his fraught muscles. This'd been a long day and he was looking forwards to just getting himself thrown down into bed, and having it all over with at last.

But first he had to do his best to save the family business.

This might well be his last chance to do so.

He had to concentrate a hundred per cent.

"Mister Neels," Argoon began, "I only came down here because your company—Rapid Rodents—they gone and done something fishy about our Working Licence, and the Business Bureau they say I gotta pay a fine if I want it back." He paused, met his eye briefly. "You get me?"

Mister Neels pursed his lips, apparently considering this. "That's quite an accusation you're making there." He tilted his head slightly to one side. "Do you happen to have any evidence to support those claims of yours?"

Argoon thought on it harder. Then shook his head. "No, sir, but who else has gone and done it? I know how these things work, know how it's important to your company to flush out the competition and to take hold of the whole thing." He paused. "My pa taught me that."

"And your 'pa,'" Mister Neels said, "he was also a ratter?"

"Yes, sir."

"Hmm."

"A family business—three generations," Argoon said.

Mister Neels tapped the rim of his envelope against his knuckles. Argoon stared at those knuckles, all fresh, unbroken, uncalloused skin—the types of knuckles that came from doing no real labour in life . . . 'no-good' skin was what his pa would've termed it.

"Yes," Mister Neels said, staring down at the envelope now, "that's the issue, isn't it? I mean, I'm all for nostalgia, in thinking back on the wonders that independent business has done for Guynur City." He glanced up. "But the times are changing now, Mister Shween, you must have noticed. You must have noticed how it's more difficult for family businesses, such as your own, to find work now, for them to find fresh clients, hmm?"

Argoon thought this over long and hard, again not wanting to show his hand, to give away all them company secrets his pa was always chewing into him not to tell a soul about.

How he had to keep the upper hand through any kind of business conversation.

But, at the same time, Argoon knew that he'd got right to the end of the path now, that there was simply no other way to go, and that it was time for him to just fess up.

To get a *solution* to this thing.

"Yes, sir," Argoon said, averting his gaze, and looking on out the windows instead, to the cityscape and to the setting sun as it came on down with its grapefruit glare over the rooftops. "It's been gettin' hard for quite some time."

Mister Neels nodded to himself as if this was the answer he'd expected.

Argoon supposed, if Mister Neels really was telling the truth about having had other ratters in here, other independent ratters coming to him, that he'd had this meeting over and over.

Mister Neels let the silence unwind about the penthouse a few seconds, and then he settled his eyes upon Argoon's once again, and said, "Look here, in this envelope I think I've got a very attractive offer, one which, I think you'll find, will rid you of all your troubles —all those stresses and strains, all those *responsibilities*," he said almost spitting the word.

He tapped the envelope against his knuckles once more, then continued, "In here, you shall find your future, an *assured* future."

Argoon felt his throat dry up. Now the smell of the cigar smoke had pretty much gone completely from the air, and he could only smell that stomach-crunching stench of polish thickening all about him. That smell that reminded him of the Business Bureau. He dreaded going on back there . . . it'd be the end of him, he was sure of it.

Almost positive.

Argoon took the envelope that Mister Neels held on out to him.

8

A S ARGOON SAT THERE, in his van, down in the underground car park of the building, the envelope torn open and discarded on the seat beside him, he read on over the letter once again.

It was an offer.

Plain and simple.

A yes or a no for him.

Mister Neels was offering cash money for his business, for the *family* business. It really wasn't anything special at all, at least not as much as his pa would have priced it at . . . but, all things considered, Argoon knew that he'd be lucky to get anything at all for the business, the state it was in at the moment.

So he was best off just taking whatever offer he could get.

The payoff would be enough to get him and his family through the next few months, get them through it with nice, full bellies and a warm house about them.

In addition to the payoff, there was a contract for Argoon to come on board with Rapid Rodents, for him to take on a job that'd pay him double what he'd earned in the last year of his own business.

It made sense.

Everything about it made sense.

But, still, he'd have to find a way of telling Pa.

He'd be devastated for sure.

There was no other way, though, not if he wanted to survive.

He would have to accept the job.

It was difficult for him to think about himself in one of them light-blue overalls, with that rucksack chocked full of poison on his back. Didn't seem like the right way to go about it . . . but, all the same, it was *their* way. There would be no more wooden mallets, none of the old ways of ratting. Wouldn't just be ratting either. He'd be diversifying right out into other pests and such.

But, he guessed, that was just change at the end of the day.

And there was nothing at all he could do about change.

Before he'd so much as slipped the keys into his ignition, and listened to the whipplesnife, the magical fuel that powered just about everything in Guynur, churn on through the pipes and pump on through the engine of his van, he had decided on what he was going to do.

He would take Mister Neels's offer—he would accept.

And that would be the end.

No matter what Pa said, he had to live in the real world now, there was no preventing it.

It was like his heart had had a weight lifted right off the top of it as he powered on up out of the underground car park and into the setting sunlight that poured out over all Guynur, and he couldn't help but give the meathead standing at the glass booth a salute and a smile as he drove on by, because everything was going to be different now.

And he had to admit to himself that he was, all things considered, fairly happy about it.

Now he could just turn his mind to the ratting.

The only part of the business that he really loved.

So, with the unfolded letter, the offer for the family business, and the contract lying there on the passenger seat of the van, he drove on down into the mounted-up, rush-hour traffic and headed on for home.

This'd be a tricky discussion, but he was certain they'd all come out of it for the better.

It was what he and his family needed right now.

Nothing could change that.

THE CAN

FEEDING TIME in the zoo, that was what it was like.
Jee-zuz.

All about Paulin his fellow inmates stamped their feet, and did their wolf whistling. Others of them were clattering their steel bedpans against the iron bars of their gaol cells.

Paulin squeezed his own bars tighter, felt that shrill tingle of nerves all the way across the bridge of his knuckles, and felt a slight ticklish surge to his bollocks. Felt the sweat soaking the back of his sallow gaol overalls.

The perfume plumed up in the air, in an invisible cloud.

All them odours were like memories more than something actually going up his nose, all them half-forgotten things, like jasmine, and roses, and lavender.

Paulin could almost get them smells so thick in his nose that he thought he could chomp on them . . . even though chomping on any of them things was a pretty bad idea.

He could feel himself salivating, could feel his spit all pooling in that gap he had in the bottom row of his teeth so he had to keep sucking it back.

His spit tasted all bitter but, at the same time, pretty tasteless.

The dozens of girls all lined up there, in the middle of the cell-block, all of them wearing their fur coats of all different shapes and sizes. Clutched up to their throats. The only flesh on show below the knees. They always came in like this. All matching. Paulin always wondered just whether they got the madam to look after that for them, if she maybe chose whatever it was that the girls were all going to wear for that evening. For the boys in the Can.

It was strange, the way that he knew that this was all public, like how all his fellow inmates were all standing up at the bars of their own cells, all of them looking down on that sad little concrete patch with all the prozzies standing about, like meat for market, but how it also felt like this was all just for him.

In his life, Paulin had always known he was the centre of the world. That wasn't *feel*, yeah, some people *feel* they're the centre of the world, but Paulin knew for sure.

Knew that the whole fucking revolving globe that was Schwyn, he knew that it went round just so that he'd be able to dance to whatever tune he wanted.

That was what had got him into trouble.

That's what had got him locked up here, in the Can.

Locked up in the biggest gaol in all Guynur City.

That'd been the reason why it'd been just fine for him to kill people when they got in his way, just fine for him to smash in their skulls, leave their crumpled-up bodies in back alleys while he went back to the pub for another drink.

Just his luck that one day he'd bashed in the wrong skull, got himself on the wrong side of the Council.

What the *fuck* had a councilman's kid been doing in a drinking hole like that, anyway?

That always beat him, to be honest, how all them rich pricks felt attracted to the dirtiest places in the city, felt like they had to gauge just how good what they'd got was.

How good they'd got it.

Well, that councilman's kid got a pretty good idea before he got his skull all bashed in, didn't he?

Paulin put them posh pricks out of his mind, and turned his attention back to the more important matter of the ladies all down there below.

His eyesight had never been all that good, and here, in the Can, in the dim light . . . others might've called it *darkness* . . . he could barely make out the prozzies' faces, could've been trannies for all he knew, thinking about it, not that that mattered, not after spending some serious time in the Can.

Anything with warm flesh would do him fine.

He could just about make out that there was a redhead among them, that was his favourite, the one that he really liked the most, though he'd never got one once, not in his whole time in the Can. His mother had had red hair, his sister too, and when he'd had hair, before he'd got all bald, his hair had been red also.

Sometimes, lying on his bunk at night, his hands all clutched on his belly bulging from the rotten scrounge they served up by way of dinner in the Can, he'd make a go at psychoanalysing himself, try to work out just why he thought the way he did . . . why he was so attracted to redheads, if it, maybe, said something about him, if he wanted to fuck his mother or his sister, or himself, maybe.

Thinking didn't get you nowhere, though, not in the Can.

And even if you did manage to get out the Can, out beyond them fifty-foot concrete walls, what with the coiled-up barbed wire and all, and the searchlights, and the search party that'd come after you . . . well, you'd still be in Guynur, and just like Paulin had worked out in all his forty-six years of life, out there in Guynur, well, you might as well have just have been in a gaol anyway.

Bastards, there was no escape.

Not really.

He could hear his bunkmate, Fworte, beside him, making this strange kind of chattering sound, almost like something between a throaty chuckle, and a hyperactive giggle. He could smell his bulky, sweaty mass from here, just like a wad of meat left to rot on a windowsill for a week, and all turned green about the edges, and all flavour of it long gone too.

Yeah, if there was any justice in the world, then Fworte could use just a little seasoning before the screws all let him rot, just like that.

Not that Paulin cared any, because Fworte fell somewhat outside his zone of attention, being that Fworte was another person, another breathing, scrabbling, struggling, other person who wasn't Paulin at all.

Fworte had that kind of wispy, clown hair, and when he got all sweaty, all hot and bothered, it got all curled up and puffier.

Though he wore his gaol overalls with the arms all cut off so as to show off his bulging biceps, and them tattoos he had all painted on of weird fairies and the like, Paulin knew he was soft, had worked him out as being soft.

Why, on the third night sharing the cell with Fworte, he'd stopped clutching his shank to his chest, ready to thrust him through the gut or the throat, whichever appeared first.

But it turned out, if Fworte was queer, that he knew who was boss about the place.

And Paulin had ideas in the way of arse-fucking.

Yeah, like *no* fucking ideas about it.

Paulin pressed his cheeks up between the cool iron bars, and looked down on the prozzies, all of them being led off in a line now, the lead screw, Gudders, leading them on their way, out off that concrete patch right in the middle of the cellblock.

This was the way they always did it, the screws always brought the prozzies into that place, in the middle of the cellblock. To begin with Paulin had wondered why, wondered at the point of it. But then he'd twigged it, got right on top of the matter. Realised it right when Paulin shanked his first victim, an inmate who'd had the fucking nerve to cut him up in the lunch queue. It was weird that, the way the screws did almost nothing, save for hold him back to keep him from finishing the fucker off, and take his shank away, but he'd discovered just what his punishment was the next time the prozzies came to visit.

How his name was just never called on the register.

He could still remember the feeling of his balls near enough busting open. Waiting for his name. How he'd been hopping up onto the balls of his feet like a little doggy all eager to get a peek at some food on the kitchen counter, some shit like that.

But the screws hadn't listened to him.

Nope, not an inch.

And then the prozzies had been led away, they'd headed back off through that concrete patch in the centre of the cellblock, and been taken away for another month.

That'd been his punishment.

That was the point of showing them off.

To show any unruly inmates just what it was they were missing . . . and make them think twice before they tried any shit again.

From what Paulin had seen of it with his inexpert eye, he thought that it was a pretty effective tactic, all things considered, what with how when an inmate got a glint in his eye, and a shank in his hand, he was just as likely to think through the whole deal twice, maybe three times, before he did something he'd regret.

The smarter ones did, anyway.

And Paulin had always thought of himself as smarter than all.

They'd just caught him, that was it.

And who gave a shit, anyway.

Guynur City was the real gaol.

2

T HE SCREWS called out Paulin's name in order, just like it should've been, and the screws came along to drag him off past the cells, to see all of the recently serviced inmates, most of them lying back on their beds, some of them blowing plumes of smoke up to the ceiling in the dribble of moonlight that managed to get on in through the tiny barred windows.

Paulin didn't pay no attention to any of the cries from any of the inmates, the ones off opposite him, to them rows of cells, all five floors of them, all of them facing into one another. He knew that some of the ones calling out were the inmates who were being punished, who wouldn't be allowed their conjugal.

And he didn't give a pissing shit.

Because he was just taking what was his.

This was the least he deserved here.

The screws padded him down, checking him for weapons or whatever else. They passed him through the double-locking doors, then along the narrow, concrete hallways that flickered with buzzing half-dead light bulbs.

The iron door, the one with the reinforced glass, with the rivets all punched in around the rim of it, it was wide open, almost like it was asking him in.

Paulin's mouth felt dry, and he could feel his gut tighten just a little bit.

Nervous?

Just a little maybe.

But soon he'd take care of that.

He cleared his throat, and popped the collar of his overalls, and tried out his best swagger, though the twinge at the base of his spine made it difficult for him to walk with anything that resembled fluidity. It was a real trick to be fluid when you got them types of pains all the time.

The screws at his heels kept up the rigid *snap* of their heels. But he could easily forget about them. He could put them right out of his mind.

He stopped when he reached the threshold to the room, he held back for just a moment, took his time, before he took that final step over and into the place.

The Whoring Room, as the inmates spoke about it among themselves, and the Conjugal Relations Conduit as it was known to the screws. It looked just like it always did, that peeling, beige wallpaper, with that spangled, wiry, black-inked design flowering out all over the place, the bricked up window, on account of preventing escapes.

Paulin turned slowly. Starting at the floor first with his eyes. Always liking to suspend the mystery of the thing. Leave himself as long as possible to suck this all up, and to tuck it all away in his mind so as to mine his memories in his bunk for the long and dry month ahead of him.

The saggy, battered-up old mattress which lay on top of the all-creaked-out, iron-framed bed. It was a kind of cigarette-butt brown, and had stuffing seeping out of it from just about every tear.

Then he moved to the bare foot. The one that was laid, sole down, on the concrete floor. And he saw the burgundy nail polish on the toes, the kind of dull shine of it from the flickering lights above.

Her skin was pale, and she had a scattering of freckles, here and there.

His heart fluttered in his chest, and he almost dared not to look up at her, to examine her for himself. But he knew that he must.

He must do it.

Because that was the reason he was here, there was nothing else other than this room. Right here and right now. And this . . . now, now was the time for him to see.

He drew her into him slowly, like he was a swimmer coming up for air after a long dive, after gliding along the bottom of the pool, feeling them slick tiles flow past against his skin.

Back to the real world, and yet also going away again.

Her throat, slick skinned, freckled like her shins, like the bare foot she'd exposed to him, and then, in a single, swift motion, he took in her face, took in her *red* hair.

Yes. She was here. She was his. That long-thought-of dream.

She was real. And now.

3

PAULIN FELT the blood rush about his system, and tickle its way through his veins. It was like he could feel himself a ticking bomb, all set to explode if someone was just to give him so much as a tap on the shoulder.

Kind of far away, he heard the twin *snap* of them screws' heels as they headed off away from him, leaving him for now. Far enough away to give them the illusion of privacy, but close enough to hear a girlie screaming out for help.

Yes, they'd come running if she asked them.

Paulin could hardly summon the courage to look her in the eye, and when he did finally, he saw that she had pale-brown eyes, what was that called? . . . Hazel, that was it, though it made him think more about walnuts, or almonds, that was what it made him think about.

She gave him a gentle smile, the skin around her mouth creasing just a little. With her gentle, fragile fingers, fingers that'd snap like toothpicks if Paulin wanted them to, smoothed down the stirred-up bed sheet beside her. It was like she was absentmindedly smoothing all the wrinkles out.

She wore a crimson corset that hoiked her breasts up into an unnatural position maybe only an inch from her throat. And her lips, too, were all painted that same shade of red. He guessed that none of the other inmates had complained, hadn't paid attention to, the slightly different tone that she had on her toenails.

Or that her hair was more of an orange, flame-red, than a crimson like the corset and the lipstick she used.

"Come on, now," she said, her voice sounding fragile, and

womanly, but one that he knew could just as easily take on a shrewish shrill if given the chance.

She could get insistent if she wanted.

Paulin had a hard time keeping his guts in his stomach. This was it. All that he'd ever dreamed about, for so long, for ever since he'd been in the Can.

"You 'right there?" she said.

Paulin managed to meet them hazel eyes of hers, and to steer them onto his own, and to stop himself from showing how much he trembled. "I . . . I been dreaming of you."

She arched her eyebrows just a touch, and her smile got just a little wider.

Only then did Paulin think of what a stupid thing that was to say and, no doubt, just about half of the inmates that'd been in here had said just the same . . . or along them lines.

"That's sweet, honey," she said, "why don't you come and sit yourself here and we'll talk about it, huh?"

Paulin stayed still. On the stilted, bricky air, he could smell her, that treacle-scented odour, and it sent a thrill right to the pit of his stomach. She made it sound so easy, so simple, and that made him think he was stupid, that he was acting like a fucking child because he was just standing about and gawping here.

Finally, he managed to get himself out of his stupor, and took them few steps over to the mattress, and he sat himself down there. Heard the very slight *creak* of the mattress beneath him. But he clasped his hands in his lap, and he faced forwards, never taking his eyes off the design of the wallpaper ahead of him. Afraid to look at her.

Maybe he thought she'd disappear.

That'd be the worst he could imagine.

She couldn't disappear, not now.

He felt her hand brush his neck, and it sent chills skittering down his spine. Her skin was delicate and soft, and he could feel that her hands hadn't been overworked. He guessed that she'd been a prozzy just about the whole of her life, yeah, that'd figure.

"You feeling all right, honey?"

Paulin feigned like he didn't hear at all, and didn't dare look around, look her in her face, in them eyes of hers. It was just too much for him to achieve.

He felt her fingers work themselves upwards, up his neck, massaging the back of his skull as she went, and he could feel a thousand different thrills, all of them springing right through him, and dancing on his nerves.

He wished the world could end, right here and now, because he was certain that, in this position, with this woman with him, that he was truly in the centre of the world.

That all Schwyn had stopped to watch this.

Out in the hallway, he heard a cough of one of the screws.

He noticed her head jerk upwards at it, and look off in that direction.

It was a warning mechanism, though Paulin had never experienced it himself before. He knew how he was acting—that the way he was acting just wasn't how a sexed-up inmate acted in these sessions, and he knew that he'd got the girl worried.

She probably thought he might lash out at any minute.

. . . When that couldn't be further from the truth.

Speak.

He had to speak.

Didn't make sense not to.

Though she continued to massage his scalp with her fingertips, he could also feel that she was growing a little hesitant, kind of like that feeling that if she stopped doing what she was doing then she might start shuddering, or something.

And he didn't want her to feel nervous.

For whatever his needs had meant to him while he'd been in the Can, *hell* while he'd been out in Guynur, a free man, he'd never go out of his way to hurt a woman.

Why, he could think of one bar fight that seemed like aeons ago now, and how he'd got started into by this drunken dicemaster, some shit like that, and how his old lady had broken this bottle right there, on the fucking table, and how she'd come a running up to Paulin, all set to slash out his throat.

Paulin had socked her in the jaw, real hard, hard enough to send her tumbling, and blood spurting. But for weeks later he'd felt terrible about it, wondering about how that dicemaster's old lady looked now, if she'd got a welt where he'd caught her.

But she'd forced him to.

It'd been a case of him versus her.

And, in the end, Paulin knew himself that it was a matter of survival, and him being the centre of the world meant he would always win out.

Because if he didn't exist, then how could the world?

He responded subtly to the prozzy's touch now, taking deep breaths and then breathing them out, and leaning into her, and gently he felt her other hand embrace him, as she squeezed him to her chest. To her withered breasts.

He could feel the warmth of her breath wafting over him. Bringing his skin out in pimples, and making his whole body tingle as she did that thing with her hands.

"You 'right there, honey?"

"Mm," Paulin said, speaking for the first time.

They just sat like that a long time, neither of them doing anything at all, not one of them making a move to do nothing else.

Paulin heard that pissing screw's cough off along the hallway again.

He'd fix him if he could get away with it.

He'd never heard of a screw biting it in the Can, so he could only ponder at what the consequences would be.

Would it be just the same as how they punished all the other stuff around here, the stuff between prisoners?

Or would they maybe be more hands on where their own were concerned, like make his life a living hell, let other prisoners lay into him with beatings, and whatever else, before one day they snuck rat poison into his food, invited all the screws round to watch him cough his last. Maybe they'd launch into him kicking him to pieces, wanting to break his bones too, to send him off into the next life with a couple broken ribs, or whatever.

But Paulin wouldn't kill the screw.

For one he had no shank on him.

And he was a prisoner whatever happened, whether he was out there, in Guynur City, or he was jammed up in here, in the Can.

"You 'kay there, honey?"

This time Paulin did manage to find his voice. Managed to answer her. ". . . Yeah."

THE SCREWS, like they always did, delivered Paulin on back to his cell, brought him back to Fworte who was already stretched out on the top bunk and smoking.

As Fworte looked off over the foot of his bed at Paulin, he dabbed his cigarette out on his mattress, on the burned-out spot, because he knew how much Paulin hated smoking. And Paulin had taught it to him, too, with a little help from his shank, and holding it at Fworte's throat. He'd even made the big man bleed for him.

That'd taught him some.

Paulin felt his whole body tingling, but not because of what he'd done back there with the prozzy, because he hadn't done anything at all. They'd just sat. And they'd just embraced one another. And he'd told her nothing of his life, and she'd told him nothing of hers.

And that'd been just fine for the two of them, or so he'd felt it.

When the screws had come to take him away, Paulin had noticed one of them looking to her, as if checking in with her, seeing if she was doing okay, and whether or not he'd pulled some kind of nutty shit. But the truth of it was that she was still clinging onto his hand, her fingers all interlocked with his, and he felt that reluctance, as she had, to let him go, and let the screws take him back to his cell.

As Paulin listened to his cell door swing shut on its rusted-up hinges, he prowled on up to the bars, and he looked out, down onto the concrete area below. And he waited. And waited. It felt like the seconds, then the minutes, were just ticking on by, not in any rush at all, till he heard that tottering of them high heels, and he saw the procession of prozzies, all them heading back into the cell block, going on that parade of theirs yet again, and he'd caught her eye, caught that redhead's eye, and he'd felt a spark pass between them, not like electricity, nothing like that . . . much *more* than that.

But he'd never be able to explain it.

Not to no one.

And so, Paulin just bucked himself away from the bars once the prozzies had all filed their way out of the Can for another month, and he dropped himself down onto his bunk, and he shut his eyes and lost himself in his thoughts.

Tried to shuck them bad things that sometimes threatened to consume him whole.

Because he, he really was, the centre of Schwyn.

The fire and soul of the fucking place.

MITT THE SCROUNGER

MITT GRIPPED on tighter to the rectangular-sawed, splinter-ridden handles of his wooden cart—all cobbled together with nothing much more than a handful of nails, and the hitting of a well-heeled boot—and he listened to the poorly-shaped wheels clack along the busted-up tarmac road.

He still had that rancid, acid taste at the back of his throat after he'd bit on something that had turned out not to be food at all. Though he guessed that was just what you got for pawing about in the rubbish for food.

His rags stuck to his skin, still soggy from where he'd taken a tumble into a canal earlier in the afternoon. He'd seen a piece of scrap with a mighty glean and he'd taken a chance on swimming out to go get it. Only, by the time he'd got about a quarter of the way to the floating scrap, his fatigue had caught up with him something horrid, and he'd had to turn back to dry land.

The rags that he wrapped about his feet to stop the glass cutting his soles had gone all squidgy and mushy, and was really no use at all now by way of protection.

But he had nothing better to put on his feet, and though a good dozen or more times he'd come across shoes, he was wary about ever using them himself—almost always opting instead to hock them at the Tip.

He'd heard stories of scroungers getting their throats cut while they slept in their carts, off in side alleys, for much less than having a pair of shoes worth stealing.

Back when Mitt was a kid, he'd often heard people sprouting that nonsense about 'sleeping with one eye open,' and he'd always thought about how it was just about the greatest pile of bull *he'd* ever heard.

That was till he'd found himself out in the streets of Guynur himself.

Out with his own cart.

As he wheeled the cart on, through the rickety streets, all seeming to take on bends and curves all of a sudden, he caught a whiff of rat piss carrying on the evening breeze.

He had always taken great care with the smell of rat piss whenever he was looking for a place to bed down for the night. Might find himself pitching up on top of a rat nest, and there were a thousand bad things that could come from doing that.

And so, he sped up just a little, despite the rumbling in the pit of his tummy, and gripped the wooden handles of his cart even tighter still.

When night rolled around, it was always better to be all pitched up. Off down a side alley someplace. Out of the way. And, preferably, not in the way of anybody special.

'Rely on nobody and nuffink,' that was what Mitt's dad had taught him. And it had been a pretty good lesson, all told. At least it'd got him this far in Guynur City. Kept him alive for a solid few winters now. Finally got him out of digging through them rubbish heaps off down the Tip, and out on his lonesome, here with a cart to call his own.

Oh, it was lonely work, to be sure, but that didn't mean that it wasn't preferable to working the Tip with all the other scroungers. He had done his time there, been under the watchful eye of Naufrenzy, the boss of the Tip, and the guards he kept there. And he would say, without question, that he much preferred being out on his own, knew that the greatest decision he'd ever made was to save up for his own cart, to take his own operation beyond the walls of the Tip. And while many of the other scroungers who worked the Tip, his workplace companions, had gone off to buy this drug or that drug, or whatever, Mitt had kept his nose clean, picked out a good spot off near the inside wall of the Tip and kept his savings there.

Waited till he'd got enough quid to get himself up and out, a cart of his own, like he had now.

As he wheeled onwards, he kept his eyes watchful of the side alleys he passed by: just as much looking for a place to bed down for the night as looking out for any trouble that might be lurking in the wings. Ready to jump him for what little he had.

Of course, he'd already hocked what he'd gathered on his cart that day, hocked it to the men at the entrance to the Tip, but he also knew well that there were men out in these mean streets that'd quite happily cut a scrounger's throat to get at what he'd got.

Especially if what he'd got was a cart.

As Mitt had.

Mitt ploughed on round another corner, hearing the side of his wooden cart brush a little against the brick wall as it went. All the windows on these streets were boarded up. Some with simply wooden planks nailed on, and others with out-and-out steel sheets.

To stop the squatters getting in.

But they *always* found a way in.

Though it was tempting at times, Mitt had enough street sense about him to know that he was much safer bedding on down in some side alley, covering himself with quite a few bulging, plastic sacks of rubbish, than letting himself into some abandoned house he had no idea of . . . where he had no idea just who might be lurking in the shadows ready to cut his throat for his cart right off in the middle of the night.

Up ahead, Mitt spied a blind alley. He liked blind alleys. It was easier to keep a watch on the comings and goings. To see just who might be approaching him in them post-midnight hours.

He wheeled on stronger still, flashing the occasional glance back over his shoulder, just checking to see if there was anyone who might've followed him this far.

Some poor soul that had spotted Mitt's cart a long while back and had the perseverance to scout him out, to keep on his trail, till he ran him down into some spot where there was no chance of any fuzz ever seeing what was going on . . . though, with fuzz, Mitt was pretty sure that they'd do next to nothing even if they saw a scrounger cut another's throat in broad daylight . . . maybe if it was out on Sunstream Avenue, but that'd be different altogether . . . that was a place where *good* folks would see, where it'd mess with their appetites for the rich meals they were having in them restaurants and cafes there.

When Mitt reached the opening to the alley, he shifted a final glance off over his shoulder and then yanked his cart off into the shadows of the alley.

2

THOUGH MITT KNEW there were some in Guynur City that wouldn't have appreciated the pungent odour of the alley, them black, plastic sacks of rubbish all piled up, sweet and sickly brown juices flowing all out of them, for him it represented nothing less than a perfect spot for a night's sleep.

Why, even when he'd got his cart all turned round, and got himself laid down flat on the base of it, feeling the sure and even surface of the wooden planks straightening out his spine curved from lugging the cart about all day, he could see the moon glowing up in the sky above him. Kind of like one of them light bulbs with the impossibly white lights they had down at the Tip for nights.

That was another thing about being out on his own account now, that he got enough quid from working the streets, from bringing in scrap to the Tip, that he had no reason to work through the night, pawing through them heaps of rubbish for something —*anything*—that might catch Naufrenzy's eye.

He could remember more than one instance when he had spent a whole night toiling through them rubbish heaps, and cutting himself a good dozen or more times on broken glass, and worse, and coming up totally empty-handed.

Them days were behind him now, or so he hoped.

They would be, at least, if he could just keep a hold of his cart.

He dipped his hand into the pocket of his rags, to where he had the paper package where he'd wrapped up a bread roll he'd knicked out of a skip behind a bakery . . . thankfully, in retrospect, *after* he'd taken the dip in the canal for that scrap.

He crunched the bread as he stared up at the moon above him, lost himself in its cheesy yellow glow. It was almost as if he could feel himself levitating. Lifting clean up off the base of his cart. Could feel the sweep of the breeze passing over his skin, cooling him, lulling him to sleep.

He chewed the bread till it went all soggy in his mouth, breathed in its rich, full taste, and listened to the gentle grinding of the muscles in his jaw.

It was a perfect night. And he couldn't help but feel optimistic for his future.

Once he scraped some quid together, he could buy himself a horse, and then he wouldn't have to drag his cart about town all on his own any longer. He'd be able to make more than one drop at the Tip every day. He'd get more and more quid till he could . . . well, that was the point where his imagination started to go all out of focus—get all blurry on him.

Because he couldn't imagine having a *surplus* of quid.

To him that just sounded indulgent.

But, if he could only just keep himself going, then that was where he was headed.

It was only when he swallowed down the chunk of bread, felt its warmth passing all the way down his throat before hearing the *groan* of his stomach as it thanked him for filling it, that he realised he was floating.

Actually floating.

Like, *in the air*.

He looked about himself. Saw the base of his cart a good three, four feet below him. And, right then, as if he had just clicked his fingers to bring reality out of whatever trance it'd gone into, he plummeted back down, landing with a *thunk* on the wooden cart.

He felt a skitter of pain through his spine, like a bunch of dancing sparks off a rogue electrical wire. And he felt the blood rushing to the point of his back which had hit the wood.

He felt a chunk of the bread lodge in his throat.

He tried to breathe.

Couldn't.

He began to panic.

Drawing hard on his lungs. Trying to draw a breath.

But mostly failing.

A tingle spread out from his chest. But the breaths didn't come. The chunk of bread acted like a stopper, preventing him from breathing at all.

He tried to calm himself down. Reassured himself with words from his father.

Rely on nobody and nuffink.

This was his mess, and he would get himself out of it.

Or else he would die alone.

He slowed things down. Forced himself to stop trying to draw breaths. Told his heart to stop beating so hard in his chest.

Gradually, he felt the chunk of bread lodged in his throat soften. Just a little. No more than a fraction.

Mitt tried to swallow.

And got it down.

It burned all the way down to the entrance of his stomach.

But he *did* get it down.

Once again he could draw breath. He had no trouble now. He could keep himself going now. The moment for panic had passed and everything was going to be all right.

As he sat himself upright on the edge of his cart, he noted the sharp pain still in his throat, and his mouth felt extremely dry.

He dug out the plastic bottle he used to collect water, usually stagnant water out of gutters. There was only a trickle in the bottom of it, but he unscrewed the cap of the bottle, and tossed the little water that was there down his throat.

It soothed him for a quarter of a second, before the burning sensation returned.

He shifted off the edge of his cart, headed for the opening of the alley.

Before he stole out into the street, he stuck his neck out, glanced both ways just to check that no one was coming, and then he headed on up, searching out a reachable gutter.

3

A S IT HAPPENED, this street turned out to be hard to find gutters. Most of the ones lower down had already been salvaged by other scroungers, hauled off to the Tip so that they'd fetch a few quid. And the gutters left close enough for Mitt to reach were invariably cracked, with holes in, and no water to be found.

It hadn't rained for a few days, so most of the standing water had got dried up.

But Mitt was determined.

It was only when he located a good gutter, back out on a street which branched off from his back alley, and he got his plastic bottle good and filled up with a fresh batch of the stagnant, brown water, that he thought on what had just happened to him.

He had flown, hadn't he?

That was, well, pretty much the only explanation, wasn't it?

At least, that was what he remembered.

He thought it over some, on his way to his back alley. Of course he'd heard of magic, everyone in Guynur City knew all about it.

And most feared it too.

Mitt certainly feared it.

And flying, it seemed to him, was just one of them things that was no doubt connected to magic.

What other explanation was there for it?

None, that was what.

As he suckled away at his plastic bottle of stagnant water, he rounded the corner to his back alley, and it was then that he saw them.

Three of them.

All wicked skinny, bony.

Two of them in beige and gold and black robes.

The other in plain black robes.

The Watch.

Them forces that kept an eye on magic throughout Guynur, tossed it out when they found it, or, at least, that was just about as much as Mitt knew about the whole thing.

He never did like to pry into matters like this.

Matters that he'd always thought to himself to be a little above his station.

He paused there, standing on the corner, the turn on into the back alley he'd scouted out with such great care, and he watched them go about their work.

All three of them were looking off towards his cart. To it there. And, Mitt guessed because he couldn't see round corners, they could see all them mounted-up black, plastic sacks of rubbish all around his cart too.

He squeezed his plastic bottle tighter, felt his fingertips burrowing right down into its plastic form. Heard a gentle *slosh* of the water from inside of it.

And maybe that was the thing that caught their attention.

That made them all, moving almost like one person, pivot round and glare off at him.

Mitt's breath caught in his throat. For a moment or more his muscles all locked up. He was paralysed. He couldn't do nothing but stare right at them. At them shadows that hung over their faces on account of their hoods, like it was midday and not the beginnings of the night.

A cold shudder passed clean along Mitt's skin. And he felt himself break out in goose bumps, and his heart hang suspended between his ribs. All of a sudden, his mouth tasted drier—*staler*—

still, and he caught a whiff of that leathered hide smell, that smell that reminded him of *them*, of the Watch . . . the few times he'd seen them about the city.

But this time, and it was a sure thing, what with that flying or whatever that'd been back there in that alley, that they had come for him.

All the same, it took a few seconds more for that realisation to properly flood upwards and kick in with his brain.

But, when it did, it seemed like his legs got the gist awfully quick.

And he took off running.

4

THE AIR WHISTLED by Mitt's ears. He could feel it all fresh up against his cheeks. He was afraid—*really* afraid—for maybe the sixth or seventh time in his life.

Before it'd been just big street kids, or an addict scrounger who'd got his hands on a piece of lead piping, and had lost all his sense someplace.

Now, though, this was much worse.

The Watch was after him.

And there was only one way it could turn out.

Or so he'd heard.

His heart seemed like it was clenching tight within his chest. Like it was moving so fast, pumping blood so hard, that it didn't feel like it was moving at all.

He couldn't hear any footsteps behind him, them three members of the Watch chasing him, because the Watch didn't walk like people . . . they *weren't* people.

They were magical beings.

Why, they just appeared to float along.

Now, thinking about it, he couldn't believe that once in a while he'd joked with other scroungers about how he'd like to float just like the Watch did. That it'd save the need for some rags on your feet, or cure the need to dig out some shoes from somewhere that'd more likely than not end up getting your throat slit one night.

Didn't seem funny anymore.

He beat on hard, limping just a little on account of the fatigue from slogging about all day with his cart. He knew that they were coming to taking him away. That the Watch had seen him doing . . .

well, whatever it was he'd been doing . . . and that was all there was to it.

If they did catch him then he'd get himself turned right out of Guynur City.

And then where'd he be?

He stole on hard about the bends, sometimes scraping his bare arm up against the brickwork, and other times near enough tripping up and over the curbs of the pavements which had mostly crumbled off, come apart in places.

Though he checked back over his shoulder a few times, he could never see them.

Could never catch so much as a glimpse of the Watch chasing him.

Maybe they weren't chasing him at all.

Perhaps it'd just been a big mistake.

Or they'd been looking for someone else

But Mitt didn't think it all that likely.

He knew that he'd been floating.

Been floating his way up to the moon.

And now the Watch'd make him pay.

There was one place that he could go now, though he'd have no way of knowing if he'd be allowed inside. If they'd *let* him inside. He wasn't well dressed, after all, to put it mildly.

But it might just be his only chance.

Because one thing was for certain, his cart was gone for good now.

Even if the Watch didn't take it away, some scrounger would be along before too long and they'd acquire it for themselves.

In that way, Mitt guessed they weren't called 'scroungers' for nothing.

He pounded on along the beaten-up tarmac, feeling each step, each scrape of the scattered rocks through the thin rags that bound his feet, and pressing right into his calloused soles.

He just had to keep going.

Just a little while longer.

Maybe he could get away.

5

A LL TOLD, Mitt must've run on for a solid hour or more and, to be honest, he really hadn't imagined he'd have that sort of strength in him. That kind of stamina to just keep on going.

To escape the Watch.

It was only when he looked up, saw that he was approaching Pikenun Park: the biggest park in the whole of Guynur City, that he knew that he was coming close to his destination.

As he passed Pikenun Park by, he turned his attention to them great, big pointed black railings that surrounded it. And to the guard booths that stood up on every corner of the four or five square blocks the park occupied. From inside each booth he could see a slight, orange glimmer, and he guessed each had a guard snoozing in there too.

Thankfully, fuzz had little if nothing to do with the Watch, and though these guards didn't have nothing to do with fuzz, it reassured him just a fraction to know that they weren't on the lookout for him.

Not as far as he knew, anyway.

The park'd been long locked up, and, anyway, it'd never been Mitt's intention to pry his way inside. The park, for him, just about acted only as a reference point for just where he really wanted to head.

Though he'd only been by here a handful of times, to come by and pick up scrap of whatever kind, before hauling it off over to the Tip, he still recognised the layout of the streets leading away, and, with a quick, shifty look over his shoulder, he headed for the alley which he knew would take him where he wanted to go.

To the only person in the city that might be able to help him out of the predicament he found himself in right about this time.

The streetlights around here were all switched up full, at least much fuller than the other, abandoned districts where Mitt was used to prowling about.

Like that abandoned district where the Watch had found him, and where he'd had to leave his cart in that back alley.

No, this place was populated. He could see that from the gentle yellowy glows that shone on the curtained windows. Keeping the insides of them places all private and the like from the outside world.

A couple of places were opened up, had their doors wide open to the night, and Mitt saw that they were bars and the like, though today there weren't many people about.

It wasn't a festival day or nothing so that wasn't unusual.

He headed on along the street, and up to a concrete streetlight post which had a splash of yellow paint on it. And Mitt knew that he'd found just the right place. That this was where he had intended to come all along.

He eyed up the roll-down, steel door before him. One of them doors people used down at street level, to stop robbers and the kind from busting right through into their houses or businesses or whatever.

He glanced back a final time, right back over his shoulder, and then rapped his knuckles a pair of times against the steel.

It felt cold against his knuckles, and the steel made a kind of hollow hammering sound.

At first, because the door didn't roll back straight off, he thought that maybe the people inside hadn't heard him, and he made to knock again.

But, when he did, he heard the *clink* and *clank* of the chain that rolled up the steel door, and then the door itself lifted a few feet off the ground. Just enough for Mitt to make out the legs of the person on the other side.

They were wearing black jeans. Had on sturdy, ankle-high boots with the laces untied, and with dried-up mud about the leather treads.

"Yeah?" came a voice from inside, gruff and standoffish-sounding.

Mitt knew that now was the time to state his business or be gone for good from here—to send himself off to go take his chances with the Watch.

Mitt liked his chances better here, with this steel door right now.

"Uh, I heard about this place you got, you know, for *disappearing*." Mitt drew a breath, and then remembered the name, and added, "I came to see Beggy."

There was a loud snort on the other side of the steel door, and then a spit.

Mitt saw the honey-coloured wad land on the tarmac, just between the pair of ankle-high boots on the other side of the door.

"You fuzz?" the voice said.

Mitt just stared on at that glob of phlegm between the man's boots for a long while, before he snapped back to his senses. "Uh, no, uh uh, not fuzz."

"Don't sound too convincin' to me."

When Mitt spoke again, he felt his voice quiver a little in his throat. Maybe on account of the bread that'd lodged in his throat, and that he was still feeling just a lingering pain from that. "I swear, I'm not fuzz."

A long pause on the other side of the door, and then, "What are ya, then?"

Mitt hesitated a moment, then realised that, really, there wasn't much point in him hiding it, since, after all, if this guy decided to open up the door he'd see him for what he was anyway. And so he said, feeling a slight flush of shame, "Scrounger."

Another pause. Then the chains that held the roll-down steel door clanked a couple of times.

Downwards.

The person was closing up the door.

Mitt felt his cheeks flush and his heart skitter. "No, wait! Please, I've got quid, if that's the issue, please, you gotta believe that I've got the money. I ain't on the look out for no charity, nor nothing." Then he remembered his dad's words. "I don't rely on nobody or nuffink, promise."

The descent of the door paused, almost like the door itself was deciding whether or not to let Mitt inside. And Mitt had to admit that he was grateful enough that the door hadn't clean slid all the way shut on him.

He still had a chance.

"On the run?" the voice said, quieter this time, maybe even a touch gruffer.

"Yah."

"From who?"

"Does it matter?"

A hard sigh. "Some."

Mitt thought it over. Again, it was better for him to tell the truth. If what he really wanted was for Beggy to help him then it was just better for him to be honest about the whole thing. "The Watch."

Mitt actually closed his eyes in anticipation for the roll-down steel door pounding down, shutting on him and his needs forever.

Leaving him to try and slip through the Watch's fingers throughout a long night . . . for the rest of his life.

Because, and this was one thing straight in his mind, once the Watch got a sniff of somebody they got *found*. It might take till their dying breath. But they did get found.

That was fine to Mitt, but he'd rather they found him when he took his dying breath than right about now when he still had a good portion of his life still ahead of him.

Still all laid out and ready for living.

He had to try all he could to get himself safe.

With another few *clanks* of the chain, the roll-down steel door jerked upwards, till Mitt could see the face of the man he'd been speaking too.

He had thick black hair, a bushy beard, and he had swift, compassionate pale blue eyes.

"Name's Beggy," he said.

6

"YOU ON THE RUN from the Watch, huh?" Beggy said.

They'd come on in from the street outside, and after he'd locked up the roll-down steel door, he'd led Mitt down a long flight of stairs to an wide-open area which Mitt guessed could at least fit a whole house inside.

It was a whole other world down here, underground. And he wondered, having been a scrounger after all, why he hadn't spent more time underground.

He guessed there must've been all sorts of scrap laying about, ready to hock down the Tip.

Beggy had led him past a subterranean stream that gushed through the middle of this dug-out chamber, which seemed to be entirely lined in clay, or some other kind of soft material, before bringing him in through a doorway, into this smaller room, which turned out to be a kitchen.

There was a fridge. And a sink. And, well, just about everything that Mitt would've expected from a kitchen in any *normal* house. It seemed that Beggy had a pretty snug setup here, all things considered.

And, delights of all delights, Beggy had warmed Mitt up some soup fresh off the stove, got it all bubbling away, before serving him it to him in a chipped porcelain bowl with a blue-and-white flowery pattern all around the edge.

The soup was chicken-flavoured, with some herbs that Mitt thought were maybe coriander and rosemary, but it'd been so long since he'd tasted them that he couldn't be sure.

What he was sure of was that he was delighted to be sat here, at this metal table that looked as if it'd been swiped from a disused hospital, and supping on this scolding-hot soup.

Even a warm, buttered bread roll thrown in for good measure.

As he felt the warmth of the stuff head down his gullet, he couldn't help forgetting the world outside, the one that he'd run from.

He'd even forgotten about the Watch, just for a moment, till Beggy had brought it up just now.

He savoured the salty flavour of the soup, swallowed down another mouthful, and then breathed in that thick, chicken taste. His last warm meal seemed almost a lifetime away now. Over on the stove, he could still hear the soup bubbling away within its stainless-steel saucepan.

Mitt couldn't shake the feeling that he might've died and gone straight up to heaven.

Something like that.

Mitt glanced up from his bowl, met Beggy's pale blue eyes, and said, desperate to take another spoonful of his soup before him, "Yah, that's right. The Watch."

Beggy gave a slight nod, and then crossed his arms over his bulging stomach. He wore a thick, dark blue seaman's sweater with a turtleneck, even though Guynur was a long way from the sea. And he had on a pair of black jeans underneath, just as Mitt had seen when he'd greeted him up at street level.

The sweater had a few frayed holes in it, and Mitt could see other places where Beggy, or someone else, had done a job of sewing it up.

Beggy glanced back to the stove, to the soup still bubbling away there. "More?" he said.

Mitt gave a slight grin, not wanting to seem greedy, but, at the same time, knowing that if it was offered, he couldn't possibly go without the soup.

Beggy took his bowl, poured him out some more, then laid it down on the table before him.

Mitt thanked him, and then picked up his spoon again.

Beggy's lips contorted in a smile beneath his bustling, black beard, and then he said, "Dunno why you're thanking me, you're paying for every one of them bowls."

Mitt felt his stomach churn. But he reminded himself about his savings. About the ones he'd stashed away somewhere no one would ever think to look. That quid would get him through for a little while, pay for a week or more. Just till he got back on his feet.

Worked out what he was going to do.

Beggy dipped into the pocket of his jeans, withdrew a half-crushed packet of cigarettes, flipped the lid, and then removed a cigarette using only his lips. He produced a lighter from somewhere else, and then lit up. Blew a cloud of bluish smoke into the brightly lit air.

With the same hand he used to hold the cigarette, he jabbed his thumb into his temple, as if deep in thought, and then said, "Gotta few that're on the run from the Watch, ya know?"

"Hmm?" Mitt said, mouth full of soup again.

"Yah, find their way to me, they do." Beggy took another drag of his cigarette, this time not taking the smoke down completely, just sucking it into his mouth before letting it loose, then said, "What's it they want to take you for, eh?"

Mitt paused a second, stared down into his bowl of soup, into the murky little puddle at the bottom of it. That brown-coloured liquid, the chicken soup still begging him to drink it all down.

Could he trust Beggy?

. . . What he wanted to ask himself was whether or not he could really tell him what had gone on.

If Beggy had wanted, he could've thrown Mitt out on his arse, but he'd allowed him in.

And so Mitt guessed that he at least owed Beggy the luxury of an explanation.

No matter whether or not he believed him.

And so he told him.

Beggy drew hard on his cigarette, making the tip glow like a scorching-hot coal, and then he blew out a thick cloud of smoke.

As it settled in over Mitt, Mitt breathed it in just like air. He was so used to smoke, breathing it every day, that he never thought twice about it. Somewhere, way off in his past, he'd somehow forgotten what fresh air was supposed to be like.

"Yah," Beggy said, "getta few like you, the ones that fly."

Mitt blinked a couple of times, hardly able to believe that. But, then again, what did he think made him so special? If someone like *him* could do what he'd done, then it stood to reason that others would be able to do it just as easily.

Why, he hadn't so much as thought about it even.

Beggy finished his cigarette, tossed it into the sink, and then made his way towards the exit of the kitchen. He turned back when he reached the doorway. "You comin' then? Gonna show you to your room, or what?"

7

MITT TOOK IN the dormitory, the room stuffed full with a dozen or more people, others that were on the run from the Watch. Standing here, he could breathe in the musky odour of all of them sleepers, caught that tangy salty taste at the back of his throat from the congealed sweat.

When he glanced to his side, to Beggy standing there, he caught him smirking at him.

"Wanna, maybe, you know, take a shower of somethin' first, perhaps?"

Mitt guessed that was a good move, and he headed off after Beggy in the direction of the bathroom.

After he'd got showered, and Beggy had left him out a fresh set of clothes, Mitt was almost certain that he'd somehow been transported into a parallel dimension.

How could it be that, just this morning, he'd been wheeling his cart along, plucking scrap out of skips and bins, then heading off to the Tip to cobble together a few quid.

But, really, it *had* been this morning.

Funny how quickly things could change.

And, as he reminded himself swiftly, he had to bear in mind that this was all temporary, that he would be giving up months and months of savings just for a few quiet days of comparative luxury.

Then he would be out on the streets again . . . praying that the Watch didn't find him.

That he wouldn't do anything again to attract their attention.

Among the fresh clothes was a too-big, light-green shirt and a pair of light brown corduroy trousers. He had no complaints, though, they were clean enough.

And once he had on the thick cotton socks, drawn halfway up his shins, he felt like a king.

So it was any wonder how he felt when he discovered the shoes underneath everything. Brown to match the trousers, and looking like they'd been recently buffed up with polish. The laces looked crisp and new. Those plastic toggles at the end of the laces shone a little in the bright light of the bathroom.

Fully dressed, he felt like a real person again.

Not like that half being he had been relegated to as a scrounger.

But, as he reminded himself over again, this was all just temporary.

Mitt was already on his way back to the dormitory when he heard a shrill, tuneless whistle.

When he looked to his right, he was surprised to see Beggy standing there, leaning up against the doorframe. He had another cigarette between his fingers. Glowing away at the tip, and smoking gently. He jerked his head to indicate that Mitt should enter.

Go into the room he stood in the doorway of.

And Mitt obeyed him.

He had no reason not to.

When Mitt took a few steps into the room, Beggy flipped a switch somewhere and a bright white glow filled the room. Chased all the shadows scurrying into the corners.

The room was neat, and tidy. A study with a pine-wood desk, and a solidly built matching chair, with, what looked like, a plumped-up, black cushion.

Beggy's office, perhaps?

Beggy sank into the chair which was pulled up to the desk, and then indicated another chair, a dark-brown one—mahogany—off up against the cement wall.

Mitt took up the offer and sat.

Though the chair back was rigid as a broom handle, he couldn't help but find it relaxing to sit himself down here. To know that everything was going to be okay now.

Beggy flipped out a few of the drawers in the desk before he found what he was looking for. A well-thumbed, spiral-ringed notebook with slightly yellow pages. It had a pencil slipped in through the rings. He slipped the pencil out, flipped through the pages till he apparently found a fresh one, and then he fixed Mitt in his gaze —with those pale blue eyes—and waited.

As if Mitt knew just what he needed to know.

In the end, Beggy decided to help him out. "The money?" he said.

Mitt snapped back to reality. He met Beggy's diluted blue eyes, peered deep into them, and he was certain there was compassion there. But also a certain pragmatism.

As Mitt saw it, he guessed Beggy didn't get just a few people off the streets, and he was used to those turning up here and not being able to pay their way.

He was just looking out for his operation, nothing wrong with that.

And, in any case, Mitt *had* promised him payment.

Mitt looked to the back of the notepad Beggy held and said, "You, uh, want me to tell you where I've got it stashed?"

Beggy smirked a little. "Well, doesn't seem like you've got it on ya, does it, now? Unless you managed to put it someplace . . . well, let's just leave it at that . . ." he said, allowing his words to taper off.

Mitt supposed this was right, seeing as the whole reason Mitt was there in the first place was to stay *off* the streets. So it'd make little sense for him to go out and fetch his stashed savings himself.

And so he told Beggy just where he had his money.

Just where he'd find it.

Beggy gave a business-like nod and then flipped his notepad closed, held it down at his side, as he got to his feet. With a slight smile, he looked to Mitt, and said, "All right, may as well get some rest, I'll have some of my boys out to bring it in right away."

It was in that moment, right when Beggy showed Mitt to the door of his office, that Mitt was certain he had made a huge mistake. That he had somehow thrown away his entire life, just like that. Because he had placed all his trust in Beggy.

Not that there was anything he could do about it now.

Now all he could do was, like Beggy said, wait and rest.

8

MITT PICKED OUT the only spare bunk in the dormitory. It was the one by the door, and he guessed that it was the only one vacant for a reason. He guessed that with people coming and going during the night, headed off down the hall to the bathroom, them that'd slept there had soon learned to take another bunk inside the dormitory as soon as it came free.

And Mitt was no different. Out on the streets, he trusted in his ability of being a light sleeper. It was important that he'd come round to even the slightest stirring. The lightest suggestion of a snatch breath, or whatever.

His life had depended on it.

Not wanting to muss his nice, new clothes with his sleeping sweat, he'd folded them up neatly at the foot of his bed. And, just as he'd got ready to lay his head down on the overstuffed straw pillow, he'd almost got hold of the notion of placing his shoes under his head while he slept, to be sure no one would steal them off him in the night.

It took him a solid few minutes to finally get round to convincing himself that, really, he had nothing to fear here. That, in any case, these clothes weren't *really* his.

He hadn't paid for them yet after all.

Though Mitt had to admit that this bed, this fairly thin and well-sprung mattress was near enough the most comfortable thing he could remember, he still couldn't find himself being swept away on an easy sleep.

Maybe it was the unfamiliar surroundings. Maybe it was the fact that, his whole life it seemed, he was naturally attuned to never going to sleep around other people.

Solitude was always the safest option out on the streets.

But he just couldn't find himself drifting off.

So he just stared upwards, through the gloom, at the knitted wire of the springs of the mattress up above him. And he simply couldn't turn off his mind.

Not till he heard muffled voices out in the corridor in what must've been the early hours of the morning.

Perhaps right before sunrise.

He recognised Beggy's voice right away, and another two with him that he didn't.

Mitt lay still for another few seconds, trying to work out just what he should do. And then, realising that he would do no good simply lying about here, listening into the conversation, he decided to get himself up. To prop himself up on the edge of his mattress and to poke his feet through the legs of his trousers. To throw his shirt about his shoulders. And to prod on his pair of shoes, taking extreme care with the laces, not to fray them with his long fingernails.

He headed out into the corridor, bringing the door to the dormitory shut with a narrow *creak* of the hinges. He heard the voices coming from a little way off. Wafting along. And, following his ears, he reached the conclusion that they were coming from Beggy's office.

The place where he'd revealed the location of all the quid he had in the world.

He stole along, taking care not to make a sound. That was the funny thing with wearing shoes, the way that the soles seemed to squeak against polished-up surfaces, like the tiled floor he was walking along.

He listened for a moment to the voices drifting out through the open door of Beggy's office, couldn't make out the muffled words,

373

and decided that, rather than steal about the place like a sleuth, that he might as well just be done with it.

See whether or not they'd managed to uncover his money.

And so, with a deep breath, he stepped into the doorway to Beggy's office, took in Beggy, sitting with his back to his desk, turned around in his chair, and then the two men, both standing, and both extremely thin, skeletal even.

For a terrifying moment, Mitt was sure that they were members of the Watch, that they had come for him, that Beggy had sold him out.

But he calmed himself, took in the sunken cheekbones of the two of them, both dressed in black hooded sweatshirts, in black jeans just like Beggy. They were both swift eyed and reminded Mitt just a little of rats.

And then he saw the crumpled-up, brown paper bag, lying on Beggy's desktop, behind Beggy.

That was it. They'd found his money.

All three sets of eyes lingered on Mitt, as if he was a ghost or something that'd just popped up out of the ground, and then, with a smile full of teeth, Beggy held out his arm to indicate Mitt. "Well, this is him."

The rat-faced men took Mitt in, and Mitt felt a stirring at the base of his gut.

What were they going to do?

Were they going to toss him out, just like that?

. . . Even though these men weren't members of the Watch, they could do him just the same amount of infinite harm by merely throwing him out on the street.

But the rat-faced men held their ground.

And then, all at once, Beggy dismissed them.

The rat-faced men slipped past Mitt in the doorway, and then trod their way off down the corridor. He listened to their footsteps echoing away before finally being sucked up by the silence of the underground chambers.

Beggy motioned for Mitt to sit in that same chair he'd sat in that afternoon. And then, with the other hand, reached for the brown paper bag which sat on the table behind him, and brought it round, laid it in his lap. It rustled a little as Beggy dug his hand inside, flipping through the quid stashed inside, and then he peered up at Mitt. "Don't mean to be rude, nor nothin', but ain't really all that much here, eh?"

Mitt felt his gut tighten. And his heart crunch in on itself.

"I mean," Beggy said, peering in through the opening of the bag, "for what I'm doin' for you, there's not really, well"—he looked up from the bag, fingers resting in the pit of his chin, nestled beneath his bustle of beard—"how'd I put it, not really a fair exchange, if you see what I mean?"

Mitt felt himself slipping downwards. As if he was toppling off a rooftop. About to land square, *slap* on the broken-up asphalt. About to smash just about every bone in his body. "I . . . I . . ." he said, trying to form the words, but Beggy was holding up his hand.

"Tell ya what," he said, "this is what we'll do, 'kay?" He dropped the brown paper bag down on the desk behind him, where it landed with a soft *scrunch*. "This is what we do with those that don't have the quid to pay up for their lodgings, what we do—right?—it's find other ways for them to give something back."

Mitt felt his gut tighten even further.

"Now, you've got something of the magic, that's the reason you're runnin' from the Watch, after all, right?"

Mitt nodded.

"So, the deal we'll strike is just this one: sometimes I gotta use for those with certain— how'd I put it?—*abilities*, got uses for them, stuff like that. And so, how we'll lay this thing out's to fix you up with the other magics about here, ones we've taken in, and they'll try to help you understand just what's goin' on with you, right?"

Again, Mitt nodded.

Beggy gave a little pout. "Good, then guess we understand each other fine, then? All decided. You'll stay here, with us, and you'll help us out however I see fit, eh?"

There wasn't anything else Mitt could say to that, except an extremely dry-throated, "Thank you."

Beggy gave a slight nod of acknowledgement, and then turned his chair around, making the feet *screech* against the tiled floor. Apparently returning to his business.

Mitt took this as his cue to get up, and to head out. To leave Beggy to whatever it was that he had to do. But, just as he stood in the doorway, he realised that he had to know. That he had to get things straight before he truly headed on out.

And so he turned to Beggy, and said, "You mean that I'm really safe now? That you'll take me in for, you know, however long you say?"

Beggy turned to him, wrinkles formed in his forehead. "You what?"

"I mean, I won't have to go back to the streets—go back to being a scrounger, nothing like that?"

Beggy held that same expression for another few of Mitt's heartbeats, and then he broke out into a glorious grin. And shook his head as he turned back to his desk, back to his work, back to the brown paper bag which contained all the quid Mitt had managed to scrape together in the entire course of his life.

"Some of 'em," Beggy said, almost to himself, "just don't get it, do they?"

Mitt held his ground another moment or so, said "Thank you," again, and then headed on out through the corridor.

And, as he approached the dormitory, the other sleepers, could hear some of them stirring, some of them moving about inside, he couldn't help but break out into a wide smile himself.

Because, as he knew, this was surely the beginning of a new life.

A life that he had never expected.

But, still, much better than being a scrounger.

THE CART TOWN SWINDLER'S SWEEP

DUST SWILLED UP and swatted down. The carts spiralled about the square, seemingly without logic or order. Creatures of all colours and creeds thrashed the horses—or other beasts—drawing their carts forwards with thick leather reins.

The combined effect was one that made it seem like the constant flow of the carts about the town square, their constant entrance and entry, was like that of a burbling stream through a narrow valley, with all its currents and spinnies.

Today was known all round here as Swindler's Sweep, the busiest day in the year in Cart Town, when the carts all barrelled into the town square looking for repairs, and for watering and feeding for the creatures that drew them on over the dust plains, along with the sustenance for the travellers themselves.

The name came from the fact that it was the day most ripe for mischief in the year, what with all the commotion . . . and the greatest chance for a criminal not to get caught.

Sheriff Diff Andchek swivelled about and drew in his domain like a briskly snatched breath.

There it was. All laid out before him. His town.

Cart Town.

Just as its name suggested, the carts all wheeled in and out of the main square spread down below, some brand-new looking while others were thatched together with whatever had come up handy. Some had hay spread to cover the expansive holes, and other owners just hadn't bothered to cover the holes at all.

Cart Town sat right in the midst of the Kunaha Desert, a rare oasis for the travelling workers headed from the East Coast to the West, changing along with the change of the seasons. Getting themselves away from those lands in the East that, in summer, were such fertile, virile lands. But when the winter winds beat into the coast . . . well, it'd take one hardy soul to survive that, or so Diff had always thought.

Nah, Cart Town was the place for him. Ever since he'd been one of those travellers himself, wading on towards the warmer climes of the West Coast for the winter, he'd got himself stuck here.

He thought he'd found someone he well and truly loved with all four of his hearts.

And he'd been wrong.

As always, the air of Cart Town carried sawdust on it, from the dozens of workshops which lined the streets, and the few hundred craftsmen who aided the carts, brought them in for repair, and all.

Water vendors ducked and weaved between the carts too, offering food and water for prices negotiated with the passengers. And though usually Diff would think hard on watching those known crooks among them, looking for petty thefts, today he had something much weightier on his mind.

Diff jabbed his forked tongue in between his two lower fangs, and thought long and hard on just what he was gonna do about the latest case. Thing was, when they'd come to him not less than an hour ago, he'd been eating.

Though the lunch was a distant memory, or so it seemed.

He vaguely recalled it had been bean soup, stuffed with something or other else. Something herby, or grass, or . . . he didn't know what *the hell* what. All he knew was he hadn't had that meaty injection into his bloodstream, that meaty injection that seemed to kick his energy up a notch—that really seemed to get him going for a day's work.

Thing was, his appetite had been waning with this murder thing on his mind. Most the time the creatures that passed on through

Cart Town behaved themselves just fine. Creatures didn't tend to kill other creatures. Not in Cart Town. Everyone was a hard-worker.

And even with the bright sun that beamed down, warming his cold blood, and the flawless blue sky which stretched off right to the horizon of the world—of *Schwyn*—he found it tough to think any straighter about this murder.

He listened to the *clickety-clack* of the cartwheels, of the carts all trundling along down below. Who was he rightly to suspect of the crime? What was his next step? The way he'd heard the victim had been done in, it just said nothing to him at all.

But he had to find the murderer.

He was the sheriff.

2

"SHARF?"

Diff ran his eyeballs on their runners so they went round the back of his head, and he eyed his deputy there, Fjourn Plutkronz, the best in the business there was and a noble successor for whenever Diff took his turn to ride off into the sunset, to leave behind this perennial rolling town.

Fjourn was a Guni, and he was all squat, kinda cartwheel-shaped, thinking about it. Whenever he spoke a green spittle squidged out of his lips, like he was allergic to talking, or something. Guni was the most common race of creatures about the deserts, and so they made up the majority of the population of Cart Town.

"Yuh?" Diff said.

"Gonna take a look?"

Diff cast his eye over the main square of Cart Town one final time, over those tens and tens of carts, all loaded up with creatures of all races and creeds, all of them passing through, none of them set on staying here too long.

"Yarp," Diff replied, still staring off down there for a few moments, before letting Fjourn take the lead, take him along those ever-crooked corridors that led down to street level, and to where things-proper kicked off in Cart Town.

He let Fjourn do the talking mostly since he couldn't muster much up in Brak-a-lak, the common tongue they used around here. That wasn't his fault, though. What with his four beating hearts and his forked tongue, he was never gonna have been a creature good with languages.

Him being a Saverak meant that he couldn't speak much, but he always thought himself much better at spotting other stuff that people just didn't notice themselves. They were too busy blabbing off in their Brak-a-lak to notice it. And that was why he supposed he made a good sheriff. Why he'd found some kinda vocation for it.

Just like always, everyone buzzed about the streets, that *clickety-clack* grew louder still, and Diff caught that sawdust scent all the stronger about the place. It clung to the whole town like a brand mark to a cow's backside, and thinking about it, when Diff lay in his bed at night, staring up at the ceiling, watching the bugs crawling up there, he smelled it till it lulled him to sleep at night.

He thought back to that bean soup of his, and wished he'd grabbed a whole cupful more. That was always his problem. Him being too polite, and all. That was what his husband . . . if he'd had one, would've ground right into him till he could hear no more.

He was no sheriff. Not the sheriff Cart Town needed, any case.

All those beans had been thick and rich, and gooey in all the right places. Warmed him up real nice and everything. But he shoulda taken more when he'd had the chance. And now he'd have to work feeling just like he did.

Nothing to do about it now, though.

Fjourn led him through a long and weaving side alley, the kind that Cart Town was famous world-round for, the ones where tourists could get themselves trapped in for days on end . . . and would, just as Diff had found out.

That was what he most got called out for, being sheriff, to go find creatures—*tourists*—that'd gone and got themselves lost. He wasn't at all accustomed to something like a *murder*.

But he had to get himself accustomed real quick.

Diff unleashed his sweat sack as they rounded the corner round to where they'd told him the murder scene was, and where Fjourn was leading him to now.

It was just good manners to empty your sweat sack before you went into someone's home, no matter if there'd been a murder committed there or not.

Thinking about it, *especially* if there'd been a murder committed there.

Fjourn held back, rocking about on his rounded feet, gently lolling back and forth in that way that made Diff nauseous, but which he'd never speak about to Fjourn since he didn't want to hurt his feelings.

No creature could account for just how he'd been created, and so it made no sense to criticise. What if someone'd said something about Diff's sweat sacks, and that pungent odour they gave off when he did? Why, he wouldn't have liked that *at all*.

And so, Fjourn kept to his rocking—back and forth, back and forth—and Diff's mind took to humming in the sweltering stale air which lurked about here, seemed to collect here in the shadows, it seemed.

Diff put it off another moment more before stepping through that doorway and onto the murder scene.

3

ARIPE, rotten-meat stench crammed itself tight into the room, and it made Diff think immediately of those canned vegetables and other sorts that they got shipped into the Cart Town General Store sometimes, and how he'd peel back that tin lid and it was like magic how that packed-in odour just leaked on out.

Those cans didn't stink of rotting Saverak bodies, of course, which was just what was laid out before his eyes.

A Saverak, just like him. He had always thought it cruel for a creature—*any* creature—to have to face the dead version of itself. Which was where he found himself now.

Three of his hearts squeezed the tremoring cold blood about his veins, while the fourth, the heart his fellow creatures named Saveronak—the *still* heart—remained true to its name. Keeping him focussed. Keeping his mind from becoming carried away. That heart which made his fellow creatures, his *race*, adept for the duty of sheriff.

He buried the memory of those beans he'd had for lunch with a packed-up blend of saliva and blood, and swallowed it down. Now he could focus. Now he could give this case his best shot.

Outside the *clickety-clack* of the passing carts, all on their way to the centre of the town, for the work that required doing, for the sustenance of their passengers, grew dimmer as Diff concentrated on the facts spread out before him.

Entrails. Blue, blotched skin. The claw marks up the walls indicating the sign of a struggle. This place itself, nothing more than a room to rent for the night. A place perhaps visited by a different soul every night of the year, while waiting to have his cart patched up, sustenance provided him, before venturing on his journey for the next day.

Where his journey might take him.

He felt Fjourn sidle up beside him, gently bobbing about on his spherical stumps of feet, his percussive breathing almost like a jabbing dagger through the stifled air of the murder scene. "Whatcha got, sharf?"

"Mardar."

"Yah?"

"Yur."

Fjourn rocked a little on his ankles, and his half dozen eyes, all static in their own sockets, and only able to be manipulated by him moving his whole head around, took stock of the place.

Diff could hear the *tic-tic* of the brain juices flowing through Fjourn's head, as he got to thinking. That was the thing about Guni, you could actually hear them thinking. And that, Diff had always thought to himself, was just a great thing to have in a deputy, one that you knew was always doing his best for the case.

And, if he weren't, then you knew that too.

On account of there being no sound of brain juices flowing.

"Lookie here, sharf," Fjourn said, dipping forwards, and reaching out his tendrils for some aspect of the splattered-up scene, of some entrails or other that, despite being part of his own species, Diff couldn't identify.

Hell, he'd never studied anatomy, so why'd he expect himself to know?

Fjourn glanced back, all those static eyes like glassy beads sunken into his skull, and he held up a chunk of what appeared like a sodden sponge, just like the ones that Diff would use to clean out his sweat sacks when they got too stinky.

Only difference with this sponge, it was a dark-blue colour, the colour of Saverak blood. *His* blood.

"Yar," Diff said, taking the sponge-like thing off him with his pincers.

He held it up to the little light that dribbled in round the boarded-up window, and ran his eyes right to the end of their runners to get a good look at it.

He still had no better idea just where it'd come from, or even any idea about where he might start with this whole thing.

He'd already thought it'd be a case of a murder, before he'd even got here, to this room. Come onto the murder scene. And so this told him nothing at all.

Fjourn's brain juices went *tic-tic-tic*.

But he didn't offer nothing about the case at hand.

Over his shoulder, back by the door, Diff heard the *scuffle* of footsteps and he swivelled his eyes round on their runners, to look round.

There, standing in the doorway, was a Porbearman.

And he looked mighty pissed off.

4

THE PORBEARMAN had slightly stretched skin all over him, and wrinkles—*lots* of wrinkles—just as with them all, with all of them having their own strengths and weaknesses, Diff guessed the Porbearmen had just the same issue as them all.

"Wat'sa goin' on here?" the Porbearman said.

Fjourn rocked a little and then his head turned to look over him. "Murdar."

"Eh?"

"Been murdar."

The Porbearman only then seemed to see the scene stretched all about them right then, and to realise just what had gone on in this place. He brought out his four flapping hands before him, and jerked all his fingers downwards. "This *my* place."

"Yarp," Diff said.

Fjourn rocked more and more, as if building up momentum, and at the same time he eyed the Porbearman, and his brain juices kept on going *tic-tic*.

Though Diff tried not to judge the other races of Cart Town, he just couldn't help it sometimes. Or he couldn't help the thoughts that just seemed to sneak to his brain. Because he could feel that pounding odour of the Porbearman, that stink of a latrine hanging off him like cloud of flies.

Diff tasted those beans again. One of his stomachs threatened to spill them out. But he crunched up his abdomen and wished for the best. And he mostly kept them down. Or enough of them down so that no one would so much as notice.

That was the important thing.

"When you finish here?" Porbearman said.

"Mardar," Diff repeated.

The Porbearman's stench got even harder to tolerate, and Diff felt another quiver pass through his stomachs. His blood ran all the colder, and the *tic-tic* of Fjourn's brain juices seemed to grow more intense and such.

"Yar," the Porbearman said, "I gotta more client here."

Fjourn swivelled about the room, his head like a rotating wagon wheel the way he did it. And Diff found himself wanting for those beans some more. It'd been a waste to turn them down. To turn the offer of seconds down.

"Who did?" the Porbearman said.

Fjourn rocked back in a shrug. "Dunno," he said, and then he pointed at Diff, a point that Diff felt at him, and yet he had nothing else to add. "Sharf gonna solve the case."

"Yarg," Diff said.

The Porbearman's hairy lips pouted out from his face, and his stench climbed up another notch, became all the more over-whelming. It was okay being Fjourn considering he had no nostrils, but Diff's nose, why it was well attuned, and extremely sensitive.

"You gunna clean?" the Porbearman said.

Fjourn looked Diff over, like he would have the answer, but Diff was just a sheriff, and he knew nothing about the protocol for such a situation. He had never run into it while he'd served as the sheriff of Cart Town.

"Yar," Fjourn finally answered him.

"Gooda, then I go," the Porbearman said, and then he went.

Diff breathed easy again, and the sifting smell of the rotting corpse, of the rotting Saverak before him returned. But it was easier—easier than the stench of the Porbearman.

He still clutched that sponge-like object in his pincers, and he saw now that this would be the clue to the case set out before him. And that he could let the murder scene go.

He nodded to Fjourn, and listened to his brain juices go *tic-tic* some more, and then the two of them left the rented room behind. Left it to whichever poor soul would come to inhabit it the next time along.

5

D IFF'S MIND bucked and weaved, and he felt the throb of his frontal lobe become almost too constant to bear. That was his logical mind working away at the case. Trying to work out just what had gone on back there.

He still held the sponge-like object in his pincers, that piece that had cropped up in the remains of the Saverak. The question, Diff was sure that he needed to ask, was how it had got there at all. Surely that would lead him directly to the murderer.

His first stop was to the Pennies-to-Hardware Store in the centre of Cart Town. It was just off a narrow alley from the central square of Cart Town, and Fjourn lingered at his heels, his brain juices still going *tic-tic*.

As Diff turned into the alley, a fluster of dust twizzled its way about before him. He breathed it all in, let his mouth filters do all the necessary filtering that needed doing to make the air any good for him to take into his body. He tasted its roughness, and felt all those grains of sand embedding themselves into him.

Sometimes he wondered if there was any division anymore between him and Cart Town, like sometimes he couldn't quite tell just where Cart Town ended and he began.

Ondermour, the keeper of the Pennies-to-Hardware Store, a Guni, just like Fjourn, cocked his head and looked out from his counter at them. Like Diff always pictured Ondermour in his mind, the keeper kept his elbows rested up on his counter and peered out into the street with a permanent frown. "Mornings," Ondermour said to Diff, and then he jabbered a greeting in the Guni language at Fjourn, who responded in kind.

Diff supposed he coulda gone out to the Cart Town General Store, but on a day like today, it being the Swindler's Sweep, he thought it being way too busy to bother the keeper there. And, besides, he liked to think that he trusted Ondermour a little more. From past cases Diff had cracked here in Cart Town, he'd noticed that Ondermour knew how to keep his mouth shut, not to go gabbing at every creature walking by.

And that was all the more important considering this was a murder they were dealing with here.

Diff gently set the sponge-like thing down on the counter before Ondermour, who reached for the eye-spectacle he kept round his neck and brought it up to one of his static eyes, then leaned over. "Hmm-ba-ba-ba," he said, with his brain juices ticking away too.

That 'Hmm-ba-ba-ba' was the sound that all Guni made when they got to *really* thinking about something, the sound that Diff often heard Fjourn making, even more than just bubbling up his brain juices real good.

Ondermour straightened up and looked over both of them. "Plunger's what this is."

"Yarg?" Diff said.

"That's right, sharf, a *plunger*." Ondermour turned his attention back to the sponge-like object—a *plunger*, apparently—and did some more hard squinting at it. "Yar, that's just it. A plunger, though it's been pretty nice and chewed up." He glanced up and looked Diff straight in the eye. "You mind givin' me jus' a little more information, sharf?"

"Yarf."

Ondermour glanced down at Fjourn, just as a lot of the towns-people were trained to do, since they knew that he was the only one that could be one-hundred-per-cent relied upon to accurately convey Diff's words.

Sometimes Diff cursed about his lack of skill with Brak-a-lak because he did practise it as much as he could. Problem was, though, his equipment just did nothing to serve him at all. He wasn't built for it.

And so, he supposed it was a good thing to have Fjourn, someone who could not only understand a healthy smattering of Diff's language, but almost never needed to. The way they worked, in their team, it meant that Fjourn near enough always could read Diff's mind.

Or appear to do so.

Ondermour lifted his arms up and Diff caught a strong whiff of oily rags back there in his shop. Just like everyone else—but especially on Swindler's Sweep—Ondermour gave his services to any wagoneer that needed them. For a fair price, of course.

And Diff knew that, though Ondermour was a Guni of infinite patience, and good manners, that he was thinking about all the money he might be losing standing here behind his counter and flapping his lips about.

Diff gave Ondermour a solid nod, and said, 'Thank you' in his own language, before retreating from the Pennies-to-Hardware Store.

Just as they headed away from the place, Diff heard Ondermour call out to them.

"Just one more thing, sharf."

Diff glanced back at the Guni, saw him leaning on out from his counter, those same elbows, rubbed almost red-raw from all the leaning, propped up beneath him. "Yarp?"

"That plunger, it ain't nothing made here, in Cart Town.

Whoever bought that, whoever used that *thang*, it weren't from here they got it."

"Yarg," Diff said, with another nod of his head, then he looked to Fjourn, who took his turn and, looking right back at Ondermour, said, "Thank you kindly for your cooperation, sir."

"Pleased to do all I can," Ondermour said, and then disappeared back into the shadows of his store.

6

S OMEONE FROM OUTTA TOWN.
Yes, that was what made sense to Diff. He couldn't rightly imagine anyone in town here—a *resident*—of Cart Town getting all wrapped up in a thing like this. Being right where they were, in the centre of the Kunaha Desert, why it meant that they all had to work together if only to survive.

And so it made sense.

Though he couldn't shake the possibility that some resident of Cart Town mighta gone out to pick up the plunger, so they could stuff it down the victim's throat. But that'd be a hell of a lot of effort just to do someone in, when there were a million other ways.

Cleaner ways.

Why, they coulda used *poison*, that'd have been Diff's first choice, if he'd been a murderer, or inclined that way. They coulda just as easily used a mite of rope. Another way. Or a sharped-up cartwheel, or coulda swindled one of the hundreds of thousands of tools used for fixing up carts all dotted about town.

Yup, it was right that this was a tough case, and one that Diff knew he'd have to use up all his wits to solve.

"Where to now, sharf?" Fjourn said.

Diff steadied his gaze, making an effort to get his head steady, so that he'd see past the heat hazes that rose off the cobblestones in the midday sun. He guessed he could do with some water, that'd be pretty fine. The way his hearts were all beating hard at him . . . well, excepting Saveronak, that heart was just as still as always.

He concentrated on that feeling now. Thinking that he could feel Saveronak squeeze a little, that sense that told him that danger was nearby. He had little knowing about his own body, he had never

397

learned much about it, or seen that it was important to know. And his race were so few through here that he could count the Saveraks he'd seen passing through Cart Town on one set of claws.

But he knew to trust the Saveronak when it got to that squeezing.

He glanced about, looked up to the rooftop over above their heads, and he saw the figure standing up there, silhouetted in the sun, and he cried out long and hard, and grabbed a hold of Fjourn and tugged him right down to the cobblestones of the alleyway beside him.

7

P AH-SHHT! *Pah-shht! Pah-shht!*

Diff lay on the hard cobblestones, feeling three of his hearts pounding out harder and harder, swelling up in his throat as if they'd conspired to choke him to death.

Blow darts.

That's what they were.

He listened to them clatter to the ground, fall between the gaps in the cobblestones all around them, fortunately having missed their target.

But they had to move now.

Acting on instinct, Diff grabbed hold of Fjourn, and set him back up on his feet, on those rounded stumps, and he pushed him up against the wall so they'd be outside of the shooter's aim.

Pah-shht!

Another blow dart flew through the air, and before Diff could quite absorb what had happened, he saw it become imbedded in Fjourn's hide, needle its way right into him.

Diff listened to the *clatter* of roof tiles over their heads as the shooter made his mistake, and he turned to his deputy—to his *friend*—to see just what could be done.

He got him laid out flat, on his back, and he saw the way that his half dozen eyes lolled back in their sockets, eyelids drooping over each one, and he knew that those blow darts had carried poison.

But what kind? And was it lethal?

From the way that Fjourn groaned about there, lying on the cobblestones, he looked in a bad way.

"Yarp! Yarp! Yarp!" Diff called out, hearing his brutalised cries echoing about him.

Further off, in the distance, he could hear the relentless *clickety-clack* of the wagon wheels, all of them still turning, the carts still coming and going.

It would be an easy getaway for the shooter, unless . . .

Diff heard another loud *clatter* from the roof tiles and he knew it was the shooter slipping off, coming back down to street level. He had to chase him, had to go after him, else all would be lost . . . Fjourn might die for nothing.

But still with that logical conclusion ringing between his ears, Diff couldn't move so much as a muscle. His mouth tasted dry and his sense of smell seemed to have stopped working. All he could smell was that poison given off from the dart which had struck Fjourn, that slightly fruity, sticky smell. He tried to place it in his mind, to put a name to it. But, no matter how hard he tried, he just couldn't.

He heard the sound of someone approaching. When he looked up, he saw it was Ondermour, who he supposed had heard the ruckus, heard his unintelligible screams.

Ondermour stalked closer, his eyes all fixed on Fjourn's prostate body there. And then, slowly, his gaze worked up from the body and onto Diff. "Wha' . . . what happen?"

It would've done no good for Diff to answer anyway—what detail could he communicate with a sole syllable?—and so he took off running, in hot pursuit of the shooter, and, he hoped, the killer.

8

DIFF GAZED OUT across the town square. The sun—Nephmur—had just hit its highest point and it shone down on them with no mercy. He could feel his cold blood warming in the sun and his mind becoming a blizzard of activity. That scent of the poison still lingered heavily in his nostrils, and he wondered if he'd ever be able to forget it, if it might be the last detail he remembered of Fjourn, if this proved to be his last day in the world, before he was taken down to the afterlife, down to Hiddersnarl.

If he was taken, then Diff supposed that one day in the future they would meet again. But he had grown attached to his friend up here on the surface of the living world . . . not to mention the capacities which Fjourn had shown as a deputy.

He flickered his forked tongue out his mouth, and tasted the dusty air that rose up off the constantly passing carts. The carts all clops of hooves and the *clickety-clack* of cartwheels and the bellowings from the creatures driving where there was any gap at all.

And then he saw him.

Just over across the town square.

And Diff took off running, putting his proud, knobbled legs to good use, and running hard.

9

DIFF HADN'T to get up all that close to see that the shooter, the creature he was pursuing, was an Ebbersdorm. Those compact, square-chested creatures with the curling horns that poked out from their bruised and battered scalps. He could already see his bare chest and the bulging muscles which rippled out from his arms and chest.

But, most of all, he saw the blowpipe which he held clasped in his hand.

He slipped off down another alley, about thirty or forty paces from where Diff was.

Diff knew he could catch him.

Knew it.

As he trotted the Ebbersdorm's trail, he caught that thick and rich scent of boiled leather, the one which always turned his mind to boiled leather. And he recalled a memory from his childhood, when he had been no more than a fledgling in his mother's nest, and how one day she had brought them each a strip of leather which she'd bought off a vendor who had been passing by.

Then she'd shown them how to prepare the material—the Saverak method of preparing it—and how she'd poured out the boiling water into that iron pail, and then watched them, one by one, Diff along with his brothers and sisters, as they each submerged their leather in that water, and made them into armour even stronger than their own skin. He still recalled the way that near-boiling water had left singemarks on his still child-soft hide.

Diff rounded the corner, and arrived in the alley. It was dark and dank, and the light scent of the sawdust was nothing compared to the putrid reek of piled-up bones scattered about the place. And he knew that the Ebbersdorm had led him right round the back of the town tavern.

He stared into the gloom and then saw the Ebbersdorm standing there, at a dead end, that blowpipe still clutched in his fist, but either out of darts or for some other reason hesisitant to fire off another one at Diff.

He guessed that the shooter had banked on being able to take a shot, to let one of those blow darts fly, from the comfort of some darkened refuge. It was one thing to remain out of sight firing blow darts and quite another to do it face to face.

Especially with the town sheriff.

Diff stalked closer to him, feeling the sturdy cobblestones through the soles of his feet, and three of his hearts hammering hard. The Saveronak remained still, just like always. As it always would do.

"Ya, ya," the Ebbersdorm said. "Whatcha lookin' for, eh?"

Diff just pressed on, feeling his eyes grow accustomed to the gloom down here in this side alley. When he stood a few paces away from the Ebbersdorm, he stopped and watched him quivering.

He could use his height to his advantage. Compared with an Ebbersdorm, a Saverak like him was a towering monster.

"Eh, eh?" the Ebbersdorm said. "Dontcha gonna tell me whatta about?"

Diff felt his skin draw taut, and his tongue glanced off the sides of his fangs as he allowed it to slide out between his lips. He could afford another few moments of intimidation, a way to get information out of this shooter.

The Ebbersdorm fixed his eyes on Diff's tongue, regarding it as if it was a well-sharpened blade or, perhaps, a rapidly rotating cartwheel. "Look, ya gettin' in the way, tha's all, right?"

Diff stayed still.

"Things about this case you shouna be, uh . . . uh, a messin' with, ya?"

Diff kept up his glare.

"Bigger than this place, than shammy Cart Town."

Diff had almost always taken exception to creatures who spoke ill of Cart Town—how they'd badmouth the place, call it a sweat-sodden armpit in the middle of the Kunaha Desert to their friends . . . but they'd always come back, come back here when they had to. When they trucked out to the East or the West. They always did.

And, at that moment, not having the luxury of Fjourn to translate for him, to put his thoughts into words this Ebbersdorm would understand, Diff took another step closer.

The Ebbersdorm's eyes widened all the more. "Nah, nah, nah," he said, holding his palms out towards Diff, as if his palms could stop him. "Ya notta see this, eh? Gotta do with things bigger than this place."

Again, this was more or less the same slight about Cart Town . . . as if it was some backwater little place, and not a necessary point in the middle of the desert, a place of refuge for those who would accept it.

The Ebbersdorm screwed up his eyes, and seemed to look at Diff for the first time, or at least to *see* him for the first time. "You'sa Saverak, ya?" He paused a second. "Ya, you'sa Saverak. You, uh, you ah don't speak so good, huh?"

Diff waited a few selected moments and then said, "Yarp."

"Ya," the Ebbersdorm said, his eyes narrowing all the more, and Diff noticed how he'd tightened his grasp on that blowpipe, made a note himself to keep an eye on this Ebbersdorm's every move. "Ya don't speak so good."

Diff just stayed quiet this time.

"Ya no heard of the Spirit Highways, out thar beyond the plains?"

Of course Diff had heard of them. He'd heard of everything about Schwyn since a great representation of every race from around the world would pass through Cart Town at one time or another, in the midst of migration.

"This'uh comes from thar, ya see?"

Diff tilted his head down at the blowpipe still clasped tight in the Ebbersdorm's fist.

The Ebbersdorm noticed his look and said, "Oh, yar, I guessa you gotta questions about this little thingy, eh?"

Diff kept his glare down on him stiff and unrelenting.

"Yar, well, I hadda keep you from makin' trouble, see? Hadda keep you from messin' this whole thing right up." The Ebbersdorm sniffed hard and Diff half prepared for him to raise the blowpipe to his lips and fire a dart into him. "I jus' cover, ya? I jus' keep this thing with that dead Saverak *hush-hush*. Yous and your partner, you'sa buzzin' about askin' the questions, makin' the troubles. But thing is that this ain't nothin' you never gonna understand." Then he paused a little while before adding, "Sheriff."

Diff fixed the Ebbersdorm with a steelier glare, and continued to keep his gaze tight on that blowpipe of his, making sure it didn't leave his sight. He'd have to make sure that Ebbersdorm didn't raise that thing up and shoot him like he'd gone and shot Fjourn.

Diff decided that enough was enough and that he had to make the arrest. *An* arrest. Otherwise he'd find himself with troubles of his own on his hands. This Ebbersdorm, why it seemed like he might well have committed a murder too, if it passed that Fjourn didn't pull through, if his blood couldn't force out that poison.

And Diff would blame it all on himself. Because it woulda been all his fault.

He took steady steps forwards, and the Ebbersdorm held still while he slipped the cuffs onto his wrists, whipped the blowpipe out from his hands and led him away, out to the main square.

10

ONCE DIFF got the Ebbersdorm all locked up in the jail, he went off to go and see to Fjourn, who was being seen to by the Cart Town doc, Yongle-stark. Another Guni.

Diff noticed that the stethoscope Doctor Yongle-stark had hanging round his neck had grown a little rusty since they'd last seen one another. Diff guessed it might've been to all the rains they'd been having in the past few days, and that it'd got into the metal of the thingy.

"Sharf," Yongle-stark said then stood back from the door to let Diff slip past him into the room.

Diff prowled about the perimeter of the wall, and he kept his eyes fixed on the bed where Fjourn was all tucked up, the blankets right up to his chin. His skin looked pale, and he had several drops of sweat running down his face. And Diff caught a sour scent in the air and, a little further back, that fruity, sticky smell from the poison.

He looked to Doctor Yongle-stark for answers, and he gave them. "Thing is, sharf, that he's been bluddered up with that thar poison real good and all. Gotta delirium and all sweeping on him."

"Yarp," Diff said.

"He gonna be okay, sharf. I gotta him just in time."

Diff felt all his hearts lift in his chest—even the Saveronak—and he cast a glance over Fjourn with fresh eyes now, glad that his deputy would be saved.

"Catch the killer, sharf?"

Diff thought it over, thought about how it had turned out. He'd caught the Ebbersdorm, sure, but he couldn't help thinking that whatever else had gone on here, with the murder and all, whatever was happening about the rest of it, that he would never truly know.

He was the Sheriff of Cart Town, and that was where his remit ended.

Though it pained him to admit it to himself.

And he had no reason to believe that the Ebbersdorm had lied to him, that he had made something up about this being bigger than him—this being *bigger* than Cart Town.

Because, deep down, he knew it to be true.

The murderer had already scarpered the town, and, if not, there was little chance of finding him, what with all the hiding places, all them nooks and crannies about the town . . . and let alone on Swindler's Sweep, with all the creatures blasting through the town, coming and then fleeing just as quick.

So far as Cart Town was concerned, he guessed the murder was just as fine as resolved. At least the killer was gone and the body would be just as gone soon.

"Sharf?" Yongle-stark repeated.

"Yarg," Diff said, feeling his forked tongue grow unruly as he tried to make it obey him, to put more words to Yongle-stark. But he knew he couldn't.

He felt drained from this. Still drained from seeing the dead body of that Saverak. It'd been kinda . . . *unnatural* somehow. Or at least that was the way he saw it.

And stricken with a mixture of failure, at having missed the killer, and gladness for the fact that Fjourn was gonna be okay.

Yongle-stark gave Diff a slight smile, and those static eyes of his seem to catch a glimmer of the sunlight that dripped in through the window of the infirmary. And the *clickety-clack* of the carts all bombing about the town square, the *squawks* and *blarwks* and *screeches*, and whatever else, all hummed up in the air.

And Diff knew he had work to do, and so, with a final glance at Fjourn, he turned away, and headed on his way out of the room.

"Sharf?" Yongle-stark said.

"Yarp?"

"Dontcha feel bad at all about this, will ya? Because, well, sharf, you're the best we got here in Cart Town. One that keeps us all safe and all."

Diff managed to manipulate his lips into a vague smile, the best he could do with his Saverak face, and then he ventured out the room, into the cool corridor, into that echoplex where all the sounds seemed to build and swill all about him. Ebbing into his head then bouncing round his skull a while before letting themselves out again.

This job, sometimes it could be brutal. And mean. And cruel. A trail leading out of town, to a place that he could not go. Beyond his remit.

Though, he supposed, it took a particular strength to resist the calling of it, the will to keep an ego in check and to stay behind—to stay faithful to your charge, to the *burden* you'd accepted so long ago.

Because the Sheriff of Cart Town had to think of the town first, and the world second. That was the charge that Sheriff Diff Andchek carried over his shoulders, in any case.

AUTHOR'S NOTE

Thank you for taking the time to read one of my books. If you would like to hear about my latest releases you can sign up for my newsletter here: www.raymondsflex.com

Thanks for reading!

Raymond S Flex

Guynur Schwyn
A Short Story Collection